Goddess of Grass

Introduction

The Story of Malinalli

I first heard parts of the story of the slave girl who helped conquer a country on the PBS series *'Conquistadors'* (2001). Coming away very intrigued, my first research book after viewing that was *"Voice of the Vanquished"* by Helen Heightsman Gordon—which eventually inspired me to write this version, and to whom I owe a great debt of gratitude.

Unlike that book and a few other scholarly works, I purposely took a decidedly more accessible approach, initially forgoing the native names of people and places in favor of the English translations to allow the casual reader to immerse themselves without struggle.

When researching La Malinche there are basically only three principal sources:

'The True History of the Conquest of Mexico' by Bernal Diaz

Cortés' Five Letters to the King of Spain

'The Aztecs speak - an Aztec account of the Conquest of Mexico' taken from the Codex Florentino.

To a much lesser extent there is Francisco de Gomara's biography of Cortés, which most scholars consider extremely flawed...

Each of these sources has its issues. The Codex Florentino is actually a translation of Aztec hieroglyphics (they had no written language) by Spanish monks and as such may have extensive errors in meaning, although most of this account corresponds closely to the account by Diaz. A reading of this document would also lead one to believe it is often exaggerated, so taking it with a grain of salt is advisable.

It must be remembered that the letters from Cortés to his king were clearly designed to laud himself and flatter the king at the same time. Cortés was in a bitter battle to control New Spain or

Mexico over the objections and greed of the Cuban governor Diego Velasquez and so much of what he writes, while similar in timeline at least, may have embellished some events while omitting others.

Bernal Diaz leaves us with the most complete historical document, but clearly it was written by a naive man some fifty years after the events took place, and appears to view those events from hindsight through rose colored glasses. However, reading between the lines and ignoring some timeline issues and outrageous remarks, this document mostly rings true. The fact that Diaz goes out of his way to call out glaring errors by Gomara, also tends to diminish that work. But most importantly, Diaz was an eyewitness and participant in the Conquest, and knew both Cortés and La Malinche (Doña Marina / Malinalli) personally, so his account must take weight over the others.

Unfortunately La Malinche herself apparently never wrote anything down, or at least nothing in her hand has survived the ages. And all the historians, scholars, and authors who wrote about the Conquest and La Malinche did so many years after the events. The fact is, not one of these people knows the real truth.

So, where do we go to for information on La Malinche? The only legitimate method would seem to use all of these sources, cancel out opposing descriptions of events, while considering those views that are in agreement to be factual. It is also important to read between the lines especially in the case of Diaz. Some of the events simply could not have happened the way he describes them and this is borne out by events that occur later or were unknown to him. He certainly wrote down what he believed, but it's doubtful he always knew the facts.

Finally, it is vital to remember that except for the Aztecs, none of the Spanish (including Diaz) knew what La Malinche actually said to the Aztecs. Cortés could have told her to tell Montezuma that he (Cortés) was not a god and both Cortés and Diaz would have recorded it that way. However La Malinche could have spoken the opposite in Nahuatl to Montezuma and none of the Spanish would have known! So since actual facts about Malinalli are few and far between, it necessitates some fictional material—especially when it comes to her actual words.

The most interesting aspect of the story is the way many actual historically recorded crucial dates intertwine in a way none of the various researchers or authors I ran across previously mentioned. In fact it wasn't until I accumulated all my notes that I recognized it myself. It now seems clear to me that the sequence of events as described herein is too obvious to be coincidental.

So while this is a fictionalized account out of necessity, it is as factual as I can possibly make it.

Finally, while much of Mexico considers La Malinche to be a traitor, I take the view she was perhaps one of the greatest and certainly most interesting female heroes of all time.

The Circle of Fate

In the same year, almost at the same time, three inter-linked events took place which would change the face of the world, create at least two heroes, and result in the downfall of an empire ruled by one of the most powerful men in the known world:

An Emperor assumes the throne of a feared and mighty empire.

A Conqueror is prevented from his quest due to an injury. He would then be delayed many years until finally arriving in the land he would conquer in the exact year a prophecy promised the return of a god.

A Heroine is born who would be inexorably bound to both their fates. She is named for the symbol of her birth day: Grass

1 The Emperor

The pungent sweet fragrance of flowers from the many gardens throughout the city mate with the soft cries of every species of the exotic birds kept in extravagant cages, and carry on the night breeze. The same wind stirs the torches in the palace, making the flames dance in a frenzied twisting of shadows. The contrasting shades cause the exquisitely carved stone surfaces to appear cold and hard, while a nearly naked handsome and muscular man tosses fitfully in his dreams.

This man, the Emperor, is catered to by six hundred servants, half of which are the first born sons of noblemen. His name is Montezuma, and although he commands an army of more than 400,000 men, no such might is able to fend off the terror that comes to him in the night. He has been the ruler of a mighty empire for three years and this marks the first ill feeling he has had in that time. And although surrounded by the trappings of royalty and power: inlaid marble, highly polished jade, opal, and turquoise jewelry, and ornaments of pure gold; he is nonetheless drenched in sweat, tossing and turning as the fearful images come to him unbidden:

A great light appears in the night and moves across the sky, shooting flames.

A temple bursts into flames. Water poured on the blaze will not put it out and the temple burns to the ground.

A soundless bolt of lightning comes with no flash and destroys another temple.

A stream of comets, so bright they are visible in the daytime, races from west to east, shooting off sparks of fire with such long tails, they fill the sky.

The lake that surrounds the city boils and rises to great height although there is no wind and destroys almost half the houses.

Two headed men roamed the city, and disappear at will.

The voice of a weeping woman is heard coming from everywhere, and from nowhere crying, "Oh my children, my children, we are lost!"

When morning finally comes, the Emperor grunts for fresh water to quench his starched throat. His wants are instantly served by a slave, who brings the water in a cold-hammered copper goblet gilded with gold. After the liquid enables him to speak again and he calms down, he calls for Coyote, his oldest and trusted advisor.

The cagey old man listens carefully, both stunned and relieved. He had the same dream and knew exactly what it meant, but had been searching for a way to tell the Emperor without incurring his wraith; after all many a messenger of bad news paid the price in death.

The wily old man also knows exactly why the Emperor summoned him instead of any one of the dozens of younger and more favored priests: he is expendable. The Emperor's secrets can be safe in his death. He decides to draw out his advice, in an effort to make his own importance shine brightly again.

"My Lord, what you have seen is of great importance and curiosity. I seek your leave to study this matter and report back." Coyote tells his Emperor.

"Very well, but make it quick. I want to know what this means. Report to me before sunset tomorrow."

And the old advisor leaves, using the time wisely, considering carefully the exact words he would use to warn of the bad times ahead...

But that very evening the Emperor, while preparing for his bath, looks into a mirror of polished copper and sees people moving across a plain, armed for war, and riding on what look like impossibly huge strange deer. He knows it is another sign and commands his guards to fetch Coyote.

When the adviser enters the royal chamber he sees the Emperor is nervous and his cheeks flushed with anxiety—and perhaps fear. He can't avoid the subject any longer.

"My Lord, you are aware the time of the Feathered Serpent is approaching. What you have seen are the signs, and there will be more: the people will go hungry; and the earth will shake, so mightily that buildings will fall. And your own sister will appear to be dead." Coyote says carefully.

"You mean the End of Days?" The Emperor Montezuma asks with his head bowed in sheer terror.

"Not necessarily, but the Feathered Serpent is due to return on One Reed, in thirteen years. The signs of light in the night sky are surely the Feathered Serpent's way of warning Smoking Mirror that he is coming to vanquish him; that Feathered Serpent will once again bring light to the blackness of obsidian. We must prepare to greet him." Coyote tells his ruler, knowing full well that past Emperors had set these events in motion.

Coyote had been against the course of actions Emperor Montezuma had continued, that others before him had put in place decades before, but the other advisers and priests had been more influential.

"What are you saying exactly old man?" Montezuma asks with a cold edge in his voice.

Coyote knows he is on dangerous ground but he has no choice. These signs are real, and soon no matter what, Montezuma will have to face his fate.

The old man knew Feathered Serpent's departure from the land was the work of his old enemies, Smoking Mirror and Hummingbird Wizard, who wanted his subjects to make bloodier sacrifices than the flowers, jade, and butterflies they offered to Feathered Serpent.

Smoking Mirror tricked Feathered Serpent by getting him drunk and then holding up an obsidian mirror that showed Smoking Mirror's cruel face. Believing that he was looking at his own black and imperfect image, Feathered Serpent decided to leave the world and sailed east into the ocean on a raft of serpents.

"The blood sacrifices are against the wishes of the Feathered Serpent. Perhaps you should bring a halt to them." He replies warily.

"Never! The offerings of human hearts and blood to Smoking Mirror and Left-Handed Hummingbird are the source of Aztec power. You would have me throw that away?"

When Coyote remains silent under his withering glare, the Emperor questions him further.

"Who is to say that Feathered Serpent is more powerful than the Lord of Smoking Mirrors or Hummingbird? Suppose I choose wrong and then we must all pay that price?" Montezuma asks angrily.

Coyote can no longer hold his tongue, no more than the sand can hold back the ocean. The human sacrifices have grown more and more extreme and it sickens his heart. The Aztecs make war solely to capture more warriors to feed to the insatiable gods. Now they have run out of brave warriors and turned to the virgin children of their former enemies. Unrest in the Empire grows every day because of it.

"The Prophecy says the Plumed Serpent will bring light to the dark. That is written, and it will happen in One Reed when all things end and all things begin again. You yourself have seen the signs my Lord. The light filling the night sky is but one portent of his return. He was and always will be the most powerful god—the only god that can vanquish the night." Coyote finds the strength to make his point even as he fears the consequences.

"Then you are saying the Feathered Serpent will replace me on the throne?" Montezuma asks bitterly.

"The Prophecy is the Prophecy, and the One Reed will be upon us in thirteen years. Nothing can change that, but you will have that time to prepare. The signs have granted you warning. Stop the sacrifices of blood so you can welcome Feathered Serpent."

"You go too far old man. Guards! Take this pitiful creature out of my sight!" The Emperor commands.

Coyote knows he will never live to see Feathered Serpent return.

2 The Conqueror

While the Emperor struggles with fevered nightmares, far away another man is bothered by different kind of night fever—one much more pleasant.

He loves the smell of her; she is a woman, older than him by ten years at least. He loves the feel of her, long silky hair she lets down only for him, and pampered skin only someone with wealth can achieve. But most of all he loves the excitement of her. She is the wife of a rich man and he has put one over on the unknown husband, he has stolen his property.

He met her in the square, singling her out because of the maid who was picking over vegetables and then showing them to her—a sure sign of wealth. He knows nothing of vegetables, or any food for that matter, except how to eat. But that doesn't hinder him in the least.

"Miss, if you please, the carrots at the stall over there have just come in from the fields within the hour. They are by far the freshest here." He suggests, without inducement or formal introduction, a grave violation of etiquette under the best of circumstances.

The woman fans herself against the mid-morning warmth, eyeing him briefly but clearly taking in his fine attire and style. He is very young but if his manners are lacking at least he cuts quite a dashing appearance.

"Oh sir, I am certain they are not the freshest thing in this square." She allows the faintest of smirks to escape her full lips. "And it is Missis. I am a married woman I will have you know."

Of course he has already deduced this fact. He does not wish to waste his time on entanglements with single ladies of no means. He removes his hat and bows deeply before her.

"Allow me to introduce myself formally; I am Hernando Cortés of Medellin, at your service." As he rises he plucks a flower from a nearby window pot and presents it to the woman, eyes level and piercing. "And you have brightened the whole of this square with your formidable beauty."

Even her maid blushes at this and must turn away before her excitement becomes evident to her employer. The three of them wander about the shopping district for a time, Cortés and the married woman making small talk, but all the while she does not disclose her name. Finally they come to the woman's carriage and she climbs aboard and the driver closes the door.

Cortés does not lose confidence however, and is rewarded as the maid passes close on her way to the other side of the carriage.

"Come at nightfall." She says without slowing and whispers an address.

For a brief instant Cortés isn't sure from whom the invitation is extended—the maid or her lady, but then he sees the married woman's eyes flash with smoldering intensity from the carriage window...

They are in the throes of passionate lovemaking, the woman is heady with the energy of the seventeen year old, and Cortés is about to moan some utterance of encouragement to spurn her on to climax when he briefly forgets her name.

"Carisa, Carisa." He remembers finally. "You are so lovely."

She moans loudly when they manage to hear noises in the courtyard and the door below them slams, announcing her husband's early return.

Hernando Cortés leaps, albeit reluctantly, from the bed and scrambles for his clothes. Then he runs to the balcony just as the husband enters their bedroom. Cortés has no option except to jump.

He twists his ankle in the second story fall, but the thrill of danger shines even through the excruciating pain. As Cortés hobbles down the cobblestone street he can still smell her perfume...

The next morning his ankle is swollen so badly he cannot put his weight on it, but he must get to the docks. Today he is to sail to the Americas with a family acquaintance and distant relative: Nicolas Ovando, the newly appointed governor of Haiti and the Dominican Republic.

Cortés breaks a leg off a side table to use for a walking stick and crutch. Every step is terribly painful, but he grits his teeth and bears it, finally making it to where thirty ships, the largest fleet every to sail to the Americas, awaits departure while the last of the supplies are loaded.

When Ovando sees Cortés limping aboard, he is sympathetic but steadfast. He needs men with all their abilities. The journey will be arduous enough, let alone what conditions they will face upon arrival. He tells the young teenager to go back home and recover and perhaps someday he can sail to the New World.

Cortés is stunned at the news, his teenage exuberance crushed as he can only stand and painfully watch the fleet depart on their adventure. He feels Fate has tricked him again—he was born of minor nobility but with no money to practice it. Now he is stuck watching the world go by without him. As the last ship disappears into the horizon, Cortés is determined to change his Fate, but he will learn that will take time.

At the age of 14, his parents had sent him to the University of Salamanca to study law. But Cortés was too restless to follow the rules. He did learn a little Latin, and became good at writing, a skill that would eventually serve him well, but after sticking it out for two years—and failing—he returned home. But the provincial small town wasn't for him, especially after stories began to come in about the mysterious 'New World'. Cortés wanted to be a part of it.

Instead, he spends the next year wandering the country, seducing rich women—another skill he seems to have come by effortlessly. But he spends most of his time in the heady atmosphere of Spain's southern port of Seville, listening to the tales of those returning from the Indies, who tell of discovery and conquest, gold, Indians and strange unknown lands.

Every story serves to strengthen his resolve to get there...

3 The Heroine

The same year that the Emperor Montezuma assumed the throne as ruler of the Aztec Empire, the instrument of his ultimate downfall was born many miles to the East. She was daddy's girl from the moment she could breathe on her own.

Her father had wished for a child for many years and finally was rewarded. Although boys were much more highly valued, he didn't care in the least. He had a beautiful child.

She is born on the 12th and named for the day of her birth: Malinalli or Grass, governed by the provider of Shadow Soul life energy. This day signifies tenacity and rejuvenation, that which cannot be uprooted forever. Malinalli is a day for persevering against all odds and for creating alliances that will survive the test of time. It is a good day for those who are suppressed, a bad day for their suppressors—a fact that will come to pass just as sure as the Prophecy of the Feathered Serpent...

Malinalli's father loves playing with her and can not wait for his duties to be finished each day so as to rush home and see her. He is the chief of their village—and a good portion of the surrounding area and as such is always busy judging minor disputes and ensuring the needs of the people are met. His position also makes him wealthy and powerful—answering only to the governor and the Empire.

Before even her first birthday Malinalli recognizes her father from his brilliant turquoise earplugs and she is fascinated watching his gold necklace shine and sway as he coos to her each night. He never kisses her of course, his gold lip jewelry would have interfered even if he wanted to, but touching lips with another is just not done. The act of kissing is reserved for more ceremonial occasions.

It is some time before Malinalli realizes her father's importance and her station in life. Her mother, the taskmaster of the family, manages to keep her from playing with the other children. But she can't help but notice her family has plenty of food and she is even able to indulge in her most favorite of all: cocoa—a drink doled out carefully by her doting father when she is especially good.

It isn't until she starts school and sees a dozen boys and herself as the only girl she understands she is special. While all children are instructed at home in the ways of the elders and the gods, only noble born attend the special school run by priest-teachers.

Females are expected to engage in activities suiting the role of wife and mother—such as cooking, spinning, and weaving. But though even noblewomen are legally subject to the authority of father or husband they are not discriminated against in any way and have all other legal status such as the right of inheritance.

Noble girls are encouraged to learn and in fact many serve as priestesses, midwives and pharmacists. First though, the class must learn about the gods—not an easy undertaking in a culture with 33 deities.

The priest begins the first day by explaining the calendars—to which the gods are inexorably tied.

"So my children, there are two calendars: the agricultural days and the sacred day-count of the gods." The priest tells the class.

Malinalli is nothing if not a free spirit and constantly tries the patience of her priest-teachers by asking endless questions.

"What is agricultural?" The six year old Malinalli asks.

"It means farming: the planting and harvesting of crops—food." The priest explains patiently. "This calendar has 365 days, each one the rise and fall of the sun and moon."

Malinalli nods, she has witnessed this of course and it makes sense.

"The other calendar, the sacred day-count calendar has 20 days…"

The priest teacher continues.

"But why?" Malinalli interrupts.

"Because there are 20 gods of the days and we must divide our time between them, so as to preserve the balance..."

"What is the balance?" She wants to know.

"Each of the gods strives for power, little ones." The Priest explains to the class, growing a tiny bit frustrated with the girl. "If one god should vanquish another then the world would surely end."

"Why would the world end?" Malinalli spouts out, clearly alarmed and frightened.

"Why if Lord Hummingbird Wizard, the Sun god, were to leave us then the world would plunge into darkness forever." The Priest replies, a little smugly, secretly hoping to silence the girl with fear. "Just as Lord Smoking Mirror tricked Lord Feathered Serpent to leave the land."

"How did he trick him?" Malinalli asks, unfazed.

"Lord Feathered Serpent's departure from his people was the work of his old enemy, Smoking Mirror. Lord Feathered Serpent was a kind god who desired offerings of flowers and butterflies. Lord Smoking Mirror mocked this and demands sacrifice of blood to nourish him and his friends. Smoking Mirror tricked Feathered Serpent by getting him drunk and then holding up a mirror that showed Smoking Mirror's cruel face. Believing that he was looking at his own twisted image, Feathered Serpent decided to leave this world and sailed east on a raft of serpents." The priest explained, upping the scare factor another notch.

Malinalli finally falls silent, but it is not from fear. She is taken with the notion of kindly god Feathered Serpent and daydreams of flowers and butterflies.

"And so the weeks are 14 days and the year consists of 260 days. Then every 52 years, a 'Reed', time starts over again." The priest continues, happy the girl at last gives him a chance to speak...

4 Cortés Makes His Move

For nearly two years Cortés continues to make conquests of his own—the female variety—and each adds to his personal treasury until he finally accumulates enough to buy passage to Haiti and set himself up as a colonist.

The ship on which he travels happens to be commanded by Alonso Quintero. It is part of a fleet, for no one dares such a journey in solitude. But Quintero orders the sails deployed to their fullest extent so as to race ahead. He signals to the rest of the fleet he will scout forward so as to clear the route of any dangers. But in fact Quintero tries to deceive his superiors and reach the New World before them in order to secure advantage for himself. Quintero's mutinous conduct will serve as a model for Cortés in his subsequent career: Seize whatever advantage you can.

Upon his arrival in Santo Domingo, the 18-year-old Cortés registers as a citizen, which entitles him to a building plot and land to farm. Soon afterwards, Nicolas Ovando, still the governor, tries to make up for the lad's disappointment at missing the original sailing, and gives him a labor force of Indian slaves and makes him a notary of a small town.

Cortés works hard and the next five years help establish him in the young colony. He works just as hard after hours and manages to sleep with every woman in sight, including more than a few of his native female slaves. Though the Spanish consider the natives no more than property, to be used as one pleases, Cortés finds himself fascinated with their caramel skin and earthy manners—always willing to please their master.

But his extracurricular activities eventually led to an STD, a mild case of syphilis which the Europeans called the 'pox'. Cortés does not know if he caught it from one of his Spanish women, who would have undoubtedly been infected by some vile and disgusting sailor, transporting it across the ocean, or one of the native women since it is said by many the disease actually originated in the New World.

In any case Cortés manages to recover just in time to take part in the conquest of Cuba.

***

Montezuma has no knowledge of the Conqueror's slow but steady progression westward, nor the Heroine's appetite for learning—after all she is merely a child and just one of a million of his subjects. But the sense of impending doom is with him always, visited upon him by those dreams years ago. His advisors repeatedly assure him there is nothing to worry about, but the Emperor realizes now they are yes men and fools. He regrets more than once having the old Coyote skinned alive, for it appears his predictions are coming to pass.

The first troubling sign is the sudden and mysterious crop failure which is leaving the people hungry. Then just last month the whole of the kingdom shook violently, toppling a few buildings and frightening everyone.

He decides to visit the 'Place of Heavenly Learning' to seek relief from his depression and answers to what he hopes are the riddles of those dreams. But the priests that practice there frighten even the Emperor's advisors, for they remain in constant trance states brought on by the Peyote cactus. The advisors attempt to dissuade Montezuma, as much out of their fear as the fear of that temple's priest gaining too much influence, but he will have none of it—the frightening dreams and warnings from Coyote are still so vivid in his memory.

The two priests that greet the Emperor would seem to be worse than the cure. Black robed and vile smelling—they believe that bathing would wash off the holy blood that encrusts their self inflicted cuttings—lead Montezuma deep into the recesses of the temple. His entourage can do nothing but wait outside.

Seated around a smoldering fire—in the 100 degree heat—the priests give him a potent mixture of Psilocybin mushrooms and ground seeds of the Rivea-corybosa plant. The psychedelic seeds are used by the Aztec priests in order to help them commune with the gods. Because of the extremely fine line between safe and lethal doses, the ground seeds are only ingested by the most experienced priests. Dosages of less than 10 seeds are employed for spiritual experiences, which last for up to 8 hours. The traditional method of preparation is to soak the finely ground or chewed seeds in a small amount of water for several hours, then consuming both the water and seeds. This time, due to the importance of the ceremony with the Emperor himself, the priests add the sacred mushrooms.

They lead Montezuma in the holy chants and then one priest hands him a razor sharp obsidian knife. The Emperor promptly cuts his tongue to draw blood and spits it into the fire. Then he makes a small cut in each arm. As both a political and a religious leader, the Emperor is expected to sacrifice more blood than any of the priests and he does so willingly. The Aztecs believe the gods give things to humans only if they are nourished by humans and according to the priests only blood will serve as that nourishment.

The chants grow louder and more frenzied as Montezuma pierces his own penis and dances around the fire dripping blood into the flames. The loss of blood, the heat, and the drugs have their effect and he falls into a deep trance exploding with images of nature and the gods. The relief for which Montezuma hoped is not forthcoming, but instead there are dark beasts flying around his head...

The priests sense their Emperor is going over the edge, he is moaning and writhing in fear and they realize the seed and mushroom mixture may have been too much. One leaves and returns with a black crane, a magnificent and rare sacred bird kept only in the temple, and present it to Montezuma, letting him hold it, hoping it will calm him.

The crane has a dazzling colorful crest and as Montezuma peers at it he see stars in reflection and sticks that spit out fire. Then the vision changes to show the advances of warriors riding great four legged beasts like huge deer which spout smoke from their nostrils. He believes they are demons sent from the gods and in fear and panic rips the bird to shreds with his bare hands, spewing its blood over the fire and the two priests...

When the Emperor returns to the palace the following day he is greeted with more bad news: in his absence his sister Paranazin has died without warning. Grief stricken at the continued course of bad events, Montezuma orders an elaborate state funeral.

Most of the Aztec capital turns out for the event in honor of the Emperor and the funeral procession winds through city's flower gardens and neat streets on the way to the royal crypt as onlookers stand silent in respect. Suddenly in the middle of the journey Paranazin sits up and screams. She is alive, back from the dead and the people watching flee in panic.

It turns out Paranazin was in a cataleptic trance for days and mistaken for dead, but even more chilling is what she reports to her brother.

"I received a vision from the gods that showed great ships coming from a distant land. These ships carried hairy faced men who arrived bearing weapons, carrying banners, and wearing 'metal hats'. These strange looking men are to become masters of the Aztecs."

The Emperor questions his sister over and over, but she does not sway in her recollection.

Then, as if to drive home the point like a spear into his head, a light with three heads and sparks shooting from its tail is seen flying in the eastward sky for many days. The prophecy is coming true.

Montezuma's advisors' response to this new vision is to suggest more sacrifices and out of fear he agrees. Since there have been few battles lately, there is a lack of captured warriors, the preferred source of human hearts and blood—for the braver the warrior the better the sacrifice. This means the villages under the rule of the Aztec Empire will have to provide...

***

Malinalli is happy. She is continuing her education and absorbing it like a sponge. Her father loves her and even her mother softens a little, teaching her weaving and spinning and cooking—apparently accepting the fact she will never have a boy, but must be content with only a girl.

She believes her father loves her more though, and this is proven when the teacher comes to visit one evening and she overhears him complaining mildly about her constant questioning.

"Not that I mind your Lord," He must treat the situation delicately and with respect, "But Malinalli never ceases to talk, never ceases to ask..."

"Is this not a good thing? Obviously you are instilling in her a curiosity beyond her years. It would seem it proves you are doing a good job." Her father says wisely (even more wisely than Malinalli realizes at her young age). Her mother serves the men drinks—cacao mixed with ground maize. As the teacher sips the rich chocolate, a drink reserved for the rich and noble, the reason for his visit dissolves into the night air.

But the subject sets her father thinking, if his daughter is so inquisitive perhaps it is better she studies at a temple where she can receive intense education from a priestess who will be more patient.

When the teacher leaves Malinalli is still listening as her father broaches this subject with her mother.

"I've been thinking it may be a good idea to dedicate Malinalli to one of the temples for a few years. Having her in class with only boys may not be the best course for her."

"Do you intend her to be a priestess then?" Her mother seems to gently mock the idea.

"No, I intend for her to marry well and bear us many grandchildren. I'm just saying I think her education is important. A girl should not spend all that time with boys, she belongs with females."

"So the question is what temple shall we seek out for her?" Her mother asks.

As usual Malinalli cannot contain herself. She bursts into the great room and interrupts her parents.

"I want to dedicate myself to Quetzalcoatl, the Feathered Serpent, a good and kind god who shall soon return." She pleads.

Before her mother can scold her for her bad manners, her father breaks into a smile.

"Then so it shall be, you will be dedicated to Feathered Serpent. I shall speak with the priestess tomorrow."

Malinalli is elated, visions of flowers and butterflies fill her young head.

Her happiness is short-lived however, even before she can begin her course at the temple of Feathered Serpent, the Emperor's tax collectors arrive in the village. Soon there is talk everywhere of the heavy burden the village will have to offer this year. The famine in Mexico City means that the tax will be double, leaving many of the families short of food themselves after a season of hard work in the fields.

And to make matters worse, Malinalli hears talk of 'sacrifices'—a concept she is only vaguely familiar with because over her brief life a few men have left the village with past tax collectors and never returned. She decides to ask her teacher.

At first he is reluctant to be blunt with the girl, but the rituals are a fact of life. And besides, she asked didn't she?

"The gods give things to us only if they are nourished by us and the gods demand hearts for their nourishment." He tells the class.

"Hearts! How can we give our hearts and continue to live?" Malinalli (of course) asks.

"That is the point child; the gods demand our life, the ultimate sacrifice." He replies and goes on to explain in some detail the exact method of the sacrificial rituals. "And the hearts must still beat, better to prove our devotion to them."

Malinalli is horrified at this news.

"Which god demands our beating hearts?" She asks with tears in her eyes, as the boys in the class sit stoically silent.

"Lord of the Sun, Hummingbird Wizard, is the giver of life and we must appease him in all his demands lest he go away and leave us in darkness forever." The teacher gestures grandly, waving his arms up to the sun beating down on them.

That afternoon Malinalli waits restlessly for her father to return so she can ask him to put an end to this sacrifice thing. She believes he can fix anything and is sure he will grant her wish. But hour after hour he still does not come home.

"Your father is busy dealing with the Emperor's tax collectors. Now go to sleep." Her mother finally commands as night falls.

The next morning she awakes to find her father with his head bowed, sitting cross-legged on the floor. Her mother is gathering bales of cotton and sacks of corn.

"Half of everything?" Her mother mutters, as much to herself as her husband.

"Yes. Half of our corn, half of our grain, half of our cotton," He answers in a bleak but firm tone. "As chief I must make an example to the people. The times are hard in the capital and the Emperor requires food to feed his subjects there."

"But how will we live?" Her mother stares blankly.

"Woman, just be happy we don't have to contribute something else." He eyes Malinalli hovering in the doorway. "Some families will not be so lucky." Then her father stands and leaves for work without another word, leaving his daughter chilled at his demeanor.

That day three young men are seen being led away by the tax collectors. Malinalli—and the whole village—know they are training to be Eagle warriors. She even knows one by name, a cousin of her mother. The whispers among the villagers confirm they are to be sacrificed.

That evening her father ignores her, frightening her even more. He is angry and red faced—a state she has never witnessed in him before. He orders Malinalli out of the room while he speaks to her mother, but she hides and listens.

"So it is true?" Her mother asks before he can speak.

"Yes, three of our best trainees." He replies with tight lips.

"And there is nothing you can do?"

"No woman, you think I didn't try? Not only will the village go hungry but they must give up their loved ones. The Emperor goes too far, one day he will regret his actions." He spits the words with venom.

"My husband, please hush. Talk like that will have you being taken away next."

Her mother's words scare Malinalli more than anything she has heard: Take away her father!

That night she cries herself to sleep waiting for her father to come and wish her good night. It is the second night in her life she misses his hug.

The next day she can barely concentrate at school. The teacher is attempting to put a good light on the situation, but that only makes it worse. Finally class is over and she goes home only to find her mother and her aunt red faced from crying.

"Malinalli go out and play." Her aunt says as her mother begins wailing loudly.

"What's wrong Momma?" She pleads, but her mother can't stop crying.

Finally her aunt takes Malinalli aside and kneels to her level. She takes her shoulders and looks into her face.

"Your father is gone little one."

"Gone? What do you mean? Did the Emperor take him?"

"No child, the gods took him. He has passed."

Malinalli's world has just ended.

5 Events Determine Fate

Montezuma is too busy dealing with one disaster after another, each one rocking his world, to notice the resentment growing in the vassal states. First the famine and now severe floods right here in the capital.

Lake Texcoco is a natural lake formation within the Valley of Mexico. The Aztecs built the capital on an island in the lake complete with causeways, floating markets and an abundance of gardens irrigated by the lake water. The Emperor always enjoyed the scent of the flowers on the night air, but now the water that nourishes those very gardens threatens to wipe out the city. The lake rose mysteriously over the course of a few days and he is reminded of the dream years ago:

The lake that surrounds the city boils and rises to great height although there is no wind and destroys almost half the houses.

And truly many of the houses and buildings on the lake shore are inundated—just as if the lake had boiled over. As a short term solution, he orders cotton bags filled with sand placed around the city in a last ditch attempt to save it.

In regards to the multiple catastrophes striking the Empire, his advisors and priests all have the same answer: more sacrifices to the gods. But the Empire is almost a victim of its own success— there are no more tribes to go to war against, and thus a scarcity of captured warriors to send to the temples to appease the gods. Over the years as many as twenty thousand at a time had been sacrificed to nourish the gods.

The Aztec strategy was to subjugate the tribes and villages and then demand tribute in the form of taxes and warriors for sacrifice. Although the Aztec military structure resembles other armies, their methods of warfare differ greatly from the tactics and strategy of any other culture. Highly organized and well trained, their main objective on the battlefield was not to force their opponents to retreat, but to capture as many of them alive as possible.

In a close pitched battle, the Aztecs would employ weapons such as bows and arrows, spears, and wooden swords studded with sharp stones. The Aztec sword was not meant to kill, but to disable the enemy with a blow to the knee or leg, so that men from the rear could tie them with ropes and take them prisoner. When an Aztec soldier captured two enemies, they were promoted in rank.

The Aztec army consisted of Eagle warriors and Jaguar warriors. The Eagle warriors generally carried spears, and had eagle plumage as their uniform. They were the rank and file troops of the Aztec army, and wore no armor.

The best of the Eagle warriors were promoted to Jaguar warrior, who carried swords and wooden shields. Jaguar warriors were the Aztec crack troops, and were highly feared by other tribes.

Consisting of groups of approximately 8,000 men, the majority of warriors were new recruits who would be anxious to increase their social standing through victory on the battlefield. The more experienced warriors would be placed in strategic locations in order to afford the greatest chance of obtaining multiple captives. As the soldiers engaged in more and more battles, they would achieve higher ranks based upon the number of captives.

The highest ranking Jaguar soldiers would be paired with a warrior of similar status and adorned with magnificent garb. They fought in pairs throughout the entire battle and should one die, it was the duty of the other to die too. This fighting team would then seek out similar or higher ranked warriors from the enemy army.

Aztecs could remain in the field for months or even years if need be. At any given time the army would consist of several hundred thousand soldiers, of whom at least 100,000 would be porters accompanying the troops, each carrying as much as 50 pounds in material.

The Aztec army once marched 500 miles south from the Valley of Mexico to the coast to defeat and kill a local tribal chief who had made the fatal mistake of executing a group of 160 Aztec merchants. At its zenith, the Aztec army consisting of 400,000 men attacked a coastal kingdom, burnt the city and captured all the inhabitants.

So according to the priests, the series of bad events demonstrates the gods demand more blood, more hearts, and that they are no longer satisfied with brave warriors but crave females and children.

Now the villages and towns under Aztec rule will have to contribute more than grain and jade—they will now be forced to give up their virgin children to the Empire so they can be sacrificed to the gods.

***

While the Emperor tries to deal with disasters and the future Heroine suffers her loss, Cortés the Conqueror, accompanies Diego Velásquez in his expedition to conquer Cuba—a prize sought by Spain since the Italian explorer Christopher Columbus sighted the island on his way to America.

Cuba is the largest Caribbean island by far and the battle for it is marked by stiff resistance from the natives. With only three ships and 300 men, including young Cortés, who was a clerk assigned to the treasurer of the expedition, Diego Velásquez decided that brute force would be the best course of action. Also along on the expedition was a Spanish cleric named Las Casas, since one of the prime objectives of the Spanish in the New World was to convert the natives to Christianity. Ironically, it was this priest who would eventually be a champion of the Indians as intelligent and sophisticated people and go on to document the horrors of the conquest and denounce those responsible.

The small expedition landed on the southern coast, where they established a settlement at Baracca. The task could have been relatively easy except that Hatuey, an Indian Chief from Haiti had paddled over to Cuba first with several hundred followers. He sought to warn to the inhabitants about the atrocities committed by the Spanish back in Haiti and the Dominican Republic, and to incite them to resist the invasion.

But in fact the Indians in Cuba were peaceful and even offered food to the Spanish, so initially he won over only few supporters. That is until Diego Velásquez made a huge mistake.

Arriving at the town of Caonao in the evening, the Spanish found two thousand people, who had prepared a great feast consisting of cassava bread and fish from the ocean. But it quickly become obvious the Indians of Caonao were frightened—not just by the Spanish, but even more by their horse—animals which they had never seen before. At least five hundred more natives were hiding in a large hut and afraid to come out.

Perhaps attempting to head off a war with Hatuey by a brutal show of force, either someone ordered a massacre or something spooked the Spanish. One of them suddenly drew his sword, then all the others drew theirs and began to slaughter the Indians—men, women, children, all of whom were seated, off guard and frightened. Within minutes, not one of them remains alive.

In a blood lust the Spanish then entered the large hut nearby and begin to kill as many as they found there, so that blood streamed in puddles on the wooden floor and ran out into the dirt.

As if Hatuey wasn't already fired up by the Spanish, now he had proof to show the Indians of Cuba what they were dealing with. He managed to gain more supporters and waged a guerilla war against the Spanish, who retreated and feared to leave their fortified settlement at Baracca.

It is three years before the Spanish gain control. Those three years are marked by stiff resistance from the natives, until Hatuey is betrayed, and Velásquez has him burned alive at the stake in front of as many Indians as he can muster.

The mission is ultimately successful however, and Velásquez is appointed governor. At the age of 26, Cortés is made clerk to the treasurer with the responsibility of ensuring that the Spanish Crown receives customary one-fifth of the profits from the expedition. He works hard and keeps meticulous records, a result of his legal schooling and writing abilities. For his efforts Cortés is granted a large estate there and more Indian slaves.

But the most important lesson Cortés learns has nothing to do with record keeping. He has seen the brutality of his leaders and comrades first hand and understands it only prolonged the conquest needlessly. The Indians would probably have accepted Spanish rule—and conversion to Christianity—without bloodshed. He vows to himself that when it is his turn he will not repeat this mistake.

***

For weeks there is a power vacuum in the village. Malinalli's father's clerk takes over temporarily as the people there and in the surrounding territory are in shock at the news of their chief's early demise. By all appearances he died a natural death since there was no trauma on the body, but he was still in his prime so it makes the situation more difficult to accept. How could a young man die suddenly? Perhaps the gods had some role in it?

Finally the people settle down and elect a veteran Jaguar warrior the new chief. After his confirmation by the Empire, one of his first official duties is to visit Malinalli's home. In fact their estate and their servants are reserved for the chief—a law instituted by the Empire so that the leadership has no need of temptation or corruption. The new chief benevolently informs her mother that they may continue to live there for the short term until they can find suitable quarters.

Malinalli takes an instant dislike to her father's replacement despite his outward kindness.

"Mama, I don't understand—we have to move?"

"This estate belongs to the chief of the village. It is only because of your father's position that we live here."

"It's not fair. What will we do?"

"Perhaps the gods will show us the way. You should pray and make an offering to your Feathered Serpent." Her mother suggests, but Malinalli senses something else in her tone. It is the first time in weeks she sees a slight softening in her features.

Within a few weeks Malinalli learns why: the new chief and her mother seem to be spending a lot of time together. In fact tongues are already waging in the village.

After yet another evening when the new chief shares dinner at her home, she confronts her mother.

"Why is *he* here again?"

"Hush daughter, it's none of your business."

"But daddy has only been gone for two months..."

"Don't questions your elders! Besides you want to stay in this house don't you?"

"What do you mean by that?" Malinalli asks, suspicion building.

"If you want to maintain the life we had then you will be silent and respect him! Don't ruin this by your whining. Your father is gone. If you were older you would inherit his title and power, but that cannot be for many years. So I must find a way to provide for us."

Malinalli studies her mother. For the first time she recognizes they are cut from the same mold, her mother is slender and tall of stature, unlike most of the women in the village, and she is lighter skinned and well, pretty.

"You intent to *marry* him?" Malinalli asks with a shocked tone, but she already knows the answer...

Thankfully Malinalli has something to take her mind off the situation: she is accepted into the temple and begins spending day and night there, only returning home on the weekends. This is required both as a means of intensive immersion and due to the long journey from her village of Paynala.

The temple of Feathered Serpent is almost exactly as Malinalli imagined it: light and airy and surrounded by flowers. As she approaches the first day a woman in a white robe bids her inside.

"I am called Eréndira and I will be your teacher and guide in your journey to understanding." She motions Malinalli to sit cross-legged face to face on the stone floor and the girl instinctively likes her.

"I am Malinalli." The girl replies politely.

"Yes Malinalli, you were born under the sign of Grass. This day signifies tenacity, rejuvenation—that which cannot be uprooted forever. Malinalli is a day for persevering against all odds and for creating alliances that will survive the test of time. It is a good day for those who are suppressed, a bad day for their suppressors. It is a good and powerful sign." Eréndira tells her.

They are briefly interrupted by a brilliant yellow butterfly flitting around the temple.

"Perhaps a sign." Eréndira smiles at the pleasant intrusion. "You know that your birthday is governed by Patecatl as its provider of life energy. He is the Lord of Healing and Medicines. He is the husband of Mayahuel."

Malinalli nods seriously, paying rapt attention.

"But did you know that Feathered Serpent himself took Mayahuel from her grandmother and the fearsome star demons in order to protect her? But the demons caught her and tore her to pieces. Feathered Serpent then buried her remains from which the first maguey plant grew so the people would have drink, rope, and sweet syrup."

Malinalli is torn between delight and horror at this information, but says nothing.

"I am very pleased you have chosen Quetzalcoatl, the Feathered Serpent, to whom to dedicate yourself. Did you know that all noble born, such as yourself, are considered to be his descendants?"

"Please tell me about Feathered Serpent. I want to know everything." Malinalli asks excitedly.

"Feathered Serpent is a giver of life and bringer of knowledge. Feathered Serpent and his three brother gods created the sun, the heavens, and the earth. Feathered Serpent's battles with Smoking Mirror brought about the creation and destruction of four suns and earths, leading to the fifth sun and today's world." Eréndira spoke with a strong but calm voice, looking the young girl in the eye.

"At first there were no people under the fifth sun. All the peoples of the four worlds had died, and their bones littered Hell. This sorrowed Feathered Serpent greatly because he felt responsible. So he and his twin brother journeyed to Hell to find those bones, but once there aroused the fury of the Death Lord. As he fled from the underworld, Feathered Serpent dropped the bones, and they broke into pieces. He gathered up the pieces and took them to the goddess Snake Woman, who ground them into flour. Feathered Serpent pierced his manhood, his penis, and moistened the flour with his own blood, which gave it life. Then he and his brother shaped the mixture into human forms and taught the new creatures how to reproduce themselves." The priestess gestured with a delicate wave of her hands at the sky and the ground as the young girl hung on her every word...

While Malinalli enjoyed her education at the temple, each time she returned home she found the chief already there, as if he had taken up residence. Three weeks later her mother took her aside and told her the news: She was getting remarried—to the new chief. This did not sit well with Malinalli who began to use her time at the temple as an escape from this depressing situation.

She endured the wedding ceremony only by thinking of how soon she could get back to Eréndira's teaching. To make it worse, there were the ugly rumors about her father's untimely death: perhaps her mother had somehow 'helped' it along? Had she poisoned him somehow? This was too much for Malinalli who hurried back to the temple the very next day after the marriage.

"But why did Lord Feathered Serpent leave us? I have heard stories at the village school." Malinalli asked Eréndira, with her own feelings of abandonment by her father whirling in her head.

"Lord Feathered Serpent's departure from our world was the result of his old enemy, Smoking Mirror, who was disdainful of Feathered Serpent's kindness to us humans and jealous of our adoration for him. Smoking Mirror tricked Feathered Serpent by getting him drunk and then holding up a magic mirror. Instead of himself, Feathered Serpent saw Smoking Mirror's cruel face. Believing that he was looking at his own cruel image, Feathered Serpent decided to leave the world and sailed east into the sea on a raft of serpents. But Feathered Serpent missed his creations, we humans, so much he threw himself onto a funeral pyre. As his body burned, birds flew forth from the flames, and his heart went up into the heavens to become the morning star Venus."

Malinalli was on the verge of tears at the story.

"Do not fret child, you may see our Lord Feathered Serpent each summer day in the morning sky as he watches over us." Eréndira assured her kindly.

"But will he return to help us?" Malinalli asks.

"It is prophesied that our Lord Feathered Serpent will return in One Reed, eight years from now..."

But eight years is a long time for someone so young and the next thing Malinalli knows her mother is pregnant! And by the end of her first year at the temple, her brother is born.

Although her step father treats her decently enough, it is blatantly obvious that he and her mother favor their new son. Her mother has finally gotten what she wanted all along—a boy. Malinalli no longer feels welcome in her own home.

She misses her father, misses him saying good night. As she remains cut off from friends thanks to her mother, she has no one but Eréndira.

A few weeks later Malinalli is summoned home for a ceremony for her brother. After a trying day and restless evening she finally falls asleep—only to be jostled awake by rough hands in the dead of night. Someone puts a coarse bag over her head and clamps a hand over her mouth and lifts her from her bed. Before she knows it, Malinalli is carried off.

They travel a long way. Malinalli squirms and struggles but here are at least two of them—against which a nine year old girl has no chance. At some point she dozes off and the next thing she feels is the warmth of the morning sun. They stop and she is dumped on the hard earth. The sack is removed, blinding her for several minutes.

Someone shoves a cup in her hands, which she realizes are bound with rope.

"Drink!" An old man's wizened face swims into view. His wicked grin is missing several teeth.

Malinalli looks around and sees there are four men—all dressed in tattered filthy clothes, and she knows they are not Aztec but probably Mayan. She also does not recognize the area which means she is far from the village.

"Why am I here? My father is chief of Paynala and my mother is noble born. You will be punished." Malinalli cries.

"You foolish girl! Your mother sold you to us—for a good price I must say—so that you wouldn't be around to inherit your dead father's power and wealth." The eldest of them yells her, his face so close she feels the spittle flying from his lips.

"That can't be!"

"Of course it is, her and her new husband want their boy to succeed to the title of chief and the estate which is rightfully yours." The vile man laughs evilly.

"People will miss me; my teacher priestess Eréndira will miss me." Malinalli reasons, almost to herself.

"No one will miss you! Your mother buried another girl, a convenient result of her slave's child's death, and told the whole village it was you. No one will ever look for you; you're mine, my slave, and my property now. And I hope to get a good price for you though you're skinny and frail looking."

Malinalli is in the hands of slave traders; her own mother sold her out! Tears fill her eyes at the pain in her heart.

"Consider yourself lucky you still live, another mother would just have drowned you in a river." The old man tells her and then shouts something to the others in a language she doesn't understand. One of them puts the sack over her head and lifts her over his shoulder and they are off again.

Several hours later they stop again and when the sack is removed Malinalli sees she is in a large city, much bigger than her own village. She is carried to a square in what must be the marketplace. The old man places a noose around her neck and she is led like a dog on a leash to a group of other people, most of them dirty and nearly naked. Although the language is foreign and she doesn't understand what is happening, the bidding has begun.

One by one the other people—men, women and children like her, slaves she realizes, are marched off after an exchange of cocoa beans or jade pieces. Then it is her turn.

A few men feel her arms, and force her mouth open to look at her teeth and comment in their unknown tongue. Then a tall man with no hair and the biggest arms she has ever seen speaks at length to her captor.

The old slave trader turns to her.

"Can you spin and weave?"

Malinalli nods.

The men exchange more words, heatedly it seems and then the tall one passes over a few pieces of jade. The slave trader hands him her leash and he pulls her out of the line.

He leads her a few steps to an old woman who has several other slaves with her and hands her the rope tied around Malinalli's neck. Before long they are all walking eastward until they come to a large stone house, one of the finest Malinalli has ever seen.

But the slaves are shoved into one of the outbuildings to lie on a dirt floor as darkness falls. There is almost total silence; no one speaks out of fear and confusion.

That night Malinalli's eyes burn with tears as despair pierces her heart. Her own mother had not only abandoned her, but gave her away to slave traders. As she tosses and turns fitfully on the hard ground, Malinalli wonders what will become of her and prays to Feathered Serpent for some guidance or sign.

Hours later, a Goddess came to her in a dream. She is a beautiful lady, not unlike a young Eréndira, dressed in pale shades with a light filling her face framed with flowing earthen locks.

"Child, why do you weep so? Look inward and imitate the strength of which you are named. Do you not know the grass cannot be tamed? See it bend with the wind and then stand upright. See it trampled under the feet of men and then straighten. See it guard the soil from blowing away in the storms. See it hide and protect the many creatures that live in its midst. Do not fear your future my child, for you are far stronger than you think, and like the grass for which you are named, you will prevail."

6 Calm Before the Storm

After years of one disaster after another, the Emperor enjoys a brief respite. The lake water has receded; the doubling of taxes in the form of food has eased the famine, and Montezuma can attend to his regular duties—which even in the best of times is no small job in an Empire with over a million inhabitants.

The Aztec people are hard workers, fierce fighters, eloquent speakers, and excel in mathematics, agriculture and engineering. The culture is based on constant growth, expansion and change. The foundation of their daily life is a series of complex laws handed down from generation to generation.

The legal system is sophisticated and includes judges who handle everything from disputes between citizens and even villages to all type of criminal offenses. Courts are held every eighty days and attended by judges from throughout the Empire.

Parties are required to swear strict oaths in the name of the god Hummingbird Wizard to tell the truth and do so by touching the ground and then their lips. In this way, lying becomes an affront to the gods and can be punished by death. Lying in court can get you the same punishment as the person you were trying to protect or lying about. Documents and other evidence are introduced into the proceeding just as in any modern legal system.

Aztec judges have a great deal of assistance in their task of administering justice. They have messengers and constables to inform or arrest the accused. Jailers are also present and prisoners awaiting trial are placed in wooden cages until their trial date. Aside from these jails no truly long term prison system exists because either the convicted are executed (by bashing their heads with rocks or involuntary sacrifice) or draw some form of home punishment such as restitution or slavery.

Scribes are a fixture in the Aztec court system and serve the important functions of recording lawsuits between villages, acting as stenographers in court proceedings and compiling codebooks. Since the Aztecs use a complex pictorial writing system this requires a high degree of skill to draw and keep up with the proceedings.

When charges are filed, the accused party is summoned before the court and given a chance to confront their accuser. And while no lawyers are present they can bring a friend or relative to help plead their case. Trials are public and based on an inquisitorial process where it is the judges that question the witnesses, defendants and plaintiffs.

But even if Malinalli's plight had become known, it is questionable what might have been done about it. Slavery is legal and slaves compose about 3% of the Aztec population. Many slaves are brought in from foreign lands to be sold in the central slave markets. The Empire strictly regulates the slave trade and once purchased, it is illegal to sell an obedient slave against their wishes.

Some slaves are sacrificial victims captured in war. The Empire engages in a continual process of expansion through conquest and sacrificial captives serve several purposes. First, the Aztecs firmly believe that their gods sacrificed themselves to keep the universe intact and believe that humans need to be sacrificed in order to keep the universe in order. Secondly, they increase the prestige of the captor as they gain special status when they captured their first four captives. Finally, the sacrifice of captives provides an example to the various vassal states of the price of defiance. Sacrificial slaves have no rights, but are expected to die with dignity.

But then there were the Aztec slaves: citizens considered commoners who had to sell themselves into slavery to survive, or became slaves in compensation for some crime they committed. Aztec citizens could sell themselves or another member of their family into slavery to support them.

Aztec slaves have a number of legal benefits, including exemption from taxation and military service. Many slaves even rose to positions of responsibility acting as overseers and estate managers, and Aztec law allows them to acquire land, property, and even slaves of their own. It is not illegal for slaves to marry and there is no social stigma attached.

In Malinalli's case, although she is a child and was sold by her mother, she is noble born and was sold into slavery unwillingly in order to deprive her of her rightful inheritance. So her mother and stepfather could probably have been accused of both theft and kidnapping—the latter punishable by death.

So despite the sophisticated Aztec legal system, no judge nor Montezuma is aware of this crime, and thus the ultimate demise of the entire Empire is set into motion—exactly as predicted.

***

It is in Cuba, Cortés finally becomes a man of substance—and not just title—with mines, cattle and the slave laborers to work them and make him wealthy.

The Governor of Cuba, Diego Velázquez, is so impressed with the hard work of Cortés as clerk-treasurer that he secures a high political position for him in the colony—he backs him for mayor of Santiago, which is the capital of Cuba at the time. In this position Cortés continues to build a reputation as a daring and bold leader and forges alliances with the Governor's secretary, Andreas de Duero and the King's accountant, Almador de Lares—two men who will be instrumental in advancing the Conqueror's exploits.

This position of power also makes him a new source of leadership, to which opposing political forces in the colony could then turn—a fact confirmed when he was twice re-elected as mayor. Cortés even leads a group which demands that more laborers be assigned to the settlers, resulting in the importation of black slaves since the natives were considered frail and in short supply after a lengthy war of attrition.

Cortés, the ladies man, also manages to find time to pursue that pastime. His own Indian slave girls willingly serve him and there seems to be a mutual attraction. Cortés is handsome, cuts a dashing figure and is relatively gentle master. The Indians females are quite different from pale Spanish women, not only in their coloring but in their direct open manner, since they possess none of the feminine wiles of European women. As many other men have discovered it is a case of opposites attract.

As time goes by however, Cuba becomes more settled and a fair number of Spanish women join the colony, providing Cortés a 'target-rich' environment for his pursuits. One of the most valuable of those targets is about to come his way, a fact he learns first hand from the Governor.

"Hernando I have a very important task for you." Velásquez tells him after summoning him to his office.

It should be pointed out here that Velásquez is not only arguably the most pompous man in all of the West Indies but has an obsession with his version of what should pass for proper etiquette to the point that not even the most distinguished persons in the colony would dare sit uninvited in his presence.

"Of course sir." Cortés says as he judiciously remains standing.

"An emissary from the Royal Court will be traveling here next month. This lady, Maria de Toledo who is a relative of our King, wishes to examine the conditions of the natives. While we certainly don't need any meddling in our affairs, we don't have a choice. Since you seem to get along with the native population, I'd like you to take the lead on this."

"Certainly sir." Cortés is leery since Velásquez is widely known to treat the Indians harshly. While it appears his boss is trying to hide behind him, he can't pass up a chance to meet a member of the royal family.

"And that's not all. There is a family of the name Juarez who will be accompanying her. Three sisters named Maria, Leonor, and Catalina are acting as her ladies in waiting. So you will be expected to look after a group of three ladies. Can I count on you?"

"Of course Governor." He replies, and sets about arranging for the women's arrival, to the point of having them stay on his personal estate.

So this Maria de Toledo, a relative of the King of Spain, and three of her lady friends are being entrusted to him, Cortés thinks to himself. And the ever ambitious Cortés quickly recognizes this is his chance not only to win more favor with the Governor, but also get an 'in' to the royal court!

When the party arrives Cortés sees to them personally, but Maria de Toledo consumes all of his time as she immediately sets about investigating the slavery of the natives. Despite his best efforts she indeed meddles into the colony's affairs, eventually resulting in a decree from the King prohibiting using the native Indians as slave labor.

In the meantime the three sisters are being courted by seemingly every man in Cuba. While Maria Juarez rejects all potential suitors to assist Maria de Toledo, Leonor catches the eye of the Governor, leaving Cortés to press his inside advantage with Catalina. Unfortunately, Catalina Juarez is not a beautiful woman. Although she possesses alabaster skin and fancy European gowns, no amount of finery will cover her horse-like features.

Still and all, the tighter Leonor and Velásquez become, the more likely they will be married and if Cortés pursues Catalina, he could end up as part of the Governor's family. So he grits his teeth and courts her.

At a grand party a few days later the Governor has thrown to present the ladies formally to the colony, Cortes finds himself studying the three sisters. Maria is plain and Catalina is just plain unattractive while the delicately beautiful Leonor seems to have received all the looks in the family.

Unable to help himself, Cortés recklessly flirts with Leonor and is rewarded with some mutual interest. But this begins to incur the wrath of the Governor and before long it is clear she has eyes on the bigger prize anyway. Guided by his blinding ambition, he has little choice but to outwardly continue his liaison with Catalina by day while secretly bedding his Indian women at night.

A few weeks later Governor Velásquez summons Cortés again.

"I have decided to wed Miss Leonor. We will be announcing our engagement next month. "

"Congratulations Governor." Cortés replies, pleased he is privy to this news but also wondering why.

"She has expressed her desire for a double wedding with Catalina."

This statement floors Cortés! He can barely look at the woman and it is much too soon. He needs to get used to her before even considering marriage. For once Cortés is at a loss for words.

"Do you not find her a suitable wife?" Velásquez questions him in the roaring silence.

What could he say—that he finds the Governor's future sister-in-law ugly?

"Well, yes, I mean she is good material, but…" Cortés stammers.

"But what? What's the problem then?"

"Well we hardly know each other and I'm not even sure Miss Catalina would accept my proposal." Cortés tries.

"Oh, I have it on very good authority that Catalina would accept your proposal of marriage." The Governor smiles briefly. "You know Hernando, you are a gentleman of means and importance in the colony, taking a wife will polish your image and help elevate your social status."

"I understand sir." Cortés replies lamely.

"Cuba is civilized now and we all need to settle down. A wife will do wonders for you—better than those native women of yours."

Cortés cringes a little at the jab.

"And remember, anything that makes my future wife happy will make me happy." The Governor fires off his last shot to nods from Cortés as he makes his leave.

The Conqueror returns to his office deep in thought and soon commits himself in the direction he must take. A marriage into the Governor's family will do wonders for him and certainly cement his status not only in the colonies but back in Spain. That evening as he returns to his estate he is determined to see it through and propose to Catalina.

But when he sets eyes on that horse face, he just can't bring himself to do it.

***

Malinalli's first days in slavery are a frightening experience. She doesn't understand the language and there are no friendly faces to comfort her. But the overseer, the man who purchased her, assigns one of the older women slaves to look after her and teach her the Mayan tongue so she can be a productive worker for the household.

Day by day, word by word, she learns while she hones her weaving skills alongside the old woman. Soon Malinalli is making dresses for all the other slaves and is able to speak to them as well. The next time the overseer pays attention he is surprised to hear the young girl speaking their language almost perfectly.

Malinalli becomes popular among the women for her beautiful garments; for she knows how to dye them brilliant colors as her mother taught her. Red dye is made from cochineal which comes from crushing tiny female coccus insects that live and feed on the prickly-pear cactus. And yellow is derived from mulberry or rabbit brush.

She has many other skills as well and begins teaching the slaves how to read. The overseer is even more stunned to discover Malinalli not only knows how to write, but also can count and do math. Within a year, the girl is helping him keep records for the household.

The next year Malinalli comes to the attention of the Lord of the house, a high chief of the town, when his wife points her out.

"She is the one who made this dress you like." She informs him, it is a bright yellow garment with a red flower woven into the fabric.

The Lord calls for the overseer to ask about her.

"Yes, that one is called 'Grass'." The overseer explains. Malinalli was called that when she couldn't speak their language and kept pointing to the grass in the field and the name stuck.

"A clever girl, a most valuable purchase Overseer; you are to be commended."

"Thank you my Lord." The overseer doesn't even want to tell his owner all she can really do.

"Where did she come from? She must have had an education."

"I do not know my Lord, I found her in the slave market. I believe she must have come from the Aztec lands judging from her language."

"Ah, that would explain it. But she was legally purchased?" The Chief doesn't want to incur the wrath of the Empire, but also doesn't mind putting one over on the Aztecs either.

The two cultures are in a constant state of wary truce dating back centuries when the ancestors of both peoples had an unfortunate disagreement. A king of the ancestors of the Aztecs asked for the daughter of the king of the ancestors of the Maya. The Mayans thought he was asking for her hand in marriage and agreed only to discover during what they thought was the wedding ceremony, that the Aztec had sacrificed her and the chief priest was seen wearing her skin. The Mayans then drove them out, but over the last century the Mayan power had declined in the face of the superior Aztecs.

"Yes sir. We paid two pieces of jade for her."

"Ah, even somewhat of a bargain. This girl is pretty and skilled; who will you mate her with?"

"She is not yet of age, my Lord. She is only twelve."

"Really? That is quite astonishing. Well, protect her well she is a valuable asset."

Malinalli continues, if not exactly to thrive (after all she is a slave without freedom), but at least to survive. She makes the best of her situation, both learning and teaching, until she comes of age and the overseer is faced with handling her journey into womanhood.

The old woman who first taught the one they call Grass how to speak takes the overseer aside one day.

"The blood came for Grass last night, she is a woman now."

"Does she favor any of the other boys?" The overseer inquires—a fact that would make his task easy.

"I do not think so, though more than a few favor her." The old woman answers with a smirk.

The overseer watches Malinalli briefly as she weaves. He is not surprised since the girl is tall and vibrantly pretty. The only problem is that she talks a lot, but given her skills...

"Have you taught her about being a woman, about how not to get pregnant?" He asks, struggling with the problem.

"If you so desire, I will see to it and teach her the ways."

The overseer has a personal stake in Malinalli: she secretly assists in certain complex tasks of the household. If she would marry he would likely lose this since her husband would discover this secret—which would be an embarrassment for him.

"Yes, teach her. I think she could use a few more years before taking a husband, but I don't want her with child before that." He commands, delaying the issue a while longer...

But the years pass quickly and soon the Lord of the house summons the overseer to inquire about her.

"This girl Grass has blossomed into a beautiful woman." The Lord says. "Are there marriage prospects?"

"There have been a few inquiries, but of course any arrangement would have to have your approval."

"Well, one of my sons has taken an interest in her."

This news rocks the overseer. While it is not unheard of for nobility to marry a common slave it is very rare. But what really troubles him is that if Malinalli marries into the family or even just shares a bed, she will gain tremendous power. His own position would be in jeopardy.

"While her lips may be pretty my Lord, they move a lot. You may find her distracting." He finally says, pondering a way to derail a possible match and calculating what he can do to get rid of her.

"I see, that is not unlike my own wife. But I shall leave it up to my son."

Malinalli is of course unaware of this discussion. That night as every night, she says her one and only prayer: That Feathered Serpent will return to save her people from Hummingbird Wizard...

7 The Stage Is Set

Montezuma strolls through the beautiful garden with balconies extending over it, supported by marble columns. There are ten pools, in which were kept all the species of water birds. Some of the pools contain salt water and others fresh water depending on the bird's needs. Three hundred slaves tend these birds, feeding them worms and seeds or fish from the salt lake upon which the city is built.

He walks through a large courtyard, paved in marble with a chessboard pattern, where large cages, each covered with a roof of tiles, contain birds of prey, from the kestrel to the eagle. The Emperor continues on into the palace where on the immense ground floor are larger cages made of heavy timbers. In these are kept lions, tigers, wolves, foxes, and every variety of large cat. Montezuma amuses himself briefly with one of the mountain lions before moving on to the grand dining hall where six hundred nobles and merchants await—as they do each and every day.

The meal is served by four hundred youths, who bring an infinite variety of dishes—every kind of meat, game, fish, fruits, and vegetables that the country can produce. At the beginning and end of each course the servants bring water for the hands, along with cotton napkins never used twice.

When the Emperor finishes his meal he retires to his chambers to change into his second of four outfits for the day, each entirely new, never to be worn again. He is bored that day, having no emergencies to which to attend, so he decides to indulge in one of his few vices.

Craftsmen and merchants bring their wares for his perusal. Montezuma studies the art and jewelry arrayed before him by the best craftsmen in the capital. The Aztec artisans are no part-time amateurs. They dedicate their lives to their craft. In a world permeated with religion and symbolism, they have no shortage of work to do. Jewelers sell most pieces in the marketplace, where a huge variety of colorful items are available, but the best are always reserved for the Emperor and other nobility. If someone important chose their work it would of course enhance their reputation.

One common form of Aztec jewelry is the large ear plugs, which were really designed to fit into the ear lobes, and are popular with both men and women. Men also often wear ornaments in their noses through a hole in the nasal septum and also jewelry suspended from a slit in their lower lip.

Aztec art is generally owned by the upper classes, and jewelry was no exception. It is very common for Montezuma to wear extravagant necklaces and earrings. Aztec jewelry is made with a rich variety of materials, and often more than one type of material went into one piece. Mosaics are sometimes created by placing bits of various precious stones like jade, quartz amethyst, opal, and turquoise into a background of clay or wood. These stones are also highly polished and used in jewelry and ornaments. Other commonly used materials are shells, clay, wood, rock such as obsidian, and feathers.

Copper, silver, and gold metals also find their way into jewelry. Copper is cold-hammered and carefully hammered into sheets or other forms. It is also cast into bells and ornaments through the lost wax process. The desired shape is modeled in clay, over which is dusted finely ground charcoal, followed by an even layer of wax. This coating is also dusted with charcoal and the whole enclosed in clay, which is perforated at the top and bottom. The molten metal is poured in at the upper hole after the wax is melted and the lower orifice plugged. When the metal cooled the cast is broken and the finished object removed.

Silver and gold is very popular due to its relative abundance in the area and serves mostly as trim and adornment. While gold is used it is in fact considered less valuable than jade or even cocoa beans. It found a place in jewelry primarily because it is an easy soft metal to work into the artisan's creations.

The Emperor chooses a few pieces and one of his attendants pays the craftsmen a few pebbles of jade. Montezuma is pleased and relaxed and retires to his private chambers to pray and then get a good night's sleep.

But it is not to be. Barely an hour after he closes his eyes, two of his priest-advisors awaken him excitedly.

"My Lord, my Lord, look outside!" One practically yells.

In the sky Montezuma sees a comet with three heads and sparks shooting from its tail flying in the eastward sky. The vision sends chills down his back. It will just be the first of many such events.

The next year, another comet, a pyramidal light, scattering sparks on all sides, rose at midnight from the eastern horizon and fades at dawn. This phenomenon appears for 40 nights, and is interpreted by the priests as the Feathered Serpent conveying a great message that presages war and mortality among the lords.

Then the following year yet another comet is sighted. It is like a rip in the sky which bleeds celestial influences onto the Aztec world. While the Emperor watches horrified, a lightning bolt strikes the temple of Hummingbird Wizard and destroys it.

Then finally a woman's voice was heard throughout the capital coming from everywhere and nowhere crying "My children, my children, we are lost!"

Montezuma knows the prophecy is coming true, the year of One Reed is upon them.

He orders more human sacrifices...

***

In the intervening years Cortés becomes restless despite his status as mayor of Santiago, the largest city in Cuba. But even worse, his relationship with Governor Diego Velásquez deteriorates badly, mostly due to his hesitation in marrying Catalina. This subject is a continual source of marital dispute in the Velásquez household because his wife Leonor, who is Catalina's sister, reminds him of it often.

As if that weren't enough, Velásquez also became wary of Cortés' ambitions and fears he might seek to replace him as Governor since he has many powerful political allies in the territory. The situation reaches critical mass when the Governor becomes so incensed with Cortés he has him thrown in jail on trumped-up treason charges.

Some of Cortés' friends quickly advise him of the condition for his freedom: marry Catalina. A deal is struck secretly, so as not to embarrass Catalina or the Governor, and Cortés reluctantly announces his engagement upon his release.

The wedding is a happy and festive occasion for everyone except Cortés. All the important people in the capital turn out and Governor Velásquez not only stands as witness for Cortés but even gives away the bride. This way not only does he make Leonor happy, but he figures the marriage will insure Cortés' loyalty and remove him as a threat.

After enduring two years of a loveless (at least on his part) marriage, Cortés is bored, restless, and desperate for a way out. Then some excitement comes to the colony of Cuba when the Governor launches a small expedition to explore westward.

Under the command of Francisco Hernandez de Cordoba three ships and 110 men including Bernal Diaz del Castillo, sail west into the unknown. After weathering a furious storm, the tiny fleet makes land on the 21st day.

They immediately run into natives they continue to call 'Indians' and discover these people are more intelligent—and dangerous than the natives of Cuba. The natives, wearing cotton garments and faces painted black and white, attack the Spanish with spears, arrows and slingshots. During several battles Captain Cordoba suffers wounds in no less than twelve different places by their arrows and Bernal Diaz is wounded himself by three arrows, which fall like rain upon them.

But the Spanish make two important discoveries for their troubles: Three temples built of stone inside of which they find idols of horrible and frightening shapes, but also three crowns and other ornaments, some in the shape of fish, others in the shape of ducks made of gold. They also run into the native priests—ten of whom came running out of one of the temples, dressed in long white robes, with the thick hair of their heads entangled and clotted with blood.

The Spanish retreat to their ships, and addition to the gold manage to capture two native prisoners, who they baptize and convert to Christians. One is named Melchior and the other Julian.

In the end the expedition loses fifty-seven men, besides two the Indians carried off alive, and five who died on ship of their wounds and extreme thirst.

The tales of fine architecture and more importantly—gold, convince Velásquez to form another expedition the following year, this time with four ships and double the men, under the command of Juan de Grijalva, since Cordoba had died of his wounds. Bernal Diaz is also on this voyage, as are the two natives Melchior and Julian, who are to act as guides.

So the fleet set sail for the newly discovered country the natives called 'Yucatan'. Once again they meet with more fierce resistance, and only a few days after making landfall they suffer sixty wounded during a huge battle. The men barely escape with their lives and press onward, finally encountering some natives who will talk. Melchior and Julian are able to communicate and tell the native chief the Spanish are only here to trade, upon which they are warned the natives have an 8,000 man army ready to repel any attempt to conquer them.

During a six day period they are able to trade for upwards of 1,500 pesos' worth of gold trinkets—a small fortune of about $18,000. When the Spanish ask for more, they are told the tribe has given them all it has, but there is much more gold to the west—in the capital of the Empire.

The expedition continues, running into both friendly and not friendly natives who constantly attack them. After months of exploring, they are exhausted and sail back to Cuba to treat their numerous wounded.

When Governor Velásquez sees the gold and hears the accounts of much more to the west, he is determined to send out an enlarged third expedition and this news spreads like wildfire through the colony.

Cortés is determined to lead this new mission, but the competition is fierce. Not only does de Grijalva want to return, but every would-be conquistador and relative of Velásquez vies for the opportunity. So Cortés enlists his friends and confidants of Diego Velázquez: Andreas de Duero, secretary to the governor, and Almador de Lares, the royal treasurer, to persuade the Governor in his favor.

His strategy is successful and Cortés is elected Captain of the new expedition, but in return is expected to finance it himself. While he manages to come up with 30%, he has spent a great deal of his wealth on the marriage so he petitions his friends and is given 4000 gold pieces plus 4000 more in supplies in exchange for a mortgage on his land and a future share of the profits from the voyage. Upon receiving these funds he has several ornate banners made, and Cortés being Cortés, custom uniforms including one coat trimmed in real gold.

With Cortés' experience as an administrator, knowledge gained from many failed expeditions, and his impeccable rhetoric he is able to gather six ships and 300 men within a month. Most importantly many of the conquistadors from the previous expeditions (those still alive) such as Bernal Diaz join him.

The choice of Cortés creates no little envy and the Governor's relatives bombard him with complaints and suspicions about Cortés to the point he is advised by his close friends and benefactors to leave immediately before the Governor changes his mind. So he leaves early—with the Governor's full knowledge and blessing—and sails to the port of Trinidad Cuba, where he plans to lay over and accumulate more ships and men, safe from the jealousy in the capital.

Here Cortés easily convinces 200 more men to join him including Pedro de Alvarado, and even some of Velázquez's relatives and gains five more ships. But with Cortés gone from Santiago and unable to defend himself, his enemies prevail and convince the Governor to rescind Cortés' charter. Velásquez sends a messenger to Trinidad ordering the expedition back.

When Cortés hears this he has a meeting with the mayor of Trinidad and along with his men convince him he has done nothing wrong. He openly writes a letter to the Governor proclaiming his eternal loyalty and promising to uphold his charter—which is to claim the lands for Spain. Of course Cortés knows that is a ruse since Velázquez's main intent is to establish trade with the Indians— cheap trinkets for gold.

The clever Cortés also suggests innocently that Trinidad may not want to be caught in the middle of a battle and this point hits home since Cortés has by then nearly 500 experienced soldiers under his command. The mayor decides to ignore the Governor's message and Cortés is smart enough to leave when he has the chance, so he takes the fleet to Havana, the final port of Cuba.

There the expedition and especially Cortés are greeted warmly and the Conqueror takes on the last of fresh supplies they will need for the journey. He seeks to purchase more horses but they are in short supply. Cortés manages to purchase one with a strip of gold from his very coat.

But when the Governor learns no one obeyed his order and Cortés has left Trinidad he flies into a rage, accusing even his secretary and the royal accountant of conspiracy in a plot with Cortés to steal the fortunes of the New World. Those two immediately dispatch a message to Cortés while Velásquez sends an aide to Havana with orders for his relatives to take him prisoner and stop the expedition.

The plan backfires completely. The messenger not only apprises Cortés of the situation but actually joins him. And the very men Velásquez ordered to arrest Cortés side with him instead—a sign of the Conqueror's considerable leadership skills.

So Cortés, after the example set by Quintero years earlier, ignores the order and slips away from the Cuban coast accompanied by eleven ships, 500 men, 13 horses and a small number of cannons and sets sail for the Yucatan Peninsula in Mayan territory with banners flying the sign of a red cross.

"Comrades, let us follow the sign of the holy Cross with true faith, and through it we shall conquer." Hernando Cortés speaks to his men.

Thus begins the conquest of Mexico. And the three cogs: The Emperor, The Conqueror, and The Heroine, meshed unknowingly for some 17 years, are turning into their final alignment.

***

Shortly after Malinalli's entry into womanhood she begins to feel the urges in herself. The old woman who serves as her surrogate mother explains the mysteries of 'grinding corn'—the native euphemism for sexual intercourse.

"It is natural to feel the tingling when certain men look at you." She tells her. "But you must control yourself if you don't want to get a baby inside you."

This surprises Malinalli a bit since she thought only the gods grant babies.

"No, the man will give you the seed to make a baby. A woman is usually able to get pregnant for about 5 days each month, about 14 days before the blood comes."

"How will I know *before* the blood comes?"

The old woman gives her a string of colored beads.

"You must keep count of your blood days for a few months and then you will know when it is safe to be with a man. The red bead is the first day of your period. Then you count each day as one bead. A dark brown bead marks day 26 and next time you will know before the blood comes." She explains.

The old woman then reports to the overseer that she has instructed the girl. He decides he must wait a few months to put his plan into action, to give the girl a chance to record her periods. The last thing he wants is for her to get pregnant.

After the time passes he arranges with the old woman to introduce Malinalli to one of the strapping slave boys. He wants her to lose her virginity before the Lord's son has a chance to bed her, hoping this will dissuade any further interest.

Once past the fumbling and painful first encounter with the slave boy, Malinalli enjoys her subsequent couplings and like any of her other undertakings, proves a quick learner in the ways of intimacy between a man and a woman.

Although the first part of his plan succeeds, the overseer has miscalculated. Besides Malinalli's intelligence and wit she now has a new weapon: her sexual power. A power she quickly grasps and uses to her advantage.

After all Malinalli does not intend to remain a slave forever.

8 The Conqueror Comes

Montezuma grows more distraught each day. Not only are the lights in the sky, the comets, a daily and frightening reminder for all to see, but now he hears reports of skirmishes with strangers coming from the sea. Unfortunately these battles take place by tribes that are not exactly allies and in areas that are not totally under the control of the Aztec Empire, so solid information is hard to come by.

He calls his high priest Crocodile (Cipactli) and his brother Cuitláhuac for a meeting to discuss these events.

"These stars come day and night now, like a tear in the sky from the next world. We hear rumors of odd warriors coming out of the ocean. I myself have had this vision. Is this the final prophecy?" The Emperor asks them.

Crocodile hesitates in speaking. He is fully aware that his predecessors met untimely deaths in connection with this subject.

"We should send an army to see for ourselves and repel the invaders if this is true." Cuitláhuac speaks out in the silence.

"You are aware the incidents have occurred in Mayan territory?" The Emperor reminds his brother.

"The Mayans are nothing! They have been nothing for a hundred years. We let them live out of pity." His brother spits out.

"They pay us tribute, they pay taxes." Montezuma says.

"Dear brother, you know as well as I they do not pay their full share. You only have to look at those fat pigs to know they are holding back."

The Emperor cannot argue that fact. It is a problem he should have handled long ago—if he were not so preoccupied.

"Send spies along with fast runners to the eastern territories with instructions to report back on the Mayans—and anything else they may encounter. At least we'll be prepared." Montezuma tells his brother.

Then he turns his attention to the priest Crocodile.

"What say you? You have been silent."

"My Lord, I do not believe there is need for worry. It is not yet One Reed so these events cannot be part of the prophecy." He feels at least he speaks the truth, even if it is a weak excuse.

The Emperor flies into a rage—a rare occurrence for him.

"Are you a fool? One Reed is only months away! You expect us to believe what is happening is not connected?"

"My Lord, the prophecies specify One Reed and since it is not yet One Reed I don't see how they can be connected." The priest tries to use logic.

Montezuma glances at his brother and sends a silent message with his eyes: It is time for a new high priest.

***

Cortés very nearly loses control of the expedition before it even begins. He orders his eleven ships to rendezvous at the cape of St. Antonio, where they would then sail together into Cozumel as a show of force. Pedro de Alvarado, a brave and ferocious fighter but a loose cannon—a trait that will continue to be a problem for Cortés, is commanding the San Sebastian, one of the fastest ships. Alvarado orders his pilot to go directly to Cozumel Island without waiting and thereby arrives two days earlier than the rest of the fleet.

Alvarado and sixty men, including Bernal Diaz, disembark but find only an empty and deserted village. The natives apparently ran and hid. So he orders his men further inland where they find another deserted village, although this time the natives left their belongings in their haste to escape the invaders. The Spanish help themselves to forty fowls and then search a temple where they take several cotton mats, and a few small boxes containing all manner of ornaments made of gold and copper. On the way back they capture three Indians who happened by.

In the meantime Cortés arrives with the remaining vessels, having been delayed by a broken rudder on one of the vessels. He scarcely steps on shore when he orders the pilot of the San Sebastian put in irons for disobeying his orders. But his anger at this is mild compared to when he learns the men under Alvarado had plundered a deserted village.

Cortés then severely reprimands Alvarado.

"How do you expect us to establish relations with these people if you rob them of their property?"

"They are savages." Alvarado says in his defense.

"Our mission is to trade with these people not to steal and murder." Cortés is determined not to make the same mistakes he witnessed in Cuba and start a war.

He then orders the three native prisoners brought in front of him and with the help of Melchior, the native captured on a previous expedition, tells them they have nothing to fear and asks to tell their chief to return to the village so they can meet. He also returns all the items and golden trinkets, and gives them glass beads in exchange for the fowls, which had already been eaten. Then in a sign of good faith he presents each one with a Spanish shirt.

The Spanish set up camp at the village and while they are waiting Cortés orders his men that no one is to harm any native and begins to enforce strict discipline on them in that regard.

The next morning all the natives return and the chief meets with Cortés in a friendly manner, with Melchior again serving as interpreter. During the meeting the Indians are heard to use the word 'Castilian', which is Spanish, and Cortés reasons they must have had contact with Spaniards among them. He tells Melchior to question them about this and they confirm there are indeed two Spanish men, who are slaves to another chief about two day's march from there.

Upon hearing this Cortés is determined to 'rescue' the men and asks the Indians to carry a message to them, paying them with gifts and promising more when they return. The chief tells Cortés though that he will have to pay a ransom and buy back the men since they are slaves.

So Cortés gives them various kinds of glass beads and letters he wrote to the Spanish captives. He sends them aboard two of the smaller ships, armed with twenty men each under the command of Diego de Ordas, to sail further up the coast with orders to remain there for eight days to give the two Spaniards time to get to the ships.

For all the trouble the Indians have caused the previous expeditions, these natives turn out to be quite conscientious and deliver the letters as promised. The first Spaniard is named Geronimo de Aguilar, a Roman Catholic friar, and when he reads the letter and receives the ransom is overjoyed. He takes the beads to his master to beg for his freedom—which is granted as legally required. Aguilar then immediately goes in search of his comrade Gonzalo Guerrero, who had been captured with him after their ship went aground and was wrecked during a storm.

It turns out that Guerrero has assimilated into the native culture much better than Aguilar. The friar is shocked beyond words to see Guerrero has native tattoos on his face and pierced ears.

"Brother, I have an Indian wife and three beautiful children; I am happy here. I have no reason to leave." Guerrero tells him, at which point his wife comes out and admonishes the friar for trying to take away her husband, basically telling him to mind his own business and leave them alone.

Aguilar leaves to pack his meager belongings and then makes another attempt to induce Gonzalo to leave, telling him to consider that he is a Christian, and that he ought not risk the salvation of his soul for the sake of an Indian woman. He then suggests he might take her and the children with him if he could not bear to leave them.

But Gonzalo cannot be persuaded and so the friar makes a long trek to the sea—only to find the harbor empty. He has taken too long and the ships have already left. He has no choice but to return to his Indian master.

In the meantime Cortés has been exploring the island of Cozumel, and it seems to have special significance for the neighboring tribes, for they come in great numbers to worship at a huge stone temple in the form of a pyramid there.

One morning the Spanish notice a large crowd of Indians and their wives. They burn a kind of resin, which resembles incense, and there is an old priest standing at the top of the temple who begins preaching something to the Indians. The Spanish are very curious at the ceremony so Cortés instructs Melchior to interpret it to him.

The Conqueror is not pleased when Melchior explains the Indians are making offerings of fruits and foods to their various gods. He went so far as to call the chiefs and priest to a meeting where he had Melchior tell them that their gods were evil and there was only one true God to which they should devote themselves.

Cortés then shows them an image of the Virgin Mary and a cross, and suggests they be put up instead, because these would bring a blessing to them and make their seeds grow and preserve their souls from eternal hell.

The chiefs and priests answer that their ancestors had prayed to these gods before them, because they were good gods, and that they were bound to follow the gods rule over man. Then they politely suggest that Cortés and his men would discover the true power of the native gods when they send them to the bottom of the sea.

Cortés ignores their threats and orders the idols to be pulled down, and broken to pieces. He then orders an altar to be built, with the help of the same Indians, out of limestone on which he places the image of the Virgin Mary. At the same time two of the Spanish carpenters construct a wooden cross and set it up in a small chapel, which is built behind the altar. When this is done, Father Juan Diaz, the expedition's chaplain, says mass in front of the new altar, and the chiefs and priest look on with curiosity.

By this time Diego de Ordas returns empty handed and without any information, and the Conqueror is not at all pleased since Ordas merely waited on the ships and never bothered to check for the missing Spaniards. Cortés decides it is time to move on and orders the fleet to set sail for the mainland. But they quickly discover one of the ships, the one carrying the bulk of their food supplies, has a hole and is sinking rapidly. The expedition is then forced to stay on Cozumel four more days to repair it.

It appears that Fate has intervened on behalf of Cortés once again, for this malfunction will prove to be a blessing in disguise. It will allow Friar Aguilar a second opportunity to join the expedition and he will prove a pivotal figure in the early stages of the conquest.

Word reaches Aguilar from the Indians who were at the temple that the strangers are still on Cozumel. So he asks the Indians who brought him the letter to hire a canoe with six rowers for himself and them. Since the glass beads they received from Cortés are considered of great value, they willingly comply and set out across the twelve mile channel from the mainland to the island of Cozumel. The Indians had never experienced glass and had no knowledge of how it was made. In fact all the glass beads brought by the Spanish originated in Venice, Italy. The closest thing the natives had to glass was jade, which had similar qualities, and to them jade was more valuable than gold. So glass was deemed more valuable than gold as well.

When Aguilar and his party of Indians finally reach the Spanish, Cortés is confused.

"I thought a Spaniard was returning, which among you is he?" All the men before him look like natives, he can't pick Aguilar out because his years in captivity have made him dark skinned and ragged.

When Geronimo Aguilar heard this, he cowered down after the Indian fashion.

"I am he." He tells the Conqueror, in Spanish he barely remembers.

Cortés helps the man to his feet in shock and then orders new clothes be given to him while he asks the man to tell his story.

He says, in broken Spanish, that his name was Geronimo d' Aguilar, and was a native of Ecija. About eight years ago he had been shipwrecked with fifteen men and two women, on a voyage between Darien and the island of St. Domingo. The ship struck a rock, and ran aground. The whole of the crew then got into a smaller boat, in the hopes of making the island of Cuba or Jamaica, but were driven on shore by the strong currents, to Yucatan where they were captured by Indians.

Most of his companions had been sacrificed to their gods, and the women died from forced hard labor. He himself had also been doomed to be sacrificed, but made his escape during the night, and fled to another village, where he became a slave to the chief.

With regard to his companion Alonso Guerrero, he had married an Indian woman, and was the father of three children. He had adopted the Indian customs, his face was tattooed, his ears pierced, and his lips turned down. He was a sailor by profession, native of Palos, and was considered by the Indians to be a man of great strength. Aguilar adds that about a year ago that a squadron, consisting of three vessels, had briefly landed, when Guerrero advised the Indians to repel the invaders at all cost.

Cortés realizes this must have been the expedition under Francisco Hernandez de Cordoba and is disturbed by the news.

"We need to get this man under our power; his staying among the

Indians will do us no good." Cortés tells his men.

Aguilar on the other hand proves his worth immediately when the chiefs of Cozumel hear him speak their language and treat him with great respect. Aguilar advised them to always honor the image of the Virgin Mary and cross his brethren set up, as they would prove a blessing to them. He also suggested they ask Cortés to give them letters of recommendation to other Spaniards who might run into Cozumel, in order that they might not be harmed by them. Cortés readily complied with this request; and, after mutual protestations of friendship, the fleet hoisted anchor, and set sail for the river Grijalva.

***

Rumors flit about the household like mad butterflies of strangers coming from the eastern sea. At first Malinalli ignores them, but soon her curiosity is aroused.

"What is everyone talking about?" She asks two other slaves.

"It is true; my own cousin has seen them and heard them at the temple on Cozumel. Strange white hairy men have come on huge floating houses of wood." One of them tells her.

"And they came from the east?" She questions.

"Yes, it is true!"

"What do they want?" Malinalli asks.

"They say our gods are no good, commanding that there is only one god we should worship. My cousin was confused because the strangers showed them a image of a woman. And a sign like this." The slave makes a sign of a cross with two fingers.

"Indeed." Malinalli says introspectively.

She doesn't understand the news either, but the strangers coming from the east—and speaking of not worshiping certain gods?

Could it be?

Her brain goes into high gear, planning...

9 Fate Smiles

While braving a fierce storm, the expedition attempt several landings on the mainland, but are driven off each time by strong winds. On the advice of his pilots who are in fear of running aground, Cortés decides to continue on further west passing several harbors, one of which Aguilar points out is near the place he was held captive.

So on the 12th of March, the Spanish under Cortés finally arrive in the New World near the mouth of the Tabasco River. The larger vessels anchor out at sea, while the smaller ones sail up the river, in order to disembark at the promontory where the palm trees grew, about four miles from the town of Tabasco—the same spot where Grijalva had previously landed.

The Conquistadors immediately catch sight of large numbers of Indians lurking among the almond trees along the shore and soon discover there are thousands more warriors assembled at the town ready to attack. Apparently the other neighboring tribes had accused the Tabascans of cowardice, for having given the previous expedition under Grijalva tribute of their gold, while they had courageously attacked and killed fifty-six of the strangers. The natives of Tabasco therefore are not about to repeat their mistake.

With his strategy of 'talk first-shoot last' Cortés orders Aguilar, who is perfectly fluent in the language of Tabasco, to ask some Indians who are in a large canoe why they are massing to fight. Aguilar tells the natives per Cortés that they have come in peace and wish to treat them as brothers and trade with them. But they promptly threaten death if the strangers even set foot on their territory. Aguilar tries again, seeking permission to take in fresh water, trade for supplies, and tell them about God. The Indians reply however, that if the Spanish pass beyond the palm trees they will kill them all.

When Cortés hears this he orders his men to prepare for battle—a brave move considering the Spanish are outnumbered by a factor of more than 20 to 1. He commands the small flotilla to halt before the palm trees and pull up next to the river bank. Three cannon are put on board of each of the forward boats, and crossbow-men and musketeers equally distributed among them. Then after posting sentries to watch the massed Indians, they wait for darkness.

Just before dawn the next morning Cortés dispatches Alonso de Avila with one hundred men, ten of which are equipped with crossbows, along a narrow road leading to the village. They have orders to attack from either side when they hear cannon fire. Cortés himself moves up river with his remaining forces.

If Cortés is hoping for the advantage of surprise, he is denied. When the Indians see the boats approaching, some leap into their canoes while others station themselves along the bank. Warriors line the shore armed with bows, spears, and crude stone hammers. As soon as the Spanish sail into view they begin their war cry accompanied by a terrible sound by blowing through large twisted shells and of pounding drums.

Cortés orders a halt for a few moments as he tries once more though Aguilar to request to come on shore to get fresh water. He also adds that if they attacked his men would defend themselves and any blood would be on their hands since he comes in the name of the one true God.

The Indian's response is a shower of arrows falling like piercing deadly rain upon the Conquistadors, wounding many. Natives in their canoes completely surround the Spanish while arrows continue to thud into the wooden boats. The Spanish jump into the shallow river and fight back in waist high water while trying to pull their boats to the shore. But the bank is thick gooey mud and they have difficulty trying to gain a foothold.

Cortés himself loses a boot stuck in mud while trying to scramble onto dry ground. This enrages the dandy, style conscious Conqueror more than the hail of arrows, and he shouts for a full out assault.

The Spaniards remaining in the boats open fire with crossbows, muskets and cannons. The flash, blast, and noise frighten the natives initially and many are cut down by iron musket balls. The Conquistadors slowly begin to drive the Indians back with superior firepower. Cortés rallies the men on shore and pursues the Indians to their village. But the natives have fallen back behind a barricade of freshly cut trees and fight back ferociously while chanting *'ala lala, al calachoni, al calachoni'*.

Cortés asks Aguilar what they are shouting.

"They are yelling *'Kill the chief'*, my Lord; meaning you."

"Then perhaps we should fight harder." The Conqueror replies calmly.

Very few of the Conquistadors have muskets, as these are expensive weapons affordable by only wealthy or those willing to make huge sacrifices to purchase one. While muskets and cannons are far superior to anything the natives possess, they are in no way an overwhelming advantage. Both muskets and cannon are black powder weapons which are laborious to fire and time consuming to reload. First a quantity of black powder is poured down the barrel, then a iron ball is dropped down, followed by a cotton or paper wad (designed to keep the load inside while it is aimed), then the load is tamped down with a long rod the soldier rammed down the barrel. At this point a small amount of black powder is poured into a hole near the breech. When the trigger is pulled, a piece of flint strikes a rough surface, causing sparks to ignite the gun powder and finally fire the ball. After just one shot this process must be completely repeated—requiring a minimum of two minutes or so by a really experienced soldier.

Military tactics attempt to get around this problem by having the musketeers fire in groups: twenty-five men would fire, while the other twenty-five reloaded. Still, this meant only 25 shoots could be fired at a time against hundreds or thousands of attacking native warriors equipped with their own bows & arrows, lances, obsidian-edged swords and slings.

But just in time Alonso de Avila appears with his men, having been held up by mud also, this time in deep pools along the road. The delay proves beneficial in that now is the perfect time to flank the Indians on both sides, while the main force led by Cortés keeps them busy with a frontal attack.

The natives fight bravely and viciously with fire hardened arrows and spears, not cowed by the Spanish weapons. But they are eventually driven back under the three pronged assault, and the Conquistadors fight their way into the main village where there are three temples. Then they realize the natives have somehow melted away into the surrounding forests leaving the town empty.

With the Indians only recently vacated but obviously lurking nearby, Cortés takes time out for the unthinkable: He formally takes possession of the country in the name of the King of Spain, by cutting a cross into a nearby tree with his sword!

Taking stock of the tiny victory, the Spaniards suffer fourteen wounded while they count eighteen dead natives. It seems the carnage should have been worse considering the numbers of combatants involved and Cortés thinks maybe the Indians have recovered most of their comrade's bodies. He decides to camp in the village for the night and posts sentries to kept watch for the main Indian force.

The next day Cortés dispatches two scouting parties with a hundred men each, one under Alvarado and the other commanded by Francisco de Lugo, to march six miles in different directions in order to explore the country and probe the native's location. Alvarado was to take along Melchior as an interpreter, but the Indian is nowhere to be found. It seems he has taken the opportunity of the Conquistadors distraction with the battle to run off, having left all his Spanish clothes behind hanging in a tree. Cortés is greatly vexed by his escape, knowing he might betray many things to his brethren.

Francisco de Lugo's party reaches a distance of about four miles when they meet vast numbers of Indians, commanded by several chiefs. The natives immediately advance and surround the Spanish on all sides, and began pouring forth a shower of arrows and stones from slings. Though De Lugo and his men defend themselves bravely, they are unable to fight such overwhelming numbers and attempt to retreat to the village. De Lugo dispatches a swift runner, to inform Cortés of their situation.

In the meantime Alvarado has marched his men about four miles in the direction he was commanded to take, but runs into a large river they are unable to cross. So they turn around and return in the direction which leads to the spot where De Lugo is under attack. Before they can catch sight of the battle, they hear gunfire mixed with the trumpeting of shells and pounding drums. So Alvarado marches in a direct line to where the noise is coming, and finds De Lugo in the heat of battle with the enemy. Both detachments now engage the Indians, who are quickly dispersed, but not cowed or ready to retreat.

Then Cortés arrives with the rest of the troops, having gotten word by the runner of De Lugo's dangerous position, and immediately came to their aid. The combined Spanish might finally routs the natives who flee back into the heavy forests again.

The Conquistadors suffer two killed and eleven wounded while the natives lose fifteen men and three are taken prisoner, one of whom appears to be a chief. Aguilar asks them why they attacked when the Spanish only want to trade. One of the Indians replies that Melchior had come over to their camp during the previous night and advised them to attack the invaders and continue to do so night and day, for they would eventually be able to conquer them since the Spanish had only a small number of men.

Cortés tries once more to make peace by sending one of the prisoners to their chief with gifts of green glass beads, but by nightfall no one returns. He then orders Aguilar to press the remaining two natives in custody and learns that the next day they intend to storm the Spanish and retake their village.

Now certain that the Indians will attack Cortés immediately orders all their horses to be brought on shore, and everyone, wounded or not, be prepared to defend their position. When the horses arrive after being at sea for weeks, they are awkward and nervous trying to regain their legs. It takes the Spanish most of the night, walking and calming the horses, before they are lively and agile again. Cortés orders their riders to hang bells around their horses' necks, and impresses on them not to rush at the Indians too quickly. The horses are valuable and are to be used for shock effect only.

The following morning is a holy day so the Spanish attend Mass very early, and then march towards the bean fields, where Francisco de Lugo and Pedro de Alvarado had fought the previous battle. One contingent under Cortés is forced to take a circuitous route to avoid some mud bogs while the other two thirds have an easy going and arrive first to find thousands of Indians coming for them. Everyone has a large bunch of feathers on his head, cotton armor on, and their faces are daubed with white, black, and red colors—a sign unbeknownst to the Conquistadors that these are crack troops.

Besides having drums and shell trumpets, they are armed with huge bows and arrows, shields, lances, and large broadswords. Some have slingshots, and others are armed with fire hardened poles. The Indians are in such vast numbers that they completely fill the bean fields, and immediately attack on all sides at once like furious dogs.

The battle is ferocious, with sleets of arrows and stones hailing down on the Spanish, and within the first minutes seventy men are wounded, and one is struck by an arrow in the ear and instantly drops dead. The Conquistadors fight back with matched fury using crossbows, muskets, and heavy cannon and force the Indians to give ground a little. But the only result is that they shower forth their arrows at a greater distance, where they figure themselves safe from the muskets and swords.

Then the Spanish artillery takes advantage of the massed Indians crowded together and fires at them, mowing them down at will. But no matter how much destruction the Spanish inflict upon the natives they will not retreat, instead throwing up clouds of dirt and grass to hide their losses from the invaders. Some of the more experienced soldiers advise a full out frontal assault, but the two commanders know they are outnumbered 300 to 1 and try to maintain a defensive position; all the while the Indians are making a terrible noise with their drums and trumpets, and their war-whoops.

When all looks lost Cortés comes galloping up with the men on horseback. The Indians, who had never seen horses before, think that horse and rider are one body. Quite astonished, bewildered, and downright frightened by this sight, they retreat to higher ground and then vanish into the countryside.

In all one man is dead and seventy-five are wounded along with eight horses. As the Spanish lick their wounds they reflect upon the first full-scale battle fought under Cortés in New Spain.

***

The household and the entire village and surrounding areas are in a complete uproar. Malinalli has never seen anything like it since she had been brought there as a slave so many years ago.

For days now, everyone was involved in furious preparations for war. All the male slaves had been pressed into duty cutting the biggest trees and building a stone wall for fortification against the invaders.

It isn't long before reports come of the battle with the mysterious invaders and the strange sights witnessed by the warriors. They talk of fire sticks and thunder logs and huge deer with two heads. But the most chilling are the invaders themselves—beings of white skin and shiny metal heads.

Malinalli instantly recalls the image of Quetzalcoatl taught to her by

Eréndira at the temple, and she is more determined than ever to see this sight for herself.

But when the dead and wounded begin arriving at the house she and the others must care for them. The wounds are devastating: arms cut off, bodies torn apart, skin sliced open. No one knows how to treat such wounds, they can only watch as the medicine men apply their herbs and the slaves attempt to bind the gaping holes with cotton.

Malinalli has second thoughts at the destruction wrought by the strangers, but she knows gods are often cruel. She still must believe in the possibility the Feathered Serpent has returned...

***

Montezuma is in one of the vast palace gardens amusing himself with an eagle when his brother Cuitláhuac finds him. The eagle is out of its cage on a perch and Cuitláhuac is wary. The bird is damned big and dangerous. He has often wondered why the bird doesn't simply pluck the eyes out of his captor and fly away.

The Emperor is obsessed with birds and the cages contain every species in the Empire. Cuitláhuac thinks his brother was changed when he visited the 'Place of Heavenly Learning' and had the vision when he held that crane. Since then he spends too much time out here.

"Such a powerful and cunning creature, eh? It dives out of nowhere and catches its victims unaware." The Emperor comments.

"You know the festival of 'The Flaying of Men' is about to begin?" Cuitláhuac reminds his brother.

This festival called 'Tlacaxipehualiztli' is a springtime festival in honor of Xipe Totec, the god of spring and new vegetation, who flayed himself so that the plants would grow.

The Emperor does not typically attend every festival since they are nearly continuous in the Aztec year, but he is obligated to at least show his face at the beginning of the important ones. Montezuma gently eases the big bird of prey back into its cage and takes his brother's arm.

"Walk with me then, you are joining me of course?" The Emperor asks, but it is really a command.

Cuitláhuac looks Montezuma in the eye—he is the only living being in the Empire that can get away with this—and thinks his brother is acting strangely today and wonders why. But he says nothing as they make their way to the arena beyond the temple.

Before they leave the palace grounds several noblemen, who are obviously waiting, join the Emperor and his brother. One of the nobles precedes Montezuma carrying three slender rods erect, to give notice of the approach of his person. When they get to the arena, the Emperor takes one of the rods and sits on the golden chair reserved for him.

The ceremony for Xipe Totec is unlike most of the Aztec religious rites. Although the holiday is marked by sacrifice, the actual method is quite different than usual. This god favors gladiatorial sacrifice. And as the Emperor peruses the arena he observes that the first offering is already in place.

A captured warrior, this one looks like a Mayan, has one foot tied to a huge stone set in the middle of the open space. He is in full war dress, with several eagle feathers on his head and black and white war paint. He is armed however, only with a ceremonial lance made of feathers.

Soon an Aztec jaguar warrior appears—armed with a real obsidian sword and a ceremonial fight to the death begins. If the sacrificial captive can best four warriors, he will be given the option of either being freed for proving himself a great fighter, or be sacrificed the traditional way in the temple. In reality, this almost never happens. The Emperor can remember only once in his lifetime such a man came forth, and that captive choose death in the temple in the end anyway. Still though, it does add some element of excitement, although today it was not to be, the victim succumbs quickly.

All those who died in sacrifices during this festival will their skins striped from them and these will be worn by priests of Xipe Totec, to symbolize new plant growth sprouting from dead husks. The priests will wear the skins for twenty days following the sacrifice, and during this time they will dance throughout the city blessing the people by touching them with a thigh bone from the victim.

While waiting for the next bout Montezuma asks his brother whether there is any news from the eastern territories.

"In fact we have heard the Mayans have been preparing for some battle. They have gathered several thousand warriors near Tabasco. At first our spies thought they might be attacking our outposts but they seem to be concentrating on the seaside." Cuitláhuac replies.

"Hmmm, keep me informed." The Emperor commands.

***

After the Spanish are back in the captured native village, they take time to bandage the wounds of their men with linen, and dress the wounds of the horses with melted fat, cut from the dead bodies of the Indians—a seemingly harsh but ultimately practical act. In contrast they count over eight hundred Indian killed and countless wounded, their swords having done most of the damage, though many were killed by cannon. In a signal of the native's ferocious bravery, only five are taken prisoner, although two of those are chiefs.

Aguilar spends a lot of time conversing with them and after a meal suggests to Cortés they be set free to act as delegates to the rest of the tribes. Cortés agrees and gives both chiefs blue glass beads, assuring them through Aguilar that even after this battle, which had been entirely of their own doing, they had nothing to fear, and asked them to assemble all the chiefs of the area so that he might meet with them.

The prisoners willingly comply and the entreaty is successful since fifteen of their Indian slaves return with fowls, baked fish, and cornbread. These slaves have their faces blackened and are wearing ragged cloaks. Although Cortés interprets the whole thing as a friendly gesture, Aguilar on the other hand suspects it is a sign of disrespect, asking them in an angry tone why they come in war paint and filthy rags. He tells the Conqueror if the Indians really wanted to talk peace the chiefs would come and meet and not send their lackeys.

Despite this Cortés treats the slaves kindly and with respect and gives them more beads—a sly way to insure his meaning gets across in the most equitable manner, but instructs them to tell those that send them of his displeasure. After sharing the food with them, another clever method to make sure it isn't poisoned, the Spanish send them on their way to deliver the message.

The Conqueror's ploy works. The next day thirty principal chiefs, evidenced by their fancy dress, appear bringing more fowls, fruits, and fresh baked cornbread. They beg permission of Cortés to collect the bodies of their dead and wounded, in order that they might not rot or become food for the animals. When Cortés agrees they signal for a vast number of slaves to burn the bodies, and bury them according to their custom.

Cortés himself watches the proceedings, taking as kindly and benevolent manner as he can manage. His attitude instills trust and the native chiefs let on they are saddened by the loss of life and that the day following all the chiefs and nobles of the territory will assemble to negotiate peace with the Spanish.

Cortés, who makes a point of taking advantage of every situation, orders special preparations for the meeting.

"It appears to me gentlemen, that the Indians stand in great awe of our horses, and imagine that these and our guns alone fight the battle. A thought has just struck me which will further confirm them in this notion. You must bring here the mare which is in heat and fasten her here where I am now standing. Then bring also the stallion of the musician Ortiz, which is a very fiery animal, and will quickly scent the mare. As soon as you find this to be the case, lead both the horses to separate places, that the Indian chiefs may neither see the horses, nor hear them neigh, until I shall be in conversation with them. Also load our largest cannon with gunpowder and ball and have it hidden but ready to fire."

A little after midday, forty chiefs, nobles, and dignitaries arrive with great ceremony. One of their actions is to burn vast quantities of incense—an act the Spanish think is part of their ceremony but even Aguilar knows is to mask the smell of the Conquistadors who haven't bathed for weeks. They then sit and ask forgiveness for what had happened, and promised to be friendly in the future.

Cortés, through the interpreter Aguilar, reminds them with a very stern look, how often he had tried to make peace, and how close his men came to killing everyone in the area. He goes on to tell them that he has come in the name of a mighty king and lord the emperor Charles, who sent him to this country with orders to favor and assist those who should submit to his imperial order. If this was not acceptable then he would have no choice but to fire off their many cannons. At that exact moment Cortés gives a secret signal to fire the hidden cannon and the bang, like a sudden clap of thunder, startles the Indians so that not a breath is heard from them.

The Conqueror tells Aguilar to comfort and assure them he had given orders that no harm should come to them. But at the same time the stallion is brought and tied a short distance from the spot where Cortés and the Indians are meeting, just a dozen yards from the mare hidden behind a tent. The stallion immediately began to neigh, stamp the ground and rear itself, while its eyes are continually fixed on the Indians who just happen to be seated in front of tent. The Indians think the massive animal is attacking them and prepare to run for their lives, but Cortés quickly steps in and takes hold of the bridle and calms the horse, assuring them again they have nothing to worry about.

Obviously the effects of all this are not lost on the natives, who signal more slaves to approach with food for the Spanish. After friendly conversation, the chiefs promise they will return the following day with more gifts.

***

Malinalli is ready.

She hasn't had much time to plan or prepare but most of all she too knows how to take advantage of any situation. When the overseer comes to the slave's quarters looking for twenty women she already guesses it has something to do with the mysterious strangers. After the battle and heavy losses all the important men in the village have been engaged in deep conversations for two days.

It's not like her life here is so bad, in reality she is a slave in name only. Her skills allow her the privilege of having the run of the household and she occasionally shares the bed of the chief's son—a not unpleasant experience. She has thought of leaving before but not certain she could endure the rigors of the long journey home even if she wanted to. After all, there is nothing for her back there. She has had no place to go until now.

There are twenty two women in the household so Malinalli sends two of them away with directions if they stay hidden, she will give them her dyes and stash of fabrics—a gift of riches beyond their wildest dreams for these slaves—thereby stacking the deck in her favor.

When the overseer begins picking the women he is not entirely displeased that Malinalli is the twentieth female and the only one left he can find.

Sure enough he explains they are to be given to great warriors from the east in tribute and that they shall conduct themselves as befitting such an honor.

Malinalli, of course cannot wait to see if Quetzalcoatl has returned...

10 Doña Marina

So it is on the following morning, one of the last days in March 1519, a number of chiefs along with the nobles of the Tabasco territory and surrounding area, arrive at the camp of the Conquistadors bearing all manner of gifts—one of which will prove more valuable than anyone could imagine.

The natives are packed in a large group and first present the Conquistadors with more food—a very welcome gift since they are leery of going hunting with all the possible enemies surrounding their temporary camp.

With Aguilar translating, the native chiefs and Cortés seat themselves and partake of the fresh fruit they brought which the Conqueror makes a grand gesture of sharing. Then the natives present a few gold trinkets: some in the form of lizards, others ducks, dogs, a few with Indian faces which Cortés suspects are idols, and finally a pair of sandals with golden soles.

Although in reality the presents are not worth much, Cortés makes a prolonged show of examining and admiring them. He soon finds out that the Mayan Empire is in decline and possesses very little gold. Through Aguilar the natives tell him that people living to the north of the Yucatan have large amounts of gold, pearls, and precious stones.

Cortés then asks through Aguilar why they attacked them three times when all he wanted was to trade peacefully with them.

One of the nobles explains that the chief of Champoton, a nearby territory, had previously accused them of cowardice for not having attacked when the previous strangers arrived off the coast with four ships under another commander, meaning most probably Grijalva. The same advice was also given them by the Indian interpreter Melchior, telling them to attack day and night, as the strangers were few in number and would bring nothing but misery to their lands. Aguilar later learns that Melchior paid for his bad advice with his life as he was sacrificed to the gods after their defeat in battle with the Spanish.

Cortés further wonders how the natives could fight so well against his superior firepower and asks the Indians from where their bravery and tactics originate. It is then Aguilar learns his old friend and fellow castaway and slave, Gonzalo Guerrero, has been training them how to repel the Spanish invaders.

With Aguilar translating, Cortés assures them that they mean the native no harm and would never attack them without cause. He then goes on to say that if the natives really wanted peace they should all return to their village so that they could trade and learn about the one true God.

His words stir considerable discussion among the natives, so Aguilar deems to explain the Christian faith and that the one true God does not condone idols or especially human sacrifice. He then shows them a small statue of the Virgin Mary holding the baby Jesus.

This image seems to hit home with the Indians and they instantly begin referring to the mother of God as *Tecleciguata,* meaning a woman of distinction. They beg Cortés to let them keep it in their village. The Conqueror is only too happy to comply and orders his carpenters to build an altar for the statue and erect a cross. Then he gets to the important matter at hand and asks through Aguilar where they got their gold.

This results in a long explanation in which the Indians use the words *Culhua* and *Mexico*—neither of which Aguilar understands. In frustration the natives finally point to the west and make signs of something big there a great distance away. Not understanding what they mean, Cortés finally calls an end to the meeting and stands up, preparing to retire to his tent out of the hot sun.

But the Indians are not finished; they have one more present for the Conquistadors. Twenty girls are brought forward and presented to Cortés with an explanation through Aguilar that these women are for 'grinding corn' and other duties to help them survive in these lands.

The concept of slaves is of course common to the Spanish as well as the natives, so he accepts them graciously, knowing his men have been apart from companionship for a long while. As Cortés accepts the slaves he studies them one by one. Most are squat and rather ugly, prized obviously for their ability to do hard work rather than their looks.

But then the last one walks up to him and immediately takes his eye. Cortés is surprised and confused. This one is not only tall and slender and striking, but she is dressed in a fine garment of pure white adorned with bright yellow flowers. And most noticeable is that she holds herself in a regal manner so that he thinks she must be a princess of the tribe and surely not a slave. She also, unlike all the others, looks him directly in the eye—a bold move for a slave, especially one so young, she can't be more then 16 or 17 years old.

The Conqueror feels a familiar stirring and a bit of light headedness at the gaze of this girl. She is at once interesting and challenging and defiant like a wild stallion.

Cortés has Aguilar question the Indians as to the girl's status and is assured she now belongs to him—a fact he guesses will be quite a distraction he can't afford right now. He will have to think carefully about how to handle this situation, not only with this one but the others as well.

Little does he know that just then two of the three cogs in the wheel of their Fate are now locked forever in place...

***

Malinalli is fairly certain the person standing before her is not Quetzalcoatl. He appears to be a man, although he certainly matches the description of the Feathered Serpent as she imagined from the teachings of the priestess Eréndira. His white skin and hairy face and his amazing shiny metal hat all fit. And he is rather handsome in an unusual way too. They way he conducts himself portrays power and confidence and it is a heady mixture for her. Besides, the look he gave her was clearly not one between a god and a mortal; it was one of desire between a man and woman.

She did have second thoughts of her actions in coming when she heard this man was responsible for over 800 hundred deaths—a horrific number among the brave native warriors. But then she heard him say through the strange little man he only wanted peace and not war, and that the Tabascans themselves were responsible for the outcome. Malinalli was also intrigued by the talk of one true God and the holy Mother.

In any case she owes no allegiance to her master, the household, the Mayans, and not even the Aztec Mexica—after all they had abandoned her. She owed no one anything, except herself.

Malinalli observes carefully as the following day the cross and altar are completed, and the figure of the holy Virgin Mother placed thereon. The inhabitants of the village also return as promised and join in the curiosity of the stranger's god, somewhat confused by their notion of one god yet displaying a baby, a mother, and a cross of wood.

Noticing the native's interest Aguilar holds Mass and explains in their language about the holy religion, and telling them that they should abandon their belief in idols, for they are not gods but evil spirits and should now adore Christ, the Lord.

Seeing this, Cortés hits upon a singular solution to multiple problems. One of his primary missions in coming to New Spain is to spread Christianity and convert the natives to Catholicism, but so far he has no converts. He also faces the problem of the girls, he cannot very well allow the men to take comfort with them and give in to sin when he is trying to show the natives the way of the Lord. So he decides to baptize the slave girls, thereby killing two birds with one stone.

Aguilar is all for this but insists he must teach them the rudimentary aspects of the Catholic religion before he can rightfully baptize them into the faith. So Cortés grants him several days to accomplish this task before they break camp and continue on. So during the next few days the girls are segregated and taught about Christ.

Many of the concepts Aguilar speaks of are oddly familiar to Malinalli and the rest of the slave girls: the notion of Jesus' sacrifice, the flaying of his skin, his ascent into heaven, and even the Virgin Mother all have similarities to their beliefs. What impresses her though is that this God does not demand sacrifices of blood and hearts from his people. Malinalli asks many questions and unlike her previous teachers, Aguilar seems particularly pleased at this, thinking she is his best student by far.

When it is finally time to be baptized, the friar tells them they must choose a Christian name, and he helps each select one. When it is Malinalli's turn she has already decided to take the name of the Virgin Mother but slightly mispronounces 'Maria' as 'Marina' and Aguilar thinks she has picked this name because they are close to the ocean, so he baptizes her Marina. And so these twenty slave girls become the first coverts to Christianity in New Spain.

After this ceremony Cortés solemnly presents each girl to one of his commanders as their companion and valet. As much as he would like to, he knows he cannot take the one now called Marina for himself and wisely gives her to Alonzo Puertocarrero, not only well born but a giant of a man and a brave cavalier, who is stout enough to protect her from any danger. Malinalli is somewhat disappointed by this turn of events but vows to get close to the charismatic leader sooner rather than later.

All in all the Spanish remain five days in the village, giving the men time to heal and the slave girls time to learn. Cortés uses the time wisely, conversing with the native chiefs. He tells them by aligning themselves with him and this King they are assured of his protection and if they ever need assistance all they need do is ask.

In these talks he also begins to understand this tribe is in decline and subjugated by a great ruler, a powerful chief to the west who demands tribute in the form of both food—and lives. He also learns these people called the Mexica or Aztecs, possesses gold and precious stones in vast quantities.

Finally on the fifth day the Spanish hold a solemn Mass and prepare to embark back to their ships with a grand ceremony and procession. Cortés makes a point to bow and pray before the new altar of the Holy Mary and reminds the natives to adore and protect it. Then with the newly baptized Indian slave girls, they board their ships. Malinalli is stunned when the small boat takes her to the largest vessel which she sees is flying a banner with a red cross—a symbol of the Feathered Serpent. This causes her to have brief doubts about Cortés, but decides to observe him closely as they set sail westward in search of treasure.

Malinalli is fascinated by the sailing ships. She has never felt the ocean air in her face before and takes to it like none of the others, who are fearful of being out of sight of the land. She pays attention, studying every detail and cleverly helping out wherever she can to learn even more.

It is not long before the Spanish soldiers pay special attention to Malinalli. Her elegant manner and pleasant but lively disposition entrance them all, and besides it is obvious their Captain and Conqueror has eyes for her too. So without much thought they all begin referring to her as Doña Marina—the title reserved for a Spanish lady.

***

It is not long before the first runner arrives at the capital with news from the east. Protocol demands that the runner report to Montezuma's brother Cuitláhuac first since any direct contact with the Emperor is forbidden.

Cuitláhuac listens carefully to the report of the runner. He is not a student of religion as is his brother but is well aware of the visions and omens. The account is worrisome and he immediately takes the man to Montezuma.

The messenger dares not look at the Emperor; he prostrates himself on the marble floor at his feet and tells him of the strange events in Mayan territory.

"Our Lord and King, forgive my boldness. When I went to the shores of the great sea, there was a mountain range or small mountain floating in the midst of the water, moving here and there without touching the shore. Then the strangers came down river in huge canoes and fought the warriors there with sticks spouting fire and balls of thunder which ripped their bodies asunder. Then came two headed stags breathing smoke from their noses and the warriors were forced to surrender. It was the most frightening thing I have ever witnessed my King."

The account sends chills down the Emperor's neck. He is instantly reminded of his sister's dream and of his own vision at the Place of Heavenly Learning eleven years ago when he saw demons from hell coming with fire sticks and riding smoke breathing four legged animals.

Montezuma dismisses the runner and instructs his brother to send a trusted nobleman from the palace to verify the story, hoping it is some fevered hallucination of a sick man.

He anxiously awaits as four days pass until the spy returns. The nobleman is almost afraid to tell the Emperor what he saw since he can scarcely believe it himself.

"It is true that strange people have come to the shores of the great sea. They were fishing from a small boat. They fished until late and then went back to their two great towers and climbed up into them. There were about fifteen of these people, some with blue jackets, others with red, some with black or green. They have very light skin, much lighter than ours. They all have beards, and their hair is fair and comes only to their ears. There were many more of these strangers in the village of Tabasco. I swear I witnessed this with my own two eyes."

After a long silence Montezuma finally speaks and orders all his principal advisors to a meeting: the Serpent Woman, the Chief of the House of Arrows, the Keeper of the Chalk, and the Chief of the South, along with his brother and his cousin and several priests.

"Find me all the magicians in the Empire and question them on these events. I want to know once and for all what this means—on the pain of death of them and their families."

After the chiefs gather all the magicians they can find, Cuitláhuac takes it upon himself to question them.

"What can we say? The future has already been determined and decreed in heaven, and Montezuma will behold and suffer a great mystery which must come to pass in his land. If our Emperor wishes to know more about it, he will know soon enough, for it comes swiftly. This is what we predict, since he demands that we speak, and since it must surely take place, he can only wait for it." The magicians answer.

The Emperor is beside himself at this response but determines they plainly speak the obvious so he must prepare. In his heart he feels the god Quetzalcoatl has appeared. He has come back. He will come here, to the place of his throne for that is what he promised when he departed.

"Send lookouts and with them messengers to every shore along the great ocean and instruct them to remain there and report back immediately of any sighting of these strangers. Now bring me in secret two of the best artists among the goldsmiths, and two who are skillful at working precious stones."

When the artisans arrive the Emperor meets them in his innermost chambers.

"I have called for you to have you make certain objects. But take care that you do not reveal this to anyone, for if you do, it will mean the ruin of your houses to their foundations, and the loss of your goods, and death to yourselves, your wives, your children and your kin, for all shall die. Each of you is to make two objects, and you are to make them in my presence, here in secret in this palace."

He tells one craftsman to make a throat band of gold chain, with links four fingers wide and very thin, and to decorate each with emeralds in the center and at the sides, like earrings; and also a pair of gold bracelets, with chains of gold hanging from them. He orders another craftsman to make two fans with the most colorful feathers, in the center of one side a half-moon of gold, on the other a gold sun, both well burnished so that they would shine from far away. He also tells him to make two gold armlets rich with feathers. Finally he instructs the last two to make bracelets for both wrists and both ankles of gold set with fine emeralds.

Then he orders his cousin to secretly bring all of the gold, plumage, emeralds and turquoises of the finest quality to the palace so the artisans can complete their work.

By the time the gifts are finished by the craftsmen, a messenger arrives with word of another sighting of the strangers in a harbor west of Tabasco.

Montezuma immediately dispatches five envoys to greet the strangers and to bring them the gifts. They are led by the priest in charge of the temple.

"Go forward, my Jaguar Knights, go forward. It is said that our lord Quetzalcoatl has returned to this land. Go to meet him. Go to hear him. Listen well to what he tells you; listen and remember. But tell no one else of your mission under penalty of death."

***

A day later the Spanish fleet arrives at the harbor of San Juan de Ulua. One of the pilots remembers this spot from the expedition under Grijalva, and leads the ships to anchor in a place where they are sheltered from the north wind. They are scarcely there a half hour when two large canoes filled with Indians approach. They head directly for the ship with the flag bearing a red cross, for they know its meaning as well, and sure enough it is the Conqueror's vessel. The soldiers observe them warily but see that they are unarmed and dressed in feathers and fine garments.

The natives climb on board without hesitation and start speaking in some language no one has heard before. The Spanish soldiers find Aguilar to talk with them, but he doesn't understand what they are saying, it is a language he has never heard before either. Cortés comes out to see what the commotion is about and is surprised to learn Aguilar can't communicate with them.

Finally Malinalli speaks up. She knows exactly what they are asking for it is the Aztec language of her birth. And instantly she realizes she has an edge.

"That is the one you are looking for." She says, pointing to Cortés.

"They are saying *Tlatoan*. They are asking for the leader." She tells Aguilar in Mayan. "They are speaking in the Nahuatl language of the Aztecs." Malinalli adds.

When Aguilar translates her words into Spanish for Cortés, several things suddenly fall into place—this girl knows what the chiefs back in Tabasco were trying to tell him, that there are powerful and wealthy people called the Aztecs to the west.

As soon as the Indians are introduced to Cortés they bow and show great respect. Then as Malinalli translates from Nahuatl to Mayan for Aguilar and he translates to Spanish for Cortés, the parties are able to communicate.

The natives tell Cortés their master, who is a servant of the great Montezuma, has sent them in order to ascertain who he is and what he came to seek in his country. He has only to inform them of what he wants, and they would see that it is provided.

This is the first time Cortés hears the name Montezuma. So he asks Aguilar to have Malinalli inquire about him. But she doesn't need to, she already knows.

"Montezuma is the Emperor of the Mexica, the Aztec Empire." She tells the Spanish.

Her knowledge confuses the Conqueror and he makes a mental note to question her later. In the meantime Cortés thanks the Indians for their kindness, through Aguilar and Malinalli, and presents them with some blue glass beads, and orders some meat and drink to be placed before them. After they have taken refreshment, he tells them he has come to make their acquaintance, and open trade with them. The envoys then leave and sail back to the shore with a promise to return after consulting with their chief.

The following morning, Good Friday, Cortés orders his men to unload the horses and set up their cannon near some sand-hills which run along the whole coast. After the artillery is placed on a strategic spot, the men erect an altar where mass is immediately performed. Then they spend the entire day constructing huts of wood and brush for Cortés and the rest of the men.

Saturday many natives arrive, who are sent by the local governor under Montezuma. They bring fowls, corn-bread, and flavorful plums, which are nice and ripe. After dining, the Indians help finish the Conqueror's hut with more branches and cotton cloth over the roof to keep the sun out. They tell Cortés that the governor himself will come the next day and bring a further supply of provisions. Cortés gracefully accepts of these presents, and in return offers various kinds of trinkets the Spanish have brought for barter, which seems to delight the Indians.

During these exchanges which Malinalli is translating, she is very curious as to why the Emperor would be so interested in the strangers and especially why they are being so well treated. She begins to suspect there is some ulterior motive which she can't quite fathom, since Montezuma has never been known for kindness or generosity.

On Easter day, the native governor indeed appears in person as promised. His name is Teuthlille, and he is one of the former generals of the Aztec empire. He is accompanied by another nobleman. They are followed by a great number of Indians, carrying presents consisting of fowls and greens. Teuthlille orders the others to stand back a little, walks up to Cortés, and bows three times as a sign of reverence.

Cortés bids them welcome and cleverly embraces them in a sign of friendship, asking them to join him in a most important ceremony, which is in fact a Catholic mass on the newly constructed altar in honor of Easter, after which Cortés asks everyone to sit down to dine on the food they have brought.

After the table has been cleared, Cortés, with the assistance of Aguilar and Malinalli, attempts to explain to them about Christianity, and the one true God, and the fact that they are here in the name of King Charles, the greatest Monarch in the world.

At this point the translation gets jumbled, for Malinalli is not quite yet able to understand the distinction between God and King Charles so she withholds some of this information. Besides, she doesn't want to insult the envoys of the Emperor by proclaiming a more powerful ruler and possibly be responsible for all their deaths.

Cortés then adds that in order that a good understanding might be established between them, they should acquaint him with the place where their monarch resided, that he might pay his respects to him.

Teuthlille orders an exquisitely inlaid chest be brought forward and has it placed in front of Cortés.

"Before you meet my Emperor, you must accept these gifts presented in his name. Then I shall transmit to him your wishes."

When the Conqueror opens the chest he finds all the gold and emerald jewelry that Montezuma had made for the occasion.

Cortés admires the skillful workmanship and his heart leaps at the sight of the rich gold, which obviously this 'Mexica' Empire must have in vast abundance.

Cortés then presents the governors with more glass beads, multi-hued ones made in Venice, which he has been conserving for an auspicious occasion. The Indians accept them, but are more interested in something else.

One of the Conquistadors has on a gilt-edged metal helmet polished to a high sheen, and Teuthlille remarks that it bears a great resemblance to a helmet which belonged to their most ancient forefathers, and now adorns the head of their warrior-god Hummingbird Wizard.

It is at that moment Malinalli realizes what is going on—like her, Montezuma has mistaken Captain Cortés for Feathered Serpent. Not only does Cortés resemble him, but he has come in the very year prophesied for the god's return. She tries to explain this to Aguilar but the friar is uncomfortable with the notion of Cortés being mistaken for a pagan idol, so he refuses to pass along her words.

In the meantime Cortés orders an ornate arm-chair to be brought forward. It is beautifully painted and inlaid with pieces of precious stones. On it are a necklace of imitation pearls, a scarlet cap, and a medal, on which is represented St. George on horseback, with lance in hand, slaying a dragon.

The Conqueror presents the chair to Teuthlille and asks that he give it to Montezuma, so that he might sit in it when they meet. That it is given in a token of friendship and as a sign of respect. And asks again where and when he could personally meet him. Teuthlille accepts the present and assures Cortés he will hasten to give the presents to the Emperor and return with his answer, but he gives no information about Montezuma's whereabouts.

The Spanish notice Teuthlille has with him very skilled painters and artists and they are continually sketching everything that transpires.

They are producing remarkably accurate images of Cortés and the clothes he wears, and all the other chief officers, the soldiers, the ships, horses, Doña Marina, and Aguilar and even two dogs, the cannon, and the cannon balls. All of these are to be part of the envoys report to the Emperor.

Seeing this, Cortés decides to put on a demonstration of Spanish power. He orders the cannon to be given an extra heavy load of powder and commands Alvarado and the other cavaliers to mount their horses, with a bell around each stead's neck, and to gallop up in full speed in front of Montezuma's ambassadors. Cortés also mounts his horse, and together they charge across the sea shore. Then Cortés orders the cannons fired and the stone balls fly with a tremendous crash along the sand-hills, re-echoing for a length of time. The Indians are terribly startled, and order their painters to capture this event that they might show it to Montezuma.

When the Indians are preparing to leave, Cortés presents the metal helmet to Teuthlille so he can show it to his Emperor and cleverly suggests he should fill it with gold and return it so he can see if it's the same as the gold in his kingdom. Then he makes a big show of embracing the natives and wishing them God speed.

Malinalli knows if the Emperor does in fact return the metal hat full of gold, it will be an unmistakable sign that he fears Cortés is the returning god. She insists Aguilar explain this to the Captain, but again he refuses—he will not be party to blasphemy. Malinalli vows to herself to learn the language of the Spanish so that she will never be in this position again. In the short time she has been with them she has already picked up a few words, but the pronunciation is difficult for her Aztec tongue.

Upon overhearing this heated exchange Cortés questions Aguilar.

"Friar, what is this about?"

"Doña Marina is speaking some nonsense about the Indian's pagan idols, which I will not bother to relate to you." Aguilar replies testily.

At this point Malinalli points to Cortés and the departing natives and tries to tell him herself using the few words of Spanish she knows and sign language.

"They, you, Quetzalcoatl…"

"Perhaps you should explain this Friar." Cortés orders Aguilar sternly, as some of the other Conquistadors including Bernal Diaz come over to see what is going on.

"Apparently the natives believe you are the personage of some god. According to Doña Marina this god departed the world many centuries ago and is prophesied to return this year." He relates with a hint of disgust.

"And you did not feel this was important? This fact could be a key advantage for us. From now on I expect you to relate to me Doña Marina's every word accurately and completely. Do you understand?"

"Yes my Lord."

"And further I would now like to know everything about this girl Doña Marina, for I do not believe she is some common slave." The Conqueror looks at Malinalli and cannot help but admire her loveliness. Her face is composed of flashing eyes mated with high cheekbones, framed by long shiny hair. Her skin is an unmarked dusky tone which is very pleasing to his eye. He finds himself wondering what secret charms lay beneath her pure white garment decorated with golden yellow flowers…

So Aguilar questions Malinalli about her past and as the other gather around closer, they hear her story through the friar.

"She was born under the sign of Grass and called Malinalli and was a ruler over a people and country, for her parents had the dominion of a township called Painala, to which several other townships were subject. This town lies about twenty-four miles from the town of Guacasualco. Her father who she loved very much died when she was very young, and her mother married another young chief with whom she had a son, of whom it appears they were both very fond, and to whom, after their death, they designed to leave their inheritance. In order that Doña Marina, the first born, might not stand in his way, she was conveyed secretly during night-time to slave traders of Xicalango. Her parents then spread the rumor she had died, which gained further belief from the circumstance that a daughter of one of her female slaves happened to die at the time. The Indians of Xicalango did not keep the young girl themselves, but sold her to the inhabitants of Tabasco, by whom she was presented to you."

This story moves the Spanish, especially Diaz and Cortés, who now have a new found respect for the girl. Not only has she overcome such adversity, but she is clever enough to hand him a key advantage to his mission in New Spain.

And the mission has taken on a whole new meaning—he has now seen the wealth of this land with his own two eyes and touched the gifts from the mysterious Montezuma...

***

While the messengers are away, Montezuma can neither sleep nor eat, and no one can speak with him. He is lost in worry. Nothing can comfort him, nothing can calm him, and nothing can give him any pleasure.

"Tell me, even if I am sleeping when the messengers have come back from the sea." He orders the palace guards.

When they finally return, he orders them taken to the House of the Serpent and orders two captives to be painted with chalk. When Montezuma joins the envoys, the two captives are then sacrificed before the group, their chests are torn open, their hearts torn out still beating, and the messengers are sprinkled with their blood. This is done because the messengers have completed a difficult mission and they have seen the god, their eyes have looked on their faces of the gods. They have even conversed with the gods!

When the sacrifice is finished, the messengers report to the Emperor. They tell him how they made the journey, and what they had seen, and even what food the strangers ate. They lay out all the pictures and images captured by the artists so that he might see what they saw.

Montezuma is astonished and terrified by their report. He is terrified to learn how the cannon roared, how its noise resounded, how it caused one to faint and grow deaf.

"A thing like a ball of stone comes out of its entrails; it comes out shooting sparks and raining fire. The smoke that comes out with it has a pestilent odor, like that of rotten mud. This odor penetrates even to the brain and causes the greatest discomfort. If the cannon is aimed against a mountain, the mountain splits and cracks open. If it is aimed against a tree, it shatters the tree into splinters. This is a most unnatural sight, as if the tree had exploded from within." One of them report.

"Their trappings and arms are all made of iron. They dress in iron and wear iron hats on their heads. Their swords are iron; their bows are iron; their shields are iron; their spears are iron. Their deer carry them on their backs wherever they wish to go. These deer, our lord, are as tall as the roof of a house." Another adds.

"The strangers' bodies are completely covered, so that only their faces can be seen. Their skin is white, as if it were made of lime. They have yellow hair, though some of them have black. Their beards are long and yellow, and their moustaches are also yellow. Their hair is curly, with very fine strands.

"As for their food, it is like human food. It is large and white, and not heavy. It is something like straw, but with the taste of a cornstalk, of the pith of a cornstalk. It is a little sweet, as if it were flavored with honey; it tastes of honey, it is sweet- tasting food." Another envoy relates.

"Even their dogs are enormous, with flat ears and long, dangling tongues. The color of their eyes is a burning yellow; their eyes flash fire and shoot off sparks. Their bellies are hollow, their flanks long and narrow. They are tireless and very powerful. They bound here and there panting, with their tongues hanging out. And they are spotted like an ocelot." Another reports.

Finally Teuthlille walks up and presents the Emperor the metal helmet given to him by Cortés.

"The chief of the strangers has told us he is the one true god. He speaks a strange tongue and his words are given to us by a woman who says she is Malinalli and looks like us. The chief demands that you fill this with gold and return it to him so that he may see if our gold is the same as in his kingdom."

Montezuma gives his brother Cuitláhuac an 'I told you so' look. He stares at the helmet and is almost afraid to hold it in his hands. It is truly the hat of Quetzalcoatl and Huitzilopochtli! He is filled with terror. It is as if his heart has fainted, as if it has shriveled. It is as if he is conquered by despair.

The Emperor orders wizards and magicians to cast spells that will destroy or at least deter the strangers from continuing toward his capital. But in his heart he knows they will fail and it will confirm that these are indeed the gods of the legend. To hedge his bet, Montezuma also decides to send more gifts…

11 The Heroine Takes Charge

After Teuthlille departs, the other chief named Quitlalpitoc, remains behind and his vassals build him a hut a short distance away from the Spanish. He orders his Indians to bake corn-bread, and procure game birds, fruits, and fish from the local province in the form of tribute, for the table of Cortés and his officers. The Conqueror thinks this is a friendly gesture and remarks to his men that this Montezuma is taking care of them. But Malinalli thinks otherwise.

"Do you think this governor Quitlalpitoc has nothing better to do? The Emperor has ordered him to stay here under the guise of providing for you, but he is really here to spy. If you were to try to leave this place he would either stop you or immediately send word to the Emperor." She tells Aguilar who translates her exact words this time to Cortés.

The girl's blunt observation is too obvious to ignore and Cortés knows he must plan for every eventuality. But he is torn between meeting the Emperor and having vast riches fall in his lap or continuing on with the expedition and doing it the hard way. He quietly orders his commanders to begin plans to explore further by ship along the coast. At the very least they must search for a good harbor and better spot to form a settlement anyway, because it is impossible to live in this sandy region on account of the clouds of gnats and mosquitoes.

In the meantime he sits with Doña Marina and Aguilar so he can learn more about this mistaken identity—something he may very soon need to use to his advantage. He also asks Father Olmedo, who is the expedition's chaplain and a Catholic priest, to listen.

"Quetzalcoatl is the Plumed Serpent..." Aguilar begins translating as Malinalli relates the legend of the Aztec god. "He is also known as Feathered Serpent and is a giver of life and bringer of knowledge. He made the people of the fifth sun and lives as the Morning Star..."

Malinalli points to the sky at Venus and relates how Feathered Serpent was tricked and left the world with the promise to return in One Reed.

"But why do the Indians mistake me for this Feathered Serpent?" Cortés asks.

"One Reed is this year, the time of your arrival in our lands. Our images of him are that of a young man full of vigor, often wearing a conical cap—similar to your shiny silver hats. He has pale skin, a dark, full beard and hair on his lip. He wears long, elaborately decorated clothing and feathers of a noble." She explains through the Friar.

Cortés is not convinced and says so, to which both Father Olmedo and Friar Aguilar can only stare back at their commander. But it is Malinalli who brings the point home to Cortés. She waves her hand down at his fine clothes and touches his mustache and the feather in his hat and looks him in the eye—and he finally sees what is obvious to everyone else.

"And what is this 'Feathered Serpent' to do when he returns?" Cortés asks her.

"He will reclaim his throne—the one that Montezuma occupies."

The Conqueror is stunned at this information, but before he can respond Malinalli continues.

"And he will end the blood sacrifices that this Emperor and those before him revel in. The vassal states of the Aztec Empire grow weary of the tribute they must pay in food and in their lives."

"We have seen some evidence of such killing, but surely it is not commonplace?" Father Olmedo wants to know.

"The sacrifices are continuous. Each February children are sacrificed to the maize gods on the mountain tops, in March prisoners fight to the death in gladiatorial contests, after which priests dress up in their skins. In April the maize goddess receives her share of children. In June there are sacrifices to the salt goddess...and on and on. In the old days it is said Feathered Serpent asked only for fruit and flowers, now the Empire makes war just to capture people for their rituals." Aguilar can barely speak her words he is so filled with horror and disgust.

"We must put an end to this Captain!" Father Olmedo tells the Conqueror indignantly.

"All in good time Father." Cortés begins to form a strategy, but has one more question.

"Why then did the Indians of Tabasco attack us if they think we are gods?" He asks Doña Marina.

"Tabasco is in Mayan territory. These people do not believe in the legend I related to you. You should also know the Aztecs and Mayans are mortal enemies and presently have an uneasy truce."

The Conqueror has a lot to think about and takes a walk along the shore. He can't help glancing towards the hut of Quitlalpitoc and wondering what the Indian is thinking right then. In a way the chief camped there is a two edged sword—he is surely a spy as Doña Marina suggests, but on the other hand as long as he is here it probably means the Indians are not going to attack. He doesn't yet know how this business of the 'Feathered Serpent' can be put to good use, but vows to have all the men wear their morion helmets at all times when the natives are about.

He also thinks about Doña Marina's touch on his face. It left him tingling, like after a bath in a cold mountain stream. And the look in her eyes, unlike other native women, was guileless...

Seven days pass when Teuthlille returns in the morning with more than a hundred slaves, all heavily laden with goods. He and Quitlalpitoc, along with another nobleman named Quintalbor, all bow deeply before Cortés, touching the ground at his feet with their hands. Then Indian priests burn incense in clay pans and wave the scent over the Spaniards.

Cortés gives them a cordial reception, and asks them to sit down at his side, while Aguilar and Doña Marina remain standing. The Conqueror notices the Indians study the girl while trying not to be obvious about it. The three Indian chiefs tell Cortés he is most welcome in their country and then some slaves lay out a mat made of reeds and throw cotton clothes over it. Then they bring out the presents.

The first is a round plate of the finest gold, about the size of a wagon wheel, and of the most beautiful workmanship representing the sun. It is a most extraordinary work of art, which will later to be found worth over 20,000 gold pesos (around $240,000 in today's value)—an incredible sum only a king could amass.

The second is another round plate, even larger than the first, this time of silver, representing the moon, complete with rays and stars and other figures on it.

The third is the morion helmet Cortés previously gave them, completely filled with pure gold nuggets, straight from a mine, valued at about 3,000 pesos ($36,000), but worth ten times that value, as the Conquistadors now know for certain there are rich gold mines in the country.

Among other things there are also thirty golden ducks of exquisite workmanship, looking exactly like the living bird and more figures resembling lions, tigers, dogs and apes. There are ten chains with lockets, all of gold. A bow and twelve arrows, and two staffs four feet in length, apparently used by the highest nobility, all cast of the purest gold. Then there are small cases containing the most beautiful green feathers, blended with gold and silver, and fans similarly worked; every with every species of game cast in gold. Finally they hand over thirty packages of cotton stuffs, woven and weaved and adorned with every variety of feathers.

"Lord Montezuma is delighted with the arrival of such courageous men in his states, according to the accounts he has received and judging from the occurrence at Tabasco. He wished very much to see this great man, who is such a powerful monarch and of whom he has already gained some knowledge, and so wished to send these gifts. He is likewise ready to furnish you with everything you might require during your stay. But as for Cortés calling upon the Emperor, this is not possible, as it is not necessary, and would be accompanied with great difficulties." Teuthlille says, as Malinalli tells Aguilar, who translates for Cortés—who realizes for certain the Emperor has spies everywhere since he knows about the battles they waged in Tabasco.

The Conqueror thanks them most sincerely for their kindness and gives each a couple of shirts made of linen from Holland, blue beads, and other trinkets. Then he begs them to return to their great Emperor Montezuma, and tell him that his emperor and master would take it very unkindly, after he had come from such distance and crossed such vast seas, merely with the intention of paying his respects to Montezuma, if he returned without fulfilling this objective.

Malinalli does not translate this statement exactly, instead she tells the Aztec envoys that the 'One True God' will be displeased in such a way as to leave open that Cortés is one and the same. She does this both out of confusion and uncertainty since she isn't quite sure who this other emperor is, as well as to throw a little fear into the haughty Aztecs.

Teuthlille is stunned at this outright statement and drops his former feigned politeness—a trait the Aztecs use to dominate.

"Who is this god?" He asks Malinalli bluntly.

"He is my master." She replies simply.

"And who are you? You appear as us, a Mexica."

"I am Malinalli, the servant of my master." She answers curtly, directly avoiding the question.

The Aztec ambassador though now knows by her name that Malinalli is an Aztec, and briefly wonders if she too is a god. He cannot take the chance of offending any of these beings. He tells

Malinalli that they will pass the request for a meeting to their Emperor, but that waiting for an answer would be a waste of the important man's time.

Cortés asks them to take his gifts to Montezuma as a token of respect and once again beg for a meeting. Both the delegates then depart, again leaving Quitlalpitoc behind in his hut.

As soon as the Aztec envoys leave, Cortés quietly orders two vessels to sail further on up the coast. The command of these is given to Francisco de Montejo, with orders to follow the same course taken by Grijalva. He is to sail on for five days. Although they do spot a fortified town named Quiahuitzlan, which has a harbor secure from the wind, thirty some miles away, they can't reach it on account of the heavy currents.

***

When his envoys return with news that the gods are still in his lands, Montezuma knows the magicians and wizards he sent to destroy them have failed.

"The god demands an audience, my Emperor, and no amount of words or excuses would seem to dissuade him from his goal." Teuthlille reports.

"You gave him the tribute?" Montezuma asks.

"Yes my lord and he in turn begged us to present you with these." The Aztec noble lays out the shirts and blue beads. "But he again asked I transmit to you his request for a meeting."

The Emperor waves the gifts away with disdain; he is both incensed and terrified the stranger wants to see him in person.

"His woman told us directly that this person is a god." Teuthlille reveals.

"You say she speaks for him, why would Quetzalcoatl not speak for himself?" The Emperor's brother asks.

"This person and all his companions speak in a different tongue, perhaps they have been away so long they speak a language from long ago." Quintalbor suggests.

"Yet this woman speaks clearly?" Montezuma asks.

"Yes, and she has the name Malinalli. She is Aztec. She carries herself like a princess, like nobility. She is direct and doesn't lower her eyes when speaking to us. She is dangerous. She may be a goddess of her own right." Teuthlille tells them. "My Lord, if you please, I do not think they will go away quietly."

"What do you think my brother?" Montezuma asks Cuitláhuac.

"You should not grant an audience to this being. He may be a sorcerer who will use the opportunity to poison or cast spells on you." His brother replies.

"Tell this person that the affairs of state prevent me from taking the time and that the journey is much too difficult for either of us to endure. Further, take them a few more gifts that my brother will provide you." Montezuma commands.

Then the meeting is interrupted by a fast runner sent by Quitlalpitoc. He whispers his report into the ear of the Emperor's brother, who then whispers it to Montezuma.

"My spy Quitlalpitoc has reported that the gods have sent two of their floating mountains farther west in search of another landing. You are to return and present the gifts and suggest that they leave. In the meantime I am instructing Quitlalpitoc not to provide any more food for them. Further, no one in the Empire is to have any contact with these strangers under penalty of death to them and their wives and children and all their families!"

"Does my lord think this is wise, after all this is Quetzalcoatl?" Quintalbor blurts out, fearful of offending a god.

Montezuma glances at his brother Cuitláhuac. Quintalbor will pay for his remark with his life.

***

About the time the scouting party returns, Quitlalpitoc although still camped near the Spanish, ceases to have his vassals bring food and is unresponsive to any requests. Cortés instantly is reminded of Doña Marina's warning of what may happen if they try to leave the area and continue. Apparently the Indians are demonstrating their displeasure with the Conquistador's explorations further up the coast. They are running out of food since all the supplies they brought with them and held in reserve have gone bad in the intense tropical heat. So the Conqueror anxiously awaits the return of the two ambassadors with word from Montezuma.

Finally a few days later Teuthlille indeed returns with a large number of Indians. He and Quitlalpitoc observe the same courteous behavior towards Cortés as before, while innocently explaining the great chief Quintalbor had fallen ill and therefore remained behind.

The envoys then bring forth their presents, consisting of ten packages of cloaks, richly worked in feathers and all kinds of gold trinkets, valued at about 3,000 pesos ($36,000). Finally they present four pieces of turquoise and jade, each of which they promise is worth more than a load of gold, which Malinalli confirms since she is stunned at the sight of so much wealth.

Then the ambassadors tell Cortés that their Emperor had graciously accepted his gifts, but is unable to meet him. And that it is unnecessary to send any more messengers to Mexico, and that this will be their last visit, so he and his subjects should return back to the lands from which they came.

"Really this Montezuma must be a great and rich gentleman and his time and duties important; nevertheless, if God be willing, we shall one day visit him in his palace." The Conqueror replies, thanking them greatly for the gifts, while hiding his displeasure at this news.

All this takes place just about the hour of Ave Maria which is announced by a bell, signaling that the Spanish should assemble around the cross. While they are all on their knees before it praying the Ave Maria, Teuthlille and Quitlalpitoc inquire why they humble themselves so greatly before this 'pole'.

Cortés immediately turns to Father Olmedo, and remarks that this might be a good opportunity to give these natives some notion of their holy religion. Olmedo first of all explains that they are Christians, and gives the basics of their beliefs. He then preaches that the native's idols are useless things, evil spirits, which fly away from the presence of the cross. On such a cross, he continues, the Lord of heaven and earth suffered death, they believe in him only, and pray to him as the only true God. And that someday Jesus Christ, who suffered death for the salvation of the human race and who rose again on the third day, and ascended into heaven, will again appear to hold judgment over the living and the dead.

Cortés then explains to them that among the many reasons he was here, one was that they should abandon forever the rituals of their cursed idols, abolish human sacrifices, and abstain from kidnapping. He asks them to erect crosses like this in their towns and on their temples, and also the figure of the holy Virgin, with her most excellent Son, so God would bestow great blessings on them.

Again Malinalli changes his meaning slightly. She tells the Aztecs in a stern tone that it is Cortés who demands they cease their idol worship and human sacrifice or face the wrath of this 'God'. The two dignitaries are visibly upset at these words, but try to hide it by going to Quitlalpitoc's hut to talk between themselves.

"Can this be any other than Feathered Serpent? Who else would dare to incur the wrath of Hummingbird Wizard and Smoking Mirror by withholding the blood sacrifice they demand?" Quitlalpitoc ponders.

"You stay nearby, you observe them daily." Teuthlille probes.

"They have those beasts; they have the firesticks and the thunder logs. They demand to be served food instead of hunting it themselves. They move on the ocean in their floating mountains. They wear iron garments. Yet they smell so awful my nose wrinkles from a distance. In any case they are extremely dangerous." Quitlalpitoc sums up.

In the meantime some of the Spanish officers trade with the Indians who accompany Teuthlille, and obtain various kinds of cheap gold trinkets , which they then pay to the sailors for catching them fish, since the Indians have not brought any food. Cortés is well aware of this and says nothing since it keeps the men happy.

The friends and relatives of Diego Velásquez are not pleased however, and the Conqueror is about to face a new challenge...

Those loyal to Diego Velásquez complain bitterly about the bartering for gold to Cortés. The Governor has not sent them here so the soldiers could line their pockets, after all a fifth of all the treasure was to go to the King. They demanded a treasurer be appointed to keep track of all the gold and valuable so the King's portion could be calculated correctly.

This is all a ruse since Velásquez never intends to pay the royal tax and certainly doesn't plan on giving any gold to the common soldiers. He will keep it all for himself and his cronies as he did before.

Cortés has no choice but to agree that they are right and proclaims no further bartering will be permitted, but as it turns out that order is to be mote anyway as the situation is about to change rapidly.

***

Montezuma is both furious and terrified when he hears the report from the final meeting: that they should abandon forever the rituals of their idols, and abolish human sacrifices. And further he is to erect the cross of Feathered Serpent in their towns and on their temples, and also the figure of this woman, and her son, then Quetzalcoatl would bestow great blessings on him. These words make it blatantly obvious that Feathered Serpent has returned to reclaim his throne—along with this woman he is supposed to worship as well!

All of which is a mixture of coincidence, complete misunderstanding, and confusion sown by Malinalli of course, who now the Emperor thinks could be the Virgin Mary. After all, though the Spanish preach the notion of 'One True God', they also display images of his son on a cross—similar to both Quetzalcoatl's symbol and that of the flag of Cortés, and this 'Holy Mother'—who appears as a young woman!

The Emperor is completely torn on his next move. Should he welcome the Feathered Serpent and lose his throne or try to repel the god?

He decides to ask the other gods themselves for advice...

Keeper of the Chalk is no fool.

His hair may be matted with the dried blood of his uncountable victims, his body may reek of the flayed human skins he wears during the ceremonies, and his skin marked with the scars of countless piercing for bloodletting, but he is no fool. He is not about to go against Montezuma. He arranges several sacrifices to the gods and he will interpret the results as he sees fit.

Tezcatlipoca (Smoking Mirror), and Huitzilopochtli (Hummingbird Wizard), after all were responsible for Quetzalcoatl's (The Feathered Serpent) departure from the land of the fifth sun, and it would be unlikely they would council welcoming him back with open arms.

And so, in the Emperor's presence, there are daily sacrifices of young children and brave warriors, that they might reveal what he should do about the situation in the east.

As the blood runs in rivulets from the temple altar, Keeper of the Chalk chants that unless the strangers leave they should be taken prisoner.

"Hummingbird Wizard says the Lord Montezuma should pay no attention to what the false god says. He must use the white stranger to teach the children of the foreign ways to set an example, and demands the blood of the rest of them—especially the Grass Goddess who speaks for him. You must take her tongue and eat it so you shall gain her skill and then rip out her heart and hold it in your hands." The priest says.

Hearing this the Emperor again issues an order to all the subjects and lands under the rule of the Empire that no one is to have any contact with the strangers under penalty of death...

12 Malinalli Shows the Way

One fine morning before anyone realizes it, the Indians who the Spanish are bartering with, have all secretly left with Quitlalpitoc in the dead of night. Their camp is deserted and empty, leaving the Conquistadors without any source of provisions.

Cortés is reminded of Malinalli's warning and expecting hostilities are now imminent, orders the men to high alert and posts double sentries all around their seaside encampment. Then circumstances take yet another turn when Diaz and another soldier who are on watch, spot five Indians approaching along the shoreline. Their appearance is quite different from the Aztec natives. They have large holes bored in their under-lips, in which they wear pieces of blue speckled stone, or thin plates of gold. The holes in their ears are larger in size, and adorned with similar ornaments. The natives seem quite friendly and make signs they want to be taken to the camp so Diaz obliges.

Neither Aguilar nor Malinalli understands their language, but when she asks whether there is a 'Naëyavatos', or interpreter, among them they reply in Nahuatl since two of them understand the Mexica language. Now they are able to converse with Cortés.

They bid the Spanish welcome, and state that their ruler has sent them to inquire who they are, and that he would be delighted to be of any use to such powerful men. The natives also explain they would have come sooner, but saw the Culhua, or Aztecs, were camped here.

At which point Malinalli explains to Cortés that these people are probably bitter enemies of the Aztecs according to their tone. And that they only came when they knew the Aztecs had left.

Cortés is most friendly to these people, and gives them various kinds of presents. Then he questions them closely through Malinalli about Montezuma and confirms what she explained previously, that this tribe like many others, chaffs under the rule of the Empire. Cortés then asks them to return to their ruler and report that he will visit him shortly in person. Though the Conqueror cannot know it now, this meeting will prove more fortuitous than he can ever imagine.

But first he must deal with multiple simultaneous problems: lack of food, swarms of mosquitoes, and growing resentment among some of the troops—many of whom are ready to return to Cuba.

Cortés orders the fleet be readied to make for Quiahuitzlan, about thirty miles or so down the coast. But while preparations are being made for departure, the friends and relatives of Diego Velásquez unite to press the issue with Cortés. They demand to know how he expects to continue without provisions and that even if they get to the next port it is the final one reachable by sea—the only alternative will be a land march.

The dissidents protest that already thirty-five men have died either of the wounds they received at Tabasco, of sickness, or of hunger. The country is too big, the population too numerous, and the inhabitants will no doubt attack in a few days. It is, therefore, most advisable to return to Cuba, and render an account to Diego Velásquez of the considerable gold they have amassed.

To which Cortés replies it is foolish to quit without seeing the country, and that such things as death and injury are to be expected when exploring the unknown. He assures them there is plenty of food around, they just have to look for it and promises to make it a top priority. While he succeeds in quieting them temporarily, the matter is merely put off, as they hold secret meetings, and commence in engaging in all manner of intrigue.

At the same time Conqueror quickly puts together a plan of his own to forestall the growing mutiny. He enlists three loyal soldiers, Escalante, and De Lugo, and Puertocarrero (the same man to whom he gave Malinalli), to his cause and persuades them to recruit more.

The first man they seek out is Bernal Diaz. They draw him from his tent at midnight with the ploy they are making rounds, but once away from camp they explain the situation.

"We have something to tell you, but you must keep it a secret from Diego Velázquez's partisans. We are of opinion that Cortés must not heed anything that Velázquez's friend say. Back in Cuba the Captain made known that he was going out to found a colony, and now those men claim that he was not empowered to do so, but was merely sent out to barter for gold, and then to return to Cuba with all we should make. If this takes place, we are altogether ruined men, and Diego Velásquez will pocket the gold, and keep it, as he has on previous occasions. And may we remind you that this is your third expedition, that you have spent your whole in them, and undergone so much, risked your life, and suffered from wounds, all for nothing. This we cannot allow." Puertocarrero tells Diaz.

"We are sufficient in number and we must insist that Cortés founds a colony here, in the name of his majesty. We must also find means to inform our King immediately about this. Promise that you also will be one of us. We have united to elect Cortés our captain-general. It would, indeed, be rendering God and our King a great service." Escalante adds.

Diaz answers that he considers it equally inadvisable to return to Cuba, and is quite ready to give consent towards electing Cortés captain-general and chief justice, until his Imperial Majesty should communicate his wishes on that point.

As the loyalist group goes round recruiting more men, the partisans of Diego Velásquez soon get wind of it, and boldly ask Cortés what is this about a plan to form a colony? And why he should shirk from rendering the account which is due to Diego Velázquez, the man who appointed him head of the expedition?

Cortés calmly replies he has not the remotest intention to act contrary to the instructions and wishes of Diego Velázquez, and immediately issues orders that everyone who had come with him should prepare to board the ships the next day.

This statement completely confuses his loyalists. They then confront Cortés and remind him in Cuba he had publicly announced that he was going out to found a colony, and now it appears the expedition is merely for the sake of trading. They beg him not to break his word, but to found a colony to promote the interests of the King and the service of God. Further, that it would be impossible to return here at any future time, as the inhabitants would certainly not permit us to land, but if a colony was once founded, soldiers from every island in these parts would come flocking as reinforcements. And that Diego Velásquez had deceived them all when he falsely announced that he was empowered by his majesty to found colonies. They were, therefore, determined to found one, and left it to the choice of the others if they wished to return to Cuba.

Cortés at first appears to refuse to support this sentiment, but finally relents after much discussion. And never one to pass up an opportunity, he makes it a condition that they should nominate him chief justice and captain-general, and that he should get a fifth of the gold after deducting the fifth for the King.

The group then holds an election in secret and elects Cortés, who then appoints each one of the loyalists some official title in the new colony to appease them. He has Godoy, the royal secretary, draw up a formal deed and they resolve that a town should be built, and called *Vera Cruz*, since the Spanish arrived off this coast on Holy Thursday, and stepped on land on Good Friday.

The partisans of Velázquez, finding that Cortés was elected captain-general, and the others appointed as officials, are infuriated. They arm themselves and confront Cortés and his loyalists, insisting that that the election is not valid because they were excluded. Their dissatisfaction rises to fever pitch and an outright mutiny appears imminent.

The two sides argue back and forth. The Cortés loyalists maintain that the King himself would insist on founding a colony in New Spain so that Christianity could be spread, trade set up, and a working government be established. The Velásquez partisans declare that that the expedition was only to gain as much gold as possible and then return to Cuba.

Cortés then secretly signals Juan de Escalante to ask that they should demand the written instructions to be produced which he had received from Velázquez. Both groups then begin shouting this demand.

So the Conqueror pulls them out from under his waistcoat, handing them over to the royal secretary to be read aloud. Sure enough the words were: *'After you have bartered for as many precious things as possible, you shall return home.'* The document is signed by Velázquez, and countersigned by his private secretary Andreas de Duero—and appears to be in direct conflict to the King's stated policies.

Upon this, the loyalists insist that these instructions should be entered into the appointment they had given Cortés in order that his Majesty might convince himself of the true state of things, and that everything that had been done was to further his sovereign interest only.

The partisans of Velázquez, however, are not to be silenced by this and as the election had been made without their knowledge, they consider it illegal, and maintain that they are not required to obey his commands and are determined to return to Cuba.

Cortés answers that he would not compel them to remain, and any who wish to leave are welcome to do so—without him.

This seems to quell the immediate storm, but a few diehards continue to cause trouble. Juan Velásquez de Leon, Diego de Ordas, Escobar, and Pedro de Escudero blatantly refuse to obey the Conqueror, so they are arrested for mutiny (a capital offence) and put in chains.

Malinalli observes all these events with a mixture of confusion and disdain. Although she has picked up some Spanish from her man, Puertocarrero, as well as Aguilar and of course Cortés, it is not enough to understand what is going on. She realizes the men are arguing and knows the words for 'gold' and 'food' so deduces that is what is at the center of the disagreements. It seems silly since both are fairly plentiful, but apparently just like the gods, they want it placed into their hands and are too lazy to seek it out themselves. She has already told Aguilar there is an abundance of maize and game in the area and he had reported this to Cortés. In fact it is because of this information from Malinalli that he assures the men they merely have to go and look for food.

Then the Conqueror acts quickly to further his purposes, while talking out of both sides of his mouth. On one hand he assures the Velásquez partisans they can leave anytime, but at the same time orders Pedro de Alvarado to make an excursion into the interior to explore the country, gain further knowledge of some villages which are known by name, and procure food of which they are in desperate need.

One hundred men are selected, strategically over half of which are adherents of Velázquez. The rest on whom Cortés can fully depend, remain with him, so that no conspiracy might be set against him.

Alvarado visits some small villages which are subject to Montezuma, but they find no inhabitants. Instead they happen on sufficient proof in the temples that boys and adults had very recently been sacrificed. The altars and walls are covered with fresh blood. The flint knives with which the unfortunate victim's chest is cut open to tear out the heart, and the large stones on which they are sacrificed, still lay in their proper places. Most of the bodies seen are without arms or legs, which, according to the accounts of the Indians, have been eaten. The men are horror-struck at such barbarity.

The expedition does find these districts well stocked with provisions, but so completely deserted that every soldier is forced to carry a load of greens and fowls back to the camp. The men are overjoyed with the provisions and when a man's stomach is satisfied he forgets his troubles; so the general morale suddenly improves.

In the meantime Cortés does not stand idly by, but does all in his power to sway the cronies of Diego Velázquez. Most are given or promised some of the gold. He then sets all of them free, excepting Juan Velásquez de Leon and Diego de Ordas, who are lying in chains on board a vessel. Cortés has a long talk with them separately to gauge their mindsets, and after playing one against the other and giving them gold for their trouble, they both are released and become true friends to him.

As soon as order is thus restored, the Conqueror orders a march to the village Quiahuitzlan, which was spotted earlier by sea. Since the ocean is too rough there because of the strong winds, the ships set sail empty for a run into the harbor, lying about four miles from the village.

They march along the coast and on the way kill a large fish, which had been stuck on the beach, and serves as the midday meal. They then come to a deep river, on whose banks the town of Vera Cruz will eventually be founded. Some of the men cross using old canoes, while others simply swim over.

On the opposite bank of the river are several small villages, but once again all are deserted. Evidently the natives have all run off to hide in fear of the strangers and especially their horses. The Conquistadors find temples stained with spots of blood, implements for incense and sacrificing, a quantity of parrot feathers, and several packages of paper stitched one over the other, resembling Spanish linen. But there is no food and they are forced to go to bed hungry—something Malinalli thinks is absurd: That these brave warriors cannot seem to fend for themselves.

The next day they march inland in an easterly direction with no knowledge of the road they are taking. The troops come to a beautiful meadow, where they find wild deer grazing, but are unable to bring any down. Malinalli is astounded that with their magical firesticks and iron crossbows they cannot nab a single deer, when her people do it every day with simple arrows. She begins to wonder how these men can be so helpless.

The next morning twelve Indians make their appearance and save the day, bringing with them some fowls and cornbread. They tell Cortés, through Aguilar and Malinalli, they have been sent by their chief, who asks that they visit his township, which lay at a distance of one sun, or a day's march, from this location.

Cortés gives them sincere thanks for their great kindness, and together they march on until they come to a small village, where it is obvious only a short time earlier several human beings had been sacrificed—a situation that will occur over and over each time they come to another village and see numbers of male and female Indians butchered. Malinalli is as horrified by this as the Spanish, but the natives provide supper and lots of information. The Conquistadors learn that the road to Quiahuitzlan passes through a place called Cempoalla and discover this is the home of the five Indians who came to see Cortés a few days earlier while he was camped at the ocean.

After spending the night in the village, where the twelve Indians provide for them, they leave very early in the morning for Quiahuitzlan. Cortés sends six of the Indians ahead to notify the chiefs of Cempoalla that the Spanish are approaching, and to request permission to visit them. The six other Indians remain behind as guides.

The Spanish march out in force and Cortés is cautious, ordering the cannon and other arms be ready for use at a moment's notice. He sends sharp-shooters on point along with the horses.

They are about three miles from Cempoalla, when they are met by twenty Indians who come to welcome Cortés in the name of their chief. They bring deliciously scented pineapples of a deep red color, which they present to Cortés and the others on horseback. They tell Malinalli that their chief awaits them in his quarters as he is too heavy to make the journey. Cortés thanks them graciously for their gifts and continues the march forward.

As they pass through the outskirts of the town the Spanish are stunned at its magnitude and appearance. It is well laid out, most buildings are made of stone and mortar and others of whitewashed adobe with roofs of straw. The houses of the wealthy people are very cool, and have many apartments. Within them they have their wells and reservoirs for water, and rooms for the slaves and dependents, of whom they have many. Each of these mansions has large courtyards, and in some there are two and three or four very high buildings, most over five stories with steps leading up to them, where they have their temples. All around are luxurious gardens and the streets filled with people.

The vanguard arrives in the great square and rides up to the buildings where they are to be quartered. The walls have been newly plastered with lime a few days earlier, and the sun is shining on them full strength so they are glowing white. One of the horse soldiers then comes galloping back to Cortés at full speed to inform him that the walls here are made of silver. Aguilar and Malinalli immediately see that this is fresh lime plaster, and begin to laugh at the man's silliness.

When Cortés arrives at the quarters the chief comes out in the courtyard to receive him. The man is, indeed, exceeding fat and will henceforth always be referred to that way from then on.

He pays Cortés the greatest respect, who then embraces him in return. After this welcome the Conquistadors are shown to their quarters, which are very comfortable, and so spacious that there is sufficient room for all the officers.

Food is set out, among which there is cornbread and several baskets of plums, which are just then in season. Roast turkey, which the Spaniards originally mistook for large chickens, is abundant. As the hungry men dig in, they comment among themselves they have not seen quantities of food like this in one place since leaving Spain. Some of them call the place Villariciosa (luxurious town), and others Seville.

Cortés gives strict orders that the inhabitants should not be harmed or mistreated in the slightest degree, and also that none of them should leave their quarters until they are told, so as not to frighten the populace.

It is much more likely the populace would frighten the Spanish however, as several officers soon discover when they begin to observe the religious practices of the natives close up. Every day, before they undertake any work, they burn incense in the temples, and then offer their own blood, some cutting their tongues and others their ears, and some slicing their skin with knives. They offer up to their idols all the blood which flows, sprinkling it on all sides of those temple, at other times throwing it up towards the heavens, and practicing many other kinds of ceremonies, so that they undertake nothing without first offering a morning sacrifice.

The self-inflicted bloodletting or cutting is nothing compared to what else the Conquistadors observe however. In order that their petition may be more acceptable, they take many grown men and women and even boys and girls, and in the presence of their idols they open their breasts, while they are alive, and take out the hearts and entrails, and bum the entrails and hearts before the idols, offering that smoke in sacrifice to them.

Prisoners taken in war are the most highly prized victims, but failing these, or for the celebration of minor festivals, slaves are easily bought, or are offered by their owners for the purpose. Small infants are also commonly sold by their mothers, and instances of free-born men offering themselves as victims, for one motive or another, are not unknown.

The victims are frequently drugged, so that they go unconsciously, or even willingly to the altar. If a great festival, requiring many and choice victims, fell in a time of peace, war would be undertaken on any frivolous pretext, in order to procure the desired offerings.

The rites are carefully prescribed, and are of the most solemn description. Different kinds of sacrificial stones were used for different classes of victims. The usual one a table-shaped stone about waist high, and standing on an inverted pyramid. Six priests would officiate, five of whom held the arms, legs, and head of the victim, who is stretched upon the stone in such way as to throw his chest well forward. These five have their faces and bodies painted black, with a white line around the mouth. Their hair is bound up with a leather band, and ornamented with tufts of colored papers; their vestment is a white dalmatic, striped with black.

The sixth priest is the celebrant whose vestment varied according to the feast, or the deity, to be worshipped. His head is adorned with colored feathers, and in his ears are golden ornaments, set with green stones, while a blue stone is set in his under lip. Pronouncing the words of the ritual, he plunges a sharp knife, made of onyx, into the victim's breast, and quickly thrusting his hand into the opening, tears out the beating heart. The heart is first elevated, and then deposited at the feet of the image of the god. Sometimes the heart is placed in a vase, and left standing on the altar, or it might be buried, or preserved with ceremonies, as a relic, or it might be eaten by the priests; the fresh blood smeared on the lips of the idols. If the victim was a prisoner taken in battle, his head was given to the priests, to be kept as a trophy, the entrails are fed to the dogs, and the other parts of the body are cooked with maize, and offered in small pieces to the guests invited to partake by the giver of the sacrificial feast.

To Cortés and his officers, it is the most terrible and frightful thing to behold that has ever been seen. They ask Malinalli about it through Aguilar, who can barely stand to utter the question. She explains, with a fierce determination, that so frequently, and so often do these natives do this that no year passes in which they do not kill and sacrifice at least fifty souls in each and every temple throughout the Empire as this is required by their strict calendar.

Malinalli's point hits home with the Conqueror and now that he has seen this with his owns eyes he is determined to put an end to it and bring Christianity to this land of New Spain.

After the Spanish are rested, the fat chief sends word to Cortés that he wants to pay him a visit, and immediately after arrives with a considerable number of distinguished nobles, who are wearing heavy golden ornaments and richly embroidered cloaks. Cortés meets them at the entrance to the quarters, and receives them graciously. After the compliments are passed, the fat chief hands him a present consisting of golden trinkets and cotton stuffs, which are actually of little value.

"Lopelucio, Lopelucio", which Malinalli explains means 'Chief', "accept this in favorable kind; if we had more to give we would have brought it." The chief repeats several times.

Cortés then instructs Doña Marina and Aguilar to tell the fat chief how grateful he is for so much kindness, and he has merely to inform him in what way he in return could be of service to him and his people. And further that he and his men are vassals of the great emperor Charles, who has dominion over many kingdoms and countries, and who has sent them out to redress wrongs wherever they came, punish the bad, and make known his commands that human sacrifices should no longer be continued.

Malinalli takes this opportunity to drive the point home about abolishing human sacrifices, telling them that Cortés is a powerful chief with vast powers who will not stand for this practice since his beliefs are against it.

The chief and dignitaries are somewhat confused by the routine of speaking to Malinalli, who then speaks to Aguilar, who then speaks to Cortés—all in different tongues. But they are even more confused by the girl herself, they recognize Malinalli is an Aztec, and probably nobility judging from her bearing and dress. They wonder among themselves how this strange white skinned chief could have enticed one of Montezuma's people to serve him. She can only be a slave or an ally and either way it means the Conqueror is powerful enough to accomplish anything

So the fat chief decides to be open, he sighs deeply, and complains most bitterly about Montezuma and his governors. It was not long ago that he had been subjugated by the Empire, and robbed of all his gold. The Aztec rule is so oppressive, that he dares not move without orders, but no one has the courage to oppose them, as the Aztecs possess vast towns and countries, huge numbers of subjects, and even more daunting—mighty armies.

Cortés answers that he will certainly relieve him of this oppression, but he will have to wait while he goes to Quiahuitzlan to establish a camp and sorts out his ships which are waiting off the coast there. Then they could get together and talk the matter over.

The fat chief is perfectly satisfied with this and the next morning sends four hundred Indian slaves to accompany the Spanish. Each of these porters is capable of carrying a weight of fifty pounds to a distance of twenty miles. The Conquistadors are delighted that each of them has a man to carry their baggage, for previously everyone had to carry his own knapsack—a situation to which they were not accustomed, since till now they traveled by sea. Malinalli tells Aguilar that according to the custom of this country the chiefs are bound in times of peace to lend their porters to anyone who requires them, and from this moment on they always demand them wherever they go.

After the first day's march they spend the night in a small village not far from Quiahuitzlan. Once again, the inhabitants have fled, but the people of Cempoalla furnish them food for supper.

The next morning they arrive in the principal township of Quiahuitzlan, which is built on a steep slope of rock, and would certainly be difficult to take since it is fortified. Seeing this, Cortés has no faith in the peaceful attitude they have so far encountered, and marches the men with the greatest precaution, preceded by cannon, so that it might be ready at hand if required.

The Conquistadors arrive in the middle of the town without meeting anyone and are not a little surprised at this circumstance. It would appear once again the natives have fled in advance of them. On the most elevated point of the fortress there is an open common space in front of the temple and there they met fifteen well-dressed Indians.

The natives go up to Cortés and bid him welcome, and beg forgiveness for not having come out to meet him. Through Malinalli they confess fear of the white iron men and their horses. So they decided to hide and observe who they were. Now that they have met each other, Cortés and his men had now only to make themselves comfortable, and they would see to it that all the people returned to their houses.

Cortés thanks them, and tells them many things about the Christian religion and the great monarch, as was customary wherever he went. Since Malinalli knew these people were not Aztecs, but under their rule, she correctly translates the concept of 'One True God' but leaves them with the distinct impression Cortés is some sort of powerful shaman in the service of this 'One God'.

Then the Conqueror presents them with a few green glass beads and other trifles he has brought from Spain, while the Indians supplied the ubiquitous cornbread and turkey in return. While the welcome reception is going on it is announced to Cortés that the fat chief of Cempoalla is approaching in a chair, carried by numbers of distinguished Indians.

Immediately upon his arrival he renews his complaints about Montezuma, in which he is joined by the chief of Quiahuitzlan and the other nobles and officials. He relates the cruelties and oppression they have to suffer, sobbing and sighing bitterly so that the Spanish cannot help being affected. Montezuma he says, demands annually a great number of their sons and daughters, a portion of whom are sacrificed to the idols, and the rest are used as slaves in his household and for tilling his gardens. His tax collectors take their wives and daughters without any ceremony if they are attractive, merely to satisfy their lusts. The Totonaques, whose territory consists of upwards of thirty townships nearby, also suffer the same treatment.

Cortés consoles them through Malinalli. He promises and assures them that he will put an end to their oppression and ill treatment. He tells them that this is one reason that his majesty has sent him to their country. They should, therefore, keep up their spirits, and they will soon see what he is about to do for their good. Although this in some measure seems to comfort them, Cortés is unable to completely allay their fear of the great Montezuma.

Then, during the lengthy talks, some Indians from the district announce that five Aztec tax-gatherers have arrived. At this news the chiefs and officials turn pale with fear. They immediately leave Cortés and hasten to receive the unexpected guests, for whom an apartment is instantly cleared and dinner set out, including cocoa in great quantities which is the principal beverage of the wealthy.

As the house of the chief is in the neighborhood, the Aztecs pass right by the Conquistadors, but ignore Cortés and his men completely. They wear exquisite cloaks and their glossy hair is combed and tied up in a knot in which are stuck some sweet scented roses. Every one carries a stick with a hook, and has an Indian slave with a fan to keep off the flies.

They are accompanied by a great number of distinguished nobles from the country of the Totonaques, who remain around them until they arrive in their quarters and sit down to dinner. After this is finished they send for the fat chief and the other chiefs of the townships, and scold them severely for having received the Spanish. They remind the chiefs that the Emperor had ordered there be no contact with these strangers and now they would have to pay dearly for all this. The tax collectors then order them to find twenty males and an equal number of females, and sacrifice them to appease the gods for the evil they have committed.

When the meeting breaks up the chiefs and nobles walk back past the Spanish quarters crying and sobbing. Cortés, seeing how upset all the natives behave, asks Doña Marina and Aguilar to explain the reason of all this, and who the strange Indians are. Malinalli already knows all about it, as the situation brings back painful memories from her own childhood, and tells him what is happening.

Upon hearing this Cortés is horrified, but also sees a unique opportunity to gain the complete attention of the elusive Montezuma. So he sends for the fat chief, and the other chiefs of the townships, and pretends to question them himself as to who the strangers and why are they treated so ceremoniously?

They answer, that these are tax collectors of the great Montezuma, who had bitterly complained to them for having received the strangers against the Emperor's direct order, and now require twenty males and twenty females for a sacrifice to the god of war, in order that he should grant them victory over the invaders. And, in the spirit of 'you're in trouble too', that the tax collectors have informed them that Montezuma would take the strangers prisoner and turn them into his slaves.

Malinalli spits out their words like venom, insuring Aguilar relates the frightening details of what the Emperor plans for them.

"Montezuma will take some of you as slaves and you will clean the droppings from the cages of his many birds and animals. The rest he will watch as your chests are ripped open and your hearts are cut out still beating so they can be roasted and eaten." She tells the Spanish. Her tone is not lost on either the Spaniards or the natives.

After hearing them out, Cortés tells them to take courage, assuring them he will punish the Aztecs for this, as both he and his troops are willing, and have the power to do so. He further reminds them he has already assured them that he is specifically commissioned to punish all those who do evil, and in particular kidnapping and human sacrifices. And since the Aztec tax collectors now demand human beings for these sacrifices, he will take them prisoner so that

Montezuma can learn a lesson and is made aware of the other violent measures committed against them and their wives and daughters.

The chiefs are extremely alarmed that Cortés would require this be their responsibility, and proclaim they dare not lay hands on the tax-gatherers of the mighty Montezuma. But Cortés cajoles them for hours until they at last gain the courage to act. The chiefs then order the tax collectors seized and fasten them to long poles by collars, which go round the neck. One of them who resists is also whipped in the bargain.

Then Cortés commands all the chiefs to no longer obey the mandates of Montezuma, nor to pay him tribute, and to make this known to all those tribes with whom they are allied and friendly. He adds that they should inform him, when any tax-gatherers arrive in other towns, so he can also take them prisoners too.

The news of all this quickly spreads through the whole country, as the fat chief dispatches messengers to relate the Conqueror's promise, and the other chiefs who had accompanied the Aztec tax collectors, rush back to their towns to report the wonderful news.

When the Indians learn this astounding and to them so important an event, they begin to talk that, such great things could not have been done by men, but only by 'teules', which sometimes means gods and sometimes demons. Malinalli is quick to reinforce this notion; blurring the difference between the Cortés and the 'One True God' every time she has the chance.

Of course though now the die has been cast, Cortés will soon have to stand up against the mighty Empire...

13 Montezuma

The leader of the Aztecs is approximately forty years of age and has a long but handsome face. Montezuma is above average height and well proportioned. He wears his hair just long enough to cover his ears and his black beard is light but well-shaped. He baths everyday in the afternoon and never wears the same clothes two days in a row.

Montezuma has many mistresses, all of them daughters of chieftains, and two legitimate wives. His chefs cook thirty dishes for every meal: pheasant, wild boar, quail, turkey, rabbit, partridge, duck, and venison—just so the Emperor will have plenty from which to choose. Two women always wait at his side in case he needs more tortillas. He loves to drink cacao—a chocolate drink the Aztecs reserve for nobility and the wealthy.

Sometimes his servants place a gold screen in front of him so that no one can see him eat. Other times while he eats he is entertained by a large troop the palace maintains for his amusement. He enjoys singing, dancing, people on stilts, gymnasts, and humpbacks who are made to look like jesters. He keeps over two hundred chieftains in his guard in rooms close to his. If they need to speak to him they are required to enter the room barefoot with their eyes down. They are not allowed to look at his face.

As much as Montezuma would prefer to bury his head in the sand and enjoy these trappings of power and try to ignore Cortés and the ramifications of his arrival, circumstances are just not going to permit it.

When he receives reports that his tax collectors have been imprisoned and all the townships have revolted, he flies into a rage never before witnessed. This god Cortés and the whole of his demons are purposely baiting him like a mouse teasing a great cat! Montezuma shouts at his brother.

But at least, Cuitláhuac thinks to himself, this situation has finally stirred his brother the Emperor, and if he shall make war upon the strangers at least he is not hiding away in his chamber, trembling like an old woman.

At his brother's instigation the Emperor orders one of his most powerful generals to go to war against the tribes that have revolted, and exterminate them to the last man.

"And I will personally lead an army of 500,000 men, commanded by a thousand generals, against these strangers and make them my slaves." Montezuma swears.

Has Cortés finally awakened the sleeping giant?

***

The Conqueror is not particularly worried about the rumblings of war—he has a few tricks up his sleeve.

All the chiefs and nobles were of opinion that Cortés should sacrifice the prisoners, and return their splintered bodies to the capital so as to demonstrate what happened to them. Cortés, however, strictly forbids this, and places a strong watch over them.

About midnight he orders one of the guards into his room.

"Pay particular attention to what I say. Take two of the prisoners who are talking the most, and bring them here to my quarters. This must be done with the utmost secrecy, so that the Indians of this town know nothing about it."

When the two Aztec tax collectors are brought before Cortés, he pretends to know nothing about them or who they are and has Malinalli question them as to why they have been taken prisoner.

The Aztec officials are very wary of Malinalli, for they know she is one of them and cannot understand what she is doing here. Malinalli herself is confused and dismayed at the actions of the Conqueror, but continues translating the tax collector's words until she can figure out what is going on.

"They say that the chiefs of Cempoalla, and of this area, have arrested them in secret understanding with you." She tells Cortés through Aguilar.

"Please assure them, that I am totally ignorant of the whole matter, and am very sorry it happened." The Conqueror instructs her and Aguilar—to which Malinalli can hardly believe her ears.

Then he immediately orders food to be given them, and they be kindly treated. While they are eating Cortés asks them through his interpreters to return to Montezuma, and declare that he and his men were all his sincerest friends and most devoted servants. Then he adds they will be set free at once and he will severely reprimand the chiefs who had imprisoned them.

It is then that Malinalli begins to realize what Cortés is about. He is playing the sides against one another with the ultimate goal of gaining favor with the Emperor. While this disturbs her somewhat since it is her goal to end the blood sacrifices of her people, and Montezuma is the main culprit, she is willing to give the plan a chance since the Conqueror has adamantly opposed sacrifice as well all the time since she first met him.

Cortés tells the Aztecs he is prepared to render them any service in his power, and he will likewise release their three companions as soon as he is able, but they had better get out of sight as quickly as possible, before they are recaptured by the warriors in the town and killed.

Both the prisoners reply they are very thankful for their freedom, but are afraid of falling again into their enemies' hands, as they must pass through their lands. So Cortés orders six sailors to take the officials in a boat to a point on the coast, twelve miles distant, where they would be out of the Cempoallan territory.

All this is managed in the dead of night, and when day breaks the chiefs and others are not a little surprised to find only three prisoners remaining. They insist these three should be sacrificed, but Cortés pretends to be highly infuriated at the escape of the two, and says he is determined to guard the others himself. To this end he orders them bound in heavy iron chains and taken away to one of the ships so they are out of sight. But as soon as the prisoners are on board, their chains are taken off again, and they receive kind treatment and are assured they will be sent back to the capital as soon as possible.

The chiefs and nobles of Cempoalla, Quiahuitzlan, and those from the country of the Totonaques, then assemble and complain to Cortés of the position he put them in, as no doubt Montezuma has already put an army in motion to exterminate them all.

But Cortés assures them, with a pleasant smile on his face, that he and his soldiers will protect and kill anyone who should dare to attack them. After hearing this all the chiefs promise to unite their armies with the Conquistadors against Montezuma and his allies. Then the expedition's secretary Diego de Godoy draws up a formal document of their treaty with Spain, and notice is sent of this to the different towns of the province. As there is no further talk of tribute and tax-collectors no longer make their appearance, the people erupt in celebration at having shaken off the Aztec yoke.

So with the alliance with the thirty townships of the Totonaque Mountains, which have revolted from Montezuma and submit of their own free will to the Spanish, Cortés hastens to take advantage of the circumstance and founds the colony of Vera Cruz.

The spot he chooses lies about two miles distance from the fortress of Quiahuitzlan, in the valley below. The Spaniards first of all mark out the ground for the church, the market, the armory and other public buildings belonging to a town. They then set off part of the ground to form a fortress—in preparation for what could be a major assault by Aztec forces.

Everyone pitches in and nothing can exceed the speed with which the walls of the foundation are built up, the woodwork completed, the turrets and gun holes constructed in the parapets. Cortés himself begins, carrying a basket filled with stones and earth on his shoulders, and works on the foundations. The chiefs and nobles and all of the Spaniards follow his example, and every part of the work is carried out quickly. Some mix mortar, fetch water and lime, and bake bricks and tiles, while others prepare the food and cut wood. The blacksmiths hammer hard at the nails and other ironwork. In a short time the church and other buildings are finished, and the fortress nearly so.

***

While preparations for war are being made, the two tax collectors who Cortés has liberated arrive in the capital. They explain that it was Cortés who set them free after the chiefs had taken them prisoner, and that he sent them to the palace with the offer of his services to the Emperor.

The Conqueror's mind games have the desired effect: Montezuma is flabbergasted.

"What is this god about?" The Emperor screams at his advisors and relatives.

"Perhaps he seeks to sow the seeds of discontent throughout the remote reaches of the Empire." Cuitláhuac suggests—a most clever observation on his part.

Nonetheless, the Conqueror's action completely breaks Montezuma's previous resolve as well as his anger, but he is determined now to discover the stranger's true intentions.

To this end he dispatches two of his young nephews, accompanied by four elders of distinction, back to Quiahuitzlan, with a present consisting of gold and cotton stuffs. These men are instructed to thank Cortés for the liberation of his two tax-gatherers, but at the same time to lodge complaints against the tribes who have revolted.

In the meantime he will consider his alternatives…

***

Cortés receives these messengers kindly and accepts their present, which is worth only about 2,000 pesos ($24,000)—not quite a fortune but also certainly not quite an insult.

Montezuma's nephews thank Cortés for releasing the two tax collectors, but at the same time make serious complaints against the tribes who had taken them prisoner in the first place and refuse to obey the Emperor or pay tribute to the Empire. They further declare Montezuma is only temporarily delaying his threat of exterminating them totally, out of consideration for Cortés, since he and his companions inhabit their dwellings.

"Our Lord Montezuma recognizes these people whose arrival in this country has been foretold by his ancestors, and who are of the same lineage as himself. However, they should not long rejoice in their treachery, for soon he should know how to deal with them." One of the elder Aztecs says to Malinalli—which confirms her suspicion that the Emperor thinks the Conqueror is Quetzalcoatl.

Malinalli translates this statement exactly, so that Cortés understands her hunch was correct—but she also wants him to hear the real threat as well.

Instead Cortés laughs off their attempt at intimidation and assures them that he and his companions are quite friendly and ready to serve Montezuma, and that it was in this spirit he had taken the three other tax-gatherers under his protection, and who are now immediately being brought forth from the ships and will be released to the ambassadors.

Then to demonstrate he is not about to cower before them, Cortés complains about Quitlalpitoc, Montezuma's governor. He accuses him of being discourteous and refusing to provide them with provisions (a complete sham since both sides know full well Quitlalpitoc was just following Montezuma's orders).

Cortés goes on to say that is was because of this mistreatment by Montezuma's governor they were forced to seek help from the local natives and therefore the Emperor should pardon them. And as to their complaints about the local's refusal to pay tribute, it is to be expected that they cannot serve two masters at once, since they have sworn allegiance to the Spanish. He finishes by adding he will now wait upon Montezuma so these matters could be discussed amicably face to face.

Cortés then presents both distinguished young nephews and their four venerable companions with blue and green colored beads, paying them the greatest possible (mock) respect. Finally Cortés orders Alvarado and other good riders to perform a cavalry exercise and go through a series of maneuvers designed to show off the power and speed of the horses.

After the Aztec ambassadors leave, the fat chief along with several other distinguished nobles from among the new Spanish allies, rush to meet with Cortés. They and the inhabitants of Cempoalla had stood in no little fear of Montezuma and believed that he would invade their country at any moment with a great army to exterminate them. But when they found that several of his relatives came bringing presents, and that they acted submissively to Cortés, they began more and more to revere the Conqueror instead.

"These beings must surely be gods, as even Montezuma himself stands in awe of them and sends them presents", Malinalli overhears them saying to one another. When she informs Cortés of this, he turns round to his men standing near him.

"Methinks, gentlemen, we already pass here for great heroes; indeed, after what has happened with the tax-gatherers these people look upon us as gods, or a species of beings like their idols." Cortés tells them with a smile on his face.

But the Conqueror's pleasure is short lived as some of Diego Velázquez's adherents again began to murmur, declaring that Cortés might proceed further with those who wished to follow him, but as for themselves they were determined to return to Cuba.

Next morning when the officers go round to the different quarters and order the men to march out with their arms and horses, the partisans of Velásquez insolently answer that they would take no further part in any expedition and wished to return home. They had already lost enough, they say, by allowing themselves to be led away by Cortés to join him in the first place. They now insist he fulfill the promise which he had made some time ago to grant their discharge and provide them a vessel and the necessary provisions.

Seven men declare they are positively determined to return home and are brought before Cortés.

"We cannot help feeling astonished that you should think of founding a colony with a handful of men in a country full of towns possessing many thousands of natives. We are all suffering from sickness and exhaustion in this dreadfully hot land and quite tired of roving about, and desire to return to our settlements in Cuba. We request, therefore, you grant us our discharge according to your promise." They tell the Conqueror.

To this Cortés answers, in a pleasant manner (always a danger signal), that he had indeed made such promise, and although they are acting in a manner tantamount to desertion, he is prepared to grant their request, and provides them with a vessel, bread, a bottle of oil, a quantity of vegetables, and such things necessary for a distant voyages.

In reality Cortés is playing one of his mind games, for when these men are about to set sail, the rest of the troops beg him to issue an order that no one should leave the country, declaring that anyone who could think of deserting as they are surrounded by numerous enemies, in the midst of battle and in the moment of the greatest danger merited death. So all the seven got for their pains was contempt and disgrace from their comrades—a result cleverly engineered by the Conqueror by letting his men do his work for him.

While this is going on the fat chief and his cohorts from Cempoalla decide to try and put one over on the Spanish and use them to settle an old score with the tribe from Tzinpantzinco. They meet with Cortés and tell him there are Aztec tax collectors and an army unit garrisoned in that area and request his assistance to dislodge them.

Trying to set an example for his new allies, Cortés takes this news seriously and organizes his men to march to the city. The first day they march twenty miles, and arrive at Cempoalla, where 2000 Indian warriors, divided into four troops, join them. The second day towards nightfall the Spanish, moving ahead of the Indians, arrive at the plantations near Tzinpantzinco, and take the road leading into that fortress, which wound up between large and steep rocks. The natives see them and immediately eight noblemen come out to them, making signs of peace. They ask Cortés through Malinalli, with tears in their eyes, why the strangers are seeking war, as they had done nothing against them?

Malinalli tells them that Cortés has come to relieve the burden of the Aztec Empire and take them under his protection because the chiefs of Cempoalla reported an Aztec garrison in the town.

She quickly learns however, that the Aztec tax collectors fled some time ago when their comrades were imprisoned. The nobles then tell her that Tzinpantzinco and Cempoalla have had a dispute over territory since ancient times and they are certain the Cempoalla tribes have come to plunder and destroy them, under protection of the Spanish.

When Malinalli informs Cortés of this, he angrily orders Alvarado to take some men and march back to the Cempoallan warriors and command them not to advance any further. Though they rush to the rear, the Spanish find them already plundering the farms and have taken several prisoners for sacrifice.

Cortés is furious at this news and orders the chiefs of the Cempoallans brought before him, and severely criticizes them for such behavior. Then he commands them to bring him all that they stole, and not to set a foot into the town. Cortés further tells them that if they commit such crimes again none of them would escape alive. After the Cempoallan chiefs return the prisoners and the turkeys they had stolen, Cortés orders them to return to their camp and remain there for the night.

When the chiefs and noblemen of Tzinpantzinco and other inhabitants of the surrounding area witness this act of justice, and see how friendly Cortés is, they are inclined to listen to his usual speech about Christianity and the evils of human sacrifice. As she translates the words however, Malinalli once again omits any mention of the 'One God' and the King of Spain and instead hints that Cortés is the god they should fear.

After hearing complaints about the Aztec Empire and Montezuma in particular, Cortés promises to grant them protection provided they abolish the worship of idols and human sacrifices. In response the chiefs declare themselves vassals of the Spanish—their very first allies in the interior of Mexico.

Malinalli also observes these kind actions of Cortés, as she has since being more or less brought into his inner circle as an interpreter, and begins to admire the Conqueror even more. She judges him a kind and fair leader, as well as feeling a growing attraction.

The next morning Cortés sends for the chiefs and nobles of the Cempoallans, who had spent the night in fear of what the Conquistador might do in punishment for their lies. But instead Cortés invites the inhabitants of Tzinpantzinco and mediates a reconciliation between the tribes and orders them to live in peace with God and each other so that they may fight the oppression of the Aztec Empire instead.

After this accomplishment, Cortés marches his men back to Cempoalla, but detours through two villages friendly with the Tzinpantzincans so he can continue to spread his message and recruit more allies. In one of the villages, a soldier named Mora steals some turkeys out of one of the huts and makes the mistake of boasting about it to his comrades. When Cortés finds out he orders a rope around the man's neck and proceeds to hang him on the spot.

"We will not treat the natives as savages! We will not plunder from them. These people are our allies!" Cortés shouts to his men.

Only the Conqueror's trusted officer Alvarado convinces him to change his mind and he manages to cut Mora down from the noose with his sword before he can be hanged. But the moment seeks to again reinforce the native's (and Malinalli's) good opinion of Cortés.

When the Spanish return to Cempoalla the following day, the fat chiefs and other nobles are waiting with a large feast, hoping to cement the alliance after their ill conceived attempt to get the Conquistadors to destroy their enemies. During the lavish meal they suggest the Spanish should look upon them as brothers, and that they should choose wives from among their daughters and relatives, so that prosperity might descend upon them all. To this end the chiefs present Cortés with eight females, all daughters of nobles.

"*Tecle*, these seven women are intended for your chief officers. And this, my own niece, who herself holds dominion over a country and a people, I give to you." The fat chief proclaims as he presents them to Cortés.

All the young women are finely dressed in beautiful gowns, with golden chains about their necks, golden rings in their ears, and even have other Indian females to wait upon them. As it happens though none are beautiful and in fact the fat chief's niece is the ugliest of all and severely cross-eyed—a characteristic that Malinalli explains to Cortés is a mark of high beauty among the Aztecs. Despite this, Cortés gracefully acknowledges the gift of the girls and thanks the chiefs, remarking that these women shall cement the bonds of brotherly union between them. But then goes on to say that the women must be converted to Christianity before he could think of accepting them and that now they should renounce their idols, and no longer conduct human sacrifices.

"All these atrocities must cease from this moment, only then can our union be sincere." He speaks through Malinalli, which she translates with a cutting edge to her tone, since the subject of sacrifice is one close to her own heart.

"It is impossible to abolish our gods and the sacrifices they demand. Everything that is good we receive from our gods. They make our seeds grow and grant us all necessities: the sun, the rain, our food, and even our children." The chiefs and nobles reply.

When their words are translated Cortés is incensed and turns to his men.

"We can do nothing which would be more beneficial to these people, and more to the glory of God, than to abolish this idolatry with its human sacrifices. It is certainly to be expected that the natives will rise up in arms, if we proceed to destroy their idols. We must however, make the attempt, even if it is to cost us our lives. Prepare yourselves for battle!" Cortés rallies his soldiers.

Upon this the Spaniards array themselves as if preparing for battle, and Cortés tells the chiefs that he is now going to destroy their idols.

When the fat chief hears this he is furious and orders the other chiefs to call out the warriors in their defense, at which point the Spanish soldiers begin the long climb up the stone steps to the main temple where the sacrifices take place.

"Why are you going to destroy our gods? Such an insult we will not suffer; it will mean destruction for everyone." The chiefs tell Cortés menacingly.

"I have already told you several times you must not sacrifice to these monsters who are nothing more than deceivers and liars. There is now, therefore, no alternative left than to lay violent hands on them myself, and hurl them from their bases. And since you put no faith in my advice you must look upon us as your worst enemies, and no longer as friends. Any opposition will cost you your lives." Cortés loses patience and answers.

Malinalli seizes upon this opportunity to remind the chiefs of Montezuma's army, which waits to crush them, and that it is only Captain Cortés that stands in the way and protects them out of friendship.

She has scarcely finished speaking when more than fifty soldiers mount the steps of the temple and reach the top. They proceed to tear down the idols from their pedestals, break them to pieces, and fling them down the steps. Some of these idols are shaped like furious dragons and are the size of young calves, others have half human form, some again are shaped like large dogs; but all are horrible to look at.

When the chiefs and nobles see their cherished idols in pieces on the ground, they set up a miserable howl, cover their faces, and beg forgiveness of their gods.

It does not end there however, for their armed warriors then come charging up and began shooting arrows at the Spanish soldiers atop the temple. Malinalli knows no fear and plunges into the melee and shouts at the Spanish to seize the fat chief, six priests, and several of the nobles. She then tells them, that if the attack is not instantly stopped they will all forfeit their lives. The fat chief then commands his men to cease, and quiet is somewhat restored.

When Cortés is able to turn his attention to those six priests he notices they wear hooded long black cloaks without sleeves, which hang down to the feet. But when he studies them closer, the real horror of the situation becomes apparent: their garments are completely clogged with blood from head to foot, so much so they have difficulty walking and even worse they smell of sulphur and putrid flesh. All this as a result of the countless human sacrifices they conducted. Malinalli explains distastefully that these priests are sons of distinguished nobles and are forbidden to marry or bathe and fast on certain days, eating very rarely.

The Conqueror is so taken aback and horrified at these men in his midst he forces them to gather the fragments of their precious idols and burn them. When this is done, Cortés delivers a speech through Malinalli.

"Now we can look upon you as our true brothers, and lend powerful assistance against Montezuma and the Aztecs. I have already informed the Emperor that he is no longer to make war upon you, nor to exact tribute. Instead of your false idols, we will give you our own Blessed Virgin, the mother of Jesus Christ, in whom we believe, and to whom we pray, that she might intercede and protect you in heaven."

Although the natives listen attentively to this and many other things, which Cortés explains to them concerning the holy religion, the concept of the 'Blessed Virgin' as mother of Jesus Christ is somewhat confusing. They think that Jesus Christ must be the brother of Cortés or a fellow god—a notion Malinalli does not bother to dispel.

In any case Cortés single-mindedly presses on in his attempt to convert the Indians and instructs the chief to order every mason in the city to bring lime to clean away the blood from the walls of the temple, and plaster them over. The next day an altar is erected and carpenters make a cross which is erected on an elevated base, well plastered over with the pure white lime. Then the altar is covered with cotton cloth and the Indians are ordered to bring a quantity of their splendid and sweet-scented roses to adorn it and are instructed that these flowers are to be constantly renewed, that the place might remain pure and undefiled.

The Conqueror then selects four priests to take charge of this, but not before he has their filthy blood-clotted hair shorn off, and fits them with white cloaks, which they must henceforth keep perfectly clean. In order that they might have someone to look over them in their new occupation, Cortés nominates Juan de Torres, an old lame invalid of Cordova, to live near the altar, in the capacity of pastor. A requirement is also made that in future a local copal tree resin should be used instead of the usual incense, and the native priests are taught to make wax candles (which they had never seen before) and these candles are always to be kept burning on the altar.

The next morning early Father Olmedo says mass and consecrates the new altar. The principal chiefs and nobles of the district and village attend mass, but the real center of attention are the eight Indian females who had been previously given to Cortés, but who had remained with their parents and relatives. These girls are now baptized after an lengthy explanation of the Christian religion. The niece of the fat chief, a very ugly woman, is named Doña Catalina, and formally presented to Cortés, who accepts her with every appearance of delight. Six other young women are given to some of the other officers.

But if the events of the past few days teach Cortés anything it is not only how valuable Doña Marina is to the expedition, but also what place she holds in his heart. Her bravery exceeds that of most men and he can't forget the fiery look in her eyes as she took control of the life or death situation at the temple. He wants her more than anything.

So in a most clever move Cortés gives the remaining girl, the daughter of a powerful noble who receives the name of Doña Francisca, and who is the most beautiful of the lot, to Puertocarrero, the man to whom Malinalli ostensibly belongs. In truth this arrangement is largely a sham since Malinalli obviously has eyes for Conqueror and him for her, but it was a situation he had to live with for appearances sake. And Malinalli has no choice but to act as she had been taught and be loyal to her master Puertocarrero. Secretly though Cortés hopes now that Puertocarrero has a new woman he might be free to partake of that which he has longed for.

The mass and baptismal ceremony being concluded, the chiefs and principal nobles take their leave, and from this moment relations are good, for they are highly pleased that Cortés has accepted their daughter as his mistress.

The Spanish then return to their new town Vera Cruz amidst joyous professions of friendship between the natives and the Conquistadors—an atmosphere which unfortunately won't persist among the Spanish themselves...

***

Montezuma's two young nephews return and breathlessly report their meeting with the god Cortés—and especially of the strange creatures that accompany him:

"The 'stags' came forward, carrying warriors on their backs. These warriors wore gleaming armor. They bore their leather shields and their iron spears in their hands, but their swords hung down from the necks of the stags. The animals wear many little bells. When they run, the bells make a loud clamor, ringing and reverberating." One nephew said.

"These creatures snort and bellow. They sweat a great deal and the sweat pours from their bodies in streams. Foam from their muzzles drips onto the ground in fat drops, like a lather of soap. When they run, they make a loud noise, as if stones were raining on the earth. Then the earth is pitted and cracked open wherever their hooves have touched it." The other reported.

In their fearful excitement the group largely forgets about what was actually said at the meeting with the stranger and instead the Emperor imagines these are creatures from the underworld which Cortés/Quetzalcoatl has brought forth with him.

Montezuma himself had looked into a mirror long ago and seen people moving across a plain, armed for war, and riding on what looked like strange deer. This can only be the manifestation of the prophecy of Quetzalcoatl's return.

Again, the Emperor is paralyzed by fear and indecision...

14 Romance Blossoms

The city of Vera Cruz is nearly complete when the Conquistadors return and all that remains is the woodwork, since all the hard work—the foundations—had been laid previously. This task does not require much effort or manpower and is quickly completed. After a week or two the soldiers soon grow bored with nothing to do, and as the saying goes: 'idle hands do the devil's work'.

While the men turn their attention to the bitter dispute between Cortés and Diego Velázquez, the Conqueror pines for Malinalli. Puertocarrero shows no sign of losing interest in Malinalli and both her and Doña Francisca clean and cook for him. Of course Malinalli usually has little time for housekeeping chores when she is acting as interpreter, but in this down time there is little else for her to do.

The monotony is broken briefly when a vessel appears in the harbor. The ship's captain's name is Francisco de Saucedo and he has sailed in from Cuba. The Spanish instantly nickname him 'The Gallant' due to his extravagant attire which rivals that of their own Captain-General Cortés. He is said to have been at one time butler to the admiral of Castile. Along with him are ten soldiers, and a certain Luis Marin, a most distinguished officer, who would became one of the chief commanders in the Mexican campaigns. Both men have horses with them—a welcome addition to the small army. As it happened, they set sail for the New World on their own and wish to join Cortés.

The men also bring intelligence that Diego Velásquez has obtained authority from Spain to trade and found colonies wherever he likes, which pleases his partisans greatly. They also report that Velásquez is livid with Cortés and plans to arrest him on sight for treason.

As the men grow tired of doing nothing a majority of them approach Cortés and beg him to undertake an expedition inland. They say that they have been in this country three months, and it is high time they all should just convince themselves how much truth there is in the boasted power of Montezuma of which they have heard so much about. They tell the Conqueror they are willing to risk their lives to find out and enrich themselves with the gold he is rumored to possess.

When Cortés seems receptive to this, the men add that perhaps they ought first to give some proof of their loyalty to his majesty, the King of Spain, and forward him a complete account of everything that had transpired since leaving Cuba. They also propose that all the gold and treasures obtained so far should likewise be sent to his majesty as proof of their allegiance.

In their proposal Cortés sees, so to speak, a way to kill a whole flock of birds with one stone:

> He can circumvent Diego Velásquez by going over his head and directly to the King.

> He can finally put to rest the jelling mutiny of the Velásquez partisans.

> He can rescind the prior commitment to give some of his men large shares of gold.

> He can do what he came here to do and move to explore inland to seek even more gold.

> And last but certainly not least, if plays his cards right he can finally have Doña Marina all to his own.

So the deviously clever Cortés tells the men that their ideas exactly correspond with his own. But there is merely one problem which causes him to hesitate: namely, that if each person took his share of gold to which he is entitled, there wouldn't be enough left to be worthy of his majesty's acceptance.

Amazingly, every one of the men agrees to give up his share and a document is drawn up to that effect. Of course, they are all hoping that the expedition to the land of Montezuma will not only replace the gold they have given up, but make them richer beyond their wildest dreams.

Everyone, without exception, signs his name to the agreement, and agents are chosen to be dispatched to Spain. Cortés slyly nominates none other than Alonso Puertocarrero as one of them—an honor the man cannot refuse, since although the Conqueror's motives are hardly pure Puertocarrero suspects nothing but having gained the leader's trust and honor.

At this point some of the men get together and write an account of their adventures. Besides relating the day to day events, they state they been persuaded to join the expedition with a promise that they were going to found a colony, and how Diego Velásquez had given Cortés secret instructions to confine himself to the trade of barter. They further report that Cortés had indeed wished to return to Cuba with the gold, but that they had begged him to remain and found a colony, and they had elected him captain-general and chief justice, and that they had promised him a fifth part of all the gold after deducting the fifths for his majesty.

They described the negotiations with the great Montezuma, mentioning his power and riches, and the gifts he had given to his majesty, consisting in the sun of gold and moon of silver, and the helmet of gold nuggets, and all the other trinkets. And they described the extent of the country, its population, the arts, customs, and religion of the inhabitants, and of the human sacrifices practiced.

The men finished with a plea: that they were only 450 armed men in the midst of so many warlike tribes and the expedition had merely been to serve God and begged the King to confer command of New Spain on Cortés, who was familiar with the situation and in whom they placed all their trust.

The men present their letter to the Conqueror, who is naturally quite pleased, and reveals he has written his own account as he feels is his duty. Puertocarrero and a second officer, Francisco de Montejo, take charge of the letters and the treasure, and are ordered not to land at Havana under any circumstances, nor run into the harbor of El Marien, where Francisco de Montejo has property. This is done that Velásquez might receive no word of their actions.

The fastest ship is outfitted and they set sail from Vera Cruz. Though neither Cortés nor Puertocarrero can predict it, this simple and presumably well-meaning gesture towards the King will quickly become 'Mission Impossible'.

The ship soon arrives near Havana. Here Francisco de Montejo persuades the pilot to sail along the coast in the direction of his settlement, where he insists he will take on a fresh supply of cassave-bread and bacon. Although Puertocarrero argues this is in direct violation of their orders and promises, they land anyway. That night a sailor swims secretly ashore, at the direction of Montejo himself, and delivers Diego Velásquez letters from his partisans, giving him an account of everything that is going on.

When the Governor of Cuba gets the news he becomes violently angry and curses not only Cortés, but his own private secretary Duero, and the treasurer Almador de Lares. Not only is he furious about the letter detailing Cortés' exploits and thereby making himself look bad, but especially at the gift of all the gold and silver amassed in New Spain to the King—treasure which he intended as his own.

Velásquez immediately orders two very swift sailing vessels to be outfitted and manned with as many armed men as could be found on short notice. These vessels are ordered to make way at once to Havana, and to capture the ship which conveys Puertocarrero and the gold. Both vessels arrive swiftly in the Havana area, but upon questioning fisherman and other sailors they learn the ship passed through some days before on a favorable wind. They search the nearby ocean for a time but with no trace of her, they are forced to return to Santiago and report failure to Velázquez.

Governor Velásquez is beside himself with both rage and fear at the news. His confidants advise him to send someone to Spain to lodge a complaint to the president of Indian affairs, who happens to be an acquaintance. Velásquez also accuses Cortés of treason before the royal court of audience at Santo Domingo, and also before the Hieronymite monks, who are viceroys of that island.

Meanwhile Puertocarrero's ship enjoys a most favorable voyage to the port of Seville, where the men hire a carriage and make haste to the imperial court residence in Valladolid. Here the Archbishop Fonseca governs at will, he being not only president of native affairs, but the main power in the region since the emperor, then still very young, resides in Flanders.

The emperor, Charles V, who is barely twenty years of age, has in fact just become ruler of the Holy Roman Empire. As the heir of three of Europe's leading dynasties: the House of Habsburg, the House of Valois-Burgundy of the Netherlands, and the House of Trastámara of Crown of Castile-León & Aragon; he rules over Central, Western, and Southern Europe; and the Spanish colonies in North, Central, and South America, the Caribbean, and Asia. An empire, it is said, "*On which the sun never sets*".

Charles V is the eldest son of Philip the Handsome and Joanna of Castile. When Philip died in 1506, Charles became ruler of the Burgundy Netherlands, and his mother's co-ruler in Spain upon the death of his maternal grandfather, Ferdinand the Catholic, in 1516. As Charles is the first person to rule Castile-León and Aragon simultaneously in his own right, he became the first King of Spain. Although technically Charles co-reigns with his mother Joanna, in reality it is a sham given her mental instability. In 1519, Charles succeeded his paternal grandfather Maximilian as Holy Roman Emperor and Archduke of Austria. From that point forward, Charles's realm, spanned nearly four million square kilometers across Europe, the Far East, and the Americas. So as it was, emperor Charles V is a busy young man and left minor disputes to the Catholic hierarchy.

Cortés' envoys wait upon the archbishop, expecting to be well received with the gratitude of the crown. They hand over to Archbishop Fonseca the letters and also the presents and gold, and request him to forward all this to his majesty by a courier, whom they would accompany themselves.

However, instead of meeting with a kind reception, they are coolly received, and dismissed with a few harsh words. Little did Puertocarrero know that Archbishop Fonseca is in the pocket of Velázquez, who is after all the legitimate Governor of Cuba.

Puertocarrero begs him to mention the great services which Cortés and his men had rendered his majesty and repeatedly urge him to send the letters and presents to the emperor so that he might learn everything as it had really taken place. Fonseca however answers haughtily that they should not worry, he will fully inform his majesty of what had taken place: namely that they had rebelled against Velázquez. To make matters worse and add fuel to the fire, Father Benito Martin, chaplain to Velázquez, arrives and makes further accusations against Cortés and all of his men.

Francisco de Montejo remains quiet through the proceedings (not so strange since he is secretly on the side of Velázquez) so Puertocarrero, as cousin to the earl of Medellin, takes it upon himself to defend Cortés and urgently insists the archbishop give them a quiet hearing, and not answer so harshly. He asks nothing more of him than to forward the presents to his majesty, which they have a right to ask since they are servants of the crown, and do not deserve the remarks which have been made.

At this the Archbishop flies into a rage and as a result has Puertocarrero thrown into prison, on a trumped up charge of having carried off a married woman to India three years ago.

Upon this some of the men contact Martin Cortés, the father of their general, who while not wealthy does have connections to the royal court by way of a man named Nuñez, who is reporter to the royal council. They decide to dispatch a courier of their own directly to the emperor in Flanders with duplicates of the letters as well as a list of all the presents they had destined for his majesty.

They also sent a separate letter to the emperor with complaints against the archbishop and details of his affairs with Diego Velázquez. Martin Cortés also obtains the signatures of other cavaliers and noblemen who were at odds with the archbishop, who had many enemies on account of his haughty behavior and abuse of power.

As a result Charles V makes inquiries into the whole affair. He soon learns not only that the archbishop had not sent all the presents and kept the major part to himself, but also had given the emperor an inaccurate and distorted account of the Cortés expedition. Soon the royal court is abuzz of nothing but Cortés, his courageous behavior and conquests, and of the riches he had sent over. The Conquistadors are then looked upon as loyal men who had rendered services to the crown. The emperor informs Martin Cortés, that he would himself shortly visit Spain to investigate the matter more closely. Puertocarrero was soon released and awaited his majesty's arrival in Spain.

Back in Santiago things are not going any better for Diego Velázquez. The Hieronymite Brothers, with whom he had lodged complaints against Cortés, are not very consoling. After reading the letters, and the great things Cortés had done, they declared that no reproach could be made against Cortés or his troops. The Conquistadors had merely addressed the emperor as master, and sent him a present of such considerable value as had not been seen in Spain for a long time. On the contrary, they merited a most noble remuneration at his majesty's hands.

In the meantime back in Vera Cruz, Cortés is blissfully unaware of the trials and tribulations of his envoys in Spain. His mind is on, shall we say, a more enjoyable objective: Marina. With Puertocarrero out of the way he feels free to approach her.

The Conqueror is first faced with the problem of communicating with her, since Friar Aguilar usually handled that chore.

"Marina." He can't bear to use her native name and insists on thinking of her under her Christian name. He makes some signs that he wishes to speak.

"Good day, my Captain." (The title she will always use for Cortés, as when she first laid eyes on him one of his men referred to him that way). Marina answers in response to his awkward gestures, as she crouches near her tent sewing—her favorite pastime.

"You are able to speak Castilian, the language of my home!" Cortés exclaims, stunned to discover she already speaks and understands a great deal of Spanish—and is eager to practice it with him.

"Yes, my Captain, it is not so... difficult." Marina replies, searching for words with only the slightest hesitation.

"You learn so quickly." In the bright morning sun her pure white smock contrasts deliciously with her dark complexion.

But it is the way Marina looks up at him, a glance acknowledging his rank without submissiveness, mixed with unmistakable interest, that causes the Conqueror's heart to race. She has everything he loves in the native women, but it is also the fact she does not lower her eyes when she speaks, but stares directly into his—this girl is so strong, so confident! She has an innate power that pulls him to her like a magnet. Cortés drags over a basket and takes a seat on it, to lower himself closer to her.

"You are quite skilled at your garment making." He comments in small talk.

"Thank you my Captain, it is a lifelong skill."

He can't help but smile at this, she is so young and it would seem has barely lived her life yet.

"Do you miss Puertocarrero?" The Conqueror asks directly.

"He is my man, so yes I feel lonely. But now that you are here my Captain, I am... pleased."

Her words and her manner would seem to indicate that his advances would not be rebuffed, so he makes another bold move.

"Marina, I owe you a debt of gratitude for all your work on our behalf. Perhaps you will join me in my tent this evening for dinner?"

A warm smile fills out her ample lips and Cortés knows he will win his prize.

"Yes, I accept. Thank you my Captain." She gives him a direct look that promises much more.

"Come at nightfall then. I look forward to it!" He says softly as he stands and walks off before drawing too much attention from the men and other native women...

Cortés of course, has no means or skills of actually preparing a dinner for Malinalli. He has no woman of his own and relies on his officer's slave girls to serve him the extras from their own men's meals. As the sun began drifting behind the hills he suddenly realizes his blunder in that he has nothing to offer her. He further doesn't feel he can ask his officers and their women for assistance in that would be too blatant.

Lucky for him, Malinalli anticipated all this. About half an hour after sunset—just long enough to cause Cortés to wonder if she was actually coming—she brushes into his tent carrying freshly hot corn cakes and some fish she managed to procure from somewhere.

Malinalli smiles in acknowledgement of the Conqueror's brief discomfort.. She is striking in her beauty with her black hair let down long and wearing a pure white dress decorated with yellow-gold embroidery around the sleeves and hem.

"Good evening Marina." Cortés searches the girl's face for some sign, hoping for an expression of happiness that she will be sharing his tent. After a brief instant he thinks he detects a fleeting smile that quickly disappears, leaving him wondering.

As she kneels before him and lays out the food, the delicious smell that fills the tent reminds him how famished he is.

"My Captain, I offer you this... humble ... meal."

"Ah Marina, you are so kind! It is I who invited you, yet you did all the work. Please permit me to at least serve you. Do you thirst Marina? Come and have some wine."

"I would be grateful my Captain."

Cortés proceeds to pour two goblets of Catalan wine, a strong, dense, and highly alcoholic drink which needed to be diluted with water. It was the last of the store they brought from Spain and he had been reserving it for a special occasion. He teaches her how to toast to victory and good fortune.

The wine is unfamiliar to Malinalli and after just one sip she feels a little light headed. She waits until Cortés takes a few bites of the food and then eats some herself to fill her stomach and counteract the effects of the wine.

At first there is only silence in the tent, but Cortés is after all a most charming man, and Malinalli an intelligent girl, and shortly they are deep in conversation about many subjects. The Conqueror is fascinated with the story of her life thus far. He in turn regales her with tales of Spain.

Soon enough though the Conqueror's thoughts turn to another type of intercourse. After all, he has one of the most beautiful women in all of New Spain, if not in all of Old Spain as well, right in front of him.

There is no question she will do anything he wants. There is no question she will obey of course. Malinalli was given to him, after all, by the Chontal Maya of Potonchan. She is essentially his property. But by the same token he would never force himself on her. She is considered noble born in this country and she is the most intelligent and strong woman he has ever known. No, he wants her to want him. He needs her to want him. And he needs her period.

Desire builds quickly in the Conqueror as he gazes upon her finely delicate face and then is lost in her intense eyes in the warm glow of the lantern. He has been attracted to this girl from the moment he laid eyes on her and that infatuation has only grown over the past months.

Our Heroine is intimately aware of almost exactly the same things her Captain is thinking, and the fact that he doesn't press himself on her only makes her want him more. She too has been fascinated by this strange man who could be a god. She is attracted to his fine clothes and confident bearing and most of all by his power—power he chooses to wield fairly and kindly.

As they kneel on the ground he feels her hand touch his and somehow she is next to him, close enough to feel her heat. Then they are on their feet and their kiss is long and deep and mutual. Her body is so firm and taunt and toned. Through their embrace he feels her unrestrained breasts press against his chest and her skin is softer than anything he has ever experienced. He kisses her neck and her cheeks and runs his hands through her thin black gleaming hair.

Malinalli breaks their embrace and taking his hand, pulls Cortés down onto the soft bedroll he had previously prepared, thinking it would only be for himself. The two of them overwhelm the small space but by then they don't notice. A familiar smell of musky flowers is nearly overpowering as her body responds to his roaming hands and lips and heats up, releasing her scent.

Her mouth beckons him and he has to partake of that moist ripeness again and again. At some point she falls on top of him as their lips press together even harder. As she straddles him on the blanket, her dress rides up revealing shapely legs, so his hands find the smooth creaminess of her sleek thighs.

They kiss and explore for a long while, teasing each other nearly to the point of eruption. Malinalli moans loudly as his hand slides higher and higher up her thigh. Leaning in, she kisses him even deeper and he feels her scolding hot tongue work its way between his lips. Their tongues play with each other until their passion rises to a frenzy of excitement.

For so long now it seemed, Cortés had waited and now their urgings and yearnings are about to be satisfied. His hands can no longer resist and he fondles and caresses her, eliciting pleasurable moans.

As their fondling intensifies, Malinalli screams and shudders almost uncontrollably, and that sends him over the edge. As their passion is quenched in the fire of sex, they both collapse into a heap of spent exhaustion.

Cortés barely has a chance to savor the incredible experience of the evening when he and Malinalli, lying in each other's arms, are disturbed by a unannounced visitor. The Conqueror is about to face another kind of stormy passion. It is a man named Bernardino de

Coria, confessing yet another conspiracy against Cortés...

***

Montezuma's spies report that the strange gods have set up a town near the ocean and seemingly are content to remain there. To his vast relief the situation appears to have resolved itself and he thankfully does not have to take any action.

The Aztec Emperor strolls contentedly through his palace courtyards and visits his animals and birds, stopping at some to feed them with morsels carried by his ever present servants. Suddenly out of nowhere a strong breeze stirs the flowers in the hanging gardens. Wind is incredibly unusual for this time of year and Montezuma immediately feels a chill run down his spine, for he instinctively knows it is another omen.

The god Quetzalcoatl is portrayed in two ways. As the Feathered Serpent, he is a snake with wings covered with feathers. He also appears in human form as a warrior wearing a tall, cone-shaped crown or cap made of ocelot skin and a pendant fashioned of jade or a conch shell. The pendant, known as the 'wind jewel,' symbolizes one of Quetzalcoatl's other roles, that of Ehecatl, god of wind and movement. Indeed some of the very courtyards in the Emperor's palace are circular in shape to minimize their resistance to the wind. It is this form that Montezuma senses has visited him— a direct warning that the year One Reed—and Quetzalcoatl—is upon them.

Montezuma remembers well that Quetzalcoatl was a bringer of knowledge, the inventor of books, and is the son of the sun and of the earth goddess Coatlicue. He and three brother gods created the sun, the heavens, and the earth. Quetzalcoatl's cosmic conflicts with the god Tezcatlipoca brought about the creation and destruction of a series of four suns and earths, leading to the fifth sun and today's earth.

The wind blows stronger as he rushes inside to seek out his brother Cuitláhuac...

15 Cortés Has His Hands Full

The suspicions of Velázquez's cronies were again aroused at the departure of the envoys and a conspiracy soon arose initiated by one Pedro Escudero and joined by Juan Cormeño, as well as a ship's pilot, some seamen, and even a priest. All are excessively embittered against Cortés because he has refused to grant them the promised discharge to return to Cuba, and others because they had lost their share of the gold by the present which had been sent to the emperor. The seamen could not forget the lashes which Cortés had given them on the island of Cozumel for stealing bacon.

The group planned to seize one of the small vessels and to sail to Cuba and acquaint Diego Velásquez with all the affairs of the envoys and how to intercept them. The conspiracy is already so far advanced that the perpetrators have stored on board the necessary provisions of bread, oil, dried fish, and water, which they had been hoarding for some time. They are to set sail the very next dawn when one of them, Bernardino de Coria, changes his mind and visits Cortés that midnight, confessing the whole plot to him.

Many thoughts and emotions whirl through Cortés's mind at these revelations—not the least of which is how the girl lying with him will reflect upon this. He instinctively knows he must act boldly, decisively, and ruthlessly.

Cortés quickly gathers his most loyal soldiers and first of all conducts an investigation to learn the names and number of the conspirators. He then orders the sails, the compass, and the rudder to be taken from the vessel which they planned to steal. Then he rounds up the accused who were named and they not only immediately make full confessions, but name others who are involved. These names are for the present held in secret, and proceedings are began against those most prominent in the affair.

Cortés sends 200 men under the command of Pedro de Alvarado

into the mountains in search of provisions, which are extremely scarce. Shrewdly included in this group are most of the partisans of Diego Velázquez, so as not to cause trouble while a military tribunal is held with all the usual formalities. Pedro Escudero and Juan Cormeño are sentenced to be hung, the pilot Gonzalo de Umbria is to have his feet cut off, and the sailors to receive two hundred lashes each. The priest would likewise have shared a similar fate if he were not a man of God, as it is he merely suffers for a time the dread of suspense.

As he signs the death-warrants Cortés puts on a genuine show of deep emotion and sorrow and cries out he wishes that he could no longer write so as to avoid this distasteful task.

The sentences are carried out swiftly and Malinalli observes them, as do all the Spaniards and natives in Vera Cruz. To her the punishment is novel and seemingly humane, since in the Aztec culture it is traditional to either sacrifice such victims by ripping out their hearts or smash their head with a large rock. She also feels that the incident demonstrates Cortés is not a commander to be trifled with.

If the incident results in anything, it convinces the Conqueror it is time to move on and conquer. It is time to explore inland and visit Montezuma and seek the riches they came here to find. So Cortés announces they are to set out for Cempoalla with 200 men and after being joined there by Alvarado and his group will then march onward to the Aztec capital.

The men cheer this plan so the Conqueror holds numerous consultations with his officers and leaders and proposes that all the ships should be run aground, in order to cut off all possibility of further mutiny when they have advanced far into the interior of the country. Also, with no ships the sailors would be of greater use as soldiers instead of idling their time away in the harbor. By cleverly obtaining the Conquistadors consent in his plan, Cortés is assured that if payment for the vessels is ever demanded, he can shift the blame on his men, and say that all was done at their own request, so that all would assist in repaying the damages.

Despite probably guessing this, the men all agree and Cortés orders Juan de Escalante, a young man of very great courage, and who was a close friend to him, utterly hating Diego Velásquez because he had neglected to give him any considerable land grant in Cuba, to take all the anchors, ropes, sails, in short everything that might be of use out of the vessels, and run them on shore, with the exception of the small boats. The pilots, the old ships' masters, and those seamen who are unable to make the journey inland, are to remain behind in the town and inform Pedro de Alvarado to meet Cortés in Cempoalla. After that they are to employ themselves in catching fish with two drag-nets in the harbor, where seafood was in great abundance according to Malinalli.

So on the morning of the day after, the ships are run aground before the eyes of the officers and soldiers just after Mass. Cortés then addresses his men at great length.

"It will only with the aid of Jesus Christ, our Lord, that we shall be victorious in all the battles and engagements which await us. Notwithstanding all our trust in God, we cannot be wanting in courage, for considering our small numbers we can expect no other assistance than from above, and that of our own arms since we have no vessels to return to Cuba. Indeed, the die has been cast and like the mighty Romans led by Caesar, we have passed the Rubicon, and have now no choice left but to proceed for the glory of God and his majesty the emperor."

After this speech, Cortés orders his company of 200 men to march onward to Cempoalla. Once they arrive the Conqueror commands the fat chief to a meeting and informs him of their plan, that they are leaving for Mexico City to visit Montezuma, to abolish all 'robbery' (taxes) and the human sacrifices. He also tells him he will require two hundred slaves to transport their cannon, and fifty of his best warriors to accompany them.

Juan de Escalante soon arrives in Cempoalla with an additional company formed of the sailors, most of whom will become very excellent soldiers. Cortés again calls the fat chief and all the other chiefs and nobles of the mountain tribes who had formed an alliance with him. Then for the first time he instructs Malinalli directly through his native tongue of Spanish, and without Aguilar in the middle, to tell the natives that they are to assist in the building of the church, the fortresses, and houses of the new town.

Then Cortés takes Juan de Escalante by the hand and announces: "This is my brother who you must obey in everything and to him you must apply if you require assistance against the Aztecs. He will himself at all times march out in your defense."

The chiefs reply that they are ready to obey him in everything and perfume Juan de Escalante with incense per their custom. And so Cortés entrusts Escalante with the command of the town and harbor, as the one he can rely upon should Diego Velásquez try anything in his absence. So Escalante returns to manage and guard the newly founded town and preparations continue for the march inland.

But just as Cortés is about to lead the Conquistadors on their epic journey to Mexico City, a soldier arrives from Vera Cruz carrying a letter from Escalante, reporting that a vessel has been seen off the coast. And that despite all kinds of signals to those on board they ignored him and sailed on. After making inquiries along the coast as to where the vessel had put in, it was found she was lying at anchor in the mouth of a small river, at the distance of about nine miles. Escalante therefore awaited Cortés' orders as to what further action he was to take.

As soon as Cortés reads the letter he gives command of all the troops jointly to Alvarado and Gonzalo de Sandoval, and for the very first time leaves Malinalli with them as primary interpreter—a clear sign of his faith in her. Then after Cortés selects four horsemen including Bernal Diaz, and fifty of the most nimble-footed men, he mounts his horse and leads the contingent the twenty miles back to Vera Cruz.

As soon as they arrive at Vera Cruz, Juan de Escalante hurries up to Cortés and suggests it would be best to take off for the strange vessel that night, otherwise she might hoist anchor and steer for the ocean. Escalante offers to let Cortés rest while he manages the search with twenty men. To this Cortés answers he cannot rest as long as there is anything to be done, and he is determined to go with the men he has brought. They accordingly set off on a march along the coast, without even stopping for food or rest.

They soon encounter four Spaniards casually walking along the road and take them prisoner. When questioned they tell Cortés they have been ordered to take possession of the country in the name of Francisco de Garay, viceroy of Jamaica.

Cortés then demands to know under what pretence has Garay sent them out to take possession of New Spain?

The men then relate that in the previous year, the ship pilots of the Cordoba and Grijalva expeditions persuaded Garay to petition the king that they be granted all the land discovered to the north of the river St. Peter and Paul. Somehow Garay managed to get himself appointed vice-regent of all this land and so fitted out three vessels with two hundred and seventy men, plus horses and the necessary provisions. He placed these under the command of one Alonso Alvarez Pinedo, who at present was lying at a distance of about 280 miles from this place, in the river Panuco, where he intended to found a colony. The four prisoners added they had merely obeyed the commands of that officer, and therefore not answerable for anything they had done.

Cortés upon hearing this enticed the four over to his side—after all he had already taken possession of the entire country in the name of Spain. He then inquires if it is possible to capture the vessel.

Guillan de la Loa, the highest ranked of the prisoners, thought it might be done, and he with his comrades, would hail the ship's skiff on shore. Although they try with all means of shouting and signals, no one moves from the vessel. No doubt Cortés and his men had been observed by them, for the captain knew all about Cortés, and he had particularly cautioned his men to be on their guard and not to fall into his hands.

When his first plan failed Cortés tries a different approach, he orders the former prisoners to exchange clothes with four of his men. Everyone else then marches behind a hill so as to be out of sight of the beach and hopefully trick the observers on the ship into thinking they had left.

The next morning the four disguised soldiers make signals to the vessel with their cloaks and hats as if they are ready to be picked up. So a skiff puts off with six sailors, two of whom immediately step on shore. Cortés waits until the four others have done the same, while his four disguised men are in the meantime washing their hands, and doing everything to hide their faces.

"What the deuce are you about there? Why don't you come on board?" Those in the boat soon cry out.

"Come on shore for a few minutes, and see what the place is like!" One of the disguised men reluctantly answers.

When they hear the strange voice, the four in the boat hastily make off back to their ship which then quickly departs the harbor.

With nothing to show for their efforts except six new recruits, Cortés and his men return to Vera Cruz, still without pausing to eat, and then immediately travel back to Cempoalla to continue preparations for the journey inland to the capital of the Aztec empire.

After giving the men a chance to rest, Malinalli holds a consultation with the chiefs of Cempoalla as to the route they should take. The chiefs prefer the road through the province of Tlaxcala, as the inhabitants are friendly with them and deadly enemies of the Aztecs. They then provide forty of their best warriors to accompany the Spanish and also give 200 slaves to transport the cannon and meager provisions.

So it is in the middle of the month of August that the Conquistadors break camp and finally embark on their fateful expedition inland to the capital of the Aztec Empire. Leading the march are sharp-shooters and the most active men. On the first day they arrive in the area of Jalapa, which is strongly situated and surrounded by numerous trained vine trees.

Malinalli, with the help of Friar Aguilar, tells the inhabitants a good deal about the Catholic religion, and how they are subjects of the great king, who sent the Spanish to this land to rescue them from kidnapping and the sacrificing of human beings. As they are friendly with the Cempoallans, and pay no tribute to Montezuma, Cortés and his men receive hospitable treatment. They erect a cross in every village, and explain its significance to the inhabitants.

From there the Conquistadors march over a mountain, through a pass, to more villages where they meet friendly natives who also refuse to pay tribute to Montezuma. It is from this area that the Spanish enter into a rugged and wild mountain district which is not only not populated but bitterly cold and they are pelted with showers of hail. Their provisions are totally gone and the wind so strong blowing across the snow mountains that the men shake with bone chilling cold. The Spanish are stunned how they just came from the hot and humid area of Vera Cruz to this bitter frozen landscape.

With only their weapons for protection, and totally unaccustomed to the cold, they desperately continue on through another mountain pass, where they found some houses and huge temples for human sacrifices. Near these are heaps of wood piled up for the use of the idol-worship, but no food as the weather continues to be bitterly cold.

Malinalli suggests to Cortés that he sent out hunting parties, saying that surely there is game in the mountains, but the Cempoalla braves accompanying them insist they move on as there are settlements not far called the territory of Xocotlan. So the Conqueror sends two Indians of Cempoalla to the local chief, to inform him of their approach, and beg him to give them an hospitable reception.

They quickly learn the inhabitants of this territory however, are subjects to Montezuma, so everything is different, and they march forward with the utmost caution and in close ranks. But when arrive at the town they are pleasantly surprised. There are numerous and beautifully whitewashed tall homes with balconies, and elevated temples wholly built of stone and lime. The Spanish call the place Castilblanco because a Portuguese soldier, who was among the troops, proclaimed it was very much like the town of Casteloblanco in Portugal.

The chief, on receiving information of the expedition's arrival, comes out to meet them with other important nobles. His name is Olintecl, and he leads them into his home, where they think they are going to be well received.

Olintecl, Malinalli learns and informs Cortés, is lord of 20,000 subjects, and has thirty wives, who are attended upon by one hundred female servants. The town contains thirteen temples, full of various shaped idols made of stone, to whom are sacrificed men, women, children, pigeons, and quails. Nearby the Emperor has a garrison of 5,000 men, and couriers are stationed at particular distances from each other all the way from the town to the capital of the Aztec empire. These nimble messengers are always deployed in pairs, that all news might be conveyed to the capital with the utmost speed. She suggests to Cortés that word of their arrival is likely already on the way to Montezuma.

But instead of the customary huge welcome feast, the chief very reluctantly provides only meager morsels and is in a bad mood, fearing he will draw the wrath of the Emperor for providing any comfort to the strangers he has been warned about.

Cortés ignores the slight and accepts the morsels gracefully, putting forth all sorts of questions through Malinalli about Montezuma. With apparent pride or possibly trying to strike fear in the strangers,

Olintecl relates a good deal about the great armies which are stationed in the conquered provinces and on the borders and even the provinces which bordered on them. He describes the great and strong capital of the empire, how it lay in the midst of a lake, and that it was only by means of bridges and canoes that a person could go from one house to another. How every house has a balcony at the top, and is so completely isolated by means of moats, that they might be considered as so many castles and as such, capable of the strongest defense. The great capital and home to Montezuma can only be approached by three roads, each of which is cut through in several places by the water and it is merely required to break down these bridges so that all access to the city is cut off. Lastly, the chief also mentions the great quantity of silver and gold and precious stones and great riches of the Emperor. There is no end to the praises he bestows upon Montezuma.

Cortés and his men listen attentively to everything the chief relates of the Aztec Emperor's power and greatness. But instead of being disheartened, they are only more earnest in their desire to try their fortune against the fortresses and bridges, for such is the very spirit of a Spanish soldier. The more Olintecl speaks of the impossibility of any enemy reaching the capital, the more they want to attempt it.

Seeing that his warnings were going unheeded, the chief advised that Montezuma is accustomed to obedience from every one, and he feared Montezuma's fury when he learns that the strangers had visited the town without his permission, and had been provided with provisions.

Instead of cowering though, Cortés, through Malinalli, tells them that he shall no longer permit kidnapping and human sacrifices, nor allow Montezuma to conquer any more territories, and that they must obey the commands of the emperor of Spain and must relinquish those human sacrifices, no longer eat human flesh, and abstain from committing unnatural offences and other abominations and customs, for these are the commandments of the one true God, from whom comes life and death, and who will someday receive us all into his heaven.

Even though Malinalli translates this as though Cortés is the god, the Conquistadors are met with only stony silence by the chief and his nobles. Despite this attitude, Cortés wants to erect a cross.

"These people, as subjects of Montezuma, are neither afraid nor shy of us, and would undoubtedly destroy the cross. What we have disclosed to them concerning our religion is sufficient until the time they shall be susceptible of understanding more of it." Father Olmedo advises against it. So for the first time no cross is erected there.

But then in a twist of fate and luck, one of the huge war dogs that the Conquistadors have with them slips off its leash and bounds for its master Francisco de Lugo, all the while barking ferociously at the natives. The Spanish had been using these dogs in Europe and they did not hesitate to bring them to the New World. The Conquistadors' dogs are a mixture of wolfhounds, deerhounds, and mastiffs, and stand about 2½ ft tall at the shoulder and weigh in at some 90 pounds. These dogs are powerful, fast and fearless. Their value to the Conquistadors is such that the Spanish protected their hounds as much as their horses.

Never having seen such a huge dog before, the chiefs cower in fear as they ask the natives of Cempoalla whether it is some strange kind of lion or a tiger which the strangers employ for the purpose of tearing their enemies to pieces.

The Cempoallans answer that indeed the gods let it loose upon those who attack them. They also tell them about the thundersticks and cannon, describing how they are loaded with stones, and kill everyone in their path; and how their horses are as nimble as deer as they run down whomever they desire.

"Certainly these must be gods!" cries Olintecl and the other chiefs.

"They are indeed as you see them now before you, therefore take great care not to arouse their displeasure. Whatever you may do, they are sure to know. They penetrate your very thoughts, and have even imprisoned the tax-gatherers of your great Montezuma, and commanded the inhabitants of the mountains and us of Cempoalla not to pay any more tribute. They have likewise torn down our gods from the temples, and replaced them with their own. The tribes of the Tabasco and Tzinpantzinco were conquered by them; and, however powerful Montezuma may be, he nevertheless sent them presents. Now they have visited you, and you have given them nothing; therefore you cannot too speedily correct the mistake you have made." The Cempoallan braves tell Olintecl and the other chiefs excitedly.

Malinalli overhears all this and doesn't bother to correct any of it, instead she informs Cortés, reporting the Cempoallans have done a good job instilling fear in the people of Xocotlan.

In fact after experiencing the vicious dog and hearing the tales from the braves of Cempoalla, the chiefs present the Conqueror with four chains, three neck ornaments, and a few lizards, all of gold. And offer four women to bake bread. Cortés, as usual, thanks them with the upmost grace for these presents, and offers to render them services in return.

Cortés then asks Olintecl, which is the best and easiest way to the Aztec capital, so that he may call upon the great Emperor in person.

He suggests they travel through Cholula, which is a very large town.

The braves of Cempoalla, however, advise him not to take that path, as the inhabitants of Cholula are a treacherous people, and Montezuma has always a strong garrison in that town.

Malinalli suspects Olintecl may have been pointing the Conquistadors to a trap so that he could gain favor with Montezuma. She consults with the Cempoallans and they advise the expedition should make its way through Tlaxcala instead; for there the inhabitants were their friends, and sworn enemies to the Aztecs. This advice is followed by Cortés, and it will turn out to be a pivotal choice in the conquest of Mexico.

Despite the possible treachery of Olintecl however, Cortés shrewdly requests twenty warriors to accompany him—a request he knows from Malinalli the chief cannot refuse, and one which insures at least a small measure of cooperation of the Xocotlans.

As the Spanish march out of the area they see a sight they will never forget: situated near the temple are a vast number of human skulls piled up in neat order, which number at least 100,000. In another corner of the square are the remaining human bones. Besides these, there are human heads hanging suspended from beams on both sides. Three priests stand sentinel on this place of skulls...

***

When Montezuma is informed by his spies that the white strangers are on the march over the mountains inland, he flies into the worst rage of his life.

Why is this god toying with me? He asks himself. Why is he testing me? Why couldn't he just have stayed where he was?

It is now obvious he wants the throne and Montezuma is determined he will not give it up without a fight. If war is what Quetzalcoatl wants then that he what he shall have.

The Emperor strides purposefully to the palace armory and shoves aside the guards and the armorer who try to assist him. He steps to the wall and examines the various weapons hung there carefully.

One of the most formidable weapons is the maquahuitl, commonly referred to by the Spaniards as a sword. It is a stout stick or club, about three and a half feet long, set with a double row of blades made of the stone they call itztli—or obsidian as we know it, as sharp as razors. The warrior carries this terrible weapon attached to his wrist by a thong, and it is capable of disemboweling, or even decapitating a man with a single blow. The blades of obsidian are quickly dulled, but, even then, such a weapon wielded by a strong man is a fearsome thing.

Then there are the darts, which are short lances, whose points are tipped with bone or copper or simply hardened in the fire. The Emperor knows his soldiers are marvelously quick and accurate in throwing these. And finally there are arrows, fire hardened and likewise tipped with copper or bone.

His army shall rain these arrows down upon the strangers as soon as they come within sight and then cut them to pieces with their maquahuitl.

None of them will be left alive...

16 Battles

Cortés and his men first arrive in the small township of Xacatcinco. From there they sent two men of Cempoalla (who Cortés well knew would sing his praise), and were on good terms with the people there, to Tlaxcala. He gave them a Flanders hat with a colored feather to present as a gift and instructions to inform the chief that they are friendly and merely want to trade.

In the meantime the men camped and noticed that grape trees are in abundance around the area. They marvel at this since they thought the vines only originated in Europe yet it is certainly true that the wild vine are growing here in the New World! These wild vines bear good black grapes, and as the men partake they remark how really good they taste.

Soon the local natives appear and present the Spanish with a golden chain for the neck, some packages of cotton stuffs, and two Indian females. But Malinalli quickly learns that the whole of Tlaxcala is up in arms against the Conquistadors. They were already informed of the Spanish progress and concluded from the number of warriors they had with them out of Cempoalla and even worse— from Xocotlan, who are well known vassals of the Aztecs, that they came with hostile intentions and would act like the Aztecs, who always under some fraudulent pretence or other, marched into their country when intent upon plunder.

While Cortés awaits the return of the messengers for two days, he uses the time to explain to the natives as usual, the nature of the Christian faith, and the sinfulness of human sacrifices, and the other abominations they practiced. He also requested twenty of their warriors to accompany him as a sign of good faith.

Not wanting to wait any longer for word, the Spanish break camp on the third day and march for Tlaxcala. On route they are met by the two messengers, who relate how they had been thrown in prison before they could deliver their message or even say a word, but had been secretly released by their friends.

All Tlaxcala was making warlike preparations against them, the messengers report. They appear quite demoralized, and can scarcely speak of what they had seen and heard. Finally the two warriors tell how they had been immediately seized and thrown into prison, and the terrible threats against the Spanish and themselves.

"Now we will rise up and destroy those whom yon term gods and spirits. We shall soon see whether they are so courageous as you claim. We will devour both you and them together, for you are come under false pretences, and at the instigation and order of the evil Montezuma." The Tlaxcalans told them.

When Cortés hears this and how they await him completely equipped for war, he does not make light of the matter, but nevertheless he leads his men in a cheer:

"Well, then, since it cannot be otherwise, forward for good or ill luck!"

The men commend themselves to the protection of God, unfurl their standard, and begin the march forward. In each small village they pass through, the inhabitants inform them that the Tlaxcalans will march against them to prevent entry into their territory.

As they travel, the Conquistadors assemble in battle formation with cavalry at a gallop three abreast, with lances fixed, so as to run at the Indians full in the face. At the same time they are instructed to be particularly on guard that the enemy does not grab hold of the lances with their hands and if such should happen, the rider was to keep the tighter hold of his lance, give his horse the spur, and either by a sudden jerk wrest it out of the enemy's grasp, or drag him along with it.

"You are aware, gentlemen, of the smallness of our numbers, we must, therefore, be the more upon our guard, and fancy the enemy will each moment fall upon us. Nor is this sufficient, we must imagine ourselves already fighting, as if the battle was begun. Every soldier is fond of catching hold of the enemy's lance with his hand, but considering the smallness of our numbers, we must now particularly guard ourselves against it. For the rest, you are not in need of my advice, for I have always found that you do things much better than I am able to instruct you." Cortés rallies his men.

After advancing about eight miles, they come upon an enormous entrenchment, built so strongly of stone, lime, and a kind of hard bitumen, that it would only have been possible to break it down by means of pickaxes. But as luck would have it, the wall is not defended and there is no one is sight.

After halting to inspect this fortification, Cortés inquires of the Xocotlans, for what purpose it stood there. They tell him that it was built by the Tlaxcalans, on whose territory they are now entering, against the great Montezuma, with whom they were continually at war, to protect against his hostile incursions.

"Let us follow our standard, gentlemen! It bears the figure of the Holy Cross, and in that sign we shall conquer. Forward! Whatever may happen, God is our only strength." Cortés cries out and leads the men over the entrenchment and onward.

But they do not advance far when they spot about thirty Indians, who had been sent out to reconnoiter. They are armed with broad swords, which are used with both hands, the edges of which are made of obsidian and are sharper than steel swords. They are also carry shields, lances, and have feathers stuck in their hair.

Cortés orders some his cavalry to attack, and try if possible, to capture one alive. These horsemen are followed at a distance by five others, to assist them should they fall into an ambush. The rest of the small army marches directly for a narrow pass with the utmost caution, as the Cempoalla warriors assure Cortés that he will undoubtedly meet with a large body of the enemy in some hiding place or other.

When the thirty Indians spot the horses approaching them they began to retreat slowly, and arrange themselves in a circle, making it harder to take any of them prisoner. They defend themselves courageously with their swords and lances wounding several of the horses.

This causes the Spanish to attack more ferociously and they kill five of the Indians. At that moment a swarm at least 3,000 Tlaxcalans rush furiously from an ambush, pouring a shower of arrows upon the Spanish horsemen. The Conquistadors open fire with their cannon, and at last the enemy begins to give ground, fighting bravely as they retreat.

The Spanish suffer four wounded, one critically, while seventeen of the enemy lay dead, with a considerable number wounded, and several prisoner successfully captured. With the sun beginning to set, the natives retreat further but the Spanish follow them.

As soon as they pass over the mountain they come into a plain dotted with numerous plantations of corn and maguey, through which runs a brook. Cortés decides to make camp there for the night. As the men make their supper off young dogs, which they find in plentiful numbers roaming the fields, they keep vigilant throughout the night. The horses stand ready, saddled and bridled.

The next morning the Conquistadors march onward fearlessly and soon come upon two large bodies of the enemy, amounting to about 6,000 men. These warriors make terrific noise with their drums and trumpets, and war cries and then let fly their arrows and lances. Cortés orders a halt and dispatches three of the captured natives to the warrior's chiefs requesting them to stay hostilities and negotiate peace.

The prisoners run off back to their fellow warriors, but the only result is that the natives attack more furiously, so Cortés orders a charge.

"Forward! St. Jacob is with us! On to the enemy!" He shouts.

The Spanish run up closer to the Indians and then let loose a volley of bullets, immediately killing and wounding scores of the natives including three of their chiefs. Then they fall back to about the distance of a musket-shot, where they take up a defensive position.

But then the Conquistadors realize there is an army of thousands of warriors waiting in ambush, commanded by their general Xicotencatl, the son of the elder Xicotencatl, who is blind from old age. These natives release arrows and lances and stones from slings, and no less annoying even throw sand in their faces.

But all this only lasts until the Spanish gain level ground and are able to return fire with their muskets killing great numbers. Still, the battle is so close and fierce, the Spaniards cannot even open ranks to assist a fallen brother or they are immediately cut down with an arrow or lance.

Cortés realizes too late that a major goal of the Indians is to capture one of his horses, when Pedro de Moron on his mare, accompanied by three other horsemen, attempts to break through the enemy's ranks. The native warriors wrench the lance out of his hand, knocking him off his horse and fall upon him with broad swords, wounding him severely. Others deliver his mare such a terrific cut with the same weapon in the neck, that the animal instantly falls down dead with its head nearly severed. Moron's three companions immediately hasten to his assistance, beating off the warriors with their steel swords and drag him back to Spanish lines.

The Conquistadors then push forward shoulder to shoulder, and wreck considerable havoc with their swords. They fight for a good hour, and their firearms do significant destruction among the massed enemy warriors. It is the worst battle the Spanish have fought in all their experience.

Finally the Indians retreat, carrying off the dead horse, which the Spanish later learn was subsequently cut into pieces and sent into every village of Tlaxcala as proof of victory over the white strangers. The horse's shoes and the Flanders hat, were used as an offering to their idols.

While scores of the Indians lay dead on the battle field, among them eight important chiefs, the Spanish could never discover the exact number killed or wounded, for as was customary, the Tlaxcalans immediately carry off the wounded and dead. In turn the Spanish suffer nine wounded, plus Moron who dies a few days later, and take fifteen prisoners, among whom are two of the most distinguished nobles judging by their costumes and feathers.

After the battle, the Spanish fall back to a temple, which is very high and like a fortress, to patch up their wounded and rest for the night.

The next morning Cortés boldly suggests a show of force.

"It would be no harm if our horses were to gallop up and down the country a little; the Tlaxcalans might otherwise think we had had enough of it in the last battle. We must show them that we are constantly at their heels." He tells his men; and they agree it is better to go on the offensive then to sit idly by and wait to be attacked.

So seven horsemen, backed by 200 men with crossbows and several muskets, along with their Cempoalla allies, set out cautiously through the area. They meet no resistance and soon capture twenty Indians of both sexes, making sure to treat them well as instructed by Cortés. Their allies, however, cannot refrain from setting fire to many houses and taking quantities of fowls.

After they return to their encampment at the temple, Cortés orders the prisoners untied, and provided food. Malinalli then talks to them at length, trying to reassure the natives about Cortés and his intentions. She gives each some glass beads, adding that in future they should not act foolish, but make peace with the Spanish.

Then Cortés sets two of the prisoners free with instructions to tell the chief of the province that he did not come to injure the Tlaxcalans, but merely wished to take the road through their country to the capital to have a meeting with Montezuma.

But the native messengers soon return with ominous word from the young and brash general Xicotencatl: 'If the invaders want peace they only have to come to his father's town and after he has satiated himself with the flesh of their bodies, and has honored his gods with the sacrifice of their blood and hearts, will they have peace.'

Despite the arrogant answer from the Tlaxcalans, Cortés takes the news calmly and even rewards the two with some additional strings of beads for their trouble, not only thinking he may use them again, but putting them in a mood to discover some intelligence. So he has Malinalli question them at length regarding the commander Xicotencatl, and the number of his troops.

The two messengers reveal the general now has five chiefs under him named Maxixcatzin, Chichimeclatecl, Topoyanco, Tecapaneca; and Quaxobcin, each of whom commands 10,000 men—altogether 50,000 warriors! Each division has its own standard and arms, the general's being a large white bird, with outspread wings as if preparing to fly, and resembling an ostrich. Besides this, every chief has his own particular insignia of war and colors, in the same way as Spanish dukes and earls. At first Cortés does not believe the natives could be so organized, but soon discovers that it is perfectly true.

With the revelation there are 50,000 warriors awaiting them, the Conquistadors begin to feel the certainty of death, and they all make confession to Father Olmedo and the priest Juan Diaz, and offer up fervent prayers to the Almighty to grant them victory.

In the meantime, the prisoners question Malinalli at length about her captain and his men, inquiring if they came from the direction of the rising sun. From this she knows even the Tlaxcalans suspect Cortés is the returning god of the prophecy and she does nothing to correct this belief.

The following morning they prepare for battle. First are the horsemen followed by the foot soldiers, and even the wounded to swell the ranks. Half the musketeers and crossbow-men are instructed to load, while the other half fire, so as to be able to keep up a steady firepower. The rest of the men, who are armed with swords and shields, are to strike at the enemy in the region of their bellies, in order to stop them from getting too close as they had the time before. Even the standard bearer is surrounded by four men to protect the banner. And everyone is particularly cautioned not to break ranks.

The Spanish scarcely proceed a quarter of a mile when they come upon fields covered with warriors. These have large feather-knots on their heads, wave their colors, and make a terrible soul wrenching noise with their horns and trumpets. In an instant the Conquistadors are surrounded on all sides by vast numbers of Indians, so that the plain, six miles wide, appears as if it contains one vast army. In the midst of which stands the small army of 400 Spanish, most wounded and fatigued, fully aware the natives would spare none of them, except those who would be sacrificed to their idols—a fate presumably even worse than death on the battlefield.

The attack commences with a hail of arrows, lances and stones and quickly the whole ground is immediately covered with stalks of spears like rows of tall grass. The native warriors fall upon them like the very furies themselves, with the most horrible yells.

The Conquistadors in turn employ their heavy guns, muskets, and crossbows, with much effect, as their cavalry with great skill and bravery, attempts to rout the Indians advance. But the Spanish line is already half broken; and all the commands of Cortés and his other officers to form again go unheeded with the Indians continually rushing upon them.

The only salvation for the Spanish is, paradoxically, the vast number of native warriors who rush at them so densely that every cannon shot takes out large groups of them. The Indians leave themselves no room to maneuver and many of the chiefs and their men, are not even able to get in the fight.

Unbeknownst to the Spanish also is that there are internal conflicts among the native chiefs—namely between the commander-in-chief Xicotencatl and another chief, the son of Chichimeclatecl. Xicotencatl has accused the other of cowardice, so that in this battle neither lends the other any assistance. Chichimeclatecl even convinces another chief Huexotzinco not to take any part in the combat, leaving fully 30,000 warriors out of the battle.

To all this must be added, that the enemy has come to fear the horses, cannon, swords, and crossbows of the Spanish and with the courage they displayed in the previous fight. And so the native warriors fall back and dissolve into the woods.

The Conquistadors then return to the temple serving as their fortress and camp, overjoyed at their victory, and offer fervent thanks to God. At Malinalli's suggestion they bury their dead in one of the subterranean caverns so that the Indians might not discover them to be mere mortals, but still continue to believe them gods. Short of food and with nothing to shelter them from the bitter wind blowing across the Sierra Nevada, that makes them shake with cold, they nevertheless keep up their spirits, and most sleep soundly from extreme fatigue.

In the battle the Conquistadors had taken three important chiefs captive, so Cortés decides to try again to make peace with Tlaxcala.

He sends those three plus the two previous envoys back to the elder Xicotencatl and his council with the message: make peace with him, and allow him and his men to march through their territory to the Aztec capital, or as much as he wants to avoid it, he promises to exterminate them all.

The five delegates arrive in the capital of Tlaxcala, and deliver this message to a full assembly of the tribal council, who they find so stunned and depressed with the outcome of the battle and the loss of sons, relatives, and chiefs, they at first will not even listen to the messengers.

The council soon comes to the decision to consult all the astrologers, priests, and conjurors, to discover by their witchcraft and spells, what sort of people they are dealing with, what sort of food they consume, and whether it is possible to be victorious. The chiefs are most interested to learn if the strangers really are gods or evil spirits as the people of Cempoalla have assured them.

The soothsayers, conjurors, and priests, after performing all manner of rituals (probably more likely by spying on the Spanish), assure the chiefs that the strangers are human beings made of flesh and bone. That they eat dogs, fowls, bread and fruits, and that they do not devour the Indians, much less the hearts of those they had slain—as the exaggeration prone Cempoallans had told them previously.

But the real damage is done after the priests claim it impossible to conquer the strangers during the day light because they draw their strength from the sun. So they suggest attacking the Spanish only at night when they lose all their powers.

The council immediately agrees to have general Xicotencatl attack as soon as possible with a large force during the dark. The general takes ten thousand of his bravest troops and marches on the Spanish camp that very night. They attack on three sides at once, not bothering to be stealthy, since they believe the strangers are weak and defenseless in the dark.

But the Conquistadors are fully on guard and prepared for battle, sleeping in their clothes with weapons in hand, the horses always ready bridled and saddled, and cannon loaded. They gave the enemy a rough reception with muskets and crossbows, and cut them to pieces with swords, such that they soon have enough and melt away into the night, but not before the Spanish captured four prisoners.

Next morning the Spanish find twenty natives dead and wounded, so that no doubt, they must have found this fighting at night time was not exactly so pleasant. But in this night's combat the Spanish lost one of their allies from Cempoalla, and two men plus a horse were wounded. As some consolation, it is also said the tribal council was so exasperated with the soothsayers and priests, that two of them were butchered for a sacrifice.

But the expedition thus far is taking a terrible toll on the Conquistadors. There is not a single one either exhausted from fatigue, wounded two or three times, or sick with fever—probably malaria. Fifty-five men have been lost in battle or from sickness, and even Cortés and Father Olmedo are suffering from fever.

Xicotencatl continues to harass them, and to all these discomforts is added the severity of the weather, and even their great want of salt, which they could find no means of obtaining. (The Spanish will later discover that even the Tlaxcalans suffer the same lack of salt.)

So it is natural the men begin to experience doubts about this expedition and campaign. If they somehow manage to escape their present circumstances, how they even possibly think of penetrating deeper into Mexico, considering the vaunted power of the empire and Montezuma? Plus they are totally unaware as to how matters stand back in Vera Cruz.

But while some of the Conquistadors have doubts, one person among them never fails to show spirit and courage: Malinalli. Though not a day passes they don't hear of being butchered and devoured by the natives, and how they have been completely surrounded by enemies, and how they are all wounded and suffering from disease; she never appears disheartened but, on the contrary, displays a courage much beyond that of any man let alone a woman. In fact Malinalli sets an example to all the men and keeps their spirits up, and since Cortés is sick, takes the lead for the first time.

When the prisoners are about to depart on yet another peace mission to the enemy, it is she who gives them detailed instruction as to what to say: That if peace is not concluded within the space of two days, the Spanish gods will march forward, lay waste to the entire territory, force their way into their towns, and into their very homes, and put every living being to the sword.

***

When Montezuma's spies report that the Tlaxcalans are making war on the strangers he is overjoyed for the first time in many months. For once the pesky Tlaxcalans, who his empire has never quite been able to completely subdue, are serving a purpose. They are doing his work for him!

Montezuma is in such a great mood he almost dances through the palace. He orders a great feast for the evening of only the most rare and succulent meats and fowl: pheasant, quail, partridge, duck, and venison and a large vat of cacao for all to partake.

There are dozens and dozens of dancers and gymnasts, and he delights in seeing them bounce and whirl and tumble.

His nagging problem is solved without having to lift a hand against the gods, they will soon all be just a bad memory!

17 Alliances

The five prisoner-delegates met with two of the highest chiefs of Tlaxcala: Maxixcatzin and the elder Xicotencatl, father of the general of the same name. After hearing the bold words of Malinalli, they call a meeting of all the chiefs and nobles of the territory. And it is the elder Xicotencatl who addresses the assembly.

"Brothers and friends! You yourselves know how often these gods, who are now in our country, ready to fight at a moment's notice, have offered us peace, and assured us that they have come as friends. Nor can you have yet forgotten the numbers of prisoners they have taken, though they never do them any harm, but always set them free to return home. Thrice have we attacked them with the whole of our forces, both by day and by night, but we have not been able to conquer them. On the contrary, they have killed many of our warriors, numbers of our sons, relations, and chiefs in these battles. They now again request us to come to terms of peace, and those of Cempoalla who are encamped with them, assure us they are enemies to Montezuma and the Aztecs, and have commanded them and the tribes of the Totonaque mountains not to pay any more tribute to him.

"We all very well know that the Aztecs for more than one hundred years have made incursions into our country. Indeed, they have completely shut us up within our own territory. We cannot get beyond to fetch salt, nor cotton for our clothing. If any one of us ever ventures beyond the mountains, he very seldom returns home alive. The treacherous Aztecs and their vassals make slaves of all our people that fall into their hands.

"Our priests have told us their opinion of these strangers; that they are very powerful and courageous we have experienced ourselves. We feel, therefore, inclined to make peace with them. Whether they are men or gods, in both cases an alliance with them will be useful to us.

"Let us, therefore, send out four of our chiefs to their camp with food, and show them friendship and a willingness to make peace, that they may stand with us against Montezuma."

Upon hearing this proposition, the chiefs all declare their approval, and resolve that a treaty for peace should be initiated, and general Xicotencatl and the other commanders shall be ordered to cease all hostilities immediately.

But when the younger Xicotencatl receives this order he refuses to obey.

"As things stand there is no need to sue for peace. Many of the gods are already dead, along with one of their fabled stags. Instead I will attack them tomorrow night and destroy them all." He informs the messenger to tell his father and the rest of the council.

When the elder Xicotencatl, Maxixcatzin, and the other chiefs receive this answer, they immediately sent orders to all the war chiefs and the whole army not to obey Xicotencatl.

When the younger Xicotencatl hears this he blocks the four old men, who were appointed to make the treaty of peace, from carrying out their mission.

In the mean time, the Spanish have no knowledge of the internal conflicts among the Tlaxcalans or of the proposed peace treaty, so after two days pass by of nothing happening, the Conquistadors are anxious so they propose to Cortés that they should make an excursion to a town situated a few miles away, and again make overtures of peace to the inhabitants and try to obtain some food and provisions.

Cortés agrees to this proposal and although sick, takes command himself, leading six cavalry, ten crossbow-men, and eight musketeers, accompanied of course by Malinalli. After traveling a distance of about six miles across the snowy mountains, two of the horses fall ill and trembling so Cortés orders them back to base.

The rest of the party arrives at the village before sunrise and the natives, seeing their approach, flee in terror. In view of the inhabitant's fear, Cortés orders a halt in a courtyard until daylight. When the sun rises, he spots some priests and other old men of distinction watching from the top of a temple. After observing for a time, they finally come down to speak to Malinalli and Cortés.

The natives apologize for not having sent food, or offerings of peace, and blame all this on general Xicotencatl, who has forbidden it, and is at that moment stationed nearby. They admit they are afraid of this man, as he has all their warriors under his command.

Cortés answers through Malinalli that they should ease their fear and tell the chiefs of the province to come and make peace with us, as war will only bring misfortune down upon them.

Recognizing that the strangers mean them no harm, the priests and chief agree to carry the message and also provide forty fowls and turkeys, plus two women to bake bread and prepare the food.

Cortés thanks them kindly for this present, and requests twenty men to carry the provisions back to camp.

These immediately come forward, carry the provisions back to the Spanish encampment at the temple, and remain until the evening. After a feast for all, the Conqueror graciously presents them with a few trifles and they return highly delighted to their homes, greatly extolling their kind treatment.

This information is sent to the elder tribal council, who order provisions and anything else the Spanish might require, to be sent daily. They also again order the four old chiefs to make peace without delay.

But the next day Cortés is met with considerable dissension in the ranks, despite the food, and better conditions, and the promise of a treaty with the Tlaxcalans.

One of men, eloquent in speech, was chosen spokesman and

addresses Cortés with a plea to consider their wounds, the excessive hardships they had to undergo day and night, and have mercy on them and return to Vera Cruz and fit out a vessel and send to Diego Velásquez for a fresh supply of men and other necessaries.

Cortés listens very calmly to these words and patiently waits until they are finished.

"Much of what you have said has not escaped my own notice, but what I have observed above all, is that the whole world could not produce Spaniards who are so brave, and fight so courageously, and who could bear hardships as well as we do." The Conqueror replies.

"Indeed, we should have been lost if we had not continually held our weapons in our hands, kept patrolling and watching day and night, and boldly borne the miserable weather. We are indebted to our Almighty who certainly lent us his aid, yet I cannot imagine to myself a greater piece of heroism, when I bring back to my recollection the vast crowds of the enemy, how they attacked us in on all sides with their troops, and fell upon us with their broad swords, particularly in that battle where they killed one of our horses." Cortés tells them.

"At that critical moment I learnt more of your noble character than on any former occasion. And since the Almighty rescued us out of that battle I have gained the hope that our future endeavors will be crowned with success. I can call you to witness, that I always fought alongside you, nor have you, I must add, ever proved unworthy of the trust I placed in you.

"Neither must you forget, gentlemen, that up to this moment the Almighty has lent us his protection, and we may confidently hope he will not desert us in future, for, from our first arrival in this country we have announced his holy religion to the different tribes according to the best of our abilities and destroyed the idols. We may also, in trusting to God and our mediator the holy apostle Peter, consider the war in this province at an end, since Xicotencatl and the other chiefs no longer show themselves, because they fear us on account of the destruction we made among their troops in the late battles, or it may be they are unable to rally their men again.

"The natives willingly furnish us with provisions, while the surrounding tribes continue peaceably in their villages. With regard to our vessels, it was, indeed, requisite they should be destroyed, and if I did not consult all of you on the occasion I had sufficient reason for pursuing that course after the occurrence on the downs, which, however, I will not enter into here. The course you advised me to adopt on the former occasion, and your present discontent, both emanate from the same bad feeling; but you should remember that there are several cavaliers among our troops who are not of the same opinion with yourselves, who request and counsel that we should continue as heretofore to repose our trust in God alone, and faithfully fulfill our duties in his holy service.

"You are, however, perfectly justified in saying that the most renowned generals of Rome even cannot boast of such military exploits as we can. Future historians will also have to relate, if God be willing, greater things of us than of them. We shall continually be reaping harvests of glory, because strict justice and Christian feeling are everywhere our guides, and also because our endeavors are exerted in the service of God and of our emperor. You cannot, gentlemen, have weighed the matter well if you suppose we could save ourselves by a retreat, for the instant these people were to observe this, and though we should depart from them in profound peace, the very stones of the ground would be raised up against us. And in the same way the Indians now stare at us as if we were beings of a superior order, or rather gods, as they term us, they would then consider us cowards. We might, you say, settle ourselves quietly down among our allies, the tribes of the Totonaque mountains! To which my answer is, that even they would rise up against us immediately they perceive we are turning back without marching on to the Aztec capital; for if we leave them, and they refuse to pay tribute to Montezuma as heretofore, he will send his armies against them not merely to subdue, but to compel them to declare war with us; and if they are not desirous of being annihilated, what other course could they pursue? In this way, where we had thought to have friends, we should be preparing ourselves enemies.

"What reflections would the powerful Montezuma make, and what judgment would he pass upon our previous speeches and the messages we sent him if we were to turn back? He would think we had been jesting with him. Thus you see, gentlemen, it looks bad one way and worse another. The most prudent step we can take for the present is to maintain our ground here in this thickly populated valley where we can obtain provisions in abundance.

"Today we have fowls, tomorrow dogs, and thus, thank God, we shall always have plenty of food. Salt and warmer clothing are really at present the only great privations we suffer. You further state, that we have lost fifty-five men since our departure from Cuba from famine, cold, fatigue, disease, and from wounds: that our numbers are very small, and all of us more or less suffering from ill health. But, on the other hand, you must remember that God has given us the power of numbers, and that war is ever accompanied by loss of men and horses. Today we have provisions, the next day none. And you must also bear in mind that we are not come into this country to seek repose, but to fight valiantly about whenever it may be necessary.

"I, therefore, beg of you, gentlemen, who are cavaliers, and who have up to this moment behaved so courageously, and whom despondency so ill suits, to drive from your minds all remembrance of Cuba and everything you have left behind there. Show yourselves brave soldiers as you have hitherto, for next to God, who is our strength, all depends upon the valor of our arms." Cortés finishes eloquently.

So the Conqueror's speech sways the men and puts an end to their fears and whining—especially since there are no ships left to outfit and return to Cuba!

In the meantime the elders of Tlaxcala again send orders to Xicotencatl not to attack, but to send provisions and conclude a treaty of peace in person with the strangers. Messengers are also dispatched to each of his officers, commanding them not to obey him in anything except a conclusion of peace. These orders fall on deaf ears as Xicotencatl assembles 20,000 warriors to mount a final attack on the Spanish.

Xicotencatl apparently also decides to have some fun while maintaining his arrogance and pride. He sends forty Indians with provisions, consisting of fowls, bread, and fruits, accompanied by four disgusting old Indian females wearing copal and parrot feathers. The general proclaims he does this so that it might not be said he conquered the Spaniards by starvation, and also that their flesh might taste savory when they sacrificed them to the gods.

"These presents are sent you by the general Xicotencatl, that you may eat, in case you are spirits, as the people of Cempoalla have assured us. If you require a sacrifice with them, kill these four women, and devour their flesh and their hearts. As we do not know what your wish is on this we have not sacrificed them for you. But if you are human beings, be contented with the fruit and the fowls; and if you are kind-hearted gods, take the copal and the parrot feathers as an offering." One of the natives tells Malinalli upon delivering the provisions.

Cortés replies that he is desirous of making peace, not war, which he has already made known to them. He killed no one, excepting when he was attacked. He is very thankful for the provisions, but now they should likewise have the good sense to send messengers of peace.

While some of the natives depart to deliver the Conqueror's reply, the rest stay in camp all day and through the night. This greatly surprises the warriors of Cempoalla, as it is not customary to stay night and day in an enemy's camp without some particular motive.

So Malinalli's suspicions are aroused and she questions the Cempoallans further, who admit they heard two of the old men from Tlaxcala talking that Xicotencatl stood ready with a large army to attack at night. At first they had laughed at the idea, thinking it a mere bragging, and had, therefore, not mentioned it.

Malinalli immediately brings this to the attention of her captain Cortés who orders the two Tlaxcalans be seized, and they confess that Xicotencatl had sent them into camp as spies to gather information respecting the access to the camp, and the number of troops, of the horses and the cannon, and everything else. Cortés has Malinalli question several more and all gave the same answer, adding that their commander Xicotencatl is just waiting their information before attacking the following night with all of his troops.

After hearing all this Cortés orders everyone on alert and to be ready for action. He also seizes seventeen other of the spies who refuse to answer truthfully and cooperate. The most arrogant of these he orders their thumbs cut off and sends them packing back to Xicotencatl with the message: 'That this is his mode of punishing such spies. He might now come whenever he liked in the night or by daytime, he would wait for him here two whole days, if peace has not been concluded, he will attack and annihilate both his army. It is now, however, high time he should desist from his folly, and send a sincere token of peace.'

The unfortunate injured would-be spies arrive in Xicotencatl's headquarters just as he is marching off with his whole army to attack in the dark. When he sees his spies before him in this condition, the general's spirit is suddenly crushed. The lack of support from his father and the elders and other chiefs, including one who has even withdrawn his men from the army, have taken their toll at last.

The Conquistadors know nothing of any of this, thinking any peace is impossible, and therefore began to prepare for battle. They clean and sharpen their weapons, make arrows, and generally try to get prepared and in the spirit for battle.

Then one of the sentries comes running up with the news that a number of Indians of both sexes are advancing along the principal road of Tlaxcala, straight to their camp, laden with packages.

The ever optimistic Cortés is delighted with this piece of news, for he is sure the natives are coming with tidings of peace. He issues orders that no alarm should be sounded, and for all the men to remain quiet in hiding as if unaware of their approach.

When the Indians arrive at the camp four nobles, who have been instructed by the elder chiefs to conclude a peace treaty, step forth from among the slaves. They make the sign of peace, which consists of bending the head forward, then walk straight to Cortés and Malinalli. They first touch the ground with their hands, and then kissed it, and bow three times. Then they address the Conqueror.

"All the chiefs of Tlaxcala, with their subjects, allies, friends, and comrades, make peace and friendship with Cortés and his brothers, the gods. They beg forgiveness for having commenced hostilities, instead of uniting in friendship with you, which had merely been done under the impression that you were friends of Montezuma and the Aztecs, who have been our most deadly enemies from time immemorial.

"What had strengthened us in this suspicion was, your being accompanied by such numbers of the tribes who are tributary to that Emperor, who is accustomed to come into our country under various pretences, and carry off our wives and children. We feared some foul plan was at hand, and therefore had put no faith in your ambassadors.

"We did not attack first when you entered into our territory, nor was it done at our instigation or command, but it was the Chontales, a rude and wild mountain tribe, who imagined they could easily overcome your small numbers, carry you off as prisoners, and send your hearts to our chiefs, in order to gain our good wishes.

"We now come to beg forgiveness, and will daily provide a sufficient supply of provisions. We hope you will accept these we have now brought, with the same kind feeling in which they are offered. In the space of two days the chief commander Xicotencatl, with the other chiefs, will come himself, and further prove how fervently the whole of Tlaxcala desires to make peace and friendship with you." Malinalli translates. After the chiefs finish speaking, they again bow, touch the ground with their hands, and kiss it.

Cortés, with great seriousness, has Malinalli translate his reply.

"We certainly have cause to refuse you of Tlaxcala a hearing, or to make any compact of friendship with you. Upon our first entering into your country, we offered peace, and announced that we intended to assist you against your enemies the Aztecs. Yet you would not believe us, and had even made a point of killing our ambassadors, and made three murderous attacks against us, and even just yesterday also sent spies into our camp.

"In the battle we just fought with you, we could have killed many more of your warriors, and even though we grieved for those whose lives had thus been lost, you have driven us to it. We had resolved to carry the war into the very town where your chiefs and nobles and elders dwell, but as you now came to sue for peace, we are willing to receive you kindly and are pleased to accept the provisions which you have brought." Malinalli announces, with an audible sigh of relief from the Tlaxcalans.

"You must now tell your chiefs to come here in person to make a formal warranty of peace. If they refuse to come, I will put my army in motion, and attack you at your very doors. Moreover, you are to approach our camp during daytime only, for if you came at night, we would put you all to the sword without mercy." The Conqueror warns through Malinalli, who translates the words with a biting edge and cold tone to ensure the natives understand the seriousness of the threat.

After Cortés has spoken he as usual presents the utmost grace and courtesy and presents the messengers with blue beads in a token of peace. The delegates then return to their village, leaving Indian females whom they had brought along with them to prepare the bread, fowls, and dinner for the Spanish. There are also twenty Indians who furnish wood and water for cooking and indeed they prepare a most delicious meal.

The Conquistadors, now convinced peace is at hand, give thanks to the Almighty God and enjoy the sumptuous meal.

In the days that follow the great victory in the battles against the Tlaxcala, Cortés' fame spreads to every territory and village. If the Conquistadors had previously been looked upon as spirits or gods, the tales of their bravery now became the more exalted, and terror seized the whole country, for Cortés had broken the great power of the Tlaxcalans with a handful of men, and compelled them to sue for peace.

***

The word of the victory and the ensuing peace treaty soon reaches the ears of the mighty Montezuma and his short lived good mood and vacation from reality is over.

Once more restrained by doubts and uncertainty, he is unable to come to any decision about Cortés, except he is convinced he is not a man but the god Quetzalcoatl. How else could he have defeated the Tlaxcalans—a people his own army can barely subdue?

The Emperor calls together his advisors and nobles and cabinet and persuades them to make a decision for him.

They decide to take the unprecedented step of sending a delegation through enemy Tlaxcala to met with Cortés one last time in an attempt to head off his approach to the Aztec capital by simultaneously trying to buy him off and frightening him into retreating...

18 From Slave to Partner

And so it happens that the powerful emperor of the Aztecs, Montezuma, dispatches five men of distinction to the Conquistador's camp in the land of Tlaxcala, supposedly to welcome them on their arrival, and to assure them of his delight at the great victories which they have won over such numerous armies. Montezuma likewise wishes Cortés to know that it is his desire to become a vassal of the emperor, and that he is in every way well disposed towards Cortés and all the gods, his brothers.

The ambassadors also coyly relay that Montezuma feels great pleasure to learn that Cortés is so near his metropolis, and also wishes to inquire what annual tribute in gold, silver, jewels, and cotton stuffs he is to forward to the great emperor, which would save them the trouble of coming to the capital. Montezuma, indeed, would be pleased to see them, but the journey there would be a terrible one, through a barren and rocky country, and the fatigue which they should have to undergo grieves him the more when he considers that he was able to remove those difficulties out of their way.

This message is accompanied by a valuable present in gold trinkets of various workmanship, worth about 1,000 pesos ($12,000), and of packages of cotton stuffs as much as twenty men could carry.

To this Cortés answers that he is very thankful for such kind feeling, as also for the presents, and the offer to pay tribute, but he must beg of the ambassadors to wait while he concludes his business with the chiefs of Tlaxcala who are due to arrive shortly.

Cortés is still conversing with the ambassadors of Montezuma, and about to dismiss them so he can rest and shake off the fever that is still with him, when it is announced that the general Xicotencatl is approaching, with several chiefs. The Tlaxcalans are dressed in multi-colored cloaks—one half of the cloak is white and the other colored—for these are Tlaxcala's national costumes in time of peace. The number of distinguished persons who accompany Xicotencatl amounts to about fifty. When they arrive before Cortés they pay him profound respect. All the Tlaxcalans however, eye Malinalli carefully, wondering what her relationship is to these strangers. How is this young woman able to converse with the gods, they ask themselves?

Then they notice the Aztec delegation sent by Montezuma and it takes every ounce of Xicotencatl's will to keep his anger in check. As it is, he literally shakes with anger while trying to keep a friendly smile on his face.

Cortés receives them in his most friendly manner, as is his custom, and begs them to sit near him. The group decides to remain standing. Whereupon Xicotencatl, a tall broad shouldered man, well built, with a large reddish colored face full of scars, and about thirty-five years of age. He appears earnest and dignified in his deportment as he begins his speech.

"I come, in the name of my father Xicotencatl, of Maxixcatzin, and of all the chiefs of the country of Tlaxcala, to beg you to admit us to our friendship. I at the same time, in their name, come to do homage, and promise obedience to you, emperor and master, and to beg forgiveness for having taken up arms against you. We had done this because we were ignorant as to who you are and believed you had been sent by our bitter enemy Montezuma, who had often before used fraud and treachery to enter our country for the sake of plunder.

"We are, however, very poor, and possess neither gold, silver, jewels, nor cotton stuffs because the Aztecs stole it all. We are even in want of salt to flavor our food, as Montezuma does not allow us to venture out of our country to procure it. So now we have nothing left to make you a present."

After this Xicotencatl goes on, showing no fear, to bitterly complain about Montezuma and his allies, in front of the Emperor's very ambassadors, who are all hostile to his country, and leave them no peace. He goes on to say the Tlaxcalans always defended themselves bravely, but found that all their endeavors were fruitless against the strangers, and although they had battled three times, found they were invincible. Hard experience taught them, and they now desire to become friends, and vassals of the great emperor. For they are now convinced, that in alliance with Cortés, they would be able to live in security and peace with their wives and children, and not be constantly threatened by the treacherous Aztecs.

Cortés thanks him most sincerely, saying he would acknowledge them as vassals of his emperor, and would, for the future, look upon them as friends. But Cortés does not catch on that Xicotencatl thinks Cortés is the 'emperor'—a misunderstanding on both sides that Malinalli not only doesn't correct but instead encourages.

Upon this Xicotencatl requests Cortés journey to the capital of his country, where all the chiefs, elders, and priests are expecting them, and will formalize a peace treaty.

Cortés answers in a harsh tone of voice, and mentions the repeated attacks they had made upon him. He will certainly bear them no malice, and freely forgive all the past, but they must sacredly observe the peace which he has granted them, and show no inconsistency in their conduct. If they do he will assuredly destroy their towns and put all the inhabitants to the sword, and carry on a war of extermination to the very last person.

These words are not only met for the Tlaxcalans, but the Aztecs as well, and Malinalli goes out of her way to present them in the harshest language possible. In so doing she gains the rapt attention of the Aztec delegation, who begin to view her as a very dangerous woman in the company of an equally dangerous god. The natives on either side are not accustomed to a female of power, in fact even their female gods are portrayed by male priests, so they are mystified by this young woman.

Xicotencatl, and all the distinguished nobles who are with him, assure Cortés they will faithfully abide by their promise, and that they are ready to offer themselves as hostages as proof of their sincerity. Upon this Cortés smiles graciously and presents them with blue beads for themselves, the elder Xicotencatl and most of the other chiefs. He promises to visit their capital as soon as possible.

After Xicotencatl and his party depart, the Aztecs envoys warn Cortés not to believe them. Surely, they say after so many of their numbers had been killed and wounded, they would try instead to defeat him with fine words and a pretend show of peace.

To this Cortés answers calmly and boldly, that he is in no way troubled about their intentions. If their suspicions prove true he will simply put the Tlaxcalans all to death—a typical show of the amazing bravado Cortés usually displays. He goes on to say that they might attack him by night or day, in the open field or in the town, it was all the same to him, and to convince himself as to how matters really stand, he indeed plans to visit their capital. Malinalli, seemingly always able to perceive the undertones of her captain (or perhaps just using her incredible street smarts), translates his words in the calmest possible manner as if it were all an absolute certainty.

When the Aztec ambassadors see they cannot dissuade Cortés, they beg him to remain for at least another six days in his present location, so that they might first send messengers to communicate with Montezuma, and would return again with his answer within that time.

To this Cortés consents, partly on account of his illness, partly because he suspects the warnings the Aztecs have given him might not be altogether so unfounded as he imagined. In that time he can also try to obtain more proof of the real intentions of the Tlaxcalans.

With the Tlaxcalans standing down, the whole country from Vera Cruz up to his present location is now on good terms, so Cortés takes the time to write a letter to Juan de Escalante, detailing all that had occurred. He also requests him to make a day of thanksgiving, and in every way to favor their allies of the Totonaque mountains (obviously hedging his bets and insuring the Conquistadors had a safe way out in case the tide turned suddenly). Lastly, he requests him to send two bottles of wine which he had buried in a certain corner of his quarters there, and some holy wafers, as they had none left for Mass. Escalante responds quickly via a courier with the things Cortés required. During these days Cortés also orders a majestic cross erected in the temple where they were staying and even has it cleansed and freshly plastered by some of the natives so they would have a place to conduct Mass, and for the natives after they depart.

In the meantime, the postponement of the Conquistador's visit greatly distresses the chiefs of Tlaxcala to the point they daily earnestly plead with Cortés not to delay his visit any longer. Yet they continue to send fowls and figs, which are now just in season, and a daily supply of provisions. They do this with the best of good will, and would not accept anything in return on the assurance Cortés will visit the capital as soon as possible. But Cortés wants to wait the six days for the Aztecs to return, so each time puts off the Tlaxcalans with some friendly excuse.

While he waits Cortés is also regaining his strength from the sickness, with Malinalli nursing him back to health. She makes sure he rests and serves him substantial meals daily with her own hands.

"You are too kind to me Marina, but I must work, I must lead the men and take care of our affairs." He tells her one morning as she brings him freshly cooked food.

"You must rest my Captain, and grow strong. The men are fine. You must be strong when we meet Montezuma, he is not one to trifle with. And you must appear healthy and in command when you meet the Tlaxcalans. We cannot lose face now." Malinalli reminds him.

Cortés knows she is right, such a strong head on such a young girl! These thoughts awaken another part of him, he has not laid with her for many days...

"I see you *are* feeling better!" Malinalli exclaims with a grin at her leader's sudden rise of passion. "One more day, you must rest one more day! I do not want to steal all your newly regained strength!" Her laughter follows her out of the hut as she twists away.

***

When the five ambassadors report on their meeting with Cortés and what transpired with Tlaxcala, Montezuma is beside himself. He had prayed to the gods that the 'problem' would be solved at the hands of his enemies, instead it now appears they will join the strangers as allies!

"You cannot allow this to happen at all costs!" His brother Cuitláhuac exclaims.

"Yes, I am most aware of the consequences of such an event, my brother. But what shall we do to prevent it?"

"The best way to feed someone poison is to mix it with honey. Give these strangers the gold they seem to crave while sowing the seeds of distrust in the Tlaxcalans." He recommends...

19 Gifts

The Aztecs faithfully keep their word and on the sixth day return to visit Cortés in his camp. This time six distinguished nobles arrive from the capital of the empire with a rich present from Montezuma.

The gifts value more than 3,000 pesos ($36,000), consisting of gold trinkets of exquisite workmanship, two hundred pieces of cotton stuffs, interwoven with feathers, and other pieces of Aztec art. When they hand over these presents to Cortés they inform him that Montezuma is greatly delighted at the successful state of affairs.

Then they urge Cortés not to allow any Tlaxcalans to get close, for whatever purpose it might be, and especially not to trust them. They are merely waiting to rob him of his gold and other valuables, as they are quite poverty stricken themselves, and possess no riches of their own.

Cortés accepts these presents with delight, and thanks them with every appearance of sincerity, with the assurance that he will render Montezuma good service in return. He tells them that if he should discover that the Tlaxcalans really bear treachery in their hearts they will have to pay very dearly for it. However, he believes that such thoughts are remote from their minds, and he will now retire to consider how much truth there is in their statement.

In the midst of this conversation several messengers arrive from Tlaxcala, bringing Cortés news that all the important chiefs of the country were on their way to pay a visit, and escort him into their city. Apparently the old chiefs, including the blind Xicotencatl, the elder, were unnerved when the Conquistadors did not arrive in their city for the peace treaty and so determined to call upon Cortés themselves, and set out, carried in hand sedans.

On learning this, Cortés requests the Aztec ambassadors to wait three days before they depart again because he is about to enter into terms of peace with the Tlaxcalan chiefs.

When they arrived in presence of Cortés they pay him the customary respect, bowing and touching the ground with their hands, and then kissing it.

"Malintzin, Malintzin often have we begged of you to forgive the hostile attacks we made upon you." The elder Xicotencatl addresses Cortés as 'Malintzin' or as the Spanish write it: 'Malinche' which means to them 'Captain of Malinalli'. The natives have taken to calling him this because Malinalli (Doña Marina) is always at his side and speaks for him. As time passes, Malinalli is referred to as 'La Malinche' to distinguish her from her Captain: Cortés.

"We have already explained to you that we imagined you were in league with Montezuma. Indeed, if we had known before what we now do, instead of refusing you admission, we would not only have marched out to meet you by the shortest route with a quantity of provisions, but have come to the very coast where your vessels lie, in order to escort you here." Xicotencatl continues.

"But, as you have now pardoned all this, I have come with all the chiefs to beg of you to accompany us immediately to our city, and to partake in the reception which we intend to give you there according to the best of our abilities. Stay all other business for the present, Malinche, we beg of you, and go with us now. We greatly deplore that the Aztecs have attempted to poison your mind with all manner of falsehoods respecting us, and that this should alone have withheld you from paying us a visit. We are quite accustomed to their slanders. You must not believe them, no, nor even listen to them, for all their actions and words are full of deceit."

"I planned for many years to visit this country." Cortés says, though Malinalli translates this as: 'I knew years ago that we would one time visit this country', knowing full well these are chilling words to both the Aztecs and the Tlaxcalans, who perceive the statement as proof of the prophecy of the return of Quetzalcoatl.

"You are a brave people, and I am astonished you have treated us as enemies." Malinalli translates, as if to say: '*I am shocked you treated your god like this*.'

"With regard to the Aztecs who are now present, they are merely waiting my command to return to Montezuma. I joyously accepted their invitation to visit their city, and thanked them for the provisions they had sent, and also for all their other kind offers." Cortés replies, with great sincerity—while shrewdly sending a underlying message that he is allied with Montezuma—as a hedge against the possible deceit of the Tlaxcalans, who he does not fully trust. Cortés is playing both sides against the other with the brilliant assistance of Malinalli.

Then he goes on to make a wild excuse that the reason he had not visited them before this was solely owing to want of men to transport the heavy cannon.

When he hears this, Xicotencatl is exceedingly pleased, and asks how is it you did not tell us? He immediately sends a messenger back to his town and then scarcely half an hour later 500 slaves arrive on the spot and begin preparations to transport the Conquistador's cargo.

So it is that early the next morning the Spanish set out for the capital of Tlaxcala. Cortés has also requested the Aztec ambassadors to accompany him with the ploy that they might convince themselves that the people of Tlaxcala are sincere, but in reality he is still playing his game. To allay the Aztec's apprehensions about visiting an enemy area, he assures them they can stay in his own quarters, and will not be harmed.

After the chiefs make sure the cannons and cargo are moving forward, they hurry back to make the necessary preparations for the reception, and prepare quarters for the esteemed visitors.

When the Spanish arrive within sight of their city, they come out to meet them, accompanied by their daughters, nieces, and other distinguished nobles of the four main tribes. The inhabitants of other towns also join them, all distinguished by specific colors, which, for want of cotton, are very prettily and neatly manufactured of nequen—a cloth woven from the maguey plant.

Next comes a large group of priests, who are in the temple service. They carry pans with glowing embers of incense and wave these over the Spanish. Some of them have on long white cloaks, like surplices with capes as Catholic priests wear during Mass. But horribly unlike Catholic priests, the nails of their fingers are uncommonly long, and the hair on their heads is long and matted together, so that it would be impossible to comb without cutting it off. On closer inspection the Spanish notice the priest's hair is completely soaked with blood, which even continues to trickle down over their ears—a sign they had been sacrificing that very day. They hold their heads down on approaching, as a sign of humility. Malinalli explains that these men are greatly revered for their religion—but is aghast at the blood sacrifices they perform.

The principal nobles and chiefs then gather around Cortés, and form an honor guard to escort him the rest of the way into the town.

As they enter the town, the streets and balconies can scarcely contain the numbers of men and women who come out to see the strangers. The air is full of excitement, and twenty baskets of roses, of various colors and sweetly scented, are presented to Cortés and the other soldiers whom they considered officers, and particularly to those who sat on horseback. Two children run up and hand Malinalli a bouquet of her own.

The procession advances to some spacious courtyards, where quarters have been prepared for the Conquistadors. Here Xicotencatl the elder and Maxixcatzin take Cortés by the hand and lead him and Malinalli into his apartments. For each soldier there is a separate bed, filled with a species of dried grass, and covered with cloaks of nequen. The allies of Cempoalla and Xocotlan are quartered in nearby in a similar manner. Cortés then requests that the ambassadors of Montezuma lodge with him.

The Conquistadors feel nothing but goodwill and friendliness, and become therefore relaxed. The officer whose duty it was to post sentries and order patrols, remarks to Cortés, that with the atmosphere here, their usual watchfulness should not be required.

"This may be very true, yet we will not relinquish procedures. Though the people here may be very good, we must not trust too much to this peace, but always be upon our guard as if we expected each moment to be attacked. Many a general has been ruined by carelessness and over-confidence. We, who are a mere handful of men, and have been warned by Montezuma himself, though he may not exactly have been in earnest, must be ready for action at a moment's notice." Cortés answers.

The two chief chiefs, the elder Xicotencatl and Maxixcatzin, are very much hurt at the military precautions instituted, and they do not hide their feelings from Cortés.

"Malinche, if we are to draw a conclusion from the steps you are taking, you either look upon us as your enemies, or at least you place no confidence in us and the treaty of peace which has been concluded between us. You post sentinels and order your men to patrol the streets as is both armies stand in hostile array against each other. This you have not done of your own accord, Malinche, but because the Aztecs have secretly whispered to you fears of treachery, wishing thereby to estrange you from us. Believe us, you cannot put any faith in what they say. You are now in the midst of us; everything we have is at your service—our own persons and our children; and we are ready to suffer death for you. Ask for as many hostages as you like, and you shall have them." Xicotencatl and Maxixcatzin say to him.

Cortés and his officers are moved at the kind and graceful manner in which the old men express themselves. The Conqueror says he requires no hostages; he can see for himself that all is perfectly safe. But he does not bother to back down either, he goes on to say that these military precautions are standard procedure even back home, and they were not to take offence on that account. He thanks them for their kind intentions, and promises to render them great services in return. After this explanation, other persons of distinction arrive with a quantity of provisions, consisting of fowls, cornbread, figs, and vegetables.

Early the next morning Cortés orders an altar to be constructed, and Mass to be said, as they now again had a supply of wine and holy wafers. Father Olmedo, lying ill of the fever which has greatly weakened him, has the priest Juan Diaz say Mass, as Maxixcatzin, the elder Xicotencatl, and several other chiefs look on. After Mass, Cortés retires to his quarters with several of his officers and the old chiefs, and of course Malinalli who is indispensable.

The elder Xicotencatl tells Cortés that it was the wish of the tribes to make him a present and they accordingly spread some mats on the floor, upon which they arrange five or six small pieces of gold, a few stones of trifling value, and several parcels of manufactured nequen, altogether worth about twenty pesos ($ 240). These presents are at the same time accompanied by a quantity of provisions.

"Malinche, we imagine that you will not experience much joy in receiving such a wretched a present. but we are poor, possessing neither gold nor other riches, as the deceitful Aztecs, with their present monarch Montezuma, have by degrees despoiled us of everything we had. Do not look to the small value of these things, but accept them in all kindness, and as coming from your faithful friends and servants." The chiefs say with smiles.

Cortés indeed accepts all with every appearance of delight, and assures the old men that, since these things came from them, and were given with such great good will, they have more value in his estimation than a whole house full of gold.

"In order, Malinche, that you may have a still clearer proof of our good feeling towards you, and to show you how glad we are to do anything which we imagine may please you, and because we desire to completely associate with such good and brave men as you; we have resolved to give you our daughters in marriage, that they may have children by you. I myself have a daughter, who is very beautiful, and has never been married, whom I have destined for you." The old Xicotencatl addresses Cortés.

Maxixcatzin and most of the other chiefs continue to also beg of the Conquistadors to take their daughters for their wives. Then after asking permission of Cortés, Xicotencatl, who is blind with age, draws his hand over his hair, his face, his beard, and the whole of his body so as to form an image of the Conqueror.

"In your opinion, would this not be the proper moment to demand these people abolish their idols and the human sacrifices? From fear of the Aztecs, they will undoubtedly do anything we require of them." Says Cortés, turning to Father Olmedo.

"It will be time enough, when they bring us their daughters, then we shall have the best opportunity of telling them that we cannot accept them until they have promised to abstain from their human sacrifices. If they comply, it is well; if they refuse, we know what our duty and our religion require of us." Answers the priest.

Cortés then tells the chiefs, with respect to the women, that he and all of his men were very grateful for them, and that he will take the first opportunity to render them a kindness in return.

The next day, the old chiefs come bringing five nicely dressed pretty young women. Each also has a young woman as maid in waiting, and all are daughters of chiefs. One girl is led out in front and presented to Cortés personally by Xicotencatl.

"Malinche, this is my daughter. She is still a virgin, and has never been married, I ask that you take her to yourself, and give the others to your officers."

There is a long moment of silence as both Cortés and Malinalli consider the circumstances of this event—from different perspectives:

The practice of giving away one's daughter is not foreign to the

Conqueror, but he can't help but wonder how the poor girl feels about it: How frightening a prospect it must be for her to give her life to some stranger from another land! There is another thing on his mind as well: Malinalli, whom he has grown to admire greatly and dares not do anything to upset that situation—either as his interpreter or his lover!

Malinalli is thinking similar thoughts. While she herself was not long ago in a similar situation and is accustomed to some native men having multiple wives, she doesn't want to share Cortés (or her own power) with any woman. So she is anxiously awaiting what his response will be.

Cortés receives the young women from Xicotencatl's hand with a broad smile. He appears very pleased, declaring that he will now consider these females as his own, but asks that they should, for now, remain with their fathers. Although Malinalli's heart jumps with joy, the chiefs are taken aback by this and ask the reason for it.

"I have no other reason than that I am bound first to fulfill my duty to the God whom we adore, which is to require of you to abolish your idols, the human sacrifices, and other abominations practiced among you, and exhort you to believe in him in whom we believe, who alone is the true God." Cortés tells them.

Then he asks Malinalli and Friar Aguilar to explain about their holy religion, Jesus Christ and the Blessed Virgin Mary, and the Holy Ghost, while showing them an image of Mary with Jesus in her arms.

"If you are, indeed, our brothers, and you are really inclined to conclude a lasting peace with us, and if we are to take and keep your daughters as affectionate husbands should do, they must abandon their horrible idols, and believe in the Lord God whom we adore.

"Rather than human sacrifices which you make to your idols, who are nothing but devils and who will lead you to hell where eternal fire would torment your souls; you will soon discover the beneficial effect of the true God. Blessings will be showered down upon you, the seasons will be fruitful, and all your undertakings will prosper. After death your souls will be transplanted to heaven, and partake of eternal glory." Cortés says through Malinalli.

"Malinche, we hear all this from you, and willingly believe that your God and this illustrious woman are good beings. But you should remember how very recently you have arrived in our country, and you have but just entered our city. You should give us time to learn more of the nature of your gods. When we have satisfied ourselves respecting their qualities, we shall certainly make choice of those we consider best. How can you ask us to abandon our gods whom we have adored for so many years, and prayed and sacrificed to them? But if we should even do so to please you, what would our priests, our young men, yes, even our boys, say to it? Believe us, they will all rise up in arms. The priests, indeed, have already spoken to our gods, who have told them not to abolish our human sacrifices, nor any other of our ancient customs, otherwise they would destroy our whole country by famine, pestilence, and war." Xicotencatl replies in a straightforward and fearless manner—an indication that it would be useless to insist any longer on this point, and that they would rather allow themselves to be killed than abolish their human sacrifices.

"My opinion is, sir, that you should no longer urge this matter with these people. It is not acting right to force them to become Christians. I could likewise wish that we had not destroyed the idols at Cempoalla. This I am convinced ought not to be done until the people have gained some knowledge of our holy religion. What, indeed, do we gain by pulling down their idols from the temples? They have merely then to repair to another temple. But, on the other hand, we should never cease to exhort them with our pious lessons. In this way the time will certainly arrive, when they will find that our intentions and our advice are good." Father Olmedo, a profound theologian, finds himself compelled to address Cortés on the subject.

In addition, the three cavaliers Alvarado, Leon, and Lugo likewise speak to Cortés assuring him that Father Olmedo is right, and that they agree with him, that it would be inadvisable again to touch upon this point with the chiefs.

So reluctantly the subject is dropped, and Cortés confines himself to ordering the idols to be taken down from a temple which had been recently built nearby. He orders it to be cleansed and freshly plastered, and the image of the blessed Virgin to be placed on it. To this the chiefs readily consent, and when all is finished Mass is said.

Afterwards the daughters of the chiefs are baptized. Maxixcatzin's daughter receives the name of Doña Elvira. She is the most beautiful of the girls, and is presented to Leon. The others are given to Oli, Sandoval, and Avila, who all legally added their Christian names to theirs as if they had been young ladies of noble birth. And finally, Xicotencatl's daughter is christened Doña Luisa. Cortés then takes her by the hand and presents her to Alvarado, saying to Xicotencatl, that he to whom he has given her is his brother and a chief officer under him, who will certainly treat her well, and with whom she will live happily. Xicotencatl agrees to this. (But it is Malinalli who is happiest of all—she feels in her heart that this proves beyond all doubt that Cortés has eyes only for her.)

These 'marriages' are not made lightly. The whole of Tlaxcala takes the greatest interest in Xicotencatl's daughter Doña Luisa's welfare, and honors her as a woman of nobility. Alvarado is blond and fair, with blue eyes and pale skin that fascinates the natives of the New World. Doña Luisa Xicotencatl becomes his longtime native companion, and follows him on most of his adventures. Alvarado, who is a bachelor, will have a son by her, who will be named Don Pedro; and also a daughter, Doña Leonora, who will marry Don Francisco de la Cueva, a cavalier of distinction, and a relation of the duke of Albuquerque. She will go on to have five sons, all valiant cavaliers. She will become a lady of class and distinction, and a daughter worthy of such a father-in-law who will be governor of Santiago and chief justice and viceroy of Guatemala. She will also continue to be important in the house of Xicotencatl, a man of the highest rank in Tlaxcala, and who is looked upon as a king.

A few days pass and then Cortés takes the chiefs aside, and puts several questions to them respecting the situation and affairs of the Aztec empire. Xicotencatl, as the more intelligent and distinguished personage, answers his queries, and Maxixcatzin, who is likewise a man of high rank, assists him from time to time.

"Montezuma has such a vast army, that when he intends to conquer any large town or province, he invariably orders 100,000 warriors into the field—a sobering and overwhelming attack army. We of Tlaxcala have often experienced this in the many wars which we have waged with the Aztecs for upwards of 100 years." Xicotencatl tells the Conqueror.

Here Cortés asks how the Tlaxcalans have managed to escape being subdued by such a vast army?

"We have often been bested by the Aztecs, and lost many of our men, who were either killed in battle or taken prisoners and sacrificed to the gods. But we have made their incursions costly and likewise have slain numbers of the enemy and taken many of them prisoner. We always receive some previous notice of the Aztecs movements and so are able to mount a strong defense. Besides this, another circumstance greatly in our favor is that the Aztecs are excessively hated in all the provinces and among all the tribes which Montezuma has conquered and plundered. Since many of his warriors are from these tribes and forced to serve in his army, they fight with reluctance and with little courage. In this way, then, we defend our country as best we can." The elders tell Cortés.

They go on to say that in fact they have more to fear from the Cholulans, whose town lies about a day's march from Tlaxcala. The people there are a most deceitful lot. In that town it is that Montezuma usually assembles his troops, from which they usually commence their march for attacks during night-time.

"Montezuma has strong garrisons in every town, besides the

warriors who march out from the capital to the battlefield. Every province is compelled to pay him tribute, consisting in gold, silver, feathers, precious stones, cotton stuffs, and crops, as well as people of both sexes. Some of these captives he takes into his service, and some are sacrificed. He is altogether such a powerful and wealthy monarch, that he accomplishes and obtains everything he desires. His palaces are filled with riches and jade stones, which he seizes wherever he goes. In short, all the wealth of the country is in his possession." Maxixcatzin adds.

The chiefs give Cortés a detailed account of the magnificence and splendor of the Emperor's court, of the number of his wives—some of whom he now and then gives in marriage to his relations. About the great strength of his capital, how it lies in the midst of a lake, and the great depth of the latter. Only limited causeways, they add, lead to this city, which are intersected in various places by bridges, that if removed, would cause the sections to each become an island and thereby cut off all access to the capital.

They explain to Cortés that nearly all of the houses in the city are built in the water, and it is only possible to get from one building to another by means of drawbridges or canoes. Balconies are attached to each house, and provided with a kind of breastwork, so that the inhabitants are able to defend themselves from the tops of the houses. Then the whole town is well supplied with sweet water from the spring of Chapultepec, which lies about two miles from the town, and the water is conveyed to the houses partly by means of pipes, partly in boats through the canals, and then sold to the inhabitants.

The Conqueror continues these meetings with the elders each day for several days so that he can glean much information from them. The second day they explain about the Aztec weapons, which consist of two-edged lances, which they threw by means of a thong, and will penetrate through any cuirass. They are excellent shots with the bow and arrow, and carry pikes with blades made of flint, which are of very skilful workmanship and as sharp as razors.

Besides these, they carry shields, and wear cotton cuirasses as armor. They likewise employ a great number of slingers, who are provided with round stones, long pikes, and sharp swords, which are used with both hands. To explain all this they bring forth large pieces of nequen, on which they depict their battles and their art of warfare.

Another day the discourse turns to subjects of history. The Tlaxcalans relate how and when they came into this country, how they settled here, and how it came that they and the Aztecs live in perpetual warfare with each other. The elders also told of a tale handed down from their forefathers, that in ancient times there lived here a race of men and women who were of immense stature with heavy bones, and were a very bad and evil-disposed people. These had for the greater part been exterminated by continual war, and the few that were left gradually died away.

In order to give the Spaniards a sense of the huge frame of these people, they display a thigh bone of one of those giants, which is very strong, and although only the part from the knee to the hip joint, measured the length of a man of good stature! (* See Appendix for more on this subject)

Then one day the chiefs also mention another legend which had come down from their forefathers: A certain god, to whom they paid great respect, had informed them that there would one time come from the rising of the sun, out of distant countries, a people who would subject and rule over them. The chiefs say if the Conquistadors are that people they would be delighted, for they are courageous and good-hearted. This old prophecy is brought up often concerning the terms of peace and it is the main reason they offered their daughters in order to bring about a relationship between them and these gods, and to obtain assistance against the Aztecs.

For some of the Spanish this is the first time they heard of the prophecy and many talk among themselves of it. For Malinalli, it is yet another validation of what she told Cortés previously, and again he realizes she was right all along.

"We come, indeed, from the rising of the sun. The emperor, our master, has purposely sent us, that we might become your brothers, as he has some previous knowledge respecting your country. May God in his mercy grant that we may be the means of saving you from eternal perdition!" Cortés instructs Malinalli to reply, but once again she slightly changes the translation, leaving out the 'our master' and leading the Tlaxcalans to believe Cortés is the only master and possibly the god. She does these things for no other reason than she believes it strengthens her leader's hand in the eyes of their possible enemies.

A few days later the Spanish notice a burning mountain nearby in Huexotzinco, which at the time is emitting more flames than usual. To the Conquistadors, a volcano is something new and they regard it with astonishment. Diego de Ordas, one of the chief officers, is very curious and entertains the bold idea of inspecting this wonder more closely, and asks permission of Cortés to ascend the mountain.

Ordas takes two of his men with him, and requests some of the chief personages of Huexotzinco accompany him. They do not refuse, but try to deter him by warning, that when he has ascended Popocatepetl, their name for this volcano, half way he will not be able to advance further on account of the trembling of the earth and the flames, stones and ashes, which are emitted from the crater. They never venture higher than to where some temples are built to the spirits of Popocatepetl.

But their warnings go unheeded and Ordas indeed ascends the volcano to the halfway point, where the native guides who accompany him refuse to go further. Ordas and his two soldiers, however, boldly continue to climb. While they are still ascending, the volcano begins to emit huge flames of fire, half burnt and perforated stones and a quantity of ash. The whole mountain shakes under their feet. Fearless, Ordas then halts for an hour, until the smoke and fire gradually clears, then they continue to the summit where they find the crater, which is perfectly round and about a mile in diameter.

From this elevation they can plainly see the great city of Tenochtitlan, the capital of Aztec empire, of Mexico. They can see its layout, the whole of its lake, and the surrounding towns, for this mountain only lies about forty-eight miles from Tenochtitlan.

After Ordas has enjoyed and wondered at the sight of Mexico and its suburbs, he returns to Tlaxcala to relate his adventure. According to the natives he is the first to ever venture to the summit and they are in awe of his courage. (Later when he returns to Spain, Ordas will request and be granted permission of the royal court to depict a volcano in his coat of arms.) The Spanish as well are completely astonished at the account which Ordas gives Cortés of his hazardous journey and what he has seen—the most important of which is confirmation of everything the Tlaxcalans have told them.

As the days pass and the Spanish become more familiar in Tlaxcala they find cages built of wood, in which numbers of Indians, of both sexes, are confined, and fattened for their sacrifices and feasts. The Conquistadors never hesitate a single moment to break them down and liberate the prisoners—an act that endears Cortés to Malinalli's heart even more if that is possible. She has met her dream god, one that rights all wrongs, and saves her countrymen from that horrible butchery of sacrifice. And as if that weren't enough: he seems to love her as well!

From this moment Cortés gives orders to break open these cages wherever they find them. The Conqueror expresses his horror of these atrocities, and earnestly criticizes the chiefs for it, who then promise no longer to kill and devour human beings. But as soon as the Spanish are out of sight the same atrocities are committed.

After having been seventeen days in Tlaxcala, and hearing so much during that time regarding the immense treasures of Montezuma, and the splendor of his capital, Cortés decides to consult with all those officers and soldiers whom he presumes are inclined to advance further on a march to the capital of the Aztec empire.

Although in this meeting, which is for all intents and purposes a council of war, it is agreed that they should commence a march without delay, not everyone is in harmony regarding this decision. Many express various opinions that it would be acting rashly to venture with a mere handful of men into a strongly fortified city, whose monarch has such vast numbers of warriors at his command. Those who opposed are the same who are relatively wealthy and have possessions on the island of Cuba. But Cortés declares that all arguing on this point is useless.

"We have resolved on every occasion and expressed our desire to pay our respects personally to Montezuma, and we cannot alter this course now that we are so close." The Conqueror exclaims.

When those who are adverse to this journey see his determination, and that the majority of the officers and soldiers are devoted to him, they cease any further opposition.

"Forward, now or never!" The men cry out, mostly poor soldiers ready to sacrifice their very existence in battle, and to undergo all manner of hardships for God and their sovereign—and hopefully strike it rich themselves.

When Xicotencatl and Maxixcatzin hear that the Conquistadors are determined to march to Mexico, they are afraid for them and urgently try to dissuade Cortés from it. They warn him not to put the slightest trust in Montezuma or any Aztec, to put no faith in his show of veneration, nor his courteous and humble talk. All their declarations of friendship and even their very presents have treachery at the bottom; for what they give at one moment they take away at another.

The old chiefs advise Cortés to be on guard night and day, for they can assure him that the Aztecs will attack when the Spanish are least prepared. Neither should they spare any of their lives should it come to battle. Spare not the young man that he might not again take up arms against you, nor the old man that he might not do you injury by his counsel, the elders tell the Conqueror.

Cortés assures them how grateful he is for their warning and advice, and divides among the chiefs a great portion of the fine stuffs which had been presented to him by Montezuma. He then remarks to the elders, that it would be the best possible thing if peace and friendship could be brought about between themselves and the Aztecs, so that at the least they might no longer constantly fear attack or continue to want for cotton, salt, and other wares.

"With the Aztecs a treaty of peace is a mere formality, as deceit is always in their hearts. It is the characteristic of this people to plot the foulest treacheries under the semblance of profound peace. No reliance can be placed on their promises, their words are empty sounds, and we cannot remind and beg you too often to be upon your guard against the snares of this vile people." Xicotencatl immediately replies.

But the Conqueror did not come this far not to conquer, so he then seeks advice on the route he should take in their march to Mexico. Montezuma's ambassadors, who still remain with the Spanish, and wished to act as guides, suggest that the best and most level trail lay through the town of Cholula, about twenty miles distant, whose inhabitants, as subjects of Montezuma, will be ready to lend any assistance.

In one of his few missteps, Cortés is also of opinion that this is the road he ought to take. But the chiefs of Tlaxcala, on the contrary, are quite upset when they learn this, and insist that he ought to march through Huexotzinco, whose inhabitants are their relatives and friends. They strongly advise that he ought not to take the path through Cholula, which is controlled by Montezuma.

Their arguments, however, fall on deaf ears as Cortés keeps to his plan on marching to that town. His reason for taking that route is because this town is heavily populated, has many beautiful towers and temples, and lies in a beautiful valley surrounded by extensive towns well stocked with provisions. Indeed Cholula even when viewed from a distance, had the appearance of the great city of Valladolid of Old Castile.

At Cholula, moreover, their allies of Tlaxcala would be nearby so it seemed a most proper spot to stage the Conquistador's small army with the goal of reaching the city of Mexico without coming into contact with the great body of its troops...

***

Montezuma is kept constantly informed by spies among his ambassadors who are staying with Cortés.

"So it would appear the strangers are coming this way despite all our efforts." The emperor relates to his brother Cuitláhuac.

"Yes but our delegates almost seem to have convinced them to travel by way of Cholula—a good strategic piece of news." His brother comments as if thinking to himself.

"*Almost* is not a certainty. But you have a plan?" The emperor asks, knowing that look on his brother's face.

"Let us send them more gold, a large amount, enough to entice them to Cholula..." He mutters, beginning to form an outline in his mind.

"Yes! Once we lure them to Cholula, we will treat them with all manner of kindness, lull them into a false sense of security, and then butcher them all! Except for this white god and his woman—I want them for my personal sacrifice." Montezuma spits out.

20 The Conqueror On The Move

With the route through Cholula decided, Cortés dispatches messengers there to inform the inhabitants of his intentions. He is having second thoughts about the route since the Tlaxcalans seem to be good and trustworthy people, and is curious as to why Cholula, being so near, had not sent any ambassadors nor shown any interest in his arrival in Tlaxcala. Cortés decides to test the waters and demand that all the chiefs and priests of Cholula visit him in Tlaxcala and swear allegiance, otherwise he will look view them as enemies.

While Cortés is making preparations and awaiting the reply from Cholula, four more ambassadors sent by Montezuma arrive with presents of gold. These gifts are much more than previous and consist of valuable gold trinkets worth about 10,000 pesos ($120,000) and ten packages of cotton stuffs beautifully interwoven with feathers.

The Aztecs also deliver a message from the Emperor that he is astonished Cortés and his brothers have stayed so long among a poor and uncivilized people, who are even not fit for slaves, but so treacherous and thievish that some day or night when least expected they would murder him merely for the sake of plunder. Emperor Montezuma requests Cortés visit Cholula, where, at least, he will enjoy the good things it offers, and where he will be regularly supplied with the necessary provisions.

The Conqueror suspects these expressions of friendship are sent by Montezuma merely in order to entice him from Tlaxcala. Malinalli suggests the Emperor is surely aware of their close friendship with its inhabitants, and that the chiefs had given their daughters to Cortés and his officers to strengthen the union. And that Montezuma knew nothing good would come from this alliance and so he wiggles the bait of gold and other presents that they might enter into his territory and leave Tlaxcala.

The Tlaxcalans are personally acquainted with these ambassadors, and inform Malinalli that all are great personages and land proprietors, who had subjects of their own. These are ambassadors Montezuma employs only on the most important matters.

Cortés gives the Aztecs many thanks, in the most flattering manner, for their civilities and the expressions of friendship. And he requests they report that in a short time he will pay his respects to Montezuma personally. He then invites them to pass some time amongst him and his men.

A day later the chiefs of Cholula send four men to apologize for not appearing themselves, on account of illness. These messengers neither bring presents nor provisions.

The chiefs of Tlaxcala, who are present when these messengers arrive, are struck with their appearance, and remark to Cortés that this was a real insult to him, since these messengers were *Macehuales*, or commoners—people of the lowest rank in Aztec society.

This situation persuades Cortés to dispatch four natives from Cempoalla to Cholula, instructing them to inform the inhabitants there that he expects a delegation consisting of men of rank and authority from them within the space of three days or he would consider the town of Cholula in rebellion against him. But if they did chose to come he would consider them friends and brothers as do the Tlaxcalans.

The inhabitants of Cholula then send word that the reason why they cannot come to Tlaxcala is because they are enemies with Tlaxcala. And that Cortés and his brothers should leave there and come and visit them and they would enjoy a good reception. Cortés considers this excuse perfectly reasonable, and therefore resolves to travel to Cholula.

When the chiefs of Tlaxcala see that Cortés is really going to depart and go to Cholula, they warn him again not to trust in the Aztecs or the people of Cholula, and offer 10,000 warriors to accompany and protect him.

Cortés thanks them for their offer of men and for their good wishes, but consults with his officers as to the idea of entering into a country whose friendship he is desirous of gaining with such a large army.

After considerable consideration, they come to the conclusion that 2,000 men would be a sufficient number to accompany them, and Cortés accordingly requests only that number from his friends.

With these matters settled, the Conquistadors break camp early the next morning, and leave for the town of Cholula. They are doubly on guard for hostilities. The first day's march brings them within four miles of Cholula, and they make camp near a stone bridge built across a river.

That same night ambassadors arrive from the chiefs of Cholula, all nobles of the first rank, to bid welcome to their territory. They bring fowls and cornbread, and announce that all the chiefs and priests will soon call to give a friendly reception, and beg forgiveness for not having come out immediately. Cortés thanks them through Malinalli, but orders sentries and patrols to keep a close watch.

At day break the Conquistadors are in motion, and march directly for the town. Within a short distance they are met by the chiefs, priests, and numbers of other Indians who have come out to welcome them. But when the chiefs see the Tlaxcalans accompanying them, they request that Malinalli remind Cortés that it is not proper for enemies to enter into the town with weapons in their hands, so Cortés orders a halt.

"I am of opinion, gentlemen, that, previous to our entering into Cholula, we should, by kind words, elicit from these chiefs what their real intentions are. They seem hurt that our friends the Tlaxcalans have accompanied us, and are indeed perfectly right in what they say. It is my intention to acquaint them, in a mild manner, with our reasons for visiting their city. You know already, from the Tlaxcalans, that these people are treacherous by nature; it is, therefore, most prudent we should first desire them to take an oath of allegiance to our sovereign." The Conqueror tells his men.

He then asks Malinalli to call the chiefs and priests around him where he sits astride his horse—a subtle power play of which Cortés is a master.

"Malinche, you must not harbor any suspicion against us for not having come to Tlaxcala to pay our respects to you there, and because we did not send you any provisions. We are not lacking in good wishes towards you, but Maxixcatzin, Xicotencatl, and the whole of Tlaxcala are at war with us. They have grossly slandered us and our great Emperor, and now they no longer abide by words, but have the audacity to be upon the point of entering, all armed, into our city, under your protection. We earnestly beg you will tell them to return to their own country, or at least command them to remain outside in the fields, and not to march into our city in such a manner. The rest of you are free to enter at any time, and are perfectly welcome." The chiefs of Cholula tell Cortés.

The Conqueror considers this a reasonable request and sends Alvarado and Oli to request the Tlaxcalans erect huts outside the town, and to remain there. These officers are, at the same time, to inform them the reason for these orders, and the great fear in which all the chiefs and priests of Cholula hold them and that they will be duly informed of the day when Cortés commences the march through Cholula to Mexico. Lastly, he implores them not to be offended about this.

When the natives of Cholula observe the arrangements which Cortés makes regarding the Tlaxcalans, they appear relieved. Whereupon Cortés explains he has come to their town because the road to Mexico runs through it, and he is going to hold a conference with the great Montezuma. He is also wishes he can consider them brothers. Cortés further tells them that other great chiefs have already sworn allegiance and he hopes they will follow their example. Then the Conqueror makes his usual demands that they longer worship idols, make human sacrifices, eat human flesh, and abstain from committing unnatural crimes, and all other abominations.

In answer to this, they say that he demands too much. Cortés has just met them for the first time and is already requiring them to abolish their gods, which they cannot possibly think of complying with. They are agreeable to a verbal promise of allegiance, but without the usual formalities.

The Conquistadors decide to take what they can get and enter into the city of Cholula. The city itself was in a valley, surrounded by the townships of Tepeaca, Tlaxcala, Chalco, Tecamachalco, Huexotzinco, and many others. The country furnishes quantities of maise and various leguminous plants, particularly maguey, from the sap of which the inhabitants make their wine. In the city itself various kinds of earthenware pots are made, embellished with burnt-in black and white colors, which it supplies to the Aztecs and neighboring provinces. In this respect Cholula is equally celebrated in this country, as Valencia is in Spain.

Cholula has more than a hundred very high towers, all of which are temples, on which the human sacrifices are made and their idols worshiped. The principal temple here is even higher than that of Aztec capital. It contains one hundred courts, and an idol of enormous dimensions, to which people came from various areas to sacrifice human beings and bring offerings for the dead.

Everywhere the tops of the houses and streets are crowded with people to see the strangers. They have never before seen men like these, nor any horses! Through this mass of people the Spanish are escorted to quarters, consisting of several large apartments, in which all, including the natives of Cempoalla and the Tlaxcalans transporting cargo, find plenty of room and are immediately supplied with abundance of good food.

For the first few days the atmosphere is peaceful and relaxed. The

Spanish have good and comfortable quarters and are regularly supplied with plentiful food, water and other necessities. Then on the third day everything changes—none of the natives come around and nothing is delivered.

Cortés asks the ambassadors of Montezuma, who still remain with him, to order the chiefs to send provisions. Some wood and water is finally brought in by an old man, but he informs the Spanish there is no more food or even corn left in Cholula.

"These people are lying and treacherous, just as our friends of Tlaxcala warned us." Malinalli says Cortés. "I fear a trap."

That very day more delegates arrive from Montezuma, and join those already there. They deliver a message from the Emperor in cold and rude terms: Montezuma instructs Cortés not come to his city, as he cannot provide sustenance there. To this they require an immediate answer, as they are in a hurry to return to Mexico.

Cortés answers these ambassadors in the most courteous manner possible as usual, telling them how surprised he is that as powerful an Emperor as Montezuma should so often change his mind. In the meantime he asks them to postpone their return until the following day, when he will give them a reply.

As soon as this meeting has ended, Cortés calls together all his officers, and orders them to be particularly on guard, as the inhabitants, no doubt have some evil plan. He then sends for the principal chief, but receives an answer that he is indisposed, and that neither he nor any other of the chiefs can come.

"The Aztecs cannot be trusted and they obviously enticed us here. This is all planned by Montezuma to rid himself of you." Malinalli warns her captain.

Cortés cannot quite bring himself to believe he was tricked and stubbornly clings to his dream of making peace with the Aztecs. He orders two priests to be brought before him, with the upmost respect, from a large temple adjoining his quarters.

Cortés begins by presenting each with a green stone which they prize. He then, in a most friendly manner, inquires what has caused the fear which has come over the chiefs, and why they no longer call upon him.

One of these priests is a superior and insists that no one fears them and he is willing to call upon the chiefs, and is certain they will come immediately.

Cortés asks him to then go and summon them and in the meantime he detains the other priest. It is not long before the chief priest returns, bringing along with him the chiefs and other nobles of the district.

Cortés questions them as to what is going on, and why they no longer bring anything to eat. Then he adds, that if his stay in their town is a burden to them, he will leave the very next morning for Mexico, to pay his respects to Montezuma.

The chiefs are so embarrassed by what Cortés says they can only stutter, but finally promise provisions, admitting they have been commanded by Montezuma to withhold supplies, and not to allow them to proceed any further on their march.

During this conference, three of the Cempoalla warriors enter, and whisper to Malinalli that they had found deep holes in the streets adjoining the quarters, which are thinly covered over with sticks and earth, so as to be imperceptible to the eye. Curious, they removed the covering and found numbers of sharply pointed short stakes, sticking up from the bottom, no doubt to wound the horses when they fell into the holes. In addition, heaps of stones have been gathered on the tops of the houses and another street is barricaded by large wooden beams. It appears preparations have been made for an attack.

At the same time eight Tlaxcalans also arrive from their quarters outside the town and report they heard the Cholulans last night sacrificed seven persons to their god of war, among them five children, in order to guarantee a promise of victory over the

Conquistadors. And also that all their goods, wives, and children have been sent out of the town.

Faced with all this information, Cortés asks his allies to return to their camp outside the city and prepare for battle on a moment's notice. Then since he needs to get detailed information on the native's plan, he asks Malinalli to question the two priests at length and bribe them with more stones.

Malinalli proves quite adept in such matters, and succeeds by means of the presents, and by reminding them, as priests and men of rank, they cannot disgrace themselves by telling lies, to disclose everything to Cortés.

The priests confess all that is planned: Montezuma has sent 20,000 warriors to Cholula, some of whom lie in wait hidden in the woods about two miles away, while another contingent are already in the city and secretly waiting in houses. All are well armed, and the balconies of the houses have been strengthened, the streets barricaded by heaps of earth and intersected by deep holes so as to render the horses useless. Some houses have even been stocked with neck-straps, ropes made of twisted hides, and long poles, to which some of the Spanish are to be bound and transported to Mexico.

But there is some small bit of good news: the priests tell Cortés that Montezuma still cannot come to a decision as to whether to kill them all or allow the Spanish to march towards his capital. He has already changed his mind several times in one day. At one time he sent orders that the Spanish are to be treated well and are permitted to travel to his city, another time he sends word that they are not.

But now his most cherished gods, Tezcatlipoca and Huitzilopochtli, have advised him to kill most of the Spanish and also the 2,000 men of Cholula. Cortés and his officers—and especially Malinalli, are to be taken prisoner to be sacrificed.

After Cortés has elicited all this information from them, he calmly presents both the priests with several beautiful cloaks, warning them to say nothing of their talk, if they did they would forfeit their lives on his return from Mexico. But Montezuma's indecision is also a two-edged sword for Cortés — to him there is still a glimmer of hope he can achieve a treaty.

That night Cortés calls a council of war, consisting of his officers and most experienced soldiers, to deliberate their next step. Opinions, as usual, are divided. Some propose that they should change the route and take the road through Huexotzinco at once. Others want to preserve the peace at any price and turn back and return to Tlaxcala.

The majority, including Malinalli and Bernal Diaz, believe the treachery of the Cholulans should not go unpunished, and that the Aztecs will only act worse if they see they can intimidate the Conquistadors. They want to make a stand here, once and for all, where provisions are plentiful, and while they have the Tlaxcalans nearby to join in the combat.

So in the end all the men agree to a plan. The soldiers are to prepare their few belongings for departure and remain vigilant all through the night. The next morning the Spanish will attack the Indians in the spacious square adjoining their quarters, which is surrounded by high walls, so they have high ground from which to unleash their firepower.

As for the ambassadors from Montezuma, Cortés plays his usual little gamesmanship and tells them, that some villains of Cholula have formed a conspiracy against him and blamed it all on their esteemed Emperor Montezuma and his ambassadors. While he cannot for a moment give credence to this, for the present he must beg them not to leave his quarters, and to break off all further discussion with the inhabitants of the town. To this end he has assigned several men to 'guard' them for their own protection. The ambassadors, of course, assure Cortés that neither Montezuma, nor they, were aware of anything about this conspiracy.

That night the Conquistadors go on high alert. Their arms are ready at all moments, the horses are saddled and bridled, strong watches are posted in various places, and one patrol follows the other, as they are sure an attack is coming by the united forces of Mexico and Cholula.

But the Conqueror still clings to the belief he can avoid a battle and secure friendly relations with the Aztecs; so he sends a fearless Malinalli out into the town on a scouting expedition. She soon meets an old woman, the wife of a chief, who takes compassion on the youth and good looks of Malinalli, and persuades her to follow her home to save her from the impending carnage that night or the following day.

The woman assures Malinalli that Montezuma has issued the most unconditional orders to this effect, and has sent an army of Aztec warriors, who are to join the Cholulans and spare none of the Spanish strangers, except those they are to take prisoners to be sent bound to Mexico. The old woman advises Malinalli to pack up her goods quickly and come and live in her house and she can have her second son for her husband.

"I am thankful indeed, good mother, for your kind warning. I would go with you this instant if I could find anyone to carry away my mantles and gold trinkets, for I have a pretty good quantity of both. Wherefore I beg of you, good mother, wait a few moments here with your son, and we will leave together during the night; for these spirits have their ears and eyes everywhere." Malinalli answers shrewdly.

The old woman believes what she says, and continues chatting with her for some time. So Malinalli questions her, as to the manner in which the Spanish are to be killed and how and when the plan had been formed? The answers which the old woman provides agree perfectly with the account of the two priests. Malinalli then asks how she has come to this knowledge which is surely a secret?

"I know all this from my husband, who is the chief of one of the quarters of this town, and who has already joined the men under his command. They are coordinating with the Aztecs and both armies will meet and cut down all the strangers. All this I have known three days ago, for my husband has been presented with a golden drum, and the three other chiefs with splendid cloaks and gold trinkets, with orders to take all the stranger's leader and his chiefs prisoner and send them to Montezuma."

"How delighted am I to learn that your son, to whom you intend to marry me, is a man of high rank! You have told me matters which were intended to be kept a secret. I will now go and pack up my things. In the meantime wait for me here, for I cannot carry all my goods alone, you and your son must assist me." Malinalli tells her, artfully concealing the real impression all this made on her.

The old woman accepts all this, and stations herself with her son awaiting her return. Malinalli then rushes back and reports on the conversation to Cortés. He now knows he can no longer deny the facts and must take action, so he goes around to all the men making sure they are fully prepared for battle.

When morning arrives, the Conquistadors are quite amused to see the air of contempt and confidence of the chiefs, the priests, and of the Cholulans in general. They appear as if they have already won and are accompanied by a large group of warriors who arrive in the square, ostensibly to join the Spanish in their march to the Aztec capital as requested by Cortés. Though the warriors of Cholula arrive at dawn, they find the Spanish ready and waiting.

A squad of Conquistadors, armed with swords and shields are stationed at the largest gate of the enclosed square. Cortés sits mounted his horse, surrounded by several men to guard him.

"How impatient these treacherous people are to get among us and satiate themselves with our flesh! But the Almighty will order things differently from what they expect!" Cortés shouts to his men when he sees how early the Cholulans have arrived. Malinalli does not bother to translate these words.

The Conqueror, seated on horseback, with Malinalli at his side translating, then faces the gathered natives and severely reprimands the chiefs and priests.

"Why do you wish to murder us all though we have not done you the smallest injury? Have we said or done anything to justify this treachery? Have we done anything more than plead with you, as we have all the tribes through whose territories we have passed, to abolish human sacrifices and abstain from eating human flesh, to commit no unnatural crimes, and to lead a better life than you have to now? I have indeed merely spoken to you about the holy religion, and certainly thereby committed no violence. So for what purpose have you collected all those long poles with the nooses and ropes in the house adjoining the temple? Why have they you barricaded the streets, dug deep holes, and fortified the tops of your houses? Why have you sent away from the town your wives, children, and all your goods?

"You can no longer conceal your treacherous plans. I am perfectly aware that large troops of warriors have secreted themselves near the town, laying in wait for us when we are on the road to Mexico. In reward for our having looked upon you as brothers, and announced what our God and our sovereign had commissioned us to reveal to you, you only wish to murder us and eat our flesh. If you intended to kill us, why not attack boldly in the open field like brave warriors, as your neighbors the Tlaxcalans had done?

"I know you have made sacrifices three nights ago to your god, that he might grant you victory over us. But all his promises are full of lies and deceit. Your gods have no power whatever over us, and your evil deeds, with all your treachery, will only come back on you."

When the chiefs, priests, and nobles hear this, all of which Malinalli most carefully interprets, they confess that all of it is true. But then swear they are not the guilty parties, as everything had been done at the instigation of Montezuma's ambassadors, in accordance with his commands.

"The Spanish laws do not allow such treachery to pass by unpunished, and now you will pay for it with the loss of your lives." Cortés answers and orders a cannon to be fired, which is the signal for the Conquistadors to attack.

There transpires then a slaughter in the enclosed square and a great number of natives are put to the sword, and some are burnt alive to prove the deceitfulness of their false gods. Then the warriors of Tlaxcala come storming out of their camp into the town, and fight courageously against the army of Cholula in the streets, taking a large portion of the city. The Tlaxcalans then wander out of control about the town taking plunder and prisoners.

The Cholulans expected that their god would come to their assistance with a miracle. They believed that by removing part of the white plaster from the temple, a strong flood of water would instantly pour out, and were therefore very conscientious in repairing any little damage that might happen to the temple, by means of chalk mixed with the blood of children, killed for this purpose. It is on this temple that the Cholulan's make their most determined stand, but as the tide soon turns in favor of the Spaniards, the natives begin to loosen the plaster off the outside, firmly believing that a deluge of water will instantly burst forth and drown the assailants. When no water floods out, and they realize their god will not save them, many commit suicide by jumping from the top of the temple.

The Spanish have their hands full and fight through the day in the area around the square as more warriors arrive from Tlaxcala. These troops commit all manner of atrocities against the Cholulans, so deeply rooted is their hatred. When he is finally able to gain control of his own situation, Cortés' compassion is aroused, and orders the Tlaxcalans to cease all further hostilities and requests them to return to their camp, leaving only the Cempoallans remaining within the town. By now over three thousand Cholulans are dead.

Soon several chiefs arrive from other districts of the town, who say they have taken no part in this treacherous conspiracy. Malinalli confirms this may have been the case, as in this large town every district had its own regiment and peculiar regulations.

These people beg Cortés to pardon them, as the real traitors have received their deserved punishment. In this prayer they are joined by the two priests, who had first revealed the plot, and the wife of the Indian chief, who was to have been Malinalli's mother-in-law.

Cortés at first is not inclined to listen to their pleadings, but after considering it for a time sends for two ambassadors of Montezuma, who are under guard. He tells them that although the whole town and all its inhabitants merit total destruction, he will nevertheless show mercy in consideration of their Emperor Montezuma, whose subjects they are. He expects in return they will give no further cause to distrust them, otherwise they will forfeit their lives.

Cortés next sends for the chiefs of the Tlaxcalans, and orders them to release the prisoners they had taken. It requires all of the Conqueror's and Malinalli's skill to persuade the Tlaxcalans to comply with this, for they maintain that the Cholulans deserve a great deal worse for the many times they had suffered from their actions. Finally though since as it is Cortés' wish, they liberate the captives, but carry off a great deal of booty, consisting of gold, cloaks, cotton, salt, and other items.

Cortés then sets about bringing a reconciliation between the two tribes—to which after many hours of discussion both sides agree, as they are equally somewhat at the mercy of the mighty Conquistadors. Malinalli is joyous at this turn of events for it shows her that her lover is really a man of peace. The Conqueror then commands the chiefs to bring all the inhabitants back into the town again, and to open the markets, assuring them that no further harm will come to them. The chiefs agree to this, but many are concerned about who will lead them so Cortés appoints a mutually agreed on chief as governor.

As soon as the town is again filled with people, and the markets open as usual, Cortés assembles the chiefs, and priests, and the principal nobles, and explains to them the nature of the holy Catholic religion, and makes clear the necessity of abolishing their idolatry and human sacrifices, and other abominations.

He tells them they live under a delusion with respect to their idols, which are nothing but evil spirits from whom they could expect nothing but false promises. They should do well to remember how these idols recently promised them the victory over him, and how all their promises went unfulfilled. They should, therefore, pull down and destroy these lying and deceitful idols. Then he requests they clear and fresh plaster one of their temples, that he might fit it for a chapel and erect a cross there.

These words seem to sink in, and they give a solemn promise to destroy their idols, but continually postpone the action. On this matter Father Olmedo sets Cortés' mind at ease, by assuring him it would be of little use if the Indians did abolish their idols, unless they receive some training of the Catholic religion and faith. He ought first to see what impression their march into Mexico would make on them. Time alone will be the best guide as to further proceedings. For the present he has done all he can do admonishing them to piety, and by erecting a cross there.

During their time in Cholula the Spanish also discover more of the infamous wooden cages, constructed of heavy timber, and filled with adult men and little boys being fattened for sacrifices. Cortés orders these diabolical cages to be torn down, and releases the prisoners. He then demands the chiefs and priests promise him, under severe threat, never again to confine human beings in that manner and for that purpose, and to totally abstain from eating human flesh.

In the meantime the Conquistador's victory over the natives of Cholula spreads like wildfire through the whole of New Spain. If the previous battles of Potonchan, Tabasco, and Tlaxcala, hadn't done enough to spread the fame of their invincible courage and fearful nature, they are now truly looked upon as gods of a superior order, from whom nothing could be kept a secret.

***

When the commanders of the troops which Montezuma had sent to lie in ambush in the immediate vicinity of Cholula learn of what has taken place there, they immediately order a return to the Aztec capital to bring the intelligence to their emperor.

Montezuma is greatly displeased at the news and demands to know how his vaunted army could have allowed this to happen.

"You had 20,000 warriors under your command and you cannot gain victory over a few hundred?" He shouts furiously at his general in charge of the battle.

"My lord, these are truly gods! They knew of everything, of all our plans before they happened. The chiefs of Cholula laid a trap for them right in the town square, but instead these white gods set it back on them and exterminated their army." The general explains.

"And what of our army? What of the 10,000 warriors you had in the city, and the other 10,000 waiting in ambush, you fool?" Cuitláhuac, Montezuma's brother, demands to know.

"I, I, felt it necessary to report back here." The general stutters.

"You retreated, you turned tail and ran from the white strangers because you fear them!" Cuitláhuac screams.

"They are too powerful..." The general attempts an excuse, but Cuitláhuac is already signaling for the palace guards, who drag him away.

Montezuma instantly orders the general and a number of his officers and men to be sacrificed to the warrior god Huitzilopochtli, that he might reveal to him whether he should prevent the strangers from marching to Mexico, or permit peaceable entrance into his capital.

The Emperor, who is a priest in his own right, spends two entire days with his high priests in rituals, bloodletting, and sacrifices. At the end of the rites he is joined by his brother and awaits word from the high priests.

The chief priest, his hair dripping with blood, stands in front of the Emperor and proclaims this is the advice of the warrior-god Huitzilopochtli, and that of the god of hell, Tezcatlipoca: They are to send ambassadors to the strange leader and apologize for the occurrence at Cholula. He is further to allow the white strangers to march into Mexico, under a glorious show of friendship. But when the white gods have entered the capital they are to deny them provisions and water, break down the bridges, trap them in, and put them all to the death, excepting the leader and his mistress. The army must attack them as one, and from all sides at once, so not one of them can escape. After the leader and his mistress are sacrificed to Huitzilopochtli, their entrails are to be thrown to the Emperor's pet serpents and tigers, which are kept in the palace, that they might be nourished by these courageous gods and enjoy superior offspring.

When Montezuma and his brother are alone, Cuitláhuac reveals he is not sure of this advice.

"Surely this white stranger is aware of your instigation in the conspiracy against him and will come here prepared to fight to the death and seize your throne. He will be on guard every moment for this trap, as is it not the very same trap the Cholulans tried and failed?"

"You may be right brother, but then what shall I do?"

"I am certain the best course is to keep this creature from the city."

While the Emperor considers his next move, several delegates arrive from Cholula with a long message from Cortés through the words of Malinalli, who together have concocted an interesting new myth.

"We have journeyed over many seas, and through far distant countries, solely for the purpose of paying our personal respects to Montezuma, the Emperor of Mexico, and of disclosing things which would prove of the greatest advantage to you. We chose the road over Cholula because your ambassadors proposed that route, and assured us that the inhabitants were your loyal subjects. We met with the best of receptions, and were well treated during the first two days of our stay there, when we discovered that a vile conspiracy had been set afoot to destroy us. Such, however, could not result in anything other than failure, as we are endowed with the faculty of knowing things beforehand, and it is utterly impossible to do anything without our knowledge." This new power of knowing their enemy's thoughts was suggested by Malinalli and quickly agreed to by Cortés, to put a little well-deserved fear and confusion into Montezuma.

"We therefore, punished a number of those who concocted that treacherous scheme, but we have at the same time, abstained from punishing all those who had taken part in it, in consideration that the Cholulans are your subjects, and from the deep veneration we entertain for your person, and the great friendship we bear you. It is regrettable that the chiefs and priests have unanimously declared that all had been done at your command, and planned by your own ambassadors. Of this we have not believed a single word, as it seemed impossible to us that so great a monarch, who always styled himself our friend, could have been complacent in such action. On the contrary, we expected from you that, in case your gods have whispered to you to treat us hostilely, you would have attacked us in the open field, although it was all the same to us whether we were to fight about in a town or in the open field, or during night or daytime, as we easily overthrew those who venture to attack us. As we are fully convinced of your friendship, and are very desirous to make your personal acquaintance, and to converse with you, we intend on marching to your capital."

When Montezuma receives this message, and learns that Cortés does not implicate him in what took place at Cholula, he begins to feel in a better position, so he fasts with his priests, and sacrifices to his gods, as he again wishes to know whether he should admit Cortés into his capital.

They pronounce in the affirmative: when the Conquistadors are here he will be able to slay them at his pleasure. His chiefs and councilors are of the same opinion, and think that if he does not admit them into the city, they might commence hostilities and call in the their allies the Tlaxcalans, the Totonaque, and other tribes who are at odds with the Aztecs. The surest way to avoid that would be to follow the wise counsel which Huitzilopochtli has given they say. Only his brother Cuitláhuac disagrees.

"These priests and councilors talk out of two mouths," he spits out in front of them, "if these white gods can read our thoughts as they say, they will certainly know what you are planning. If you invite them into your city, you are inviting trouble into your own home."

Montezuma considers what was said by the white gods concerning their friendship towards him, and the confident manner in which they expressed themselves. He is amazed at the idea that nothing could be concealed from them, and that he might attack them whenever he liked, within the city walls or in the open field, by day or by night, it was all the same to them. He thinks of their war with the Tlaxcalans, of the battles they had fought at Potonchon, Tabasco, Cingapacinga, and Cholula, and loses his spirit once again.

After changing his mind back and forth several times, he finally decides to send six of his principal courtiers with a present of gold of exquisite workmanship, and several packages of beautifully manufactured cotton stuffs.

21 Onward To Mexico

After a restful two weeks in Cholula, during which the Conqueror and the Heroine are able to indulge their passion and strengthen their feelings for each other, the Conquistadors are ready to move on to their ultimate goal: The capital of the Aztec empire.

It is obvious any further stay in Cholula would be a waste of time. All the inhabitants have returned to their homes, and the markets are again filled with goods and merchants. Peace has been established between Cholula and their neighbors the Tlaxcalans. A Catholic chapel has been constructed in one of the former temples and a cross erected, and much of the holy religion explained to the inhabitants.

Besides this, the Spanish soon discover that Montezuma has sent spies into their quarters to gain intelligence as to their future plans, and whether they really intend to travel to his capital. At the root of this spying are of course, the Aztec ambassadors, who are still in Cholula under the 'protection' of Cortés, who is using them at Malinalli's suggestion, to control that flow of information.

This works so well that on the very day set for the Conquistador's departure to the capital, six more ambassadors arrive with presents from Montezuma. When these messengers are introduced to Cortés, they touch the ground with their hands, and kiss it as their sign of respect.

"Malinche, our ruler and emperor the mighty Montezuma, sends you this present, and hopes you accept it with the same friendship he bears you and your brothers. He also desires us to express his regret for the events here at Cholula, and to assure you it would please him if you would rebuke these evil-minded and lying people more severely, since they had tried to place blame for their vile proceedings upon him and his ambassadors.

"You should then be rest assured of his friendship, and journey to his capital as soon as you are ready. Being as you are men of vast courage, Montezuma will receive you with due honors, and only regrets that, owing to the situation of his country in the midst of a lake, he will not be able to furnish your table with the food he otherwise could wish. The greatest respect will everywhere be shown you, and he also sent orders to the different townships through which you will pass to furnish you with everything you require." The ambassadors declare.

When Malinalli explains this message to Cortés, he accepts the present with every appearance of delight and embraces the ambassadors, and presents them with various articles of cut glass. All the Conquistadors congratulate themselves on this favorable turn of events, and Montezuma's invitation to visit Mexico, for their desire to see that city grows daily.

But Malinalli is both immediately suspicious and confused and points out that the Emperor is saying he cannot feed them once they get there. She warns the Conqueror that this 'invitation' is not what it seems.

"To think that the Emperor has no food is laughable. He is lying."

But Cortés, blinded by his ambition to visit the Aztec capital, only hears what he wants to hear in Montezuma's message. He replies to the ambassadors that he will be delighted to take up Montezuma's offer and asks all of them to return with his answer, but cagily requests that three of them remain with him to show the way.

When the two old chiefs of Tlaxcala learn Cortés is bent on marching to Mexico, they are very upset and join Malinalli in warning him this trip is a ploy of Montezuma's to murder them all. When they see they can't dissuade the Conqueror, they offer a force of 10,000 of their warriors, under the command of their most able generals, with a sufficient supply of provisions, to accompany him.

Cortés thanks them for this kind offer, but explains it would not be proper to enter Mexico at the head of so large an army, particularly because of the hatred between themselves and the Aztecs. Instead he requests a thousand men to transport the cannon and baggage, and clear the road before them.

While final preparations are being made to depart for the Aztec capital, the chiefs of Cempoalla weigh in and call upon Cortés to return with them to their territory. They cannot join march to Mexico, as they are quite convinced it would be the mutual destruction of them all. And further, they need to return home and see to their people and protect them against Montezuma's tax collectors.

Cortés tries to allay their fears and states he is sure no harm will befall them, for they will march in his company and who would dare to attack them? He begs of them to change their minds and remain with him, and promises them all manner of riches. But all his entreaties, including Malinalli's friendly advice (whose heart is plainly not into it), are fruitless, and they refuse to go along.

In the end Cortés cannot hold a grudge against people who have rendered such valuable service, or force them to go. So he presents several packages of the very finest cotton stuffs, given to him by the Aztecs, to be divided among them, and likewise sends his old friend the fat chief two packages for himself and his nephew Cuesco, who is also a powerful chief.

The Conqueror also sends a message to Juan de Escalante, who remains in Vera Cruz, detailing everything that happened so far, and that he is on the march to Mexico. He particularly cautions him to keep an eye on the locals of the territory, hasten the completion of the fortress, and to take the inhabitants there under his protection against the Aztecs if necessary. This letter is then given to the Cempoallans to take to Vera Cruz. And so with this final act and sincere thanks and goodbyes to the Cempoallans, the Conquistadors set out on their final push into the heart of the Aztec empire.

On the march from Cholula, Cortés does not take the dangers of the journey lightly and the Spanish enforce their usual precautions. A few cavalry are always in advance to explore the territory, and these are closely followed by a number of the best foot soldiers to assist them in case of an ambush. The cannon and muskets are kept ready loaded, and more cavalry ride three and three together on the flanks of the troops to lend immediate assistance.

On the first day they travel nine miles and arrive at a spot of a few scattered dwellings on a rising ground under the control of Huexotzinco, which is friendly with the Tlaxcalans. Here they find all the chiefs and priests of Huexotzinco assembled. They are joined by other tribes from the neighborhood of the volcano, and present Cortés with a quantity of provisions and a few trinkets of gold, begging him to consider not their small worth, but the good will with which they are given.

This group also attempts to talk Cortés out of going to the Aztec capital, warning of the vast number of warriors there and all the dangers. When they see they can't change his mind, they instruct him as to the trail to take, and that when the Spanish come to the mountain pass, they will see two broad roads, one of which leads to Chalco, the other to Tlalmanalco, both of which are subject to the Aztec empire.

The natives explain the path to Chalco is in excellent condition, and passable, and so it would be the best route to take, but that a little way further up the mountain, Aztec warriors are lying in wait to ambush the Conquistadors. They report the trail to Tlalmanalco has been made impassable by numbers of large pine trees which have been felled and thrown across the road to prevent traveling that way. They therefore advise Cortés to leave the good road, and turn into the one leading to Tlalmanalco, and they would lend a hand to clear away the trees so he can pass.

Cortés is confused by this report since he still believes Montezuma will welcome him with open arms, so how can this be?

"This Aztec Emperor is lying and deceitful, he only invites you to your own death. I beg of you my Captain, listen to these good men and turn back." Malinalli once again tries to open his eyes.

"My little goddess of grass, you worry too much. Our God almighty will protect us for doing his good work." He answers playfully with a huge smile, trying to reassure her. But the Conqueror calls a halt for a short time to consider what he has been told.

Cortés then calmly questions the Aztec ambassadors as to which of the two roads they would advise him to take, the one to Tlalmanalco, or the other to Chalco? They tell him to take the latter, because it leads to Chalco, a town of considerable size, where we he will meet with a good reception, as it is subject to Montezuma. The other road they say, is mysteriously 'blocked' by fallen trees and is very dangerous in places.

Finally wary of the Aztec's intentions and with Malinalli's advice never having been wrong so far, Cortés decides for the Tlalmanalco road. The Conquistadors march through the mountains in the closest possible order, as their Indian friends diligently work to clear away the heavy trees. When they are near the summit of the mountain, it begins to snow heavily and the ground is quickly covered. As nightfall approaches they make camp for the night in some scattered huts, which are apparently for the accommodation of native merchants. The huts are thankfully stocked with an abundance of food, and despite the severity of the weather, they post sentries as usual, and make regular patrols.

The next morning very early the Spanish continue on up the mountain, and by noon reach the summit, where they come upon the two roads exactly as described by the natives of Huexotzinco, and make their way to Tlalmanalco, where they are met with a warm reception.

Upon news of the Conquistador's arrival, large numbers of people gather from all over the territory to see the white strangers. These tribes make Cortés a present in common, consisting of a little gold, some cotton, and eight females.

"Malinche, may it please you to accept the present we bring you, and from this moment we hope you will look upon us as your friends!"

Cortés goes through his customary routine of accepting their gift with every appearance of delight, and promises to assist them whenever they might require his aid. Then as usual, he asks Father Olmedo and Malinalli to explain some of the Christian religion, and demand they abolish their idol-worship.

The natives agree that this is all very good, but these people have other more pressing concerns: namely Montezuma and his tax collectors. The Aztecs rob them of everything they possess, abuse the chastity of their wives and daughters before their eyes, and if they were pretty carry them off forcibly away to toil in slavery. They go on to complain that the whole tribe is forced to transport wood, stone, and maise, both by water and by land, to the Emperor's extensive corn plantations, while neglecting their own land.

Cortés listens intently as Malinalli translates and is very consoling regarding their situation. He promises they will certainly be relieved of this state of oppression in the future, but for now they will have to bear these hardships a little longer until he is fully able to help them.

He then requests two of them to travel with him to the spot where the two roads intersect to see for himself if there are Aztec troops stationed there. But the chiefs assure him that it is not necessary to journey there, as all the fortifications have been taken away. The Aztecs had indeed come through some six days ago, and stationed a large body of troops there to prevent his passing, but then they had been ordered to allow him to march forward and not to attack until he and his brothers are within the city, where they will kill them all.

"Believe us, you must not go to Mexico, for we know how great the strength of that city is, and what large numbers of troops are there. If you enter that city, you will all be put to death." The chiefs beg

Cortés to remain with them, and promise they would provide him with everything he might require.

"These people confirm everything we have heard: Montezuma is lying in wait to kill you and eat your heart the moment you are within his grasp." Malinalli reminds Cortés.

"Yes, it would seem that way, but this Emperor suffers from indecision and has changed his mind several times. We shall trust in God that he shall change it again!" Cortés replies, proving the only thing bigger than his ego is his courage. He is also a military man imbued with a strong practicality—since he did not personally see the Aztec warriors supposedly waiting in ambush, there is a possibility that it was all a ruse to slow him down.

The Conqueror goes on to thank the chiefs for their advice, but assures them that neither the Aztecs nor any other people have the power to deprive him and his men of life—this is in the hands of the God in whom he believes. He then asks for twenty of their men to accompany him as a show of solidarity, saying he will do his utmost for them, and demand justice; and that neither Montezuma nor his tax collectors will continue to oppress them much longer.

Just as the Conquistadors are about to continue their march, four distinguished Aztec delegates arrive, with a message from Montezuma—accompanied as usual by a present of gold and cotton.

"Malinche, our Emperor, the mighty Montezuma, sends you this present. He desires us to express his sorrow for the many hardships which you have been compelled to undergo on your tedious journey from such distant countries to behold his person. He now extends an offer to pay you a quantity of gold, silver, and jade, as tribute to you and the other gods who are with you. But, at the same time, he again demands of you not to advance any further, but to return from where you came. In exchange he promises to send this abundance of gold, silver, and jewels, to the harbor on the sea coast. There you will be presented with four loads of gold, and your companions with one each (this is estimated to be a staggering 50 pounds of gold, which in today's value would be a considerably more than one and a half million dollars). Montezuma forbids you to enter into Mexico, as all his troops are under arms to oppose you and the only access to the capital is by one narrow causeway."

"I confess I do not understand this Montezuma! He now seeks to buy us off from seeing his great city!" Cortés remarks to Malinalli when she finishes translating.

"Perhaps he is worried if you get too close you will know his thoughts: that he is frightened that you will take back his throne." She suggests. "And he continues to have second thoughts if he can defeat you, the god Quetzalcoatl, in battle."

Cortés thinks this is a brilliant deduction and he must use it to his advantage.

So as unpleasant as the message from Montezuma is, Cortés nevertheless embraces the ambassadors affectionately, and accepts the presents.

Cortés then remarks to them that he is surprised how their leader, who has proclaimed himself a friend so very many times, and is so powerful a ruler, could so often change his mind.

With respect to his offer of the gold, he is thankful for his kind intentions, as also for the presents they now brought with them, and he would certainly someday render the Emperor valuable services in return. But he is determined to speak to the mighty Montezuma face to face and pay him the respect he deserves as a visiting dignitary from a far away land.

So with this answer Cortés sends the ambassadors back to their Emperor, and continues his journey—doubly on guard and making short marches.

***

When his ambassadors quickly return from Tlalmanalco, Montezuma is joined by his two most trusted relatives, his nephew

Cacamatzin and his brother Cuitláhuac, as they learn his final attempt to buy off Cortés has failed. He can barely concentrate as he listens to the message they bring from the Conqueror:

"Montezuma must ask himself if it would be acting right after we have advanced within such a short distance of his capital, to turn back without fulfilling our mission to meet the leader of this great country? Montezuma should place himself in our position and consider, if he had sent ambassadors to a monarch of his own rank, how he would like it, if they returned home after arriving almost at his palace, without once seeing that monarch or fulfilling their commission to him? How would he receive these ambassadors when they appeared before him? Would he not look upon them as cowards and spiritless beings? Our king would not look upon us in any other light, and treat us accordingly if we returned so to his court. We now have no choice left, and we must get into his capital one way or other. In future, therefore, we beg Montezuma not send any more ambassadors with such messages.

"I, Cortés, am determined to see and speak to Montezuma himself personally, to acquaint him with the object of our mission. All we require of him is merely an audience, for the moment our stay in his capital becomes irksome to him we will leave and return to the place from where we came. With regard to the alleged scarcity of provisions, we are accustomed to content ourselves with little. We therefore, urge Montezuma to receive our visit, as we cannot possibly relinquish our purpose in seeing Mexico." The ambassadors recite.

The Emperor has no answer to this statement, on its surface it is entirely logical. Paralyzed with indecision, he turns to Cuitláhuac.

"What shall we do brother?"

"We should have wiped them out in the mountain pass as I suggested. Now they approach the very door to your palace. You dare not admit them into the city or you will surely forfeit your throne. You must destroy them now!" Cuitláhuac replies with anger—the only man in the empire that can get away with such a tone.

"I fear this person is indeed Quetzalcoatl, how else can it be explained he comes this far and shows no fear? He reads our minds, he knows our plans, he even knew to take the other route through the mountain and avoid your ambush. How do you explain that?"

Cuitláhuac smolders in anger but remains silent because he has no answer either.

"I agree. If their demands displease Montezuma, you can punish them by sending your legions of brave warriors against them." Cacamatzin advises.

Montezuma immediately announces that he agrees with his nephew.

"I am of the opinion we should welcome this god with the respect his rank would warrant. If he is indeed Quetzalcoatl then to do anything else could only result in angering him for all eternity. In any case, once he is among us we may be able to work something out and install him in some position of power." Montezuma ponders wistfully.

"I pray to our gods that you will not let the strangers into your house. They will cast you out of it and overthrow your rule. When you try to recover what you have lost, it will be too late." Cuitláhuac tries one more time to sway his brother the Emperor.

"I have decided to welcome these strangers as friends. Perhaps you should go and greet him and escort him into the city my brother. You are the only one I can trust." Montezuma tells his brother.

Cuitláhuac is aghast at this suggestion, but even he cannot refuse the Emperor directly.

"That may not be wise, this is not the time to be divided. What is this stranger falls upon my party and kills me? It would leave you alone to face him." Cuitláhuac replies.

"Ah, perhaps you are correct. But we must send someone of high rank and distinction. I think the task must then fall to you Prince Cacamatzin."

22 The Conqueror Arrives

So Montezuma dispatches his nephew Cacamatzin, a prince in his own right, with great pomp and ceremony, to bid Cortés welcome.

News of this prince's approach is brought in by scouts, who send a message to Cortés that a great number of Aztecs are advancing, arrayed in their most splendid attire. It is still early in the day, just as the Conquistadors are about to break camp, so Cortés orders a halt, until he can learn the purpose of this visit.

First come four distinguished persons, who make signs of profound respect, and announce that Cacamatzin, prince of Tezcuco, and nephew to Montezuma, is approaching, and they beg Cortés to await his arrival. It is indeed not long before this prince arrives in splendor and magnificence as the Conquistadors have not seen until now, in fact many of the Spanish soldiers think surely this man must be Montezuma!

Cacamatzin is seated in a beautiful sedan, decorated with silver, green feathers, and branches made of gold, from which hang numbers of precious stones. This sedan is carried on the shoulders of eight distinguished chiefs who have their own townships. When the procession arrives in front of Cortés, they assist the prince out of the sedan, and sweep clean every inch of ground before him, and then introduce him to the Conqueror.

"Malinche, I and these chiefs have come here to wait upon you, and to provide all those things you and your companions may require, and to conduct you to the quarters we have prepared for you in our city. All this is done at the command of our Emperor, the powerful Montezuma." Cacamatzin addresses Cortés.

When Cortés and his men contemplate the splendor and majesty of the nephew, they cannot help remarking to each other, what must the power and majesty of the mighty Montezuma himself be like!

After Cacamatzin is done speaking, Cortés embraces him and plays diplomat, complimenting the prince and the nobles around him, and presents them with polished stones and blue glass beads. After thanking the prince for all the attention, he immediately asks what day he can thank Montezuma in person?

Cacamatzin assures Cortés that he is to escort his party there now and the procession continues, but with all the chiefs and their entourage and the inhabitants of the surrounding area joining in, they can scarcely move along in the vast crowds of people. Indeed, it is not until the next morning they reach the broad high road of Iztapalapan, a town of considerable size, built half in the water and half on dry land.

It is from this vantage point the Spanish are able for the first time to view the numbers of towns and villages built in the lake, and the still greater number of large towns on the mainland, with a level causeway running in a straight line into the Aztec capital of Tenochtitlan. The Conquistadors are astonished at the view as the temples, towers, and houses of the town, all built of massive stone and lime, rise up so high, majestic, and splendid out of the midst of the lake, they resemble the fairy castles they read of as children. Indeed, many of the men think it is all a dream.

Malinalli grows concerned with the Conquistadors as it seems they are blinded by the sights of the Empire.

"My Captain, you must be on guard now more than ever. Do not let these great sights and symbols of power lull you into thinking you have nothing to fear from these people." She tells him.

Cortés reluctantly tears himself away from the magnificent view, knowing she is right, but Almighty God he has finally made it!

As they approach Iztapalapan, two more princes come out with great ceremony to welcome Cortés and both are close relatives of Montezuma. Cortés thanks them through Malinalli and the three princes cannot help but notice this beautiful girl, always whispering into the white stranger's ear, and speaking for him.

"His woman holds herself like one of us, a princess. How can this be?" One prince remarks.

"She is called Malintzin and we believe she is one of us." Cacamatzin informs them. "But we do not know from where she came."

"This Malintzin has allied herself with a god! She wields much power then, she is one to watch carefully." The other prince suggests.

"Yes, she is dangerous. We have heard all through this god's travels she speaks for him. She indeed may be the tool by which the white stranger can know our thoughts, so tread carefully around her." Cacamatzin advises the others.

The three princes lead Cortés and his party into the town of Iztapalapan, where they are quartered in what can only be described as palaces of large dimensions, surrounded by spacious courts, and built of hewn stone, cedar and other sweet-scented wood. All the rooms are hung round with cotton cloths to reduce the heat of the sun.

After settling in, the Spaniards visit the astonishing adjoining gardens, walking about enjoying the numbers of trees, the rose bushes, the different flower beds, and the fruit trees; which give off delightful fragrances. There is likewise a fountain of sweet water, which is connected to the lake by means of a small canal, constructed of stone of various colors, and decorated with numerous figures, and wide enough to hold the largest canoes. In this basin various kinds of water-fowls are swimming about. Everything is so charming and beautiful that they are overwhelmed. Bernal Diaz remarks he doesn't believe a country was ever discovered which was equal in splendor to this.

While his men roam gleefully, Cortés and Malinalli partake in the many delights of their private quarters, including a bath, which she insists they use to wash off the dirt of the road before meeting the Emperor. But the Conqueror is so happy it is not long before he must indulge himself in other delights: his lovely mistress. She has never looked more beautiful, lying naked in the sun drenched pool. Cortés thinks he is surely one of the luckiest men alive.

The following morning the Conquistadors leave Iztapalapan accompanied by all princes and chiefs on their final leg to the Aztec capital of Tenochtitlan. The road is eight paces wide, and perfectly straight in a line to the capital.

As wide as the road is, it is still much too narrow to hold the vast crowds of people who continually arrive from different parts to gaze upon the strangers, and the procession can scarcely move along. Besides this, the tops of all the temples and towers are crowded, and the lake is completely covered with canoes filled with natives, all clamoring for a glimpse of the strange persons and horses.

As the Conquistadors gaze upon all this majesty they doubt whether all that they behold is even real. A series of large towns stretch along the banks of the lake, out of which still larger ones rose magnificently above the waters; innumerable canoes are plying the lake waters, at regular distances they pass over new bridges; and in the distance lies the great city of Tenochtitlan in all its splendor.

Passing through these innumerable crowds of human beings, are a mere handful of men, 450 in all, their minds now full of the warnings from the natives of Huexotzinco, Tlaxcala, and Tlalmanalco, not to expose their lives to the treachery of the Aztecs. Bernal Diaz takes a moment to ask himself whether any men in this world ever ventured so bold a stroke as this?

When they arrive at an intersection of two causeways they are met by a number of chiefs and distinguished nobles, all attired in their most splendid garments. They explain they have been dispatched by Montezuma to meet and welcome them in his name; and in token of peace they touch the ground with their hands and kiss it.

Here Cortés halts for a few minutes, while the princes rush in advance to meet Montezuma, who is slowly approaching, surrounded by other nobles and chiefs of the Empire, and seated in a sedan of uncommon magnificence. Though a fairly young man, the Emperor is helped out his sedan by the chiefs who support him under the arms, and hold over his head a canopy decorated with green feathers, gold, silver, jade stones, and pearls.

Montezuma himself, is sumptuously attired and even his sandals are richly set with jewels, and have soles made of solid gold. Other nobles go before him, and spread cotton cloths on the ground that his feet might not touch the bare earth. Not one of these ever looks the Emperor in the face, everyone stands with eyes downcast.

23 The Conqueror, The Heroine, and The Emperor

The circle of fate has finally joined and the three powerful characters are aligned in the same place and moment in time: Montezuma, Malinalli, and Cortés. Yet none of them are aware of their ultimate effect on each other.

The Aztec nobles, chiefs, and officials looking on document the Conquistadors' arrival:

'Four stags (horses) came in front like leaders. They prance, turn, look backwards, then from side to side. Then come dogs, their noses to the ground. At the very front, there is only the banner. The bearer carries it on his shoulders. He waves it from side to side. Following him are those with unsheathed swords shining and glittering. They carry their shields on their shoulders. Now come stags with riders on their backs These riders wear cotton armor, carry shields covered with leather. Swords hang from the necks of the animals. Then come bowmen, musketeers and finally their native allies.'

When Montezuma approaches, Cortés alights from his horse and advances to meet him out of respect. The Emperor is about forty years old, of good height, well proportioned and toned, and though of the usual native complexion he is not very dark. He wears his hair just over his ears, and has a short black beard, well-shaped and thin. His face is rather long and cheerful, he has fine eyes which can express friendliness or seriousness.

Montezuma bids Cortés welcome, who replies in turn through Malinalli, that he hopes his majesty is in good health. But Malinalli has a little fun with the Emperor, and asks instead:

"Are you Montezuma? Are you the king? Is it true that you are the king, Montezuma?" Acting as if she and Cortés don't know who he is.

Malinalli is in fact in the pivotal position here: She is the only one who understands both sides of the conversation. The Spanish know what they hear Cortés say, and the Aztecs know what they hear Montezuma say, but Malinalli can say anything she wants and neither man would know the difference.

"Yes, I am Montezuma." The Emperor replies, taking the question seriously—and doesn't fail to notice the woman is staring directly at him!

Malinalli for her part is completely unafraid of the mighty Emperor, and purposely looks him in eye defiantly as her form of retribution for the things that have gone on under his rule.

Her action nearly unhinges the Emperor, as he and the Conqueror size each other up.

The Conqueror for his part is thrilled to have made it finally! All around him is magnificence he could never have imagined, and at last he is face to face with the most powerful and feared ruler of New Spain. Cortés then displays a necklace of precious stones, of the most beautiful colors and shapes, strung together with gold wire, that he has been saving for just such an occasion, and places it about the neck of Montezuma. The Conqueror then moves to embrace the Emperor, but his attendant chiefs and princes restrain his arms, as touching the ruler is improper.

So Cortés asks Malinalli to tell the Emperor how he congratulates himself on his good fortune of seeing such a powerful ruler face to face, and of the honor he has bestowed him by coming out to meet them himself.

Montezuma listens absentmindedly, as all he can think of right then is if this white stranger is really a god. He certainly looks the part of Quetzalcoatl: white skin and beard, and he even has a feather in his hat! Around him are his other spirits wearing the shiny metal helmets portrayed in many images of Feathered Serpent. And then there is this damnable woman who refuses to look down as she speaks to him, but indeed stares him in the eye unflinchingly! These strangers are so bold! Such a paltry few, yet they bring themselves into the midst of his Empire, as if they fear nothing, as if they are invincible!

Disturbed by these two powerful personalities, Montezuma answers:

"Our lord, you are weary, the journey has tired you, but now you have arrived on the earth. You have come to your city, Mexico. You have come here to sit on your throne, to sit under its canopy."

"Montezuma thinks you are the god of the prophecy." Malinalli tells Cortés straight out. "He believes you are Quetzalcoatl, the Feathered Serpent, come to take back your throne, his throne."

Now that he is actually in the presence of the Aztec Emperor, the Conqueror is horrified that he should be mistaken for a pagan god.

"No, no, you must tell him I am not a god, but we believe in the one true God! And we have come here to teach him." He tells Malinalli.

"I do not believe that is wise, my Captain. As long as Montezuma thinks you are the god Quetzalcoatl, he will not dare move against us."

While Cortés thinks this over, she instead makes some trivial remarks of thanks. So the Emperor, anxious to gather his own thoughts, takes his leave and orders two of his princes to escort the Conquistadors to their quarters, and returns to the city, accompanied by his brother Cuitláhuac.

As the Conquistadors proceed onward, the lay of the land of Mexico is before them. It is in the form of a circle, surrounded on all sides by lofty and rugged mountains, its floor comprises an area of about 200 miles in circumference, including two lakes, that encompass nearly the whole valley. One of these lakes contains fresh and the other, which is the larger of the two, salt water. On one side of the lakes, in the middle of the valley, a swell of hills divides them from one another, through which runs a narrow strait. This strait is about a 100 yards wide, and connects the two lakes. The salt lake rises and falls like the sea; during the time of high water it pours into the other lake, when the tide has ebbed, the water runs from the fresh into the salt lake.

This great city of Tenochtitlan is situated in the salt lake, which is six miles across. There are four avenues into the city, all of which are formed by artificial causeways, eight feet in width. The city is as large as Seville. Its principal streets are very wide and straight; some of these are water, and are navigated by canoes. All the streets at intervals have openings through which the water flows, crossing from one street to another. At these openings, some of which are very wide, there are also bridges, composed of large pieces of timber, well built and of great strength, wide enough that ten horses can cross abreast.

As the Spanish enter into the city, they see many public squares, in which are situated the markets. There is one square twice as large as that of the city of Seville, surrounded by porticoes, where more than sixty thousand people gather daily to buy and sell all kinds of merchandise and food, as well as jewels of gold and silver, lead, brass, copper, tin, precious stones, bones, shells, snails, and feathers. There are also for sale stone, bricks, and timber.

Another part of the market has game, where every variety of bird in the country are sold: fowls, partridges, quails, wild ducks, turtledoves, pigeons, parrots, sparrows, eagles, hawks, owls, and kestrels. They even sell the skins of some birds of prey, with their feathers, head, beak, and claws. There are also rabbits, deer, and little dogs like the Chihuahua, which are raised for eating. Another street has herbs, where may be obtained all sorts of roots and medicinal herbs that the country affords. There are apothecaries' shops, where prepared medicines, liquids, ointments, and plasters are sold. Barber shops, where they wash and shave the head; and restaurants that furnish food and drink. There are laborers for carrying burdens. Wood and coal are seen in abundance, and braziers of earthenware for burning coals; mats of various kinds for beds, others of a lighter sort for seats, and for halls and bedrooms.

All manner of vegetables are available, especially onions, leeks, garlic, watercress, sorrel, and artichokes; and fruits of numerous descriptions, including cherries and plums. Honey and wax from bees, and sweetener from the stalks of maize, which is as sweet as the sugar-cane; and wine made from the plant called maguey, is for sale.

Malinalli takes special notice of the different kinds of cotton thread of all colors displayed for sale in another quarter of the market, along with all varieties of cotton and deerskins in colors as numerous as can be found in Spain.

There are earthen-ware pots of a large size and excellent quality; large and small jars, jugs, pots, bricks, and endless variety of vessels, all made of fine clay, and all or most of them glazed and painted. Maize, or Indian corn, both on the ear and in the form of bread; pâté of birds and fish; great quantities of fish: fresh, salt, cooked and uncooked. The eggs of hens, geese, and of all the other birds in great abundance, and even cakes made of these eggs.

The Spanish learn that each kind of merchandise is sold in an assigned street or quarter exclusively, and thus order is preserved. They sell everything by number or measure and several inspectors roam the market to insure the measure is correct and no one is cheated. There is even a building in the great square that is used as a courthouse, where ten magistrates, sit and decide all controversies that arise in the market, and order violators to be punished.

The Conquistadors are soon led to a large building where there is room enough for them all, and which had been occupied by Montezuma's father when he was alive. This palace contains rooms big enough for one hundred and fifty Spaniards to sleep, each in a separate bed. The apartments and halls are very spacious and every inch is remarkably clean, the floors are covered with mats, and the walls are hung with tapestry of cotton decorated with feathers, and in every room incense burns, giving off a delightful smell. Near this building there are important temples, and they are told this place had been purposely selected because they were deemed teules, or spirits, and as such should dwell among their own kind.

When they arrive in the great courtyard adjoining this palace, Montezuma comes up to Cortés, and, taking him by the hand, escorts him personally into the apartments where he was to stay, which have been beautifully decorated after the fashion of the country. The Emperor then places about his neck a necklace of gold with figures all representing crabs. Cortés thanks Montezuma profusely for so much kindness.

"Malinche, you and your brothers must now do as if you were at home, and take some rest after the fatigues of the journey." Montezuma tells him and then returns to his own palace, which is located nearby.

So the Conquistadors settle in, placing their cannon in strategic positions, and made sure that their cavalry, as well as the infantry, be ready at a moment's notice. They then are invited to sit down to a plentiful and sumptuous meal.

Later Montezuma, accompanied by a number of nobles, generals, and all his relations including his brother Prince Cuitláhuac, pay the Spanish a visit. Cortés, being informed of his approach, immediately gets up to receive him. Montezuma takes him by the hand and leads him to a pair of beautifully ornate chairs, inlaid with gold, which slaves have brought in, and invites Cortés to sit with him. Everyone else, including Malinalli, who stays by the Conqueror's side at all times and of course is translating for both men, remains standing.

Montezuma begins by expressing his delight to entertain in his empire such courageous warriors as Cortés and his brothers. Then he goes on to say:

"This was foretold by the kings who governed our city, and now it has taken place. You have come back to us; you have come down from the sky. You have graciously come on earth, you have graciously approached your water, your high place of Mexico, you have come down to your mat, your throne, which I have briefly kept for you. You have graciously arrived, you have known pain, you have known weariness, now come on earth, take your rest, enter into your palace, rest your limbs; may our lords come on earth. Rest now, and take possession of your royal houses. Welcome to your land, my lord." Malinalli translates.

The Emperor would like nothing better than to question her about Cortés, but is stymied by the possibility that the stranger will read his thoughts and know he is going behind his back. Besides, he cannot bring himself to speak directly to this impertinent young girl, who refuses to show him respect.

"Montezuma firmly believes you are Quetzalcoatl of the prophecy." Malinalli tells Cortés again.

Cortés is completely torn by this idea. On the one hand he knows she is right and abhors giving up such a strategic advantage; but on the other it is almost certainly blasphemy to prolong this idea he is a pagan idol. In the end he gives a speech for the benefit of his men and doesn't press Malinalli one way or the other. Let the stones fall where they may.

"We indeed came from the rising of the sun, and are servants and subjects of a powerful monarch, called Don Carlos. Our monarch had received intelligence of Montezuma, and of his great power, and had expressly sent us to his country to beg of him and his subjects to become converts to the Christian faith, for the salvation of their souls; and that we only adored one true God, as he had previously, in some degree, explained on the downs to his ambassadors Teuthlille, Cuitalpitoc, and Quintalbor, all of which, however, would be more fully explained to him at some future period." Cortés says out loud but the erstwhile Malinalli says something different to Montezuma:

"We indeed come from the rising of the sun to beg of Montezuma and his subjects to become converts to the Christian faith, for the salvation of their souls. We only adore one true God, as we have previously explained to your ambassadors Teuthlille, Cuitalpitoc, and Quintalbor. We therefore demand that you order the abolishment of human sacrifice as it is abhorrent to our belief."

Montezuma doesn't quite know what to make of this. Has Quetzalcoatl some new ritual or ceremony they call 'Christian faith"? In any case, as a high priest himself and having been thoroughly educated in the gods, he is aware that the Feathered Serpent did not demand blood sacrifices as does Huitzilopochtli, the Hummingbird Wizard.

"Tell Montezuma that we are his friends. There is nothing to fear. We have wanted to see him for a long time. And now we have seen him and heard his words. We have to come to your house in Mexico as friends.. " Cortés tells Malinalli to say.

Montezuma then presents various kinds of valuable gold trinkets to Cortés, and three packages of cotton stuffs, splendidly interwoven with feathers to each officer, and to every soldier two similar packages.

He then inquires, after the presents had been distributed, whether they are all brothers, and subjects of the great emperor? He also is trying to find out who Malinalli is in a roundabout way. To which Cortés replies yes, that they are all united in love and friendship towards each other—a vague enough statement that Malinalli translates as is.

Montezuma, seeing he is not going to glean much information, orders his personal steward to provide the necessary provisions, consisting of maise, fowls, and fruits, and also grass for the horses. He also instructs women provided to grind our corn with stones, and bake the bread. After which the Emperor courteously takes his leave with Cortés and all of his officers escorting him to the door.

The Conqueror then issues strict orders that no one is to leave these palace grounds until he can determine the actual situation.

***

Montezuma is relieved to be back in his palace chambers, away from the strange god and his teules, and especially from that defiant woman, who acts as though she wields great power.

Cuitláhuac soon joins him to discuss the day's events and develop some strategy.

"You looked upon him brother, what is your conclusion?" Cuitláhuac asks.

"As did you! Surely it is him: Quetzalcoatl. How can there be another answer?"

"I saw no magical powers of a god." Cuitláhuac replies sarcastically.

Montezuma angrily pulls out a tile with an image of Quetzalcoatl and holds it up to his brother.

"Do you see the light skin, the beard, the unique hat with a feather? You are aware this is the year of One Reed? This god is undefeated, he has vanquished many of our enemies and our allies! He comes boldly into our capital, the heart of the Empire with a few hundred warriors! How else can you explain all this brother?"

"It is difficult for me to believe this smiling fool is the Feathered Serpent."

"Pray that he cannot read your thoughts, brother!" Montezuma warns. "He smiles to disarm us."

Cuitláhuac sees he is about to drive his brother over the edge and wisely holds his tongue to let the situation cool.

"And what of that woman they call Malintzin? She dares to look me in the eye, as if my rank of Emperor means nothing to her! Yet I know she is one of us, a Mexica, an Aztec." Montezuma is not done venting his anger at a situation he cannot control.

"She obviously shares his bed, you can see it in their eyes. No doubt this Malintzin knows if the stranger Cortés is a mortal or a god."

Cuitláhuac speculates.

24 Worlds Collide

Across the way at the nearby palace Cortés is struggling for answers too.

"Marina, I cannot in good faith allow Emperor Montezuma to continue to think I am a god. We came here in the name of God, to bring these people the Christian faith. I must set him straight."

Malinalli explains to Cortés the entire legend of Quetzalcoatl, how he was portrayed, and the prophecy of his return.

"As long as Montezuma believes you are Quetzalcoatl, he is obligated to turn over his throne to you. Once you have attained that, you can accomplish everything." She suggests.

"I cannot continue this deceit, I cannot lie, it is against our religion. Are you with me on this Marina?"

"I am your woman, you are my Captain; of course I stand with you."

The next day Cortés is determined to visit Montezuma in his own palace. He respectfully first sends word through Malinalli to one of the guards to inquire after the Emperor's health, and request an audience. When this request is granted, the Conqueror takes with him four of his principal officers, namely, Alvarado, Leon, Ordas, and Sandoval, and five soldiers, of which Bernal Diaz is one, and of course Malinalli.

Montezuma's palace has twenty doors, which open into the large square and into the principal streets of the city. It has three large courts, and in one of them is a pool, supplied with water by the aqueduct of Chapultepec. The palace contains a number of halls, and a hundred rooms twenty-five feet long and as many wide, each provided with a bath. Everything is built of stone and lime. The walls are covered with beautiful stones, marble, jasper, porphyry, and a block stone, which is highly polished to a mirror finish. There is also white stone, almost transparent. All the woodwork is made of white cedar, palm, cypress, pine, and other fine woods, adorned with beautiful carved-work. One of the rooms, which is one hundred and fifty feet long and fifty wide, serves as Montezuma's chapel, and is covered with plates of gold and silver almost the thickness of a finger, and decorated with innumerable emeralds, rubies, topaz, and other precious stones.

When they arrive Montezuma gets up to greet them, solely attended by his nephew Cacamatzin, as the other nobles are not allowed to enter his private living quarters. Montezuma shows Cortés to an elevated seat, placed at his right hand. The rest are seated in chairs which are brought in for them. Cortés then addresses Montezuma at considerable length through Malinalli.

"All our wishes are now fulfilled, as we have reached the end of our journey, and obeyed the commands of our great emperor. There only now remains to reveal to you the commandments of our God. We are Christians, believing in one true God only, Jesus Christ, who suffered and died for our salvation. We pray to the cross as an emblem of that cross on which our Lord and Savior was crucified. By his death the whole human race was saved. He rose on the third day, and was received into heaven. By him, heaven, earth, and sea, and every living creature was formed and nothing existed but by his divine will.

"Those figures, which you consider as gods, are not gods, but devils, which are evil spirits. It is very evident how powerless they are, since in all those places where we have planted the cross, those gods no longer make their appearance. Of this your ambassadors are fully convinced, and you will also, in the course of time, be convinced of this truth."

Then Cortés intelligently explains through Malinalli how the world was created, how all people were brothers, and sons of one father and mother, called Adam and Eve; and how grieved our emperor was to think that so many human souls should be lost, and sent to hell by those false idols, where they would be tormented by everlasting fire. For this reason he had sent him here to put an end to so much misery, and to urge the inhabitants of this country no longer to adore such gods, nor sacrifice human beings to them and also to abstain from kidnapping and committing unnatural offences. In a very short time his emperor will send men of great piety and virtue, who will explain these things more fully. Of all this he is merely the first messenger, and could only beg the Emperor to support him in his mission, and assist him in its completion.

Malinalli attempts to translate this word for word but some of the Spanish words do not have exact corresponding meanings in the Nahuatl language; and besides she doesn't know the political structure of Europe anyway. As a result there is confusion over the person Cortés calls the 'emperor', and Montezuma assumes Cortés is the 'emperor' since he is clearly in command.

"Malinche! What you have just been telling me of your God has, indeed, been mentioned to me before by my servants, to whom you made similar disclosures upon your arrival off the coast. Neither am I ignorant of what you have stated concerning the cross and everything else in the towns you passed through. We maintained our silence, as the gods we adore were adored in bygone ages by our ancestors. We have for all time acknowledged them as good deities, in the same way as you have yours. Therefore let us talk no further on this subject." Montezuma replies, before going on.

"Respecting the creation of the world, we likewise believe it was created many ages ago. We likewise believe that you are those people whom our ancestors prophesied would come from the rising of the sun, and I feel myself indebted to you, and to whom I will present a present of the most valuable things I possess. It is now two years ago that I received the first intelligence of strangers by some vessels which appeared off my coast belonging to your people, the people on board of which likewise called themselves subjects of a great emperor. Tell me, now, do you really all belong to the same people?" The Emperor once again demands to know.

Cortés assures him that they are all servants of the same great emperor, and that those ships were sent out in advance to explore the seas and the harbors, and to make the necessary preparations for his present expedition.

Montezuma remarks that even back then he was very curious to see these visitors, and had intended to pay them great honors. But now the gods have fulfilled his greatest wishes, and new visitors inhabit his palace, which you should look upon as your own, and where you can rest from your fatigues, and enjoy yourselves, and not want for anything.

Then the Emperor apologizes, that although he had sent word not to visit his capital, he had done so with great reluctance. He had been forced to act so on account of his subjects, who stood in great awe of you, and believed that you whirled fire and lightning around you, and killed numbers of men with your horses; that you were wild and unruly teules, and like nonsense.

"Now that I have met you, and convinced myself that you are made of flesh and bone, and men of great understanding, with great courage, I have an even a more elevated opinion of you than previously, and am ready to share all I possess with you." Montezuma says, but this is really all a fishing expedition—he wants Cortés to confirm straight out he is made of flesh and bone.

Upon this, Cortés assures him that he felt vastly indebted to him for the very kind feelings—which Malinalli translates, purposely not taking the bait and thereby avoiding the unstated question.

So Montezuma continues in a more humorous style.

"I am perfectly well aware, Malinche, what the people of Tlaxcala, with whom you are so closely allied, have been telling you respecting myself. They have made you believe that I am some evil spirit, and that my palaces are filled with gold, silver, and jewels. I do not think, for an instant, that reasonable men as you are can put any faith in all their talk, but that you look upon all this as nonsense. Besides which, you can now convince yourself, Malinche, that I am made of flesh and bone as you are, and that my palaces are built of stone, lime, and wood. I am, to be sure, a powerful monarch. It is likewise true that I have inherited vast treasures from my ancestors, but with regard to anything else they may have told you respecting me, it is all nonsense. You must just think of that as I think of the lightning and burning flames which you are said to whirl about in all directions." He says with a smile, but the Emperor is still fishing: he wants Cortés to agree that he is also flesh like him, and that he does not possess weapons that shoot fire. And also trying at the same time to dispel any notion he has unlimited treasures of gold.

"We knew, from old experience, that enemies neither tell the truth nor speak well of each other. We had, however, long ago convinced ourselves that there was not another such a noble-minded and illustrious emperor as yourself in this quarter of the world, and that the great idea our emperor had formed of you is well founded." Cortés answers, likewise laughingly. While he has not caught on to the game, he is back to his usual cajoling and flattery, since no one in Spain had ever heard of Montezuma up to now.

During this conversation, Montezuma instructs his nephew to order his house-steward to bring in some gold trinkets and ten packages of fine stuffs, which he divides among Cortés and the four officers who are present. The five soldiers each receive two gold neck chains and two packages of cotton garments. The gifts are not extremely valuable—just enough not to be insulting, but not so much that the Spanish think he has much more.

As it is already past noon, Cortés fears that any longer stay might be burdensome to the Emperor.

"We are daily becoming more and more indebted to your majesty for so many kindnesses; at present it is time to think of dinner." He says, and the Spanish take their leave.

Over the next few days Malinalli uses her looks and charm (and not to mention people's fear of her) to gather much information about the Emperor and the daily routines at the palace.

In the halls adjoining his private apartments there is always a guard of 2,000 men of quality, who serve both as guards and servants, and with whom he never has any conversation unless to give them orders or to receive some intelligence from them. Everything that is communicated to him is to be said in few words, the eyes of the speaker must always be cast down, and when leaving they must walk backwards out of the room.

Montezuma is particularly clean and takes a bath at least every evening, and never wears the same garment twice. Further, no person is permitted to dress in attire on an equal or better level than the Emperor in his presence, and frequently anyone visiting him had to change to more average garments. Besides a number of concubines, who are all daughters of nobility, he has two legitimate wives of royalty he only visits secretly without any one daring to observe it, except his most personal servants.

This penchant for intense privacy extends to his meals which he almost always eats alone. Montezuma insists that a wide variety of food be prepared, which are placed pans of porcelain filled with fire to keep them warm, from which he can chose. Four pretty young women acting as servants hover with pitchers filled with water to wash his hands in and then they present him with towels to dry them. Two other women bring him maise-bread baked with eggs and Montezuma's favorite drink is a kind of liquor made from cacao, or chocolate.

Before Montezuma begins his dinner, a wooden screen, gilt with gold, is placed before him, so that no one can see him eating, and the young women stand at a distance. Occasionally elders, counselors of high rank, are admitted to his table to discuss important matters. It is considered a mark of great favor if the Emperor offers them some of his food, but they are required to eat it standing, without daring to look at him full in the face.

Sometimes during dinner time, he would have ugly native humpbacked dwarfs, who act as clowns and perform antics for his amusement. Often there would also be jesters and singers and dancers, who if they especially amused the Emperor would be rewarded with his leftover food and pitchers of cacao liquor.

After the main meal, the young women bring in small cakes, as white as snow, made of eggs. They then present him with a beautifully painted and gilt tube, which is filled with liquid amber, and a dried leaves of a plant the Indians call tobacco. After the dinner has been cleared away and the singing and dancing done, the tube is lighted, and the Emperor takes the smoke into his mouth, which after a while relaxes him so he can fall asleep.

Only after Montezuma has dined, is dinner then served up for the men on duty and the other officers of his household, which number in the thousands. Next his personal servant women dine, and then the numerous butlers, house-stewards, treasurers, cooks, and managers of the palace.

While the Conquistadors are not permitted to leave their palace and go into the city, they are free to roam the extensive grounds. They wander a variety of aviaries, home to every species of bird, from the largest known eagles and hawks to the little sparrows, in their full splendor of plumage. Here also can be seen the birds, which resemble jays and the natives call quetzals, from which the Aztecs take the green-colored feathers which they use for many decorations.

There are vast numbers of parrots, of every variety, and geese of the richest plumage, which are periodically stripped of their feathers, in order that new ones might grow in their place. All these birds have places to breed, and are under the care of several natives of both sexes, who keep the nests clean, feed them, and set the birds for breeding. In the courtyard belonging to this building, there is also a large pool of fresh water, in which various water fowls and flamingos live.

The palace grounds also contain many gardens for the culture of flowers, trees, and vegetables. These gardens are irrigated by a series of baths, wells, basins, and ponds, constructed of stonework, and full of clear fresh water, which regularly ebbs and flows. The gardens are enlivened by endless varieties of small birds, which sing among the trees. All this is maintained by a large body of gardeners.

After having been in the capital for four days already, but stuck in the palace, Cortés is anxious to tour the city. So he sends Malinalli to Montezuma, to request his permission to leave the palace and see the sights of Tenochtitlan. Perhaps sensing that the Emperor might try something with her, he asks Geronimo Aguilar and one of his pages named Orteguilla, who is trying to learn the Mexican language, to accompany her.

***

Cortés' instinct in not sending Malinalli alone proves intuitive, for when Montezuma received notice she was coming, he had indeed looked forward to questioning her alone and asked Cacamatzin and Cuitláhuac to join him. He does this mostly so he doesn't have to speak to her directly since he abhors her haughty attitude.

The Emperor receives them in his throne room and is frustrated to see the other two. While he and his nephew and brother remain seated, he does not bother to bring in more chairs, so the three are forced to stand. While this gesture is a puny victory over the defiant Malinalli in the Emperor's eyes, it does not bother her in the least, she is used to standing. For her small revenge, she looks him straight in his eyes again.

"My Captain desires to visit the city and see the markets and all the wonders it has to offer, and therefore out of respect requests your permission in this matter." Her words are chosen very carefully, insinuating that Cortés has the power to do anything he wants and only asks permission as a favor to the Emperor.

This is not lost on the clever Cuitláhuac, who unlike his brother, has no problem conversing with Malinalli directly.

"What is your chief's intention here?" He asks bluntly, not meaning the tour at all, but as to why Cortés has come to Mexico.

"To end the murder of the people to the blood thirsty gods!" She replies instantly.

"Because he is Quetzalcoatl?" Cuitláhuac fires back.

"Because it is right!" She avoids the question.

At this point, while Aguilar doesn't understand what is being said, he has been among the natives long enough to know that the Emperor and his princes are becoming upset. For his part Orteguilla knows just enough simple Nāhuatl to make himself understood, but he too knows it is not going well.

"Can someone else speak?" Montezuma then asks, looking at the two men, one old and one very young, with Malinalli.

Only Orteguilla understands the question but is terrified at the thought of speaking to the Emperor.

"Ah, sir, my lord..." He stutters, not even knowing how to address Montezuma. Then he mumbles that Cortés wants to visit the city but only knows a few words, including 'temple'.

"The temple! Why does he desire to visit our temple?" Montezuma asks suspiciously.

"You seek to pick on a girl and a young boy. Is this the mighty Montezuma of which we have heard so much about?" Malinalli tries to deflect the focus from Orteguilla.

This enrages the Emperor, but he manages to keep his temper in check.

"You will show some respect woman!" He tells her coldly.

"You are doomed..." Malinalli begins to threaten. Aguilar—alarmed at the heightening tension, touches her arm.

"Doña Marina, please. We must not let this endanger our mission." He tells her quietly.

"Very well. My Captain respectfully asks permission to visit your esteemed city." She tries again.

"This request is granted so that your chief may partake of the splendor and power of the Empire, but we shall accompany and escort your party lest you commit some outrage to one or other of the gods." Montezuma tells them, and then dismisses Malinalli and her companions.

"We should crush them now!" Cuitláhuac seethes. "Kill them all and sacrifice the fake god and his woman to Huitzilopochtli while you have them in your grasp. To pander to them is madness."

But Montezuma still is not sure.

***

Cortés, intent on seeing the sights, has no problem with the royal escort. Besides, he thinks he is making good progress with Montezuma, and believes they will form a peace agreement and have rich trade. So a large group of the Conquistadors with some cavalry, set out for the market where they are met by a number of chiefs.

The Spanish are astonished at the vast numbers of people, the profusion of merchandise, and at the order that exists throughout this immense market. The chiefs who accompany them point out the smallest details, and give full explanations of everything. Each type of merchandise has a specific spot for its sale. There are places in the market for the sale of gold and silver wares, of jewels, of cloths interwoven with feathers, and of other manufactured goods.

In another part are the skins of tigers, lions, jackals, otters, red deer, wild cats, and of other beasts of prey, some of which were tanned. In another place are food and vegetables and meats. Next to these are furniture dealers, with their stores of tables, benches, cradles, and all sorts of wooden implements, all separately arranged. They even see for sale 'pipes' or cigars made of paper like Montezuma smokes after his meals.

Then there is the slave market, where people of both sexes are for sale—some captives, but some willingly to pay off debts. Many are fitted with halters about their neck to prevent them from running away, though some are allowed to walk free.

On the way out they observe numbers of other merchants, who deal in gold dust, which is for sale in tubes made of the bones of large geese. The value of these tubes of gold is estimated according to their length and thickness, and are sold in exchange for so many cotton mantles, cacao beans, nuts, slaves, or other merchandise.

Then the Conquistadors enter the spacious yards that surround the chief temple. These are marked by a double wall, constructed of stone and lime, and paved with extremely smooth large white flag-stones. The area is so very clean that there is not the smallest particle of dust or straw to be seen anywhere.

Montezuma is just arriving at the temple of Huitzilopochtli and gets out of his sedan so he can approach on foot in respect to the gods. His entourage walk before him, holding up two rods, resembling scepters, which is a sign that the Emperor is approaching. He himself, holds a short staff in his hand, one half of gold, the other of wood. Then he ascends the many steps to the top accompanied by numerous priests. This temple, as are all in the land of Mexico, is in the shape of a pyramid, but with steps leading to the top where the altars are placed.

As the Conquistadors gather below, Montezuma, who is sacrificing on the top to his idols, sends six priests and two of his principal officers to assist Cortés up the 114 steps to the summit. Fearing that Cortés would be too fatigued by climbing the steep steps, they move to assist him by taking hold of his arms. Cortés, however, shrugs off this proffered aid and climbs to the top with many of his fellows including Bernal Diaz, and of course Malinalli.

Lying stretched out on many large stones are those who are doomed for sacrifice. Near these stands a large idol, in the shape of a dragon, surrounded by various other abominable figures, with a quantity of fresh blood. Montezuma himself then steps out of a 'chapel', accompanied by two priests. The Emperor greets Cortés and the rest very courteously.

"Ascending this temple, Malinche, must certainly have tired you!" But his words are more of a question, since he is surprised the Conqueror doesn't appear winded.

Cortés, in fact, assures him, through Malinalli, that it is not possible for anything to tire him or his men. A statement that reinforces Montezuma's notion that these are not mortals.

Upon this the Emperor takes his hand and invites him to look down and view his vast capital from the highest point in the city.

Indeed, this infernal temple commands a 360 degree view of the whole area. They can see the three causeways which lead into Mexico, and the aqueduct which runs from Chapultepec, and provides the whole capital with fresh water. They also distinctly see the bridges crossing the canals and causeways. The lake itself is crowded with canoes, which are bringing provisions and other merchandise to the city. The immense market is clearly visible with the astounding thousands of people gathered there. In all it is a splendid sight.

"I have just been thinking that we should take this opportunity, and apply to Montezuma for permission to build a church here." Cortés says to Father Olmedo.

"This would, no doubt, be an excellent thing if the Emperor would grant this. But perhaps that it would be hasty to make a proposition of that nature to him now, as such consent would not easily be gained at any time." The level-headed Father Olmedo replies.

"Your majesty is, indeed, a great Emperor! It has been a real delight to us to view all your cities. I have now one favor to beg of you, that you would allow us to see your gods and teules." Cortés says to Montezuma through Malinalli.

Instantly on the alert, Montezuma answers that he must first consult his chief priests, to whom he then addresses a few words. Malinalli overhears enough snippets of this conversation to know the Aztecs are nervous and on edge at this request. But the Emperor decides to permit it, if only to gauge Cortés' reaction.

The group is led into a small tower with two large stone altars, on each of these rests gigantic figures. The one on the right is the god of war Huitzilopochtli. This idol has a broad face, with distorted and furious eyes, and is covered with jewels, gold, and pearls. Large serpents wind round the body also studded with gold and precious stones. Around Huitzilopochtli's neck are figures representing human faces and hearts made of gold and silver, and decorated with blue stones. In front of it are several incense pans and three fresh hearts of recently slaughtered victims.

On the left is another figure of the same size with a face very much like that of a bear, its shining eyes were made of glass. This figure is also completely covered with precious stones, and is called Tezcatlipoca, the god of hell or the underworld. A circle of figures wind round its body, resembling tiny devils with serpents' tails.

Every wall of this chapel and the whole floor are almost black with human blood, and the stench is abominable—worse than any slaughter-house.

In another chapel there is another idol, half man and half lizard, completely covered with precious stones, half of which is hidden from view, representing the earth. In this place there is also a drum of enormous dimensions, the tone of which is so deep and melancholy that it is like the drum of hell and can heard for miles. The drum-skin appears to be made from that of an enormous snake. The smell and the horror overwhelm the Conquistadors so they must go outside for fresh air.

Despite Father Olmedo's advice, Cortés cannot keep quiet.

"I cannot imagine that such a powerful and wise Emperor as you are, should not have yourself discovered by this time that these idols are not divinities, but evil spirits, called devils. In order that you may be convinced of this, and that your priests may satisfy themselves of this truth, allow me to erect a cross on the summit of this temple; and, in the chapel, where stand your Huitzilopochtli and Tezcatlipoca, give us a small space that I may place there the image of the Holy Virgin; then you will see what terror will seize these idols by which you have been so long deluded." Cortés tells Montezuma with as much a smile as he can muster considering the circumstances. But Malinalli is horrified and disgusted at the sight of all the blood, and translates the words in a furious bitter tone, adding that the Virgin Mary would vanquish these false gods and see to it that not another soul was lost to them.

Although Montezuma has seen the benign image of the Virgin Mary, he and the priests are furious and insulted at this suggestion.

"Malinche, would I have guessed that you would use such reviling language as you have just done, I would certainly not have shown you my gods. In our eyes these are good gods. They preserve our lives, give us nourishment, water, and good harvests, healthy and growing weather, and victory whenever we pray to them for it. Therefore we offer up our prayers to them, and make them sacrifices. I earnestly beg of you not to say another word to insult the profound veneration in which we hold these gods." The Emperor says coldly.

"It is time for us to depart then." Cortés realizes by his tone there is no arguing the point.

Montezuma replies that he is now obliged to stay some time to atone to his gods by prayer and sacrifice for having committed the offence of allowing them to ascend the great temple, and insult the gods.

"If that is the case, I beg your pardon, great Emperor." apologizes Cortés and the Conquistadors descend from the temple.

On their way out through the splendid courtyards, the group encounters smaller temples likewise containing idols. One has figures like an open-mouthed dragon with huge teeth, and other statues resembling devils. Next to this temple is another in which human skulls and bones are separated into endless piles, and priests clad in long black hooded cloaks, their ears were pierced and the hair of their head was long and stuck together with coagulated blood.

Nearby are also large buildings, serving as cloisters in which great numbers of young women live secluded, like nuns, until they are married. These house female idols, who protect the marriage rights of the women, and to whom they prayed and sacrificed in order to obtain good husbands.

Cortés soon grows tired of the sight of so many idols and implements of sacrifice, and orders a return to quarters, accompanied by a great number of nobles and chiefs, whom Montezuma had sent to keep an eye on them.

When Cortés has a chance to reflect on the incident at the main temple, he realizes that Montezuma will never consent to him erecting a cross there, so he decides to ask the Emperor's house-steward to have his workers build a church in the Conquistadors' quarters. This man states that only Montezuma can make such a decision, so Cortés sends him with Malinalli and the page Orteguilla to ask permission.

***

So Malinalli again faces the mighty Emperor, and because the subject concerns the holy religion, she tries to be respectful this time.

"Lord, my Captain desires to build a church to our God in our apartments so that we can worship properly." She is careful to omit the customary '*My* Lord' when addressing Montezuma though.

The Emperor is still confused about the whole situation with Cortés. His derision of Huitzilopochtli, Hummingbird Wizard and

Tezcatlipoca, Smoking Mirror was certainly not altogether unexpected as the two and Quetzalcoatl are mortal enemies, of course. But this idea of building a temple in his own quarters is perplexing. In fact this whole idea of a virgin goddess mother and someone named Jesus and one God is puzzling—why would Quetzalcoatl worship someone else or are these deities his spirit allies? He decides to let them do it just to see where it goes.

After Malinalli and Aguilar leave, Montezuma must attend to pressing business. Cacamatzin and Cuitláhuac are there, along with many important functionaries of the government.

"The vassal states in Almeria, and the Totonaques, as well as the Cempoallans, and all the mountain tribes have refused to pay taxes because of this Cortés. This situation cannot be tolerated!" Cuitláhuac declares and the others present voice their agreement.

Montezuma, seeing he is outnumbered in this matter, is faced with no choice but to enforce the laws of the Empire. But he has the stranger Cortés right next door! If he is indeed Quetzalcoatl then such action could be disastrous. He tries to mitigate the blow by going after the smallest fish.

"We have a garrison in Panuco; have them pressure the town of Almeria and if necessary use whatever force is required. Surely once these other tribes hear this, they will see the error of their ways and things will return to normal." The Emperor suggests.

Cuitláhuac privately thinks this is too little but sets the order in motion...

Within days Montezuma receives word from his generals that the deed is done and the rebellious tribes are back in the fold of the Empire. Along with this report, he receives something else: the head of the captured Spanish soldier Arguello!

Montezuma is quite horror-struck at the sight of this enormous head with the thick curly beard. He could not bear to look at it, and will not allow the head to be brought near any of the temples in the capital, but orders it to be presented to the idols of another town.

Both disgusted and furious that the 'battle' appears to have been so one-sided, he inquires how it could be that his thousands of warriors, had not been able to overthrow such a handful of men? His chiefs reply, that despite their courageous fighting they had not been able to get the upper hand or exterminate the Spaniards, because a great Spanish *goddess* had stood at their lead, and filled the Aztecs with fear, and rallied the enemy with her speeches.

Montezuma is immediately convinced that this illustrious warrior was the Virgin Mary, who, he had been told was the stranger's strong rock. He is now even more convinced that Cortés and his army of teules are too powerful to defeat.

(Later several of the Conquistadores spoke of this apparition as a fact; and that the blessing of the Virgin Mary was upon them that day.)

25 Downfall

All of these events are as yet unknown to the Conquistadors as they work on building their chapel. While the church is finished in three days, and a cross planted in front of their quarters, in the process the Spanish make a startling discovery: As Yañez their carpenter, is looking for a proper spot to erect the altar, he finds the traces of a doorway in the wall of one of the apartments, which had been carefully walled up and neatly plastered over.

Yañez communicates his discovery to the chief officers, Leon and Lugo, who then report it to Cortés. So late that night with all secrecy, the doorway is broken open, and Cortés, with some of his officers, enter the hidden room. Inside they find a vast quantity of gold bars and trinkets and precious stones that leaves them speechless at the sight of such immense riches. The Conquistadors have stumbled upon the long lost treasure of Montezuma's father Axayacatl, who used to reside in that palace.

The room soon becomes known to all of the men, who take turns visiting this secret treasure. Many remark that the whole world put together could not produce such a vast collection of riches. However, everyone unanimously agreed to leave everything untouched, and that the doorway should be walled up again as before, and Montezuma not to be informed of the discovery.

But this momentous event sets the men on edge. They have already been cooped up in this probably hostile city too long, as if they had been caught in a net or cage, and their fate lie fully in the hands of Montezuma. So they appoint some officers and soldiers to take their concerns to the Conqueror.

They beg him to remember how they had been warned by every tribe about Montezuma, and that Huitzilopochtli had advised him to allow them to enter the city quietly, and when once there to destroy them. They reminded him of the real risk of being cut off on the wrong side of the bridges and causeways, where they could not count on assistance from the Tlaxcalans. Taking all this into consideration their only solution is seizing the Emperor as a hostage!

"I believe they speak the truth. I have seen a change in the Emperor, a suspicion that he may no longer view you as a god and therefore will not hesitate much longer to refrain from putting us all to death as a nuisance to his rule. You know that the Emperor's chief house-steward has become haughty in his manners, and he has not supplied our table so abundantly as on the first few days. Lastly, our friends of Tlaxcala have secretly informed us that the Aztecs, for the last two days, appeared to have some evil plan on hand." Even Malinalli joins in and tells him quietly on the side.

Cortés listens carefully to their pleas and the advice of his mistress, but all the same is horrified at the idea of kidnapping the Emperor.

"Do not imagine, gentlemen, that I sleep so peaceably, or that what you have just been stating has not also caused me much anxiety. But we ought first to weigh whether you think we are sufficiently strong in numbers for so bold an attempt as to take this mighty Emperor prisoner in his own palace, in the midst his body-guards and other warriors. I cannot see how we can manage this matter without running the risk of being attacked by his troops." The Conqueror says.

The four officers, namely, Leon, Ordas, Sandoval, and Alvarado, suggest that the only way to accomplish this would be to entice Montezuma out of his palace by some means, and invite him to their quarters, where he would be made prisoner. If Cortés objects to have any hand in it, they beg him to give them permission to carry it out themselves. After hours of deliberation, Cortés reluctantly gives consent to the plan.

As fate would have it, the following morning two Tlaxcalans sneak into the city dressed like Aztecs and make their way to the Conquistador's quarters. They deliver a report from Vera Cruz, announcing to Cortés that Juan de Escalante has been slain along with six other Spaniards and all the Totonaques who had fought with him, in an battle with the Aztecs. Further, all the mountain tribes as well as the Cempoallans had turned against the Spanish. They refused to furnish the town with provisions or assist in building the fortifications.

As Malinalli had feared, Cortés' insistence on declaring he is not a god and his preaching about his religion had backfired. Apparently, the natives now believed the Spaniards were mere mortals, and were on the verge of open rebellion because Cortés appeared to aligning himself with Montezuma.

The report stated that soon after Cortés left the area, Aztec tax collectors backed by warriors, descended on a tribe in Almeria, who are in alliance with Cempoalla, and demanded tribute. When the tribe refused saying they were under the protection of Cortés, the Aztecs declared they would destroy every township which refused to pay the tribute, and carry off the inhabitants as slaves, as they were bound to obey the commands which Montezuma had recently issued.

On hearing these threats the Totonaque tribes requested assistance from Escalante. So he sent messengers to the Aztecs, demanding they leave these tribes at peace, as that was the wish of Montezuma, with whom Cortés is on very friendly terms. The Aztec fired back that Montezuma himself gave the order.

With no other choice but to demonstrate the Spanish will, Escalante set out against the Aztecs, with two cannon, three crossbow-men, two musketeers, and forty Spanish soldiers, along with 2,000 Totonaque warriors. The Aztecs were double that number and at the first attack the Totonaques deserted and ran, leaving Escalante and his few men to fight alone. After a fierce battle, in which one man was captured and Escalante was badly wounded along with most of his men, they retreated back to Vera Cruz where he and six others of his men died three days after their arrival.

Cortés is extremely shocked and saddened by this news. Not only was Escalante one of his favorite officers, but now it appears Montezuma is indeed plotting against him. He comes to the determination that seizing Montezuma as a hostage is his only recourse.

Cortés, as on prior occasions, sends Orteguilla before him to announce his intention on visiting, so that Montezuma will not become suspicious at the unexpected visit. Despite knowing what had taken place at Almeria, he sends word that the visit is agreeable.

The Conqueror, accompanied by five officers: Alvarado, Sandoval, Lugo, Leon, and Avila; plus Malinalli and Aguilar, then proceeds to the Emperor's quarters. After Cortés enters his apartment, and the usual compliments have been exchanged, he addresses Montezuma:

"I am greatly astonished that a Emperor of such power, who calls himself our friend, should command his warriors to take up arms against my Spanish troops, and presume to demand men and women for the sacrifices from those towns which have put themselves under my protection. Not only that, but they have even killed one of my brothers, and a horse." Cortés says through Malinalli.

"I had put faith in your friendship, and ordered my officers in every way to comply with your wishes. You, on the contrary, have commanded your officers the very opposite. I also am aware you dispatched a large body of troops to Cholula to destroy us all there. At that time, in the desire of friendship with you, I held my tongue. But now at this very moment your generals have the audacity to plot in secret to put us all to death. Despite this treachery, I will refrain from making war upon you, which would only end in the total destruction of this city, but you must make your own sacrifice, which is to place yourself under house arrest in my quarters. There you will receive the same attention, and be treated with the same respect as if you were in your own palace. But if you sound any alarm now, or call out to your attendants, you are a dead man." The Conqueror tells him.

Montezuma is speechless for a long time, finally though he declares he has never given any one orders to take up arms against Cortés. He will send for his generals, and learn from them the truth of the whole matter, and see to it they receive punishment accordingly.

However, he cannot believe you would presume to take him prisoner, and lead him away out of his palace against his wishes. No one can demand that of him, and he has no intention of complying.

Cortés, ever the negotiator, lays out his reasons for coming to this decision, while Montezuma argues back. This goes on for half an hour, until the officers began to lose patience.

"What is the use of throwing away so many words? He must either quietly follow us, or we will cut him down at once. Be so good as to tell him this; for on this depends the safety of our lives. We must show determination, or we are inevitably lost." One of the officers, Alvarado, says in a loud and harsh tone of voice.

When Montezuma hears this, and sees the dark looks of the officers, he asks Malinalli what the man has said who spoke so loud.

"Great Emperor, if I may be allowed to give you advice, make no further difficulties, but immediately follow them to their quarters. I am confident they will pay you every respect, and treat you as becomes a powerful ruler. But if you continue to refuse, they will cut you down on the spot." She tells him point blank.

"Malinche, since then you repose no trust in me, take my son and my two daughters as hostages. Only do not disgrace me, by demanding my person. What will the chiefs of my Empire say, if they see me taken prisoner?" Montezuma pleads, somewhat cowardly, with Cortés.

The Conqueror then insists that only the person of Montezuma himself would be the guarantee of their safety, and there will be no further negotiation.

Finally Montezuma makes up his mind to go quietly. The Spanish officers treat him with civility, and tell him to inform his generals and his body-guard that he had chosen, of his own free will, to take up residence in their quarters.

Malinalli then adds that the Emperor should tell his chiefs that he does this on the advice of Huitzilopochtli and his priests, who consider it necessary for his health, and for the safety of his life. His exquisite sedan is then brought in, and his servants carry him in it to the quarters of the Conquistadors. And there begins one of the strangest hostage situations in history—an ancient forerunner of the Stockholm Syndrome and the case of Patty Hearst...

It isn't long before Aztec officials including Montezuma's nephew Cacamatzin and his brother Cuitláhuac descend on the Conquistador's quarters to inquire as to the reason for the Emperor's imprisonment, and ask him if they should commence hostilities. But Montezuma tells them he wishes to have the pleasure of passing a few days with his visitors, and that if he found reason to complain about his treatment he would certainly let them know.

Soon it is as if everything is totally normal in the alternate palace. Montezuma is surrounded by the whole of his household and servants, and even has all his wives and concubines with him. He is daily visited by twenty of his generals and counselors, and disputes from the most distant parts are brought before him, as usual, for his decision. He continues to attend to the most important affairs of state as if nothing has changed.

After some time, the Aztec generals who had fought against and killed Escalante are brought in as prisoners to the Emperor at Cortés' insistence. But Montezuma sends them to Cortés to pronounce judgment himself. These men confess to the Conqueror they had acted on the command of their Emperor, which was to levy the tribute by force of arms, and if the teules interfere, to attack them also.

Cortés then plays a masterful mind game on Montezuma. He informs him of what his generals said, but tells him he believes the Emperor when he told him he didn't have anything to do with the incident. When Montezuma remains silent, Cortés tells him that according to the laws of Spain, any man that killed another had to suffer death as punishment. Then he adds that he will not require the Emperor to order this because he respects him so much, but he will take on the responsibility himself. But then Cortés orders Montezuma to be put in chains. At first he resists vehemently, but in the end quietly submits, and grows more docile. Without further ceremony, Cortés sentences the generals to death, and has them burned at the stake in front of Montezuma's palace. After the executions have taken place, Cortés goes to the Emperor, tells him that he loves him like a brother, removes his chains, and tells he him he is free to visit any of his other palaces.

This drives Montezuma to tears and he thanks Cortés for his kindness, adding he feels no inclination to go anywhere. The Conqueror then assigns his page Orteguilla, who has already learned some of the Aztec language, to attend to the Emperor. This young man is very attentive and teaches many things about Spain to Montezuma, who grows very fond of him. Although this outwardly appearing act of kindness by Cortés is really so Orteguilla can spy and pass back information about conversations between the Emperor and his generals, it will ultimately prove to be a disastrous mistake. Montezuma will learn a little too much about the Spanish—something that Malinalli would never have permitted.

In the meantime, the example which Cortés has made of the Aztec generals has quite an effect. The news spreads like wildfire through the whole of New Spain, and the coastal and mountain tribes who turned their backs on the Spanish at Vera Cruz were now terror stricken, and again pledged alliance.

But now an odd sort of routine settles in at the Conquistador's quarters in the palace at Tenochtitlan. Montezuma is a pampered hostage who Cortés doesn't seem to know what to do with. So every morning after prayers, the Conqueror and some of his officers visit the Emperor with Malinalli, to inquire after his health and his wants, and otherwise to amuse him in every way.

The Spanish regularly play Aztec games and gamble for gold trinkets and glass beads and the Emperor frequently loses to them, since some of them, especially Alvarado, often cheat. This even amuses Montezuma and he asks Orteguilla to explain the rank of every Spaniard.

It is also during this period that Malinalli distances herself from contact with the Emperor. She is more than content to allow Orteguilla to conduct all the communications with a man she considers vile and evil—a point that her and Cortés cannot agree on.

Montezuma even one day declares that his confinement is not irksome, as Huitzilopochtli had allowed the Conquistadors the power to take him prisoner. He further gets to know quite a few of his guards and rewards those he likes with gold and even pretty girls from his stable of concubines.

But the Conquistadors are playing an incredibly dangerous game. Their lives are in the Emperor's hands, and at the slightest wink his body guards and warriors would rush to his rescue. He is continually surrounded by many distinguished officials, and numbers of princes who come to visit from distant parts of his empire.

"Can it only be a matter of time before Montezuma decides to take matters into his own hands and rid himself of us?" Malinalli warns Cortés.

"But he enjoys our company and we amuse him. After all we are here to establish relations and trade." He replies.

"This man is used to getting his way, his people obey his slightest whim without question." She tries to express the danger that Cortés keeping Montezuma hostage is ultimately going to end in disaster.

Cortés shrugs off her words initially, but after reflection begins to feel vulnerable and decides to build two ships or brigantines, ostensibly to sail the lake, but really to be used as a means of escape. When he sends a new officer to led Vera Cruz, he also orders the blacksmith there to make two heavy iron chains, and to forward them, along with the anchors taken out of the scuttled ships, back to him in Mexico City.

After those materials have arrived for constructing the two boats, Cortés informs Montezuma that he intends to build two pleasure yachts to navigate the lake of Mexico, and requests him to allow his carpenters to cut wood for the purpose, and assist his ship carpenters, Martin Lopez and Alonso Nuñez, in the building of the vessels. The Emperor agrees, wanting to see how the Spanish go about it and excited to sail himself.

There is plenty of wood about sixteen miles from the capital, so the building of the ships goes very fast, as the men are assisted by numbers of natives. The brigantines are quickly completed and rigged and each is provided with an awning to keep out the heat of the sun. Both vessels turn out very good, and sail uncommonly fast.

About this time, Montezuma expresses a wish to visit his temple. His motive for this is not only to fulfill his religious duties, but also to convince his generals and particularly some of his relatives, who daily want to rescue him from his confinement and initiate hostile action, that it is his own choice to stay where he is. Cortés grants this request, as long as no human beings are sacrificed.

Montezuma agrees and makes a procession to the temple, dressed in splendid garments, and surrounded by distinguished officials, with the usual display of pomp and ceremony. Cortés sends four officers, Leon, Alvarado, Avila, and Lugo, with 150 soldiers, to accompany him as a guard, and Father Olmedo to insure there are no human sacrifices. But this was in vain since the previous night the priests had sacrificed four victims in secret in preparation for the Emperor's visit.

When Montezuma returns, he appears in better spirits, and presents each Spaniard who accompanied the procession with trinkets of gold. Then he expresses a wish to take a trip by water to his personal hunting ground in the newly launched vessels.

Cortés grants this request as well and so the two ships set sail. One with a great number of nobles and the Emperor's a son, attended by numbers of chiefs; and in the other Montezuma and Cortés, along with his officers, and many soldiers, and even four cannon. The Conqueror is concerned that the Aztecs may attack and rescue their Emperor, so orders everyone to be on guard.

A stiff breeze rises just as the brigantines are leaving, filling the sails and sending the ships flying across the lake. so that canoes, filled with the huntsmen and other Mexican chiefs, could not keep up. This amuses the Emperor no end, who is thrilled and excited to be sailing for the first time.

The ships quickly reach the hunting grounds where Montezuma bags deer and rabbits, and has a great time. Afterward, when the ships return near the capital, the Emperor begs Cortés to fire off the cannon as a signal of his arrival, which terrifies the people nearby and further gives him great pleasure.

But all this bliss is about to come to an end. Montezuma's nephew Cacamatzin, is determined to put an end to the Conquistadors' little adventure before they should likewise take him prisoner. He secretly calls a meeting of all the chiefs of Tezcuco, and with them the prince of Cojohuacan, who was his cousin, and nephew to Montezuma; likewise the princes of Tlacupa and Iztapalapan, and the powerful prince of Matlaltzinco. These powerful chiefs, with other Aztec generals, plan a day when all their warriors are to group and attack with their united forces.

But prince of Matlaltzinco, who is considered to be the most courageous man in the Empire, only consents to join the conspiracy on condition that he be elevated to the throne. He declares that he will handle the situation himself, force his way into the capital with the whole of his army, and drive the strangers out of the city, or put them all to death. Cacamatzin, however, thinks the crown should pass to him, as nephew of Montezuma, and that he should be able to overcome the Spanish without paying so dearly for the prince of Matlaltzinco's assistance.

With the throne in dispute and sliding out of his grasp, the prince of Matlaltzinco hedges his bet and informs Montezuma of the conspiracy. The Emperor then summons the participants who confess that Cacamatzin initiated such a plan, but it was only to liberate his uncle.

Not wanting a bloody rebellion in his own capital, Montezuma then informs Cortés of the plot. The Conqueror's suggestion to Montezuma is that he should put all his troops under his command, and then in concert with his soldiers, he would invade Tezcuco, destroy the town and lay waste the whole province.

But Montezuma wisely declines that advice, so Cortés instead sends word to Cacamatzin, that it was his wish to live in friendship with him, but that if he started a war it would be his death.

Cacamatzin, however, is a young hothead, and supported by a great number of chiefs, who constantly keep urging him to rid the country of the Conquistadors. He replies to Cortés that he has already heard too much of his smooth talk and not to bother sending more messages. There would be time enough for that when their armies met on the battlefield.

When Cortés receives this answer he requests Montezuma to use his own authority against the rebels. He should issue orders to the officials of Tezcuco to take Cacamatzin prisoner and transfer the sovereign power over Tezcuco to Cacamatzin's brother.

Montezuma agrees and sends messages to Cacamatzin inviting his nephew to the capital to discuss peace. He also orders the other chiefs of Tezcuco to thwart all attempts of the young hothead to start a war.

On the receipt of this message, Cacamatzin meets with his principal adherents met to consult what steps they should take. He opens the assembly with a haughty and angry speech, assuring them he will destroy the strangers all within four days. He declares his uncle is a faint-hearted old woman for not having destroyed the invaders when they were descending the mountain of Chalco when all their warriors stood in readiness. Instead his uncle Montezuma, indeed, had invited them into the city and then gave them all the gold that was collected by tribute, and they had even broken open the secret treasury of his ancestor Axayacatl. They imprisoned the Emperor, and continually admonished him to abolish the gods and adopt theirs in their place. Further, there is no reason to fear the strangers, for his uncle's generals had a few days ago killed several of the teules and one of their horses, near Almeria. Both the dead horse and head of one of the strangers has been shown to everyone in Mexico. In the short space of one hour they should be able to capture the whole of them and sacrifice their hearts at the main temple.

When Cacamatzin is done speaking, the generals stand gazing at each other in silence, each one waiting to hear the other's answer first. At last a few of the most distinguished generals break silence declaring, they cannot possibly commence hostilities in the very capital of the Empire without Montezuma's permission.

This answer infuriates Cacamatzin, and in the heat of his anger he throws three of the generals into prison. As there are a great number of his relatives and boisterous young men like himself at the meeting, the majority are for supporting him to the death.

Cacamatzin, therefore, sends a message to Montezuma, that he might have saved himself the trouble of making friends with people who have insulted him by keeping him prisoner. The only way to account for such action is that he must have fallen under the enchantment and witchcraft of the Spanish woman, they term their protector (the Virgin Mary).

"It is my intention to pay both you, my uncle, and the strangers a visit, and speak words of death to all of you." Cacamatzin ends.

Montezuma is incensed at this impudent answer, and sends six of his most loyal generals, with his royal seal, to Tezcuco with orders to secretly show his signet to all his relations, and those chiefs of the city whom are not inclined towards Cacamatzin, to seize him, and those who supported him, and bring them to him.

These officers accordingly fulfill their orders promptly and capture Cacamatzin in his own palace and five of his supporters, and return them to the capital and into the presence of Montezuma.

Cacamatzin shows even more audacity than before and when the Emperor learns from the other five prisoners that he had designed to deprive him of the crown, and place it on his own head, he orders his nephew to placed into the custody of Cortés.

Upon this, Cortés thanks the Emperor for this show of trust and with the approval of Montezuma, raises the brother of Cacamatzin to the throne of Tezcuco with great ceremony. Soon thereafter the princes of Cojohuacan, Iztapalapan, and Tlacupa, who joined in the conspiracy, are also captured; and scarcely eight days have elapsed before all are securely locked in chains.

As peace is again restored to the country after the imprisonment of the petty princes, Cortés brazenly reminds Montezuma of the offer he had made to pay tribute to his emperor. And that it would be good therefore, if he with all his subjects, likewise acknowledged themselves vassals of his emperor, and as was customary for this act of submission, to be preceded by payment of tribute.

Montezuma still thinks Cortés is referring to himself as the 'emperor' and Malinalli does nothing to correct this notion. In answer to this, Montezuma replies he is quite willing to assemble all the princes and nobles of his empire, to discuss the matter with them. And ten days later the greater part of the chiefs from the surrounding districts assembled together.

The page Orteguilla, who is the only outsider at this meeting since he never leaves the Emperor's side, reports that Montezuma opened the assembly by reminding the chiefs of the legend that Quetzalcoatl would one time come from where the sun rose, who is destined to rule this country, and put an end to the Empire. He then concluded that this tradition refers to Malinche. The priests had expressly requested an oracle of Huitzilopochtli on this point, and had offered sacrifices for that purpose, but the god had refused. We may therefore conclude, continued Montezuma, that Huitzilopochtli meant to say we were even to take the oath of allegiance to this king, whose subjects the teules are. For the present we cannot do otherwise than act accordingly. He therefore suggests, for their own good, to willfully give some proof of their allegiance to Malinche, who demands it, and it would not be well to refuse him.

After this reasoning and statement of Montezuma, all present declare their willingness to comply with his wishes, but all of them break out in tears at thought that the Empire is at an end. With this agreement Montezuma dispatches one of his principal officers to Cortés with the information that they would take an oath of loyalty.

"Montezuma and his council have decided to pledge their allegiance tomorrow." Malinalli announces to the Conqueror after hearing the message.

"That is indeed fine news!" He answers with a big smile. "Now we can get on with what we came here for."

"You must be aware the Aztecs only do this because they think you are their god, who has returned as prophesized."

"This is not righteous!" Cortés exclaims.

"These people are deceitful and liars. Montezuma has already lied to us many times. He swears he didn't send warriors to Cholula. He swears he didn't have his warriors wait in ambush in the mountains. And he lied again when he said he didn't order the battle against your garrison in Vera Cruz when they interfered with his tax collectors. They say one thing and mean another. The instant you expose your back to him, he will run you through with a blade." Malinalli says calmly, not letting emotion mar her words.

"Still Marina, it is a lie, and a sin against God and my own emperor." Cortés says, more weakly than before, his resolve dissolving away.

"The only thing keeping us alive in this capital of the enemy is Montezuma's belief that you are Quetzalcoatl. Does it matter how your ends are accomplished, or merely that they are? You should let this matter lie where it will."

Her words strike a chord with the Conqueror, but he is not comfortable with this. In any case his own emperor can never know this, for it could be considered treason.

The next day accordingly the allegiance is given in the presence of Cortés, of the officers, and the greater part of the soldiers. All the Aztecs seem deeply grieved, and Montezuma himself cannot refrain from shedding tears. Malinalli recites their words of a pledge of loyalty and obedience to 'Malinche' and no one questions it—not even Cortés.

Not long afterward Cortés, sitting with Montezuma, innocently inquires about gold. He wants to know where the gold mines are, and which rivers where gold dust is found, and how they collect it.

Montezuma answers, that gold is found in three different parts of the country, but is most abundant in the province of Zacatula, which is twelve days' journey south of the capital. There the earth is washed in wooden troughs, and the gold dust sinks to the bottom.

The Emperor offers to show the Conquistadors the areas and even presents Cortés with a finely detailed map, covering an area of almost 600 miles, drawn on on a piece of nequen cloth. This map not only shows the gold mining locations but also all the rivers as well as coves along the coast.

Cortés is instantly drawn to a previously unknown river called Guacasualco, which the Aztecs described as very broad and deep. Cortés immediately decides to send someone there to make soundings at its mouth, and further explore the country. Diego de Ordas, a born adventurer and the same man to first climb the volcano Popocatepetl, quickly volunteers to lead an expedition there.

Montezuma warns that this journey is dangerous, as the land of Guacasualco is not part of the Aztec Empire, and inhabited by a very warlike people. He cautions Ordas to be particularly on guard. But Ordas sets out anyway on his journey, accompanied by two Spaniards and several distinguished Aztecs. Cortés also dispatches several men to each of the gold mining regions to reconnoiter and explore.

Eventually all the expeditions return with samples of gold, and accounts concerning the wealth of the country. They also report the overwhelming dissatisfaction of all the tribes with Montezuma and the Aztecs. Everywhere in the country it seems there is great unrest.

Instead of immediately and directly exploiting this widespread discontent, Cortés embarks on a risky scheme: he demands that Montezuma require all his chiefs and every town in his Empire bring in tribute in the form of gold. In this way he will both gain the gold he came here for and anger the subjects of the Aztecs even more.

Montezuma reluctantly agrees, but warns that many of them would be unable to fulfill this order because they have already been taxed and were poor. The Emperor then sends several tax collectors to the districts where there are gold mines, ordering the inhabitants to pay him the usual weight of gold bars they were accustomed to pay as tribute. So after twenty days all the tax collectors return, but the tribute they have brought back is meager.

So as not to antagonize Cortés because the collection came up short, Montezuma tells him that he will contribute the whole of his father's treasure, which he knows the Spanish have discovered and covered back up, as his share of the tribute. Cortés and his men are astonished at this generosity, but as Malinalli points out,

Montezuma knew it was only a matter of time before the Conquistadors seized it, so this way the Emperor made himself look good.

In any case, within the hour servants open the secret chamber and begin bringing the treasure to Cortés. There is so much it requires three days to remove it all out of the different corners of the secret room and inventory it. The gold alone is found to be worth around 600,000 pesos or more than seven million dollars! That doesn't include the gold bars and gold dust contributed by the other provinces. Cortés has the Aztec goldsmiths melt all this treasure into three inches square bars, stamped with the Spanish coat of arms.

Then the men insist that the treasure be divvied up immediately so each could get their share, as they already notice about a third of the original store has disappeared—into the pockets of Cortés and his officers they suspect.

First of all, one fifth (20%) of the treasure is set apart for the crown, and a second 20% for Cortés, as had been agreed when he was elected captain-general. After this has been deducted, Cortés takes out the expenses of fitting out the armament at Cuba, then the sum due to Velasquez for the ships that had been destroyed, and then the travelling expenses of the agents sent to Spain. Next are deducted the several shares due the seventy men back in Vera Cruz, then even the value of the two horses which had been killed, one in the engagement with the Tlaxcalans, the other at Almeria! Next, double shares are also set apart for the two priests, the officers, and the cavalry, likewise for the musketeers and crossbow-men. Not until all this has been deducted are the rest of the average soldiers allowed to take their shares, which by this time amounts to almost nothing—naturally resulting in some extreme grumbling and bad morale.

When Cortés is apprised of these complaints, he calls all the men together and attempts to defuse the situation by telling them there is much more gold in the country and further that he is quite ready to bestow something on those who are in need. While he goes on for some time in flattering the men and promises them riches are coming, he fails to change many attitudes and so secretly buys some off with gold, and others with shares of the abundant provisions sent everyday by Montezuma.

With the rumblings of rebellion calmed for the time being, it is not long before a number of the stamped bars come into circulation for the purposes of gambling, after a certain Pedro Valenciano managed to manufacture playing cards from parchment, which are as well painted and as beautiful to the eye as those manufactured in Spain.

26 Montezuma's Revenge

The Emperor soon has another surprise for the Conqueror—one designed to accomplish multiple purposes: to ally himself more closely with Cortés, while at the same time causing Malinalli great pain.

"Malinche! in order to prove the great affection I have for you, it is my intention to give you one of my prettiest daughters in marriage." Montezuma announces, which of course Malinalli is required to translate.

Cortés takes his cap off, and thanks him for the honor, but says he is already married, and that the religion and laws of his country do not allow a man to have more than one wife. Nonetheless, he will accept her and treat her with the respect due to her high rank, but it is requisite she become converted to Christianity. While Montezuma readily agrees to this, the situation quickly sets up an unintended confrontation about religion in general and human sacrifice in particular—thanks to Malinalli.

"Montezuma is willing to allow his own daughter to worship the one true God, while he continues to butcher people for sacrifice." She points out to Cortés.

The Conqueror has no response to this. Every day since their arrival, humans have been sacrificed in the nearby temples, despite all his requests and demands to the contrary. Doña Marina was entirely right—it is time for action.

He then calls a meeting of the friars, Father Olmedo, and his top officers and rallies them to a call of action. They vow to throw down the idols from the top of Huitzilopochtli's temple, but if that met with too much resistance, then to content themselves with demanding permission to build an altar on one side of the temple and erect there the image of the Holy Virgin and a cross. So the group marches in to confront Montezuma.

"Great Emperor, I have already so many times begged of you to abolish those false idols by whom you are so terribly deluded, and no longer to sacrifice human beings to them; and yet these abominations are continued daily. I have, therefore, come to you now, with these officers, to beg permission of you to take away these idols from the temple, and place in their stead the Holy Virgin and the cross. The whole of my men feel determined to pull down your idols, even should you be averse to it; and you may well suppose that one or other of your priests will become the victims." Cortés tells him.

"Alas, Malinche! Why is it you wish to compel me to bring down total destruction on this capital? Our gods are already angry with us, and who can tell what revenge they contemplate against you? I will, however, assemble all the papas, to know their opinion." The Emperor replies after seeing the determination in the faces of the Conquistadors.

Cortés then dismisses his men, so he and Father Olmedo, and of course Malinalli, can speak privately with Montezuma. Once they are alone, he tells the Emperor he can avoid open rebellion, and the idols from destruction, by granting permission to erect an altar, with the cross and Virgin Mary, on the top of the great temple. This will silence the murmurs of his men, and the Aztecs themselves will soon be convinced how greatly such a change would benefit their souls, what great blessings will be showered down upon them, and how abundant their harvests will be.

With a deep sigh, and great sorrow, Montezuma agrees to discuss the matter with his priests. After a good deal of arguing between the priests and Montezuma, consent is given to erect an altar, with the cross and holy Virgin, on the top of the temple, opposite the cursed idol Huitzilopochtli. While the Spanish rejoice at their first high Mass conducted there, they are blissfully unaware a storm began to gather over their heads.

No sooner is that first Mass over when the temple priests retaliate by proclaiming the gods Huitzilopochtli and Tezcatlipoca are leaving the country, as the teules have treated them with such great contempt, and that it was impossible for them to dwell in the same spot with that image and cross. If the Aztec people want them to remain in Mexico, they were to kill all the strangers. There would be no further communication until this was done. After hearing this, Montezuma sends word to Cortés he should like to see him, as he had things of the utmost importance to discuss.

"Alas! Malinche, how grieved I am at the commands which our gods have imparted to our priests. They demand that we put you all to death, or drive you away from this country by some other means. My advice is, that you had better leave of your own accord, than allow hostilities to commence. This, Malinche, I could not avoid telling you, as I have no doubt that all your lives are at stake here." The Emperor warns.

Despite what appears to be imminent danger, Cortés hides his fear and thanks Montezuma for his information. Then he adds that he is sorry they have no ships left in which to leave the country. But if Montezuma can appease his priests long enough, his men will construct three ships along the coast for their departure. As proof of their desire to leave, he asks the Emperor to supply carpenters and manpower to assist in this.

Cortés then orders Martin Lopez and Andreas Nuñez to march to Vera Cruz with the Aztec carpenters, where all the necessary materials, consisting in iron, rigging, tar and tow would be found and build the three ships.

During this time though the Conquistadors grow much alarmed at their situation in this great capital, and expect an attack at any moment. So the men are on constant alert, sleeping in their uniforms, with their horses saddled and weapons at the ready. At night they put on some many sentries, that each of them has at least one watch.

But Cortés troubles are about to get a lot worse.

Months before, Governor Velásquez accused Cortés of treason before the order of Hieronymite monks, who are viceroys of Cuba. While they eventually would come to favor Cortés, they first commissioned the licentiate Zuazo, to investigate the matter. He took the matter to heart and wanted to demonstrate his worthiness, so put much effort into the task, and seeks to outfit every ship in the island, and to enlist every officer and man he can find with the intention to send out such a powerful fleet as would easily overwhelm Cortés and the whole of his expedition.

Then the bishop of Burgos, who favored Velasquez, jumped into the fray and commands him to assist with the fleet, for which he himself would be responsible to King Charles. The governor of Cuba accordingly used the utmost exertions and assembled a flotilla, consisting of nineteen sailing ships, on board of which were 1400 soldiers, above forty cannon. To this was added eighty horses, ninety crossbow-men, and seventy musketeers. Velasquez visited every township in Cuba, to hasten the preparation of the flotilla, and invited every inhabitant who had either Indians, relations, or friends who could manage their estates, to join the standard of Narvaez, and share the honor of taking Cortés and all of his men prisoners, or at least to kill them.

With the departure of the fleet imminent, Zuazo thinks the whole situation has gotten out of hand and the operation is wildly excessive, so he sends word to Hieronymite monks. They quickly take the view that Velasquez is not justified in fitting out an armada to seek revenge but should pursue this in a court of law. These impartial men well foresee how this situation will impede the conquest of New Spain. They dispatch Lucas Vazquez de Aillon, who is auditor of the court of audience at St. Domingo to Cuba, with instructions to command Velasquez not to allow the flotilla to leave the harbor.

But Diego Velasquez, who has spent all his funds in fitting out this fleet, ignores the order, relying on the good favor of the bishop of

Burgos to protect him. Upon this Vazquez de Aillon boards one of the vessels himself, to try at least to prevent hostilities between Narvaez and Cortés.

It is this confrontation between Cortés and Narvaez, unlike any of the battles fought so far, that will have unintended consequences that prove ultimately devastating to the Aztecs and the entire country of Mexico. For one of the ships is carrying an unwelcome passenger: smallpox...

The flotilla loses one ship off the mountains of San Martin when it is bashed against the coast in high winds, but the rest arrive safely in the harbor of San Juan de Ulua. The considerable fleet is quickly spotted by some of the soldiers whom Cortés had sent out in search of gold mines. Three of these, Cervantes, Escalona, and Alonso Carretero, joyfully rush on board the commander's ship, and praise the Almighty for having rescued them out of the hands of Cortés and the Aztecs, where they faced death daily. Narvaez then plies them with meat and drink as he questions them about Cortés.

The three are all too willing to comply, and Cervantes tells him about the 700,000 pesos, and how his men are so enraged with him for his having cheated them out of their gold. They likewise inform him that thirty-two miles further up the coast is Vera Cruz, which has a garrison of sixty men, all invalids, and he all he has to do is show up with a few men and they would immediately surrender.

Montezuma is quickly informed of the arrival of this flotilla by his spies, and without saying a single word to Cortés dispatches several of his chief officers and artists to Narvaez, with a present in gold, telling him he is being held captive, and orders the nearby tribe to furnish him with provisions.

Narvaez replies back that Cortés and his party are nothing but a pack of thieves, who had fled from Spain without the knowledge of their emperor, who then had ordered him to repair here with his flotilla and troops, to put an end to these disorders and liberate

Montezuma. And that he has orders to put Cortés and all his men to the sword, or take them alive and send them prisoners to Spain, where death awaited them.

Montezuma is overjoyed with this news. Not only does he now have confirmation that Cortés is not the god Quetzalcoatl, but also has an accurate description of the whole armada from his artists, who have painted on cotton cloth everything they saw. He knows there are eighteen ships, many cannon, and 1,300 soldiers; which he believes will easily overcome the troublesome Conquistadors camped out in his palace.

When Cortés, as usual, the next day pays a visit to the Emperor, he finds him in particularly good spirits, and asked him what was the occasion. Montezuma replies with a grin, that he found himself in better health than he had for some time. Cortés, is very much surprised at this sudden change in the Emperor, who for the past weeks has been severely depressed.

" Montezuma is hiding something. Perhaps the plan to attack us is underway as we speak." Malinalli tells the Conqueror after the visit.

Cortés is in total agreement with her and checks on his men and the palace where they are quartered, but everything seems normal, if still strained. So he calls upon the Aztec ruler a second time that day, and now Montezuma begins to fear Cortés knows of the arrival of the flotilla. To remove suspicion from himself, he thinks it's better to break the news.

"I have just this moment, Malinche, received information that a fleet of eighteen vessels, with a great number of soldiers and horses, has arrived in the harbor where you first landed. This, no doubt, is not news to you, and I thought from your second visit to me this day, you came to bring me the intelligence yourself, and that now there is no need for you to build new ships. I am delighted at the arrival of your brothers, with whom you can now return to Spain and thus remove all difficulties at once." Montezuma tells him, and displays the painting his artists had rendered.

Thinking these are reinforcements, Cortés is delighted

"Praise be to God, whose assistance always comes at the right time!" He tells the men who are also overjoyed at being 'saved'.

Cortés, however, soon begins to suspect something is amiss. Not only is Montezuma much too pleased, but surely by now he should have received some message from this fleet. He is very much worried this armada was sent by Velasquez.

In the meantime, after Narvaez received the information about Vera Cruz from the three deserters, he dispatches a priest named Guevara, and a certain Amaya, a man of great distinction, and a relative of Velasquez; a secretary named Vergara and three witnesses, to the settlement to demand surrender.

Sandoval, who had replaced Escalante, is aware of the arrival of Narvaez, and concludes it was outfitted by Velasquez, and that his object was to gain possession of Vera Cruz. He therefore sends all the invalid soldiers to the Indian township Papalote, retaining only those who are in good health and able to fight. He then posts watches along the road leading to Cempoalla, which Narvaez will be obliged to take if he marches to Vera Cruz.

When the outposts signal that six Spaniards are approaching the town, he waits in his own house and issues orders to his men not to leave their quarters, nor exchange a single word with the strangers.

Soon the priest Guevara and his companions arrive in the town, but they see only some natives, who are working at the fortifications. With no Spaniards to speak with, they walk into the church to pray, and only later find Sandoval's house.

The priest begins by declaring Cortés and all of the men, had turned traitors to the governor and concludes by saying that he came to summon him in the name of Narvaez, whom Velasquez had appointed captain-general, and to deliver up the town to him.

When Sandoval hears this he can scarcely speak.

"Venerable sir, you are wrong to term men traitors who have

proved themselves better servants to our emperor than Velasquez has, or your commander; and that I do not now this instant punish you for this affront, is merely owing to your being a priest. Go, therefore, in the name of God, to Mexico; there you will find Cortés, who is captain-general, and chief justice of New Spain. He will answer you himself; here you had better not lose another word." Sandoval exclaims.

When the priest tries to order the secretary Vergara to produce the appointment of Narvaez, and read it to Sandoval, and the others present, Sandoval begins shouting.

"You lie, you infamous priest!" Then he orders his men to seize all six of the envoys, and carry them off to Mexico. A number of natives employed at the fortifications, then tie them hand and foot, throw them on the backs of slaves and transport the captives to Mexico.

These men are more than a little surprised at this rough treatment. But the deeper they advance into the country during the four day journey, the more astonished they grow at the sight of the large towns and villages. They begin to wonder if it is all a dream.

Sandoval sends one of his men along with a letter detailing everything that is going on at the coast, and the name of the captain who commands the flotilla. The man arrives a day ahead with the letter so that Cortés is apprised of the situation when they are still at some distance from the capital.

Cortés knows he can't defeat the superior force in battle. Narvaez has more cannon, more muskets, more crossbows, and almost three times his men. Instead he must use his considerable wit and charm. So he immediately dispatches some men with a quantity of food, and three spare horses, with orders that the prisoners should be immediately released from their bonds.

The Conqueror greets them courteously when they arrive and in the space of a few days turns the people sent to arrest him to his side with kind words, fair promises, jewels, and bars of gold. Father

Guevara even informs Cortés that Narvaez's men are not on the best terms with their commander, and that a few bars of gold would pave the way to their coming over to his side as well. So, those who had come like furious lions, now return back to Narvaez as harmless as lambs.

Cortés is a man who never allows the smallest advantage to escape, so with the six envoys firmly encamped in his favor, he transmits a message by native couriers to Narvaez. This letter, written in a very friendly tone, is an offer of services to him, and requests him not to incite a rebellion in the country, which would certainly be the case if the natives observe the Spanish are at odds with each other. which would be the destruction of both his troops and ours, as we should be overwhelmed by numbers.

Cortés at the same time writes secretly to Andreas de Duero and Vazquez de Aillon, and accompanies these letters with some gold for themselves and their other friends. In addition, he also dispatches a secret weapon to Narvaez's camp in the form of Father Olmedo, along with a good supply of gold and precious stones.

The native couriers arrive first with the letter and Narvaez makes a great show of humorously reading it aloud to his officers, who all enjoy making jokes at Cortés' expense.

Soon after though, Father Guevara and his companions return, and begin singing the praises of Cortés, and what a faithful servant he had proved himself to King Charles, and that Cortés would gladly submit to Narvaez. They tell about the great power of Montezuma, and the number of towns they saw. Guevara also adds, that it was for the advantage of both to remain on friendly terms with each other. New Spain was large enough to afford room for them both, and Narvaez might choose which part of the country he would occupy with his troops.

While these statements irritate Narvaez to no end, the effect on the troops is quite different. When they see the gold these two men return with, and hear so much good about Cortés, and about the wondrous things they had seen, and the vast quantity of gold, and how his men played at cards for gold only, many of them think about switching sides.

Then Cortés' third salvo arrives as Father Olmedo calls upon Narvaez to pay him respect, and tells him how the Conqueror is ready to obey Narvaez's commands, and remain on peaceful terms. But this enrages Narvaez's even more than before and he refuses to listen. This does not deter Olmedo from his secret mission: Distributing bars of gold among Narvaez's principal officers.

After the auditor Aillon carefully reads Cortés' letters, and of course received the bars of gold, he makes no secret of his sentiments, and is eloquent in his praise of Cortés and his companions. Added to this, is the fact that Narvaez kept all the presents sent by Montezuma for himself, without offering anything to his officers or men. All this almost leads to open insurrection. Narvaez views the auditor as the cause of all this bad feeling, and imprisons him, with his secretary and all his attendants, throws them on board a ship bound for Spain.

After this Narvaez decides on a more pro-active strategy and marches all of his men and the cannon, to Cempoalla and sets up a headquarters there. His first act there is to take away from the fat chief the cotton stuffs, gold trinkets, and other fancy articles. He likewise forcibly takes the native females away who had been given to Cortés, who had left behind with their parents and relatives. Narvaez then dispatches his secretary, Alonso Meta with three other officers, to the Aztec capital, commanding Cortés, by virtue of the copies of his appointment by Velasquez, to surrender.

Cortés, who by now is receiving daily intelligence of what is going on in Narvaez's headquarters and at Vera Cruz, is informed about how Narvaez has thrown Vazquez de Aillon into chains, and sent him to Spain. Cortés also learns that five of his enemy's principal officers have switched sides, over fear of retaliation by the royal court over Aillon's treatment.

After hearing all this and sensing he has a small but solid tactical advantage, Cortés rallies his most loyal supporters to march out against Narvaez. He leaves Pedro de Alvarado, along with eighty-three partisans of Velasquez and not trusted, to remain behind to guard Montezuma.

Montezuma of course, has his own spies everywhere, and quickly figures out their plan against Narvaez, with whom he has been secretly communicating.

"Malinche, I have observed all your officers and soldiers going up and down in great uneasiness. Even you do not visit me so frequently as you once did. Orteguilla informs me that you are about to march against your brothers who have just arrived, and that you are going to leave Alvarado behind, to guard my person. Do tell me if there is any way, I can be of service to you in this matter, it will be a great pleasure to me. I have great fears of your success, for you are too few in numbers in comparison to those just arrived. They have five times the number of troops you have. They also like you, maintain to be Christians, and they pay homage to the same image and cross, and read the mass as you do. Yet everywhere spread the rumor that you have fled away from Spain from your emperor, and that he has sent them to take you back again, or put you to death. Really I scarcely know what to think of all this. I must tell you, to use great circumspection in what you are about to do." Montezuma tells him through Malinalli—who has her own concerns about all these events seemingly spiraling out of control, especially now that the whole matter of a Spanish emperor is out of the bag.

In reply to this, Cortés tells him that he has avoided mentioning anything to spare him the anxiety. It is very true, the newly arrived men are also subjects of their emperor, and Christians; but it is a falsehood to say he had fled away from Spain. On the contrary, their great emperor had expressly sent him out to visit Montezuma. The Lord Jesus Christ and his blessed mother would lend him and his men strength, and provide them with superior power to those bad men who came with evil intentions. Finally, Montezuma need not worry as he would soon return victorious. In the meantime he requests him to remain on friendly terms with Alvarado, who would remain behind in with eighty men to prevent any insurrection. After this explanation, Montezuma and Cortés embrace each other twice.

The Conquistadors then march out on the road to Cholula.

27 Reversal

The Conqueror is nothing if not bold, brazen, and daring. He relies on his wit and charm time after time to overcome the most daunting obstacles. Certainly after his unbelievable feat of taking the Emperor of the Aztec nation hostage, his most daring exploit, and one that may even qualify as absolutely reckless is his march on Narvaez. This armada, with a much more superior force of Spaniards, has landed on the gulf coast with orders from Governor Velásquez, not only to neutralize Cortés, but to capture him and bring him to trial in Cuba for disobedience and treason towards the governor.

Leaving only one hundred and forty men under Alvarado to hold the capital of the Aztec Empire, he sets out against Narvaez, who has over a thousand soldiers, while Cortés can muster only about two hundred and sixty. But the Conqueror doesn't rely only on military tactics, he has also unleashed a combination of psychological warfare and bribes to soften up his opponent first...

From Cholula Cortés sends a message Xicotencatl, Maxixcatzin, and the other chiefs of Tlaxcala, asking them to send 4,000 warriors to assist in the coming battle. Their answer comes back that if he was going to war with the Aztecs they would gladly supply these warriors and more; but if he intended fighting against teules, like himself, they must refuse as the task is impossible.

Cortés then sends a courier to Sandoval, ordering him to meet as soon as possible with all his men, at a location about forty-eight miles from Cempoalla, in the province of Chinantla.

The Conquistadors then march forward with extreme caution, ready for action at a moment's notice. Two men are scouting ahead by two days while a small detachment of sharpshooters is in the lead of the main body. It is not long before they came up on a certain Alonso Mata, who terms himself a royal secretary, and was commissioned by Narvaez, to show Cortés the copy of his appointment. Mata is accompanied by four others, who are to act as witnesses on this matter. When these people are brought up, they greet Cortés in a humble manner, and he dismounts when he learns who they are.

Alonso Mata immediately begins to read his documents, but Cortés interrupts, asking him whether he is indeed a royal secretary. He adds if this is all regular he would certainly be shown the courtesy due him as a servant of the emperor.

When Mata replies in the affirmative, Cortés demands he produce his appointment. This completely takes Mata aback, for he in reality is no royal secretary, and is therefore unable to utter a single word, and those who accompany him remain silent as well. Cortés then informs them where he is going and if someone wishes to find him that is where he will be.

The Conquistadors continue their march, and arrive in Chinantla, where Sandoval appears the following day with his small detachment, consisting of sixty men. He brings along with him the five officers who had defected from Narvaez.

Cortés then sends Father Olmedo to Narvaez with another letter, demanding he forward within the space of three days by a royal secretary, the original papers of his appointment, signed by his majesty. If this was not forthcoming, he hereby summoned him, by virtue of his office as Captain-General and Chief-Justice of New Spain, to appear before him and answer the charge preferred against him of *criminis læsæ majestatis*. Lastly, he demands he return the cotton stuffs and gold trinkets he had forcibly taken away from the fat chief; to deliver up the Indian females who had been presented to us to their parents; and to command his men in no way to touch the property of the natives.

As soon as Father Olmedo arrives at Narvaez's headquarters, he makes secret disclosures in Cortés' name to a number of cavaliers in Narvaez's camp and gives them gold bars. He likewise requests Andreas de Duero to pay a visit Cortés a visit, and then finally calls upon Narvaez himself.

Although Olmedo acts humbly and respectfully, Narvaez suspects he is up to no good and decides to throw the Father into prison. But when Duero, private secretary to Velasquez, is secretly informed of it, he calls upon Narvaez to say that no good could come from such a step because Cortés had honorably received all those whom Narvaez had dispatched to him, and even dismissed them with presents.

With these and other kind words, Duero succeeded in softening Narvaez's anger; upon which he then sent for the Father to dine with him. Father Olmedo, a remarkably judicious and shrewd man, requests Narvaez with a smile, to join him for a walk together in the courtyard. At which time he attempts to sow some seeds of confusion by pretending to side with Narvaez. Olmedo then finally presents him Cortés' letter over dinner.

All these communications, bribes, and confusing statements though are beginning to have an effect. Many of Narvaez's most important officers beg him to consider a truce and ask Duero to try and persuade Cortés to meet them at an Indian village on the road between the two encampments, where they might come to an understanding with each other respecting the division of the country and the boundaries of their respective territories. This information soon comes to the ears of Father Olmedo, who immediately informs Cortés of it.

Malinalli is not standing idly by either, considering she would seem to have little translating to do in a Spanish against Spanish situation. In fact, in the meantime she is making other contributions. She manages to form an alliance with the Tchinantecs, where some of the Spaniards had gone in search of gold mines, and who are deadly enemies of the Aztecs. These people used a kind of lance, which was much longer than Spanish lances, and tipped with a sharp double-edged point made of flint.

When Cortés sees this weapon, he has Malinalli ask the Tchinantecs for three hundred of them, and inhabitants of every township of that province set diligently to work. The lances are soon finished and then the Spanish replace the flint with points made from copper, with is found in abundance in Mexico, and they turn out most satisfactorily. Besides this, Malinalli asks the Tchinantecs to send 2,000 of their warriors, all armed with similar lances, in a few days to Cempoalla...

After arriving at a brook, about four miles from Cempoalla, the Conquistadors halt in a beautiful meadow near a river. Cortés takes stock of his troops, and finds they number 260 men, among whom are only five cavalrymen, a few crossbowmen and musketeers, and two artillerymen. The rest are equipped with the new lances.

Cortés, seated on horseback, orders all the officers and men to assemble around him; he then asks for a few moments' silence, and addresses the men with flattering expressions and vast promises. The Conqueror praises their courage and reminds them that no one knows whether Narvaez was really commissioned by the emperor himself, but he doubts it. For he suspects this all this was done at the instigation of our most deadly enemy, the bishop of Burgos.

"But we, as honest cavaliers, are bound to defend the honor of his imperial majesty, as well as our own, and all our property, I have marched out from Mexico, reposing my trust in God and your assistance, to bid defiance to such injustice." Cortés tells them.

Several of the officers and soldiers then answer, in the name of the rest, that he can rely upon their determination either to conquer or to die.

Cortés is naturally very pleased at this reply, and says he had not expected less. They should find no cause for regret, as wealth and honor would be the reward of their courage and valor. He then reminds them that, in battle and time of war, prudence and experience accomplish more than bravery, and that their primary objective must be to capture the eighteen pieces of ordnance which Narvaez has arranged in front of his camp.

To accomplish this he selects sixty of the youngest men, of which Bernal Diaz is one, and places them under the command of Pizarro, who is a daring young fellow. As soon as they capture these cannon, they are to storm Narvaez's quarters, which are on the top of a very high temple.

Sandoval, with other sixty men, is ordered to capture Narvaez himself.

Cortés at the same time promises a reward of 3,000 pesos to the first man who lays hands on Narvaez, 2,000 to the second, and 1,000 to the third—just to encourage some friendly competition.

Leon likewise receives the command of sixty men, with instructions to seize Diego Velasquez, with whom he has had words. Cortés himself retains twenty men under his direct command, to render assistance wherever it might be needed.

"I am fully aware that Narvaez has four times the men we have, but most of them are not accustomed to fighting. A great number are adverse to their general, many are sick, and we shall fall upon them unawares. All opposition on their part will be fruitless, and I am fully confident the Almighty will grant us the victory. Narvaez's men also know they will lose nothing by siding with us, and would fare better in every respect by being with us than with him. Thus, gentlemen, after God, our lives and honor entirely depend upon the valor of our arms. The praise of future generations lies in our hands, and it is more honorable to die on the field of battle than to lead a life of dishonor." With this Cortés ended, as it is getting late and beginning to rain.

After a rest, the Conqueror's contingent moves out at late at night and crosses the river, which is swollen by the rain, and very difficult to traverse due to the darkness and slippery rocks covering the river bed. Just on the other side the enemy's cannon are set up.

Narvaez's men are not prepared. Many of his officers are ready to switch sides, others believe Cortés will surrender. Narvaez himself thinks he is going to meet Cortés at a neutral spot so they can divide up the country. More than a few of his men are disgruntled and can't even understand what they are fighting for.

Cortés orders the attack. His Conquistadors immediately lower their new metal edged lances and make a violent a rush at the cannon. The artillerymen barely have time to fire off four shots, three of which pass over the heads of the attackers. Only one is effective and kills three of Cortés' men.

Several of Narvaez's cavalry rally and offer some resistance, but it is short-lived. Pizarro's group captures all the cannon and turns them on the cavalry to keep them occupied. Narvaez now fully awake, takes control and orders his men to rain down arrows and musket-balls from the top of the temple. Then Sandoval's contingent comes up and despite the fire continues advancing up the steps of the temple.

Seeing this, Pizarro rushes to Sandoval's assistance. They join in the assault just as Narvaez's men has beaten him back down five or six of the steps, and the combined group fights with renewed vigor. Still unable to gain entire possession of the temple, Martin Lopez the ship builder, hits upon the idea of sending flaming arrows into the straw that lay on the top of the temple. This succeeds spectacularly well, setting the whole top of the temple ablaze.

Within minutes Narvaez's men now come pummeling down the steps one after the other, then the enemy leader himself is taken prisoner. Cries of glee fill the air.

"Long live the emperor and general Cortés, in his imperial name! Victory, victory! Narvaez is dead!"

The battle, however, still smolders on as several of Narvaez's officers maintain positions on the tops of other temples. Cortés boldly sends a messenger around to each ordering them to submit to the Imperial Standard of King Charles under pain of death. This has the desired effect until only two officers still hold out. Sandoval, however, is not deterred by their advantageous position. He attacks them so vigorously that they finally surrender.

Cortés soon rides up to check on Narvaez, who has lost an eye and is dangerously wounded, as he asks Sandoval to allow the surgeon he brought with him to dress his and the other officers' wounds. Cortés unhesitatingly nods his approval, and while the surgeon is dressing Narvaez's wounds, someone mentions that Cortés is standing nearby.

"Indeed, general, you have reason to be proud of this victory, and of my being taken prisoner!" Narvaez grimaces through his pain.

"I am every way thankful to God for it, and likewise for the brave companions he has given me; but I can assure you that this victory is the least brilliant we have yet gained in New Spain." Replies the Conqueror, as he leaves to tend to his wounded.

Late in the evening of the day of the victory, the 2,000 native warriors which Cortés had requested arrive and march into Cempoalla two abreast. Intended as ace-in-the-hole reinforcements, they nevertheless put on a grand show. They are all tall and powerful men, armed with their immense-sized lances and huge shields and every lancer is followed by a bowman.

"*Long live the emperor! Long live Cortés!*" They cry out continually and Narvaez's men are not a little grateful they didn't have to face them. Cortés receives the warriors and their chiefs kindly, thanks them for their trouble and sends them back to their homes,

After Narvaez's troops have been disarmed, Cortés dispatches Francisco de Lugo to the harbor where the flotilla is at anchor, in order to bring all the captains and pilots of the eighteen vessels to Cempoalla. He is likewise ordered to seize all the sails, rudders, and compasses, so as to render it impossible for any of the ships to set sail and provide the governor of Cuba with information respecting the fate of his armada.

When the captains and pilots of the several ships appear before Cortés, he makes them take a solemn oath to obey his commands in all matters, adding a few gold bars here and there as incentive. The Conqueror then regroups the ships and men and assign some of them to further explore the coast, and another expedition under the eager explorer Diego de Ordas, to form a settlement on the river Guacasualco.

Cortés then orders all of Narvaez's officers and soldiers to be freed and their weapons returned. When some of his officers are critical of this, Cortés, who is never wanting for an answer, states that while he is most grateful to his own men, it is also vital that they join his force willingly and the best way to achieve that is to treat them kindly like the brothers they are.

During these events the royal auditor, who was sent prisoner to Spain, prevails upon the ship's captain, by means of threats to hang him immediately on their arrival in Spain, instead to steer for St. Domingo. As soon as the auditor arrives at St. Domingo, and the royal court of audience and viceroys there are informed of Narvaez's scandalous and presumptuous ill treatment of fellow Spaniards, a scandal begins brewing which will affect the bishop and Velasquez--especially regarding the fleet which had been sent out without his majesty's permission.

Back in Cempoalla however, dual crises are also brewing which will rock Cortés to the core.

Narvaez happened to have a negro slave with him carrying smallpox, a dreadful and deadly disease previously unknown in Mexico.

He also receives word that all Mexico has risen up in arms, that Alvarado is besieged in his quarters, and that seven men have already been killed, many are wounded, and immediate assistance is required.

28 Beginning or End

How quickly the wheel of fortune turns, and trouble and sorrow follow peace and joy! Information that all Mexico has risen up in arms, and that Alvarado is besieged in his own quarters and requesting immediate assistance is brought by two Tlaxcalans.

Ready to set out on a rush trek back to the Aztec capital, Cortés is met by four envoys sent by Montezuma to complain about the conduct of Alvarado. They claim that without any provocation, he had attacked a peaceful celebration in honor of Huitzilopochtli and Tezcatlipoca, which Alvarado himself had previously given his consent to holding. Many of their chief priests and nobles had been killed and wounded, and in the course of defending themselves, six Spaniards were killed.

"On the eve before the festival we built a statue of Huitzilopochtli, dressed it in feathers, clipped on earrings of turquoise and fashioned a nose of gold and fine stones. A magic feather headdress, a cloak with pictures of skulls and bones and a vest, decorated with pictures of dismembered human parts, completed the costume. The next day unarmed Aztec warriors filed into the temple courtyard and started the 'Dance of the Serpent.' At the very height of the fiesta, the Spaniards attacked. They came on foot, sealed off all escape routes. They ran among the dancers, stabbing them, spearing them. They attacked the man playing the drum, cut off his arms and beheaded him. The blood of the dancers flowed like water. The stench of blood and entrails filled the air." Malinalli translates to Cortés, but she is not at all sympathetic, to her Alvarado merely prevented yet another bloody sacrifice.

"Once word of the massacre spread, a great cry went up. 'Mexicanos, bring your spears and shields! The strangers have murdered our warriors.' Attacked, the Spaniard retreated to their palace and began to shoot at the Mexicans with crossbows,

cannons and arquebuses. Now they were besieged in the palace."
The envoys finish.

After some convincing by Cortés, Narvaez's troops join in the journey back to the capital, and the combined force set out immediately. When they get to Tlaxcala, Malinalli learns that the Aztecs had continued their hostilities against Alvarado as long as Montezuma and his generals believed the Conquistadors were at war with Narvaez. They had killed seven men and burned down a portion of their quarters there, and had only stayed hostilities when they heard of the victory. They still, however, refused to supply Alvarado with either water or food.

In Tlaxcala Cortés' small army, consisting of 1,300 men, ninety-six horses, eighty crossbows, and a like number of musketeers, is supplemented by 2,000 Tlaxcalan warriors. So they quickly continue their march and came to Tezcuco. It is here they began to discover the bad feeling of the native population. Not the slightest mark of respect is shown nor do any of the chiefs come out to greet them.

The Conquistadors march to their quarters un-opposed and Montezuma, somewhat facetiously, comes out into the courtyard to welcome them, and congratulate the Conqueror on his victory over Narvaez. Cortés is not interested in small talk right then and retires to his quarters to learn the real cause of the insurrection of the Aztecs.

Several soldiers, who are none too pleased with Alvarado, swear that Montezuma was upset over what occurred, and were confident none of their lives would have been spared if he had not interceded on their behalf.

For his part, Alvarado related a different version: Namely that several different factors were at work in the situation. First, the Aztecs had risen up in arms to liberate their Emperor, and to take revenge by the express command of Huitzilopochtli, for having erected a cross and the image of the Holy Virgin on his temple.

Secondly, when Montezuma learned Narvaez was not coming to rescue him and further that Cortés had won and was in possession of a sufficient number of ships to leave, but didn't appear to be doing so; he realized he never intended to leave the country. At that point Montezuma decided to kill all the Spanish under Alvarado, and prepare to defeat Cortés when he returned.

Alvarado considered this sufficient justification to strike first, and chose the celebration, after hearing intelligence that the Aztecs intended attacking immediately after the feast had ended. The only thing he was guilty of, he maintains, is that he underestimated the strength of the Aztec counterattack, and as a result had been holed up in the their quarters for days without food.

The entire situation puts Cortés in a terrible mood. On the march back to Mexico, had often bragged to Narvaez's former officers of the great power he possessed among the natives. They will see how the inhabitants would come out from all parts to meet him, and receive him with every splendor. That he was now complete master of Mexico, and Montezuma would not dare to dispute him, but would bring him gold instead. But when they received no reception, let alone respect, Cortés lost face and hurt pride. Then Alvarado let the cat out of the bag regarding the Emperor's secret communications with Narvaez, which he didn't know about until now, and this enrages him all the more.

Now the situation was dire and seven men were dead and many wounded. And to add salt to the wound, Malinalli sides with Alvarado and suggests to Cortés privately that Montezuma is behind it all—a man he wanted so badly to trust. The Conqueror's anger spills out when Montezuma sends two messengers to request paying Cortés a visit.

"He might go to the devil! since he would not allow any weekly markets to be held, nor any provisions to be sent us." Cortés screams at them.

"Moderate your anger, general, and remember what great honors this Emperor has heaped upon us, the kindnesses we have received from him, and how amiable his disposition. If not for him the Aztecs would long ago have feasted on our bodies. Nor ought you to forget that he has sought your alliance by offering you his daughter in marriage." The chief officers: Leon, Oli, Avila, and Lugo tell him— all of them having of course, benefited greatly from Montezuma's generosity or bribes depending on how one sees it.

"Why should I stand upon any further ceremony with this dog? Did he not secretly connive with Narvaez, and now refuses us provisions?" The Conqueror spits at them.

Cortés cannot be pacified in any way and tells the two messengers to tell their master that he must issue immediate orders for the re-opening of the markets, and supply him with food, otherwise he should find himself obliged to take other steps.

Malinalli, for her part, is in no mood to be gentle either, and translates this message with harsh words and cold tones. Both the Aztec messengers also understood the tone used by Cortés against their Emperor, and that there is disagreement among the officers, and report all this in detail to Montezuma.

Barely an hour has gone by when a heavily wounded soldier is brought in, and reports there are warriors everywhere in the streets. They attacked him when he tried to escort Montezuma's daughter and her handmaidens back from where they were staying in the outskirts of the city.

Cortés then dispatches 400 men, heavily armed with crossbows and muskets and a few horses, to reconnoiter the situation and scout along the main causeway. They scarcely reach the half-way point down the causeway when they are met by a vast body of Aztecs, who instantly attack and kill eight men and wound most of the others.

Almost simultaneously another large group of Aztec warriors attack the Conquistador's quarters with lances, arrows, and stones, and in an instant, forty of men are wounded, twelve of whom subsequently die. The scouting party has to fight their way back through that melee and lose fifteen more men in the process. The Aztecs never let up and throw fire into the Spanish quarters, while one group attacks from the front and another from behind. The Conquistadors would have been suffocated by the smoke if they had not succeeded in putting out the fire. The combat continues the whole day until late at night, during which time the Aztecs throw such a quantity of stones and lances that the palace is literally covered with them.

As soon as dawn breaks, Cortés is determined to break out with all of his troops and the cannon, either to beat the enemy back altogether, or at least to give them a greater show of power than he had been able to do on the previous day. The Aztecs, it seem, are just as determined to prevent that, and not only fight with uncommon bravery but come in overwhelming numbers, so that every instant they pour in fresh men to attack. All the volleys from the Spanish cannons and muskets seem to have no effect. They kill from thirty to forty warriors at a time, but their ranks just close again, while their courage seems to increase with every loss.

Then the Aztecs initiate a new strategy: They allow the Spanish to push them back down the streets and as soon as are drawn further away from their quarters, they surround and attack, making escape impossible. Even the most experienced veterans among the Spanish have never faced such a ferocious enemy! It is no easy matter to retreat to back to their headquarters, so fierce is the assault with the most horrible sound of drums, pipes and trumpets. They lose another twelve men, and none of them escape without a wound.

That night the Conquistadors lick their wounds and prepare for another attack. They build two moving towers, of strongly put together wood, so constructed that under each of them twenty-five men could stand to move them along. These towers have ports from which cannon can be fired, and there is space enough for a number of musketeers and crossbow-men. At the side of these towers will march a number of musketeers and crossbow-men, and all of the cavalry, who will from time to time to charge the enemy at full gallop. The construction of these towers and the repairing of several small breaches in the buildings where they are quartered, takes all night and the following day.

The enemy continues their attacks the whole time and the Spanish have to beat off assailants who have fixed ladders to try to breech through the roof. The assaults are accompanied by continuous promises, translated calmly by Malinalli, that all of them would be sacrificed to the gods, their hearts were to be torn from their bodies, the blood was to be drawn from our veins, and their arms and legs were to be eaten up at their festivals. The remaining parts would be thrown to the tigers, lions and serpents, which had not been fed for two days, in order that they might devour their flesh more greedily.

When day breaks the Conquistadors move out with the war-towers, the objective being to push forward to the great temple of Huitzilopochtli and capture it, hoping to break the spirit of the Aztecs.

After a bloody and prolonged assault, they succeed in fighting their way up to the foot of the great temple. But then 4,000 more of the enemy rush up the steps in its defense. For a length of time the guns in the war- towers and the attacks of the cavalry make no impression on the enemy. Though cannon mow down ten or fifteen warriors at a time, and a great many others are cut down by sabers, the Spanish cannot make them yield and are forced to abandon the towers, which by now are almost broken into pieces, leaving them at the foot of the temple. The Spanish then begin fighting their way up the steps.

With forty-six of his soldiers dead at his feet, Cortés displays astonishing courage and charges up the temple to the point where they had erected the image of the Holy Virgin. But it is gone, and so he and his men smash and burn the idols of Huitzilopochtli and Tezcatlipoca. During this time the battle continues relentlessly by so many Aztec warriors, the Spanish don't know which way to point their arms.

But they take two chief priests as hostages, and this plus the destruction of the temple of the gods seems to weaken the will of the Aztecs and the Conquistadors are able to fight their way back to their quarters. They arrive just in time to stave off a large group of warriors who have already breached the walls and are inside.

After disposing of those invaders, they spend the night tending to the wounded, burying the dead, repairing the numerous breaches, and trying to rest despite the Aztec war-cries and yelling all night. To all this is added the grumbling of Narvaez's soldiers, who curse Cortés, and the governor of Cuba in every possible manner, who they said had torn them away from the delightful repose and security which they enjoyed on their respective farms, to be harassed to death in this country.

After lengthy deliberation, the Conquistadors decide to sue the Aztecs for peace, and ask their permission to quit the city. Cortés determines that Montezuma should address the infuriated multitude from the top of the building, and request they stay hostilities so the Spanish can leave. But Montezuma obstinately refuses to comply with this request.

"I will neither see nor hear anything more of this man. I put no longer any faith in his deceitful words, his promises, and his specious lies."

Upon this Father Olmedo tries to reason with him and receives some disturbing news.

"Alas! For all this, it is now too late. Whatever my wishes might be I am convinced that the people will not grant any cessation of arms. They have already raised another Emperor to the throne, and are fully determined that none of you shall leave this place alive. I am convinced you will every one of you meet with your death in this city." Montezuma answers grimly.

Malinalli then learns the truth and tells Cortés the Aztecs have named a new Emperor: Cuitláhuac, and it is he who is providing new leadership for the attack on the Spanish.

Cortés refuses to believe Montezuma has no power and prevails upon him to address his people from the roof of the palace. Montezuma finally agrees and so asks the people to stand down and allow the Conquistadors and their allies and friends to leave the city peacefully.

"Who is Montezuma to give us orders? We are no longer his slaves." They shout at him and then loose arrows and stones at the former emperor.

Several of the Spanish had been covering Montezuma with their shields while he was addressing the crowds, but let down their guard and before it could be prevented, he is struck by an arrow, and three stones from a sling. He is wounded in the arm, leg, and in his head, and so must be carried back to his palace quarters. The Conquistadors attempt to bandage his wounds, and feed him, but he refuses everything and dies three days later.

Cortés, his officers, and all of the men, shed tears at his death; and many who knew him personally mourn for him as if they had lost a parent. Even Father Olmedo himself, who notwithstanding all his efforts, had not been able to convert him to Christianity, cannot refrain from shedding tears. It seems as though only Malinalli sees the Emperor as the brutal, treacherous and conniving man he really was.

Montezuma reigned eighteen years up to the day of his death. Now the intersection of three figures has wound apart and the third cog in the wheel has dropped out.

29 Fall of An Empire

After various deliberations on their present critical position, Cortés decides the best course is to send one of the priests they had taken prisoner to the new Emperor Cuitláhuac. The priest is to announce the death of Montezuma, and explain the circumstances. Cortés also requests they take charge of the body so as to pay it the last honors. And finally, that he is ready to make peace with them, and quit Mexico. Then he brazenly suggests they not pass up this opportunity of concluding peace, for, up to the present moment, he had refrained from destroying the city merely from our love and respect of the deceased Montezuma. If however, they forced him to continue fighting, he would burn it to the ground.

Soon a delegation of six other Aztec chiefs and a large body of priests receive Montezuma's body, and report to Cuitláhuac how the Aztecs themselves had caused his death by the shot of an arrow and three stones from a sling.

But as soon as the people see the dead body of their former emperor being taken out, they break out into loud cries and bitter moans.

"Now, we will make you pay dearly for the death of our ruler, and the insult you have offered to our gods! Is it now you beg peace of us? Only come out, and we will show you what terms we mean to make with you! Don't trouble yourselves about his burial, but think of your own graves, for, in a couple of days, not a single one of you will be left alive!" The crowds yell as Malinalli translates for the Conquistadors. Then the natives rush forward and hurl sticks wrapped in flaming cotton into their quarters, trying to burn them out.

As it is very evident that the Conquistadors cannot hold out much longer, it is decided in a council of war, that they should abandon the capital, and continue the war outside on the main land, where they can wreck havoc with their cavalry and cannon. In this proposed retreat, the cavalry would form the vanguard, and no matter what the stakes, break through the enemy's ranks, even if they have to sacrifice all the horses in the attempt.

The plan is carried out the following day with unbelievable bravery. They fight their way down to the causeway losing twenty men in the process but cannot gain possession of any of the bridges, which are either burnt down, or defended by large numbers of the enemy warriors.

With water and food supplies dwindling, they decide to try again during the nighttime when the Aztecs didn't like to fight. But first they had to overcome the obstacles of the destroyed bridges. Their solution is to construct a moveable bridge out of strong beams. This will be placed over the water and as soon as everyone is across, moved to the next gap.

The Conquistadors arrange themselves into three groups. Sandoval, Lugo, Ordas, and Tapia, form the vanguard and are to clear the streets of the enemy, with one hundred of the strongest and most nimble young soldiers. Cortés takes the middle, supported by Oli, Avila, Bernardino de Tapia, and fifty soldiers. This group has the baggage, the native female servants and the prisoners. As usual, he keeps Malinalli close. She and Doña Luisa, the companion of Alvarado, are also guarded by 300 Tlaxcalans and thirty Spaniards. The rear-guard is commanded by Leon and Alvarado, consisting of the main body of the cavalry, and the remaining 900 or so foot soldiers.

Then Cortés orders all the treasure brought out. After loading as much as they could on the native porters and the eight horses, he distributed the rest to any man that will carry it so it doesn't fall into the hands of the Aztecs. As soon as Narvaez's men and many of the old soldiers hear this, they stow away as much as they could.

With all possible preparations made, they begin to move forward. It is about the hour of midnight, and rather dark. A thin mist hangs over the city, and a gentle rain is falling. It is the time that will later be called: '*La Noche Triste*'

Sandoval and his men manage to get the moveable bridge fixed, and his group and that of Cortés pass across before the Aztecs sound the alarm. Canoes loaded with warriors instantly fill the lake in a rush to stop the evacuation.

The Spanish scramble across the bridge in a desperate attempt to reach the mainland, but two of the horses slip on the wet planks in the commotion and fall into the lake. This causes the bridge to become unbalanced and fall down into the water as well. Under fierce attack, the Conquistadors are unable to recover the bridge. But those behind keep pushing on those in front, and soon the opening in the canal is filled with baggage, cargo, and dead horses and their riders, who are lost if they cannot swim. The unmerciful Aztecs now attack from all sides and a number of Tlaxcalans and the native Indian female servants are carried off, along with the baggage and cannon.

Cortés, with his party, manages to gain the mainland. But many are trapped behind, exposed on all sides to the enemy's arrows and lances, and pelted with stones from the housetops. They also encounter a forest of their own swords, which the Aztecs have captured and fixed to their long lances. To make matters worse, the Spanish muskets are useless in the water when their powder becomes wet.

Sandoval in the vanguard makes it to safety on the mainland. Malinalli and Doña Luisa—Alvarado's companion (whom Malinalli protected, as the princess is more fragile than she) are with him. But then he rides up next to Cortés and tells him they have to go back and rescue the third group.

"We are here indeed on safe ground, but there are still such numbers of our men in the streets behind the bridges, who will be inevitably lost unless we hurry back to their assistance. Up to this moment but few have been able to cut their way through, and these are all covered with wounds." He begs the Conqueror.

"It is a real wonder any one of us escaped. If we turn back to the bridges, we will certainly be lost with horses and all." Cortés replies, but can't bear the thought of leaving the rest die.

So Cortés, Oli, Avila, Sandoval, Morla, and Dominiguez, turn back with six of the cavalry and a few on foot who can still run. They don't get far before they come upon Alvarado. His horse is gone and is limping on one foot, heavily wounded, with a lance in hand. With him are left only seven of his Spanish soldiers and eight Tlaxcalans, all dripping with blood. Alvarado tells them that he leapt across the open canal and will become famous for this unbelievable feat, but most of the Conquistadors think it is much more likely he scrambled across on the floating baggage and dead bodies.

Alvarado also tells Cortés there is no sense in going back. He confirms that Leon, with twenty horses and at least two hundred men, had been cut to pieces by the enemy at the bridge. The greater part of the native females, who had been given by the Aztecs and Tlaxcalans, also perished at the bridges. It was merely through God's mercy that he had saved himself, as all the canals and streets were overrun by the enemy.

The Spanish left something else behind at the bridge as well: One of Cortés's men had contracted smallpox during the battle with Narvaez. The soldier was killed, and likely when his body was looted or perhaps even sacrificed, Aztecs caught the disease. Quickly, smallpox will spread among the population. The people have no resistance and no idea how to treat it. In many cases, everyone in a house dies. With no time to bury so many people, houses are simply demolished over the bodies.

'A great plague broke out in Tenochtitlan. It lasted for seventy days, striking everywhere in the city and killed vast numbers of people. Sores erupted on our faces, our breasts, our bellies.' The Aztecs wrote...

But the Spanish are unaware of all this; they are not out of the woods yet, the Aztecs are at their heels, rushing in reinforcements from all the surrounding towns, and their only concern is to get to safety and find food.

Some of the Tlaxcalans know a short cut to Tlaxcala, and they guide the Conquistadors to a row of houses on a rising ground while the Aztecs continually harass them with their arrows, slings, and lances. The Spanish make camp there in a temple, which almost looks like a fortress, where they are able to defend themselves successfully. Here they light several fires, and dress their wounds, but find nothing to eat.

Chilled by the cold, with empty stomachs, the Spanish look around at their miserable conditions. Most of Narvaez's men met with their death at the bridges, from the weight of the gold with which they had overburdened themselves. Leon, Salcedo, Morla, the brave lancer Lares, and several other officers are gone, along with most of their horses—only twenty-three remain. Everyone is wounded, all the cannon are lost, and they have not a grain of gunpowder left. Only a few crossbows remain with arrows.

With the Aztecs constantly attacking, they also wonder how they stand with their allies of Tlaxcala. Nevertheless, Cortés resolves to march onwards to that country, and they set out at midnight. The Tlaxcalans, serving as guides, travel out in advance. Those who are more severely wounded, require the support of a stick, are placed in the center. Those who are not capable of moving at all are bound fast to the horses of those who are unable to fight. All who can bear arms are stationed in the flanks, and have some of the cavalry to support them.

Unfortunately, every village they pass through is loyal to the Aztec Empire and they are met with insults, stones, and arrows, all of which they must patiently endure. That night they rest in a few abandoned huts and try to ignore their hunger. The daily allowance of a soldier during this time is only fifty grains of maise!

The next morning early they continue along, with half of the cavalry in advance. They march about four miles across an open plain where they believe themselves safe, when three horsemen come galloping warning that the fields ahead are covered with Aztecs waiting in ambush.

Cortés gives orders for the cavalry to rush in a group at full gallop at the Aztecs and break their line. The infantry is then to follow up with thrusts at the enemy. He then rallies the troops by crying out it is their chance to avenge the dead and wounded.

The level ground is favorable for the maneuvers of the horses, which gallop up at full speed in upon the enemy, and then fall back waiting for another favorable opportunity. Although most horses and riders are severely wounded, they continue to fight valiantly. Cortés, Oli, Alvarado (who has borrowed a horse from one of Narvaez's men), and Sandoval, though all covered with wounds, are always striking where the Aztecs are trying to regroup.

Cortés continues to cheer his men on and tells them what fine booty they shall make of the enemy's rich apparel and ornamental weapons. Then Sandoval cries out, 'On, my fellow soldiers this day the victory must be ours! Our trust is in God! We shall not lose our lives here, for God has destined us for better things!'

Some of the men swear that in the heat of battle they are assisted by an apparition of St. James mounted on a white charger. Later, even a few of the Aztecs will claim they saw this spirit among their enemies at Otumba.

At this moment Cortés' attention is be drawn to where the Aztec general is positioned with his standard flying, clothed in the richest armor, shining with gold, with a cluster of large white feathers on his head. As soon as Cortés spots him, he cries out to Alvarado, Sandoval, Oli, and Avila.

"Follow me, my brave companions, these are the men we must attack!" The words are scarcely out of his mouth, when they pledge themselves to God, and gallop full charge at the enemy position.

Cortés makes a rush with his lance poised at the Aztec commander, who drops the standard in a panic, while the other officers cut down the chiefs surrounding their general.

The Aztec general is about to snatch up the standard again and flee, but Juan de Salamanca rides after him on his splendid horse, and brings him to the ground, wrestles the standard from his hand, and the rich bunch of feathers from his head, and presents both to Cortés.

(Salamanca is subsequently rewarded for this piece of heroism when afterwards the Spanish emperor will allow him to depict a bunch of feathers in his coat of arms, which his descendants bear to this day.)

After the Aztec general has fallen and their royal standard is lost, the warriors lose spirit and flee in confusion. The Spanish cavalry, with the taste of victory on their tongues, pursues and punishes them severely. Even the Tlaxcalans have changed into lions, and furiously hack at the retreating enemy with the broad swords they have captured.

When the cavalry returns from the pursuit, the Conquistadors offer up thanks unto the Almighty God for this victory, and their escape from the hands of the Aztecs. This terrible and bloody battle was fought near the town of Otumba, by which name this battle will be known through all times to come.

Not long ago the Conquistadors marched to Alvarado's assistance in Mexico with an army of nearly 1,400 men, among which there were seventy-nine horses, eighty crossbow-men, and a like number of musketeers, along with above 2,000 Tlaxcalan warriors, and a fine array of artillery. By the time they are victorious at Otumba, they lost 870 troops, and more than 1,200 Tlaxcalans. In addition, 72 men and five Spanish females, all of Narvaez's group, were put to death by the Aztecs in Tustepec.

After this miraculous victory, they dine off some gourds which grow wild in the fields, and continue the journey to Tlaxcala. They carefully avoid any villages, as the enemy is still operating in the area.

Soon the range of hills near Tlaxcala comes into view, and they feel the same joy at this sight as if they are seeing their native country. But many are concerned as to what the present feeling of Tlaxcala towards them might be; and also as to how matters stand at Vera Cruz, where the enemy might also have cut the garrison to pieces.

All they have left is 440 men, twenty horses, twelve crossbows, and seven muskets with no gunpowder. Yet Cortés reminds them that this is the same number of men with which they first set sail from Cuba, and ventured into the very capital of the Aztec Empire. He also warns them to be particularly cautious not to give the Tlaxcalans any reason for complaint. This is especially intended for the few remaining of Narvaez's men, who are not so accustomed to subordination. For the rest, continues Cortés, he hopes to God they will find the Tlaxcalans as faithful and true as before. If, however, they should have turned against us, we were not therefore to lose courage, but to trust in our strong arm, which had the power to overcome any foe.

They soon arrive at the ruins of some ancient temples which mark the boundary between Tlaxcalan territory and the Aztec Empire and finally feel safe. When news of their arrival reaches the capital of Tlaxcala, Maxixcatzin, the old Xicotencatl, and Chichimeclatecl, accompanied by the principal nobles, immediately set out to welcome them. They gave the Spanish a hearty reception, and several of the chiefs weep aloud.

"Alas! Malinche, how deeply we take your misfortune to heart, and lament the death of so many of your brothers, and of our countrymen, who have perished with them! The only thing you must think of at present is, to cure your wounds and strengthen yourselves with good food. Do just as if you were at home in your own country. Rest yourselves a little and then proceed to our town, where we will find you quarters. We previously looked upon you as men of extraordinary courage, we do so now in a even greater sense. We will all now that mourn the loss of our sons, our husbands and our brothers. You have great reason to be thankful to your gods who have conducted you here in safety, and who gave you power to gain the victory over that vast army."

Cortés and his officers and soldiers then embrace these men affectionately and make them presents in gold and jewels, to which every man is glad to contribute. While Maxixcatzin shows extreme grief at the loss of Doña Elvira his daughter, and of Leon, to whom he had presented her; they are also extremely happy to find that Malinalli and Doña Luisa have escaped the carnage. Xicotencatl especially thanks Malinalli for looking after his daughter during the terrible and bloody retreat from Tenochtitlan.

Then in the company of all the chiefs, the Conquistadors march into the city of Tlaxcala. Cortés and Malinalli are quartered in the house of Maxixcatzin, and Alvarado and his companion in the home of her father Xicotencatl. They dress their wounds and patiently rest but four more men succumb to their battle injuries.

After barely resting, Cortés soon inquires about the 40,000 pesos worth of gold which he had forwarded to Tlaxcala for safekeeping, intending it for Vera Cruz. Maxixcatzin informs him that a certain Juan de Alcantara, with two others of the garrison in Vera Cruz, had arrived with a written permission signed by Cortés, and taken all the gold with them.

The Conqueror is not pleased at this news and dispatches three Tlaxcalans to Vera Cruz with a letter, in which he reports all that transpired in Mexico, and warns them to be extremely cautious about the Aztecs, keep a close watch on Narvaez, and not to allow any ships to depart the harbor. He further asks them to send every man they can spare with all their store of gunpowder and crossbows.

The three messengers soon return with an answer from Vera Cruz, that everything was peaceful there, but they also report that Juan de Alcantara and his companions had been murdered and all the gold stolen by unknown parties. In the end the reinforcements sent by Vera Cruz consists of just seven men, all of whom are sick with small pox, which has begun to engulf the whole of New Spain.

In the meantime the younger Xicotencatl, who still hates the Spanish and can't forget his humiliating defeats on the battlefield, sees a perfect opportunity to annihilate them while they are weak. So Xicotencatl calls a meeting of his relations and friends, and proposes that they should form a friendly alliance with the new Aztec Emperor, Cuitláhuac and together kill all the Spanish. Then they would have all their gold and cotton and become wealthy personages by such booty.

When the elder Xicotencatl and Maxixcatzin and Chichimeclatecl hear of this rebellious movement, they order the younger Xicotencatl to appear before them, and after a heated exchange throw him out of the tribal council and relieve him of his command.

After resting twenty-two days, and healing their wounds, Cortés grows restless and talks about making an incursion into the neighboring province of Tepeaca, where several of Narvaez's men and some of his had been killed on their march to the Aztec capital. He wants revenge for these actions, supposedly to maintain order. Malinalli is concerned about his behavior, she sees him as a kind hearted and relatively gentle man, it is not like him to think such murderous thoughts. She tries, but can't talk him out of it.

When Cortés tells his officers about this plan they all think he is crazy too, but Narvaez's men are worse and flatly refuse to fight. They only want to return to their comfortable former lives in Cuba. They point out how they are in dire need of horses, muskets, crossbows, and even cords for the latter; in short everything necessary to carry on a war. They further go on to say, that all of them are covered with wounds, and that only 440 men remained of the united troops of Narvaez and Cortés. That the Aztecs occupy every pass and every mountain, and the ships will rot away if they lay any longer in the harbor; and so on.

Cortés, as usual does not soon give up trying to persuade them to join him in this campaign. He speaks to them over and over in a very quiet and kind manner. When they found that all their arguments are fruitless, and Cortés maintains they are imperatively called upon to remain, both for the service of God and of our emperor, they at last consent to stay, and declare their willingness to join in the expedition.

Cortés then asks the chiefs of Tlaxcala to furnish him with 5,000 men to join him on his march into the province of Tepeaca, whose inhabitants he is going to punish for the murder of several Spaniards.

It turned out the inhabitants of the province of Tepeaca had done great damage to Tlaxcalan plantations, so they are willing to immediately contribute 4,000 warriors. However all the provinces which Cortés intends to invade are quite prepared as the Aztecs have anticipated this move and stationed warriors everywhere. Despite this, they commence their march without either cannon or muskets, as there is not a grain of gunpowder left.

The small army consists of seventeen horse, six crossbow-men, and 420 Spaniards, most of whom are only armed with swords and shields, and 4,000 Tlaxcalans. The Conquistadors make camp the first night about twelve miles from Tepeaca. The inhabitants have all fled, and carried off everything they could with them.

The Spanish soon encounter the Aztecs nearby and a savage battle ensues the day after. As the ground is level, consisting entirely of corn and maguey plantations, it is particularly favorable for cavalry maneuvers, and the enemy is quickly routed. Considerable numbers of Tepeacans and Aztecs are killed, while the Conquistadors' side loses only three Tlaxcalans and twelve wounded.

The Tepeacans, seeing that the Aztec garrison is not much protection now send messengers of peace without consulting the Aztecs. These are very kindly received by Cortés and take an oath of allegiance and send the Aztecs away.

The Conquistadors then enter Tepeaca, and found a town there, to which they give the name of Villa de Segura de la Frontera. It is very productive of maise, and because it is neighboring Tlaxcala, a regular government is formed.

They then visit all the districts where Spaniards had been murdered, seeking revenge and brand all the suspects they can find with the letter G, meaning *guerra*, (war). And turn a vast number of them into slaves of the Tlaxcalans.

About this time another Emperor is elected to the Aztec throne, as the former, Cuitláhuac has died of smallpox. The new Emperor is a nephew of Montezuma, and was called Cuauhtemoctzin. He is about twenty-five years of age, and a very well-bred. He soon makes himself so feared among his people that they tremble in his presence. His wife is one of Montezuma's daughters, and passes for a great beauty in her country.

When Cuauhtemoctzin receives news of the overthrow of his troops at Tepeaca, and of the consequent submission of that province, he begins to fear for his other provinces. He therefore dispatches messengers to every township, commanding the inhabitants to hold themselves ready for action. And in order that he might make sure of their obedience, he sends one chief at present, and another he absolves from paying tribute. His most able generals are sent with troops to protect the boundaries, and he warns them to perform better than they had at Tepeaca.

Then miraculously, the Conquistadors' fortunes change again. Letters arrive from Vera Cruz with the information that a ship has run in there, commanded by a good friend of Cortés named Pedro Barba, who had been sub-governor of the Havana under Velasquez. He has brought with him thirteen soldiers and two horses, besides letters for Pamfilo Narvaez, whom Velasquez thought had by this time taken possession of New Spain in his name. In these letters, Velasquez orders Narvaez, if Cortés is still alive, to transport him, with all of his principal officers, to Cuba, whence he would send them to Spain to stand trial.

The letter goes on to say that Caballero, the man Cortés appointed admiral of the fleet, went on board to pay his respects to Barba. The ship he went on was well manned with sailors, and their arms were carefully hidden from view. After both parties had welcomed each other, Caballero inquired after the health of the governor of Cuba, and Barba, on his side, asked after Narvaez, and what had become of Cortés. Caballero pretends to still be allied with Narvaez and so gives him the most favorable account, spoke about his power, wealth, and his vast authority in these countries. As for Cortés, he tells him he had escaped with twenty men, and was wandering about from place to place.

Caballero then suggested to Barba that he should disembark where he would meet with excellent quarters. This he readily agreed to, and stepped into Caballero's skiff, and so all went on shore. But the instant Barba set foot on land Caballero and his men grab him.

"Sir, you are my prisoner, in the name of the captain-general Cortés!" Barba and his men are completely taken by surprise and there is nothing they can do. Caballero then has the sails, compass, and rudder removed from their ship, and sent to Cortés at Tepeaca along with Barba.

Cortés welcomes Pedro Barba with every mark of distinction. Barba immediately agrees to join him, and Cortés gives him a company of crossbow-men to command. He also learns that there is another smaller vessel at Cuba, which was taking in a cargo of provisions, and is also destined by the governor for New Spain. This vessel soon arrives at Vera Cruz and has on board eight soldiers, a horse, six crossbows, and other kinds of ammunition. It is quickly captured by Caballero in the same manner, and sent to Segura de la Frontera.

There is much joy at the arrival of these new guests and the provisions they carry. Cortés receives them most kindly, grants each a command, and thanks God most heartily for this reinforcement of men, arms, and horses.

30 Cortés Consolidates His Power

While the Conquistadors are operating in the province of Tepeaca, the new Aztec Emperor throws more warriors into all the townships which lay on the boundaries as he is sure Cortés will try to enter his territories at those points. These garrisons take excessive liberties under their new master, and commit so many atrocities against the inhabitants, that they are determined to bear it no longer. They are not only robbed of their garments, their maise, their fowls, and their gold, but that the Aztecs kidnap the prettiest of their wives and daughters.

When these tribes see how peaceably and the Cholulans live without a Aztec garrison, they secretly send four nobles to Cortés, begging him to rid them of their oppressors. Now Malinalli gladly resumes her role as translator / diplomat, a job made much easier since Cortés is not so obsessed with converting every tribe to Christianity, but more with revenge. The Conqueror even finally shares with her his master plan: To retake the Aztec Empire.

Now Malinalli reigns supreme over her own people and dispenses peace or war at her pleasure, for she alone can shape the results of the negotiations and treaties between Cortés and the chiefs. She is a princess plucked from the degradation of slavery, into which an unnatural mother had delivered her, into the Conqueror's realm, where she has become the mistress of a nation's destiny.

Malinalli then negotiates a mutual aid pact, and these people agree to join the Conquistadors with their own warriors, so the combined forces should easily overcome the Aztec troops. Cortés then agrees to send, under Oli, a detachment consisting of 300 men, with part of the cavalry and crossbow-men, along with a large group of Tlaxcalans, who are clamoring to join since the rich booty they made in Tepeaca.

Oli arrives within four miles of this place, when he is met by the chiefs, who point out to him the best mode of attacking the Aztecs, and assure him he will be reinforced by the inhabitants. They barely finish speaking when the Aztecs attack. The battle rages, and the Aztecs fight courageously for a considerable time, wounding several Spaniards, kill two horses, and wound eight others. But after an hour Oli's men, along with the Tlaxcalans, and the local natives wreck carnage and take a large number of prisoners, driving the Aztecs to retreat.

They flee to a fortified township named Iztucan, which has another garrison of Aztecs. Oli pursues them and with his new allies routs the Aztecs, who flee in disorder. Here again two horses are killed, and Oli himself is wounded in two places.

Then a series of Spanish ships arrive at Vera Cruz. Some sent by Velásquez to find out what is going on, one sent from Jamaica to support an abortive settlement on the Panuco River north of Vera Cruz, and one from Spain. In all cases the crews are talked into joining Cortés and slowly rebuild his army.

The Spanish soon get reports the inhabitants of nearby towns called Zacatemi and Xalatzinco had been the ones that plundered and killed Juan de Alcantara and his two companions who were returning from Tlaxcala with the gold. Cortés then orders Sandoval, with 200 men and a large army of Tlaxcalans to punish them and retrieve the gold.

After a fierce battle Sandoval forces them to break out and flee, and soon they sue for peace. But the gold is nowhere to be found, the chiefs say that the Aztecs had taken away all the gold, and presented it to their new Emperor. Hearing this Sandoval refers them to Cortés, and he marches back with a great number of women and young men, whom he had taken prisoners, and marked with the iron.

One by one the chiefs of the surrounding tribes now came to Malinalli to beg Cortés for peace. In return she requires them to take an oath of allegiance and furnish provisions. Soon the whole territory is neutralized, and word of Cortés' justice and bravery spreads throughout the whole of New Spain. Everyone fears him, not the least of which is Cuauhtemoctzin, the new Emperor.

Indeed Cortés' authority is such that the natives came from the most distant parts to lay their disputes before him, particularly respecting the election of chiefs, right of tenure, and division of property and subjects—just like the Aztec Emperor. About this time thousands of people are killed by smallpox, among them numbers of chiefs, so it falls to Cortés to appoint the new chiefs.

But it is no wonder the Conqueror is so feared because he seems to have changed and become a cruel general. Perhaps it is due to the terrible beating he took from the Aztecs at Tenochtitlan, or his dismay and depression over Montezuma's treachery, or he is heavily influenced by his friends the Tlaxcalans, but suddenly makes a habit of obtaining slaves in every battle.

After peace is thus restored to the whole province, Cortés is determined to mark all the prisoner/slaves with the iron, and set apart a fifth of them for the Spanish king. Notice is given that every person is to come with his slaves to a certain place, that they might be marked with the red-hot branding iron. Every man, accordingly, brings the females and young men he has taken prisoner. Adult men are exempted as they are too difficult to guard. After all the slaves had been brought together and branded with the letter G, the emperor's fifths and then Cortés' are deducted. When it comes time to distribute the rest to the men, it seems as all the pretty females are already allotted, so once again the lowly soldier is cheated.

This results in severe grumbling among the troops, but then Cortés discovers that some of the men managed to hang onto the gold he had asked them to carry on the retreat from Tenochtitlan. He then demands everyone pay him a third of what they have or he will take it all. While most flatly refuse to comply, Cortés still manages to extort a good deal of it.

About this time Cortés also dispatches several trusted officers to Cuba, Santa Domingo, and Spain to give an account of all that happened and defend and answer all sorts of charges being brought against him. A number of Narvaez's men also leave and the remaining Conquistadors are glad to be rid of them.

With peace and tranquility in all the outlying territories, Cortés puts his plan into action to re-take the Aztec capital. He orders wood and parts for thirteen brigantines to be gathered so they can transport them to the Aztec lake, where they will be constructed and used in the assault. Once again he gives Martin Lopez the task. The Conqueror is convinced the best way to attack is by water so they don't get trapped again by the bridges over the causeways.

Cortés then heads back to Tlaxcala, where he learns Maxixcatzin, like thousands of others, has succumbed to smallpox. The Conqueror grieves at this loss as much as if he had lost his own father.

In the meantime, the timber had been felled and trimmed, tar had been made from pine trees in the local forest, and the iron work, anchors, sails, and ropes taken from the ships Cortés had destroyed, arrived from Vera Cruz. 1,000 Tlaxcalans are assigned to transport all these things to Tezcuco, which Cortés planned to capture and use a base of operations to construct and launch the ships.

Just as the Conquistadors are about to set out on their march, news arrives from Vera Cruz that a large Spanish vessel has run in there from the Canaries. It is carrying a quantity of crossbows, muskets, powder, and other ammunition, besides three horses and thirteen soldiers. The owner of the cargo is a certain Juan de Burgos, and Cortés immediately bargains with him for the whole of the ammunition and cargo.

With a renewed supply of muskets, powder, crossbows, and horses, the Conqueror requests 10,000 warriors from Tlaxcala. The elder Xicotencatl not only grants those, but assures him many more troops are at his service, under the leadership Chichimeclatecl. And so they set out for the Aztec capital once again, on the fourth day after Christmas.

They make camp the first night about eight miles from Tezcuco, and leave early the next morning, soon encountering seven natives, all unarmed, bearing a golden banner at the point of a long lance, which they lowered on approach in a sign of peace.

"Malinche, our lord and master Cohuanacotzin, the king of Tezcuco, has sent us to you to beg of you to take him into your friendship. He awaits you in his city of Tezcuco; and, in token of peace, he sends you this golden banner: at the same time he requests you will command your brothers and the Tlaxcalans not to commit any depredations in his country, and wishes you to take up your quarters in his city, where he will provide you with everything you may require." Malinalli translates.

She questions them further and learns that Aztec warriors lay in wait in the mountain passes. Cortés is appreciative of this information and makes a great show of embracing the ambassadors and ordering the Tlaxcalans chiefs not to allow their men to commit any atrocities in this country, nor injure any one, as we were at peace with the inhabitants. Cortés, however, suspects the Tezcucans are not in earnest in their plea for peace.

Over that night Malinalli learns that Cohuanacotzin had murdered his elder brother, in order to place himself on the throne. And further that there was one young man, Ixtlilxuchitl, who was indeed the rightful heir. He was the lawful son of the former prince of Tezcuco. Cortés then installed him on the throne. And that he might be thoroughly confirmed in the holy religion, learn the art of governing, and the Spanish language, Cortés gives him Spanish stewards. Ixtlilxuchitl is greatly esteemed and beloved by his subjects.

The first thing Cortés requires of him is a sufficient number of men to assist in launching the brigantines when they are completed, and to lengthen and deepen the canals where they are to be launched. The Conqueror makes no secret of the intended use of these vessels. They not only declare their willingness to cooperate, but even send messengers to the neighboring towns, inviting them to seek the friendship of the Spanish, and declare war against the Aztecs.

To Cortés' delight, several tribes which were subject to Tezcuco came to ask for peace and beg forgiveness, if they had been any way implicated in the late murders of our countrymen. Malinalli handles all these meetings and swears them all to allegiance to the Spanish. Cortés receives them most graciously, and makes them allies, astounded that all these tribes so close to the Aztec capital are capitulating without a fight.

The building of the brigantines is now fully underway on the lake, and every day there are 8,000 Indians employed to lengthen and deepen one of the canals. In the meantime Cortés takes an equal number of Tlaxcalans, who are itching for battle and booty, in expeditions against any tribes who don't fall into line.

Soon enough the towns of Chalco and Tlalmanalco, are desirous of making peace, but are prevented from doing so by the Aztec garrisons stationed there. They complain bitterly of the treatment which they suffered from them. Under these circumstances, Cortés decides that the natives of Tlalmanalco and Chalco, warrant immediate assistance, that they might be enabled to form an alliance.

While the main force stands by to protect Tezcuco, Lugo and Sandoval receive instructions to march out to dislodge the Aztec troops from Chalco and Tlalmanalco, and clear the road leading to Tlaxcala and Vera Cruz, along which the enemy has stationed small detachments to harass the Spanish if they should try to escape.

This plan is secretly conveyed to the inhabitants of Chalco so that they might attack the Aztecs at the same moment as the Spanish. Nothing was more agreeable to inhabitants of Chalco, and they accordingly prepare to rise up against the enemy at the proper time.

15,000 Tlaxcalans, under the command of an ambitious, and very courageous general begs Cortés to allow him to go to battle to avenge the death of so many of his countrymen. The Conqueror thereupon invites him to direct an attack against the town of Xaltocan, which lay twenty miles from Tezcuco, in the midst of the lake, and connected with the mainland by a causeway.

Cortés considers this expedition against the Xaltocans of no small strategic importance, and is therefore decides to command it himself. He takes with him Alvarado and Oli, two hundred and fifty Spanish foot soldiers, thirty cavalry, a good number of musketeers and crossbows ; accompanied by the 15,000 Tlaxcalan warriors, and a company of the best warriors of Tezcuco.

Near Xaltocan, the army comes upon a large body of Aztecs, in fortified positions. Cortés leads the cavalry, and after the musketeers and crossbow-men have fired in among the enemy, he charges their line full gallop, and kills several of them. The Aztecs then retreat to the mountains, where they are pursued by the Tlaxcalans, who slay thirty more. The first night Cortés encamps in a small hamlet, where he learns from Malinalli that the Aztec Emperor has dispatched large bodies of troops, stationed in canoes on the lake, to the assistance of Xaltocan.

Very early next morning they are attacked by the joint forces of the Aztecs and Xaltocans. They rain showers of arrows and stones on the Spanish from the small islands which rise among the marshes, wounding ten Spaniards and numbers of Tlaxcalans. Here the cavalry is completely useless, as they could not pass through the water. Even the muskets and crossbows are of little use since the Aztec learned to shield themselves by raising up boards alongside of their canoes.

Then two natives of Tepetezcuco, which are mortal enemies of Xaltocan, point out a spot which is shallow enough for them to wade through into the town. On receiving this information Cortés orders the crossbow-men, musketeers, and several of the Tlaxcalans, to step boldly into the water, which reaches only to their middles, and push forward, while he himself takes up a position on the mainland, with the cavalry to cover their rear, should the Aztecs attempt to attack from behind.

Although the enemy falls furiously on those advancing through the water, and wounds several of them, the men are not daunted by this, and move forward steadily until they reach the dry part of the causeway. With the road to the town now open to them, they wreck terrible havoc among the enemy's ranks.

The Aztecs, with the inhabitants, now took refuge in their canoes, and flee back to Tenochtitlan. The men take considerable booty, in cotton, salt, gold, and other items, and set fire to some houses, before returning to the mainland, where Cortés is stationed.

When Emperor Cuauhtemoctzin learns of this defeat he is furious; and the more so as the people of Chalco are his subjects, and had now for the third time taken up arms against him. He is determined to be revenged and assembles an army of upwards of 20,000 men, and sends these in 2,000 canoes to Chalco.

Sandoval has scarcely entered Tezcuco, and had just seen Cortés, when messengers arrive from Chalco to request his immediate return. Sandoval and his men then must march all the way back to assist them in their defense.

The panicked Chalcans, in the meantime, beg assistance from their neighbors the Huexotzincans and Tlaxcalans and these two powers arrive that very night, with an army of more than 20,000 men. This instills the Chalcans with fresh courage and they attack the Aztecs in the open field and rout them. This defeat is most humbling to the Aztecs, and they are more ashamed of it than if they had suffered it from Cortés.

In the meantime Cortés promises Chalco he would himself march with his troops to their relief, and not rest until he has completely driven the enemy from their territory. He therefore immediately sets out with 300 men.

During his absence a conspiracy had been set afoot by a close friend of the governor of Cuba, named Antonio de Villafaña, in conjunction with others of Narvaez's troops. The object of this conspiracy is to murder Cortés on his return.

The conspirators plan to hand a letter to Cortés while he sat at dinner with his officers, which was to be securely fastened and sealed, purporting to come from his father, with a vessel that had just arrived from Spain. While he was occupied in the perusal of this letter, he and all of the officers who sat at table with him, were to be stabbed to death.

The conspiracy is disclosed to Cortés by one of his soldiers a couple of days after his return to Tezcuco, and he thus has sufficient time to adopt measures for suppressing it before it spread further. This man also informs him that there are several high ranking men among the conspirators.

Cortés, after handsomely rewarding this man, communicates the whole affair to his most trusted officers: Alvarado, Oli, Lugo, Sandoval, Tapia, and Diaz. He then orders them to arm themselves, and proceed without further delay to the quarters of said Antonio de Villafaña.

On entering his apartment they find him in conversation with several of the conspirators, and they immediately arrest him. The rest instantly flee, but Cortés has many of them seized. Cortés thrusts his hand into Villafaña's shirt, and withdraws a paper containing the whole plan of the conspirators, to which all their names are attached., On perusing this paper, Cortés finds the names of several men of importance among the list of conspirators and wanting to save them from dishonor, he afterwards releases the information that Villafaña must have swallowed the paper, and that he had not read it himself, nor even so much as seen it.

A criminal indictment is then instituted against Villafaña,

whereupon he, with several others who were implicated in it, makes a full confession of the whole matter. Cortés then pronounces Villafaña guilty, and sentences him to be hanged. After he has taken confession with Father Juan Diaz, he is promptly executed in front of his own quarters.

Cortés now begins to make active preparations for the siege of Tenochtitlan. The brigantines are finished and need only to be rigged with sails. The canal in which these vessels are to be launched, and conveyed into the lake, is now also sufficiently deep and wide.

He issues requests to all the towns of Tezcuco, and all those in alliance, to furnish 8,000 copper points for arrows, to be made after the model of Spanish ones. They are also to furnish an equal number of arrows, which are to be made from a wood particularly adapted for that use, and they receive some Spanish arrows to work from. He allows them eight days for the making and delivery of these, and indeed both the arrows and the copper arrowheads arrive at Tezcuco in the time specified. The stock of these now consists of 50,000 pieces, and the arrowheads made by these people are even better than those from Spain. This is all mostly due to the intelligence and determination of Malinalli, who transmitted and explained all these requests and sees them through.

After Cortés thus acquaints his allies with his plan against the Aztecs, he determines to review the troops, and selects the second day of Easter for this purpose. This review is held in the large square of Tezcuco, and the following are mustered: Eighty-four horses, six hundred and fifty foot soldiers—armed with swords or lances, and one hundred and ninety-four crossbows and musketeers.

Out of these troops he selects the men who are to serve on the thirteen brigantines. Each of which requires twelve rowers and a captain, with twelve crossbow-men and musketeers. In this way the thirteen brigantines have two hundred and eighty men, who, with the additional number of artillerymen, amount to three hundred and twenty-five.

Cortés now divides the troops into three divisions. The first division, consisting of one hundred and fifty foot soldiers, all well armed with swords and shields, thirty horsemen, and eighteen musketeers and crossbow-men, is commanded by Alvarado. To this division 8,000 Tlaxcalans are added. Alvarado receives orders to take up his position in the town of Tlacupa.

The second division is placed under the command of Oli, and consists of thirty horsemen, one hundred and sixty-five foot soldiers, and twenty crossbow-men and musketeers. To this division, likewise, 8,000 Tlaxcalans are added, and they are to take up their position in the town of Cojohuacan, about eight miles from Tlacupa.

Sandoval is appointed to the command of the third division, consisting of twenty-four horsemen, fourteen crossbow-men and musketeers, and one hundred and fifty foot soldiers armed with shields and swords. To this division are added 8,000 Indians from the townships of Chalco, Huexotzinco, and other places in alliance. This division is to take up a position near Iztapalapan, and Sandoval's mission is to attack that town, and do as much damage as possible until he receives further orders.

Cortés takes command of the brigantines. On this flotilla there are altogether 325 men. The next morning is fixed for departure.

Cortés and his officers decide in an overnight planning session that it will be impossible to fight to the city along the causeways, unless the troops are protected on each side by a couple of the brigantines. The Conqueror therefore assigns four ships to Alvarado's division, while he retains six others near his headquarters. Two others are assigned to Sandoval. The thirteenth is deemed too small and taken out of service, and the men distributed among the crews of the other twelve.

31 The Aztec Reign Is Over

The attack begins at day break. Two ships are positioned on each side of the causeway to cover the troops as they advance and repel the Aztec canoes, preventing them from flanking the Spanish. But the fighting is no less horrendous then it was when the Conquistadors retreated weeks before.

The Aztecs quickly adapt to the Spanish ships and counter them by driving numbers of stakes into the water, whose tips are just below the water. It is difficult for the brigantines to avoid them, and they consequently get hung up, and leave the troops open to attacks by the canoes. The battle goes on the whole day and the Aztecs do not let up until night falls.

In the morning the Aztecs counter-attack in force and since the cavalry is useless on the narrow causeway, the Conquistadors are forced to retreat once again. And once again the bridges are gone and they are forced to swim across the gaps where the Aztec canoes are able to do considerable damage. Five Spaniards are taken prisoner, and most of the rest are severely wounded. The brigantines make every attempt to assist, but are unable to come near enough because of the heavy stakes.

The Aztecs are so elated with the victory they then attack the Conquistadors main staging area and it is only due to the cannons that they are driven back.

Again and again the Spanish attack down the causeways, only to be forced to retreat back to the mainland. The Aztec defense system of the narrow causeways and bridges just works too well to overcome. It is a grinding war of attrition Cortés can't win.

The Conqueror himself is wounded in the leg, sixty Spaniards are captured, and six horses dead. Then several Aztecs grab Cortés, who with great difficulty tears loose. Christobal de Olea comes to his rescue, cutting down one of the warriors, and pulls him to safety assisted by another soldier, named Lerma. But this heroic deed costs Olea his life, leaving only Lerma to cut through the enemy, but both men fall into the water. Antonio de Quiñones, the captain of the guard, hastens up and succeeds in dragging Cortés out of the water, and places him on the back of a horse. At this instant his major-domo, Christobal de Guzman, comes up with another horse for him, but the Aztecs capture him. The enemy pursues Cortés and his troops up to their very encampment, hooting and yelling.

Sandoval and his group fare no better and he is also forced to lead them to retreat. When his troops are out of danger, and after his wounds are bandaged, he pays Cortés a visit telling him the battle plan was a disaster and they are just wasting men.

Then while the Spanish are fairly secure at their encampment, they all hear at the same moment the large drum of Huitzilopochtli. It resounds mightily from the summit of the temple, accompanied by the hellish music of shell trumpets, horns, and other instruments. The sound is truly dismal and terrifying, but still more agonizing is when they all look up and see how the Aztec priests are mercilessly sacrificing their unfortunate comrades who had been captured to their idols.

The terrified and anguished Spanish can plainly see the platform with the cursed idols. They can't look away as the priests adorn the heads of the victims with feathers, how they stretch them out at full length on a large stone, rip open their breasts with flint knives, tear out their palpitating heart, and offer it to their gods. They are forced to be spectators of how they then seize hold of the dead bodies by the legs and throw them headlong down the steps of the temple.

Cuauhtemoctzin, after winning this victory, sends the feet and hands of Spanish victims, with their beards and skins, and even the heads of the horses they have killed, to all the Conquistadors' allies, with assurances that more than half of the Spaniards have been killed, and that he would soon have the rest in his power. He then orders those tribes which had entered into alliances to immediately send ambassadors to Tenochtitlan, otherwise he will put them all to death.

This has the desired effect and many of the tribes that sent warriors to join Cortés suddenly pick up and return to their homes. The Conqueror is greatly alarmed at this desertion, but takes care to hide his real feelings from those few allies who remain.

Malinalli is heartbroken at all these defeats, yet never gives up and manages to find the brother of the king of Tezcuco, the brave Suchel, to give Cortés some advice:

"Malinche, you should not throw your men against the Aztecs day after day. In my opinion you should rather lay siege to the city and cut off all its supplies of water and provisions. There are so many thousands of warriors that their store of provisions must soon become exhausted. The only supply of water they have is from the rain that falls. What can they do if you cut off their supplies of provisions and water? A war against hunger and thirst is the most dire of all calamities!"

Cortés thanks him for this advice and sends word by means of brigantines to Alvarado and Sandoval to desist from the daily attacks and instead concentrate on the aqueducts. While the siege is progressing, the men are tasked with filling up the wide opening in the causeway in front of their camp. Two companies repel the attacks of the enemy, while the third fills the gap. In this way they advance nearer and nearer to the city.

While the three divisions are steadily carrying on their operations against the city, the brigantines are diligently chasing away the convoys of provisions and water going to Tenochtitlan. They continually capture large canoes filled with food and take a great number of prisoners.

Thirteen days after the defeat and the start of the siege, Suchel, is quite convinced that the advantage has swung to the Spanish, and at Malinalli's urging, sends word to his brother to dispatch as many warriors from Tezcuco he can spare to aid in the siege. The king of Tezcuco complies with his brother's wishes, and two days later more than 2,000 of his warriors arrive. Cortés rejoices at the arrival of this considerable body of men, and bestows his praises on them.

With Malinalli continuing her diplomacy, the Tlaxcalans soon followed the example of the Tezcucans, and shortly after return in great numbers, under the command of Tecapaneca. In the same way large bodies of men arrive from Huexotzinco, but very few come from holdout Cholula.

Cortés then assembles all the native warriors and addresses them through Malinalli. He assures them he had never doubted their being faithfully inclined towards him, from the time they had become subjects of our emperor, and experienced our bounty. When he invited them to join him in this campaign against the Aztecs, he had had no other object in view than that they might reap a real benefit by it, and return home laden with booty; and have an opportunity of revenging themselves on their old enemies.

Then, as usual for Cortés, he brazenly attempts to tell them off: He says, though they had fought bravely, and assisted him on every occasion, they should nevertheless bear in mind that the Spanish drew their power from the Almighty God and as such could defeat the Aztecs without them. For the rest, he is bound to make the observation to them that, according to the strict articles of war, they deserve punishment of death, because they had deserted their general at a time when the battle was at its height. He would, however, pardon them, on account of their ignorance of our laws and articles of war. He likewise forbids them, for any reason whatever, to kill any Aztecs that might be taken prisoners; for he was anxious to make himself master of the city by pacifying its inhabitants.

Malinalli chooses to only translate portions of this speech, leaving out most of the last part so as not to offend these allies in the time of the Conquistadors' greatest need.

The battles continue day after day but then it begins to rain very fast every evening, and the heavier the showers the more welcome they are to the soldiers since the Aztecs wouldn't fight. Unfortunately the rain also supplies the enemy with fresh drinking water so they hold out for ninety-three days.

Cortés grows impatient and decides on perhaps the boldest move yet of his military career. He orders Sandoval to penetrate with all twelve brigantines into that quarter of the city where Emperor Cuauhtemoctzin has retreated with the crux of his army and the principal nobles and chiefs of the Empire.

The Conqueror, along with his other principal officers Alvarado, Luis Marin, and Lugo, then ascends to the top of the chief temple on the Tlatelulco, in order to view Sandoval's maneuvers.

When Sandoval appears with the brigantines in the quarter where Cuauhtemoctzin's palace stands, the Emperor panics and orders an evacuation by the lake. The Aztecs began to carry off all the property they can take with them in their canoes, and take to flight so that the lake is covered with numbers of canoes. When Sandoval realizes that Cuauhtemoctzin, with the chief personages of Mexico, has fled, he immediately orders the brigantines in pursuit of the canoes.

Garcia Holguin, who is an good friend of Sandoval, commands the swiftest ship with the best rowers, so he is ordered to go after Cuauhtemoctzin. He soon recognizes the canoe in which the Emperor rides by the beautifully carved work, by the tent, and other decorations. Holguin signals it to stop, and when they do not comply, he orders his men to level their crossbows and muskets at it.

Emperor Cuauhtemoctzin then fears for his life and cries out.

"Forbid your men to shoot at me. I am the king of Mexico, and of this country. I only beg of you not to touch my wife, my children, these females, or anything else I have with me here, but take me alone to Malinche."

Holguin then brings his ship alongside and actually embraces the Emperor, and assists him courteously into his brigantine, with his wife and twenty of his nobles. Soft mats and cloaks are then spread out on the poop of the vessel for seats, and what food there was on board set before them.

Amazingly, Sandoval and Holguin get into a brief argument as to which one will have the honor of bringing the Emperor in to Cortés, so Holguin escorts him by the hand while Sandoval accompanies them.

When Cortés receives news of this unbelievable feat, he is overjoyed and orders some elevated seats to be erected, and covered with soft cushions and mantles, and a good meal to be prepared. Holguin and Sandoval soon after arrive with the Emperor, and escort him into the presence of Cortés, who receive him with the utmost respect, and embraces him affectionately. Once more Malinalli, still a teenager, is face to face with her second Aztec Emperor, and handles all the translation.

"Malinche! I have done what I was bound to do in the defense of my capital, and of my subjects. My resources have now become entirely exhausted. I have succumbed to superior power, and stand a prisoner before you. Now draw the dagger which hangs at your belt, and plunge it into my bosom." Cuauhtemoctzin says, with tears in his eyes.

The Conqueror doesn't yet know the real truth:

Smallpox devastated the Aztec population. It killed most of the Aztec army and 25% of the overall population. As the natives did not know the remedy of the disease, they died in heaps, like bedbugs. In many places it happened that everyone in a house died and, as it was impossible to bury the great number of dead, they pulled down the houses over them so that their homes become their tombs. The Aztec army's chain of command was in ruins. The soldiers who still lived were weak from the disease. The Spanish will soon enter the city and they will not be able to walk through the streets without stepping on the bodies of smallpox victims...

Cortés assures Cuauhtemoctzin, through Malinalli, in the most kind manner, that he values him the more for his bravery, his powerful and courageous defense of his city, and that far from making any reproaches, he honored him. He certainly could have wished that he had accepted his offers of peace, to save the city from destruction, and the lives of so many of his subjects that had been sacrificed in battle. He ought no longer to grieve, but compose his mind, and strive to raise the desponding spirits of his officers; assuring him he shall remain lord of Mexico, and of the other provinces attached to it.

Cuauhtemoctzin and his officers thank Cortés for this promise. Then the Conqueror inquires about his wife and the other women, who he had been given to understand, had accompanied him in the brigantine. Cuauhtemoctzin said that he had begged Sandoval to leave them behind in the canoes until Malinche's pleasure was known. Cortés then sends for them, and regales them with the best of everything he had at hand. Cuauhtemoctzin was between twenty-three and twenty-four years of age, and could in all truth be termed a handsome man, with skin inclined more to white than to the copper-brown tint of the Indians in general. His wife was a niece of his uncle Montezuma and is a young and very beautiful woman.

Cuauhtemoctzin then surrenders the city of Tenochtitlan and thus the entire Aztec Empire to the Conqueror...

Cortés soon begins to make the necessary preparations for the rebuilding of the great and celebrated city of Tenochtitlan, which will eventually be called Mexico City. He marks out the ground for the churches, monasteries, private dwellings, public squares, and assigns a particular quarter of the town for the Aztec population.

This city is rebuilt with so much splendor, that, in the opinion of those who have travelled through the greater part of Europe, Mexico, after its restoration, is a larger and a more populous city than any they had seen, and the architectural style of the houses more magnificent.

32 The Heroine Triumphs

The Aztecs are defeated and human sacrifice is forever abolished in Malinalli's country, which will soon be called Mexico. She is happier than at any time in her life.

Her Captain and lover Cortés built her the most graceful house in the town of Coyoacán, on Higuera Street, where he sits even now, planning the rebuilding of Tenochtitlan, and writing his long letters to his emperor.

The only cloud on her life is that she doesn't know if she is loved. He has never said that word to her. She knows he had a Spanish wife, but Catalina died soon after arriving here.

But right now Malinalli wants only one thing. She is hesitant to ask, but up to now she has never asked for a single favor, so she decides to go through with it.

"My Captain, may I disturb you for a moment?" She has never stopped calling him that.

"Of course my dear." He responds with a genuine smile.

"I want a child." She says bluntly.

Cortés stares at her for a long moment and she cannot fathom what he is thinking. Finally he smiles again.

"Shall you give me a son?" He asks.

"I will pray to God every day for both of us that he will grant us a boy."

The Conqueror takes her by the hand and leads her upstairs.

He never tires of her beauty, but wonders what would become of her in Spain?

33 Mexico

Tenochtitlan had been destroyed and the treasure of Montezuma lost. What gold was found in the ruins was distributed among the Spanish soldiers, but did not satisfy very many. The King's royal fifth was sent off to Spain, but was captured by a French pirate while in transit.

Following his victory over the Aztecs, Cortés immediately started constructing his new city of Mexico on the ruins of Tenochtitlan. The main temple square was transformed into a typical Spanish central town plaza and a church was erected in place of the main temple.

Land was given to Cortés' followers and Indians were provided to work that land. The encomienda system was established in spite of Royal orders banning its use in the Indies. Cortés justified it to the King as being necessary to sustain Spanish political control and to establish the conditions necessary to accomplish the religious conversion of the local populace to the tenants of Christianity.

At Cortés' request, twelve Franciscan friars were sent to Mexico. Numerous parties were sent out into the countryside to search for treasure and to learn about the country that they now controlled. At Zacatula on the Pacific coast he began building four ships with which he intended to explore the 'South Sea' and to find a route to the Spice Islands. He imported livestock, seeds, and other agricultural supplies to strengthen the economy. He ordered all who were married to bring their wives to New Spain within eighteen months and all who were not yet married to find a legal wife within the same amount of time. His own wife, Catalina, arrived from Cuba - much to Cortés' surprise. She died three months after her arrival and suspicion immediately arose that Cortés had poisoned her.

Although he had subjugated the Aztecs, Cortés still had problems with his position within the Spanish hierarchy in the New World. On November 13, 1518, Velásquez had been appointed Governor of Yucatan by the King of Spain. Velásquez continued to want Cortés out of the way and one of his own men put in his place. Cortés had countered Velásquez by sending the original large shipment of gold to Spain in the hope that the King would reward him by leaving him in power in what Cortés was now calling New Spain.

In Spain Cortés had another powerful enemy in the Bishop of Burgos and Head of the Council of the Indies, Juan Rodriguez de Fonseca. In April 1521, Fonseca convinced Adrian of Utrecht, then acting as Regent during the temporary absence of the King, to issue an arrest warrant for Cortés. Cortés avoided arrest by bribing the man sent to execute the warrant. In July 1522 Charles V returned to Spain and ordered an inquiry into charges that had been made against Cortés. On October 15, 1522, the board of inquiry cleared Cortés and the King signed a decree in his favor.

In November 1522 Cortés marched north to the Panuco River and did battle with the Huastecos Indians. Following their defeat he established the town of Sanesteban del Puerto and garrisoned it with one hundred foot soldiers and thirty cavalry under the command of Pedro de Vallejo. Cortés did this in order to head off a colonizing effort by Francisco de Garay, the governor of Jamaica.

On June 26, 1523, Garay sailed from Jamaica with a sizeable force bent on executing a royal grant engineered by Fonseca to establish a colony on the mainland north of Veracruz. When he landed and found that Cortés had already established such a town he complained vigorously. Cortés sent reinforcements under Pedro de Alvarado and it was decided that Garay should go to Mexico City to consult with Cortés. The two worked out a compromise. It was agreed that Cortés would assist Garay in establishing a settlement at Rio de Palmas north of Sanesteban del Puerto, but Garay died a few days later of a mysterious illness. Once again suspicion arose that Cortés had committed murder by poisoning Garay. A bit later Indians attacked the men that had accompanied Garay and killed a number of them as well as some of Cortés ' garrison at Sanesteben Del Puerto. Cortés dispatched a force under Sandoval and annihilated the rebel Indians.

By royal decree signed by Charles V on June 26, 1523, Cortés was ordered to search for a strait connecting the Atlantic and Pacific Oceans.

On January 11, 1524, Cortés gave Cristobal de Olid command of five ships and one brigantine together with a four hundred man force in search of the long rumored strait. Olid sailed first to Cuba to obtain necessary supplies. While in Santiago Velazquez convinced Olid that he should ignore Cortés and carry on as an independent conquistador.

In May 1524 Olid established a settlement at Triunfo de la Cruz, Honduras, and announced his independence of Cortés. Cortés responded by sending Francisco de las Casas and a strong force to deal with Olid's rebellious action.

In October 1524, Cortés decided to take a strong force and travel overland to Honduras himself. On this expedition, he arranged a marriage between his mistress Malinalli and Juan de Jaramillo, a wealthy hidalgo. No one knows the reason for this except that probably Cortés needed a Spanish wife to enhance his social and political position and viewed Malinalli as a liability in that sense. One would hope his motivation here was to make sure she was well provided for by a rich landowner.

In order to avoid the possibility of an Indian uprising in Mexico City during his absence he took along with him several prominent Aztec leaders including the present Aztec King - Cuauhtémoc. Along the way these Aztec leaders developed a plot to kill Cortés. He discovered it and hanged two of the leaders including King Cuauhtémoc. In Honduras, Olid had captured Francisco de las Casas, but Las Casas had managed to kill Olid and escape through Guatemala, which was then controlled by Pedro de Alvarado.

On the expedition to Yucatan there was a dramatic encounter

between Malinalli and her perfidious mother and the younger half-brother in whose interest she had been sacrificed. While Cortés was staying in Guacasualco, he ordered all the caziques of the province to assemble, and advised them to adopt our holy religion. On this occasion the mother and brother of Malinalli also made their appearance with the other caziques.

The recognition seems to have been instantaneous and mutual; the mother, fearing vengeance, threw herself at her daughter's feet, begging forgiveness, which was accorded, with the philosophic assurance that when she had so treated her child, she did not know what she was doing (as indeed it appeared), and that she thanked God for the boon of the Christian religion and the happiness of having given her master a son and the joy of possessing an excellent husband in Juan Jaramillo. Malinalli's Christian morality betrayed its recent adoption and weak growth at this point. She loaded her relatives with gifts and sent them home rejoicing. Bernal Diaz was reminded by this incident of the meeting between Joseph and his brethren in Egypt. Jaramillo became an alcalde in Mexico, and in 1528 a grant of land was given to him and Malinalli near Chapultepec.

While Cortés was away from Mexico City the situation deteriorated badly. The Spanish were arguing among themselves and the Indians were rebellious. Cortés decided that he had to return and did not have time to march back overland. He took ship in Honduras and landed at Veracruz on May 24, 1526.

On his return to Mexico City he was greeted enthusiastically by large numbers of Indians and his Spanish loyalists. He quickly reestablished control of the city, but rumors had raised serious doubts in the royal court as to his loyalty. Charles V dispatched Luis Ponce de Leon to investigate the situation. Ponce arrived in Veracruz in July 1526 after spending several months studying financial records in Espanola. On reaching Mexico City, Cortés hosted a banquet for Ponce and his delegation after which several persons sickened and died. Nine days after convening the investigation, Ponce died of a mysterious illness. Once again suspicion arose that Cortés had used poison - this time to eliminate the threat posed by the royal investigation. Marcos de Aguilar succeeded Ponce as head of the investigation, but he too died of a mysterious illness before he could conclude his work. Once again suspicion fell on Cortés but nothing could be proven.

In the spring of 1528 Cortés decided to go to Spain so that he could explain things directly to Charles V. He sailed from Veracruz on March 17, 1528, and arrived in Palos, Spain, forty-one days later. He met the King in the fall in Toledo and the meeting went smoothly. Charles reconfirmed Cortés ' title as Captain General of New Spain and extended his command to include the South Seas. He also conferred the title of Marquis of the Valley of Oaxaca on him, but he did not reinstate Cortés as Governor of New Spain nor did he grant his wish to be viceroy.

After meeting with Charles, Cortés managed to secure a papal bull that legitimized his three bastard children including his favorite Martin, the son of Malinalli. Before returning to New Spain he consummated a marriage that had been arranged years before with Doña Juana de Zuniga. Doña Juana was the daughter of Count Aguilar and the niece of the Duke of Bejar, two of the most influential men in the royal court. Meanwhile in New Spain the investigation into Cortés ' actions continued under Nuno de Guzman. Guzman overplayed his hand and was severely chastised by Fray Juan de Zumarraga, Bishop of Mexico. A new investigation was ordered and Cortés was urged to return to Mexico City.

The veteran Conquistadores had always been sure that, as soon as Cortés should receive the appointment of governor of New Spain, he would remember the day when he set sail from Cuba, and that he would bring back to his mind the great troubles by which he was immediately after surrounded, and that he would have remembered all those of the men who, soon after he had landed with his troops in New Spain, had procured him the appointment of captain-general and chief justice of the country, and have borne in mind that we never for a moment left his side in all the subsequent battles and dangers. We were the same men who marched with him into Mexico, who assisted him in taking the powerful Montezuma prisoner in the midst of his warriors, who lent him such efficient aid against Narvaez, and then instantly marched back with him to Mexico to the assistance of Alvarado. But he never repaid them wrote Bernal Diaz

Cortés arrived back in New Spain before the second investigating team arrived and was forced to wait for their arrival in Texcoco. Before the second investigation could get under way Guzman launched a new expedition into Jalisco and thus avoided a confrontation. Cortés turned his attention to the South Seas and ordered the building of more ships. He financed several unsuccessful voyages of discovery, before deciding to command one himself.

Early in 1535 he sailed out of Sinaloa and landed at a place that he called Santa Cruz (today La Paz, Baja California). He found a few pearls but little else of value and after a year of exploration returned to Mexico City where Don Antonio de Mendoza was now established as viceroy. Cortés continued to plan expeditions and wanted to head one in search of the Seven Cities of Cibola, but Mendoza refused to grant him the necessary authority. In 1540 he decided to return to Spain to appeal in person to the king. Unfortunately the king was absent and the officials he had left in charge decided to do nothing.

In October 1541, Cortés was part of the armada that Charles sent against Hassan Aga, an ally of the Barbary pirate Barbarossa. The attacking Spanish fleet was destroyed in a huge storm and Cortés ' ship went aground off the Algerian coast. A council of war to which Cortés was not invited decided not to press the attack and the survivors retreated to Spain. Cortés offered to lead a small band of men and overthrow Hassan, but he was laughed at. He remained in Spain for the rest of his life.

At the end he lived in the home of a magistrate in the town of

Castilleja de Cuesta, outside of Seville. Cortés died on December 2, 1547

34 Aftermath

From 1521 to 1524, Cortés personally governed Mexico

Following the fall of Tenochtitlan in late 1521 Malinalli stayed in a house Cortés built for her in the town of Coyoacán, 8 miles south of Tenochtitlan, while it was being rebuilt as Mexico City.

Don Martín Cortés, was born in Coyoacán in 1522, son of Doña Marina (La Malinche or Malinalli), called the First Mestizo; about him was written The New World of Martín Cortés

Malinalli was settled in Coyoacán, when she joined Cortés on his 1524 expedition to Honduras in wasteful pursuit of the renegade Cristóbal de Olid. Cortés took Malinalli along so she could serve again as interpreter (suggestive of knowledge of more dialects).

While in the mountain town of Orizaba in central Mexico, Cortés arranged for her to marry Captain Juan Jaramillo, a Spanish hidalgo in Tiltepec on the encomienda (estate) of the conquistador Alonso de Ojeda. As a dowry she received the encomienda of Olutla and Xaltipan in the Coatzacoalcos region.

On the return trip, in 1526, Malinalli gave birth to a girl, her second child by a Spaniard. The first was Martín Cortés (Cortés's son)— known as "el grande," for his Spanish half-brother was given the same name.

Two years later, in 1528, Cortés departed for Spain with his mestizo son, but not with the Malinalli—although that is disputed by some historians. Nothing much more is known about Malinalli although she is depicted in a painting in 1537. Mention of her in the historical records surfaces on May 16, 1542, when Maria Jaramillo (Malinalli's daughter) sued her father (who tried to disinherit her) for the valued encomienda of Xilotepec. Maria was granted half the encomienda, in part due to her mother's distinguished achievements.

Historians such as Prescott generally lost track of Malinalli for some time, even the year of her death being in some dispute. However, Sir Hugh Thomas reported that her death occurred in Spain in 1551.

Soon after his birth, Martín Cortés was separated from his mother and put into the care of a cousin of Hernando Cortés, Juan de Altamirano.

Martín traveled with his father to Spain where he was admitted into the Order of Santiago and was a page under Philip II of Spain. In 1529, Cortés had his illegitimate children legitimated by Pope Clement VII.

Martín Cortés returned to New Spain with his two half-brothers in 1563, and as his half brother was the heir to the Marquesado Del Valle de Oaxaca, he was received as would correspond to his status. Hernando Cortés's children entered Mexico City on January 17, 1563.

The New Laws of 1542 effectively impeded the inheritance of encomiendas. Martín's half brother (also named Martín Cortés) led a protest against these laws known as the Conspiración de Martín Cortés, "el Mestizo" participated in the movement.

The Real Hacienda denounced the acts to the Viceroy as a direct attack upon King Philip II and the conspirators were arrested. Amongst those arrested were Cortés' three sons. Several members of the conspiracy were executed. A few days later the Viceroy Gastón de Peralta intervened directly and released Cortés' three sons.

The Real Hacienda, wanting harsher action complained directly to King Philip II of Spain and falsely accused the viceroy of subversion. The Viceroy was removed from office, tried for disloyalty, and sent back to Spain.

Cortés was subjected to torture and was sentenced to indefinite exile in Spain. His torturer was reproached by King Philip II personally, sent back to Spain and found dead in his room one day after having met with the king.

In 1574 the king offered condolences to the children of Hernando Cortés and they were all exonerated of any wrongdoing.

"El Mestizo" married Bernardina de Porras and had one son named Hernandodo. He died in Spain sometime before the turn of the seventeenth century (1595 is mentioned as a possible date).

35 The Heroine Becomes The Legend

Eventually Malinalli returns to her hacienda in Mexico. She could not abide her time in the civilized world, it is too settled. The clothes the fine Spanish ladies adore are not comfortable, and she hears them laughing at her behind her back. She will never fit in there. She even understood why her beloved Captain let her go and arranged for her to marry someone else...

She discovers adventure is in her blood, she longs for the wildness and yes, danger, of the country.

Each day she walks about her land, seeking something new and remembering her adventures and her son and her lovers.

One day she finds herself very far from the hacienda, in the hills, out of sight of civilization.

It is quiet here and she is relaxed.

Too late, much too late, she realizes she is not alone.

The mountain lion springs from a high rock.

Her last thought is that she is home...

Time Line

1502   May 12 - Malinalli is born

1502   Montezuma II assumes the throne of the Aztec Empire

1502   Hernando Cortés misses an expedition to the New World, delaying his conquest of Mexico until 1519 - One Reed

1504   Cortés arrives in Haiti

1507   Crop failure causes a famine in Mexico

1507   An earthquake occurred following the "Lighting of the New Age" ceremony

1508   Montezuma visits Tlillancalmecatl ('Place of Heavenly Learning')

1508   Montezuma's sister Paranazin collapses into a trance

1510   Severe floods strike Tenochtitlán (Mexico City)

1510   Malinalli's father dies

1511   Cortés takes part in the conquering of Cuba

1511   Malinalli is sold into slavery

1515   Cortés marries Catalina Juarez

1517   The appearance of a comet, believed to signify impending doom

1518   Cortés departs Cuba for the New World

1519 when   The Aztec year One Reed corresponds to the year 1519, Cortés arrives in Mexico and is believed to be Quetzalcoatl.

1519   A comet hangs over the capital city of Tenochtitlan.

1519   A thunderbolt burns down the temple of   Huitilopchitli.

1519   The last omen comes to Tenochtitlan. A woman's voice was heard crying "my children, my children, we are lost!'

1519   Cortés lands on the Yucatan peninsula

1519   Cortés meets Malinalli

1519   Cortés arrives in Tenochtitlan

1520   Cortés allies with Tlaxcala and the assault on the Aztec empire begins.

1520   On July 1st, the Spanish forces are driven back and suffer heavy losses.

1520   Montezuma is killed by his own people

1521   Tenochtitlan (Mexico City) falls to Cortés

1522   Malinalli bears Cortés a child - don Martin Cortés

1524   Malinalli and Cortés take part in the Honduran campaign

1537   Malinalli dies ???

1547   Cortés dies

Origin of the name La Malinche:

The many uncertainties which surround Malinche's role in the Spanish conquest begin with her name and its several variants. At birth she was named "Malinalli" or "Malinalli" after the Goddess of Grass, on whose name-day she was born. Later her family added the name "Tenepal" which means "one who speaks much and with liveliness."

Before the twenty slave girls were distributed among the Spanish captains to serve them in "grinding corn", Cortés insisted that they be baptized. Malinalli then took the Christian name of "Marina," to which the soldiers of Cortés added the honorific "Doña," meaning "lady." We do not know whether "Marina" was chosen because of a phonetic resemblance to her actual name, or she meant for it to be "Mary", after the holy Virgin.

Possibly, a Nahuatl mispronunciation of "Marina" as "Malin" plus the reverential "-tzin" suffix, formed the compounded title of "Malintzin," which the natives used for both Marina and Cortés, because he spoke through her. One possible reading of her name as "Mãlin-tzin" can be translated as "Noble Prisoner/Captive" - or "Marina's Lord" - a reasonable possibility, given her noble birth and her initial relationship to the Cortés expedition. "Malinche" was a Spanish approximation of "Mãlin-tzin."

It seems much more likely that "Malin-che" was a version of her birth name "Malinalli".

To distinguish the masculine "Malinche" from the feminine, the prefix "La" gives us the name by which the historical and legendary figure is best known: La Malinche. We may assume that her preferred name was "Marina" or "Doña Marina," since she chose it and it has not acquired the negative connotations that engulfed the name "Malinche" after her death.

There seems to be wildly different beliefs as to what year La Malinche was actually born. Sources give any time from 1495 to

1505. Her age is unfortunately not mentioned in any of the important source texts, but we can assume she was a young woman at the time she was presented to Cortes. Some people (us included) believe she was a teenager. Others maintain that is not true because she wouldn't have been mature enough to carry out some of the exploits in which she participated. But it is in fact entirely possible she was very young because at this time in history girls were married at very young ages. One of Montezuma's own daughters was already married twice by the age of 12 years!

But on the other hand if sources such as Wikipedia are correct and she was born in 1505, that would have made her only 14 years old when she was given to Cortes, and that does seem a bit young. Could a 14 year old girl have faced down hostile native tribes and negotiated with them? Could a 14 year old have faced the Emperor Montezuma? More importantly would anyone have paid attention to such a young girl?

To home in on the correct year let's examine the best possible clue: her name. Some historians maintain that Malinche was a derivative somehow meaning "Marina's Captain", (Marina being her Christian name), but that seems unlikely since many, many other sources give Malinalli as her native name. If we accept Malinalli as being her name then the other variations Malintzin or Malinche by which she is referred make a lot more sense. Malinalli, Malintzin, or Malinche: the similarity seems too close to be coincidental.

So if we accept that Malinalli was probably her native given name, then we can use the Aztec calendar itself to help pinpoint her birthday. It was quite common to name people after their 'day sign' on the Aztec calendar. Hence the day sign Malinalli refers to a specific day: the 12th day or tonalli of the twenty day period. Malinalli also is the 8th sign of the thirteen day trecena. So it would make sense if Malinche was born on the 8th trecena on the 12th day.

Because of the manner in which the Aztec calendar is constructed the daysigns do not occur on the same date. The calendar consists of two rotating wheels which do not conform to our calendar. In other words the daysign Malinalli falls on a different date each period (it only repeats every 52 years), so there are only so many days/years Malinalli could have been born.

Since the 20 daysigns are used in the 13 periods, the weeks, the months, and the years one should be able to narrow down the date the daysign Malinalli intersects. For example on May 12, 1502, the daysign and the month period are both Malinalli. The only dates that conform then are: 3/17/1505, 12/02/1505, 6/30/1504, 10/14/1503, 5/12/1502, 8/25/1501, 3/23/1500, 7/7/1499, 2/2/1498, 5/18/1497, 8/31/1496.

The other important point was that Malinche was educated: She knew the Aztec Nahuatl language and the Spanish recorded that she was refined and conducted herself like a 'princess'. This would seem to indicate she was sold into slavery sometime after at least a partial Aztec education- which probably means she had to have been at least 8 to 10 years old. It appears she was a slave for some time, probably at least 5 years, that would have made her between 15 and 18 when she was given to Cortes. If she had been born from 1495 to 1500 it seems she would have been too old because under the Aztec legal system she could have inherited her father's title at age 12 so she had to have been sold into slavery before that- let's say around age 8 – 10.

1495 +8 = 1503 (she would have been a slave for 16 years – unlikely she would have survived).
1496 +8 = 1504 (15 years in slavery age 23 when given to Cortes)
1497 +8 = 1505 (14 years in slavery age 22 when given to Cortes)
1498 +8 = 1506 (13 years in slavery age 21 when given to Cortes)
1499 +8 = 1507 (12 years in slavery age 20 when given to Cortes)
1500 +8 = 1508 (11 years in slavery age 19 when given to Cortes)
1501 +8 = 1509 (10 years in slavery age 18 when given to Cortes)
1502 +8 = 1510 (9 years in slavery age 17 when given to Cortes)
1503 +8 = 1511 (8 years in slavery age 16 when given to Cortes)
1504 +8 = 1512 (7 years in slavery age 15 when given to Cortes)
1505 +8 = 1513 (6 years in slavery age 14 when given to Cortes)

It is very unlikely a girl would have survived slavery for more than ten years, at the least she would have rather haggard from hard labor so it would seem we can disregard birth dates before 1501. We can also probably disregard dates after 1503 because she just would have been too young. That narrows it down to 10/14/1503 or 5/12/1502. Since October is the month of Fall while May is Spring and the grass is growing, we are going to select May 12, 1502 as her birthday.

The Aztecs

Culhuacan survived the fall of Tollan and maintained its prestige until the mid-14th century. According to the Cronica Mexicayotl in 1299, Culhuacan's tlatoani, Cocoxtli, helped the Tepanecs of Azcapotzalco, the Xochimilca and other cities expel the Mexica from Chapultepec. Cocoxtli then gave the Mexica permission to settle in the barren land of Tizapan, southwest of Chapultepec, and they became vassals of Culhuacan. The Mexica subsequently assimilated into Culhuacan's culture and their soldiers provided mercenaries for its wars.

In the early 14th century, the vassal Mexica asked for Achitometl's daughter, in order to make her the goddess Yaocihuatl. Unbeknownst to Achitometl, the Mexica actually planned to sacrifice her. As the story goes, during a festival dinner, a priest came out wearing her flayed skin as part of the ritual. Upon seeing this, the king and the people of Culhuacan were horrified and expelled the Mexica. The Mexica found their way onto a small island in Lake Texcoco, where they founded their capital, Tenochtitlan.

The Nahuas are a group of indigenous peoples of Mexico. Their language of Uto-Aztecan affiliation is called Nahuatl and consists of many more dialects and variants, a number of which are mutually unintelligible.

The Nahua peoples are supposed to have originated in what is now the southwestern United States and northwestern Mexico. They split off from the other Uto-Aztecan peoples and migrated into central Mexico at some point around 500 CE. They settled in and around the Basin of Mexico and spread to become the dominant people in central Mexico. Some important Mesoamerican civilizations were of Nahua ethnicity, for example, the Toltec and Aztec cultures, as well as the Tepaneca, Acolhua, Tlaxcaltec, Xochimilca, and many more.

The name Nahua is derived from the Nahuatl word nāhuatl, which means "clear", "intelligible" or "speaking the Nahuatl language". It was used in contrast with popoloca, "to speak unintelligibly" or "speak a foreign language". Another, related term is Nahuatlaca, literally "Nahua people".

The Nahuas are also sometimes referred to as Aztecs. Using this term for the Nahuas has generally fallen out of favor in scholarship, though it is still used for the Aztec Empire. They have also been called Mexicanos or Mexicans, after the Mexica, a prominent Nahua group.

Giants in America

This isn't the only time Giants were mentioned by prominent people who visited South America. Don Cieza de Leon and Agustin de Zarate published texts on South American Giants in 1553 AD and 1555 respectively. These books came just after the arrival of the conquistadores and were published within twenty years of Pizarro.

They said that the native traditions told the incoming Spanish that the giants came to the Americas on raft-like boats. Some of these men were so tall that from the knee down they were as big as a man. Their eyes were the size of plates. Some were clad in skins and others were mostly naked. They said that there were no women on these boats, which was strange indeed. These giants dug deep wells for water that still exist today through solid rock. Cieza de Leon said that when Don Antonio de Mendoza went to Cuzco Peru in 1560 that he found tombs with extremely large bones, similar to the ones that were already found in Mexico City at the time of Montezuma. Padre Acosta found similar large bones in 1560 in Manta Peru where they later found similar bones in 1928 when constructing the railroad to Ecuador. They were hidden behind stalagmites in caves.

Glenn photographed the mummies of two of these giant men in Lima Peru in 1969. These giants are still in the gold museum in Lima Peru today and can be seen by anyone who visits. They were mummified because their golden robes are prominently on display. Their crowns could fit around Glenn's waist. Their golden gloves have fingers ten inches long. Their mummies can be measured with a tape and they were both around nine and a half feet tall. The actual bodies are there incased in glass for all to see. The news media has never photographed anyone nine and a half feet tall.

In the summer of 1931 Monsignor F. Lunadi organized an expedition into the jungles of San Agustin. He found traces of a very ancient South American empire known to the old British buccaneers of the seventeenth century. These men were giants who had knowledge of electricity which they used in various forms.

This race of ancient white giant men with beards was called the Viracochas. Pedro Cieza de Leon said that they came long before the Incas began to reign. The Indians also called these white men Titicaca, like Lake Titicaca today located high in the mountains between Bolivia and Peru. Glenn Lived in Juliaca Peru on the shores of Lake Titicaca, very close to the ancient city of Tiauanacu where there are huge statues to the giants with six fingers and toes to this day.

Human Sacrifice and the Eating of Flesh

Many scholars and historians debate the idea of the Aztecs and other tribes even performing human sacrifice let alone the eating of the victims. But the multiple eyewitness accounts would seem overwhelming evidence that was in fact true. Why would the Conquistadors make up such tales? Especially Bernal Diaz who seems intent on documenting the true account of the Spanish conquests.

Diaz mentions the sacrifices and cages containing humans being fattened (for what other purpose would these people be fattened if not for eating?) many times throughout his account. While it is pretty clear the eating of flesh was not strictly cannibalism but performed only by priests during rituals, it is impossible to deny it happened.

Some historians like to admire the Aztecs as an advanced and sophisticated people who were wiped out by the Spanish before their time. While they might have been those things, it is also important to understand they were so loyal (addicted might be a better word) to their bloodthirsty gods that they regularly sacrificed humans to them mostly by tearing out their beating hearts while they will still alive and then burning them. It is also well documented that women and children were often used in these sacrificial rituals.

Notes & Translations

A Peso is equal to about $12.00 in 1520

Quetzalcoatl [ketsaɫˈko.a:tɫ] – The Feathered Serpent or Plumed Serpent

Tezcatlipoca - Smoking Mirror, chief god of the Aztecs in general

Huitzilopochtli - Hummingbird Wizard, the war and sun god. This god demanded human sacrifice in the hope he would not go away and take the sun and leave the world in darkness forever.

Malinalli Tenepal, Malintzin, Doña Marina, or La Malinche

Tenochtitlan – Capital of the Aztec Empire (Now Mexico City)

Tlillancalmecatl - Place of Heavenly Learning

Nezhaulcoyotl – Coyote, a priest and astrologer

Nahua is derived from the Nahuatl word nāhuatl, which means "clear", "intelligible"

Morion helmet – The cone shaped metal hat known as the Conquistador helmet.

About the Author

Ed Morawski is a veteran of the U.S. Air Force and served eight years in various locations from Virginia to California and Vietnam. He grew up in Cincinnati and presently resides with his family in Southern California where he is an expert in electronic security. He enjoys music, photography, and writing.

See his website at **morawski1**.com

No act of kindness, no matter how small, is ever wasted.

-Aesop, *The Lion and the Mouse*
Greek slave & fable author (620 BC - 560 BC)

Visit us at morawski1.com and sign up for free stuff!

Other books by Ed Morawski:

Newhope – a mind bending tale of a small community

FLIT – the true story of teleportation

Afterlife – there are too many people in the world

Bloodsucking Vampires – murdering vampires vs. the LAPD

ALoner – he likes being the last man on earth

Perceiver – a paranormal romance about Remote Viewing

Probe – sexy alien invasion

Made in the USA
Lexington, KY
12 December 2019

58453918R00214